PENGUIN BOOKS

CONFESSIONS OF AN INDIAN WOMAN EATER

Born in 1939, Sasthi Brata grew up and was educated in Calcutta, reading physics at Presidency College. He left India soon after and has lived in London and various other capital cities in Europe and America.

CONFESSIONS OF AN INDIAN WOMAN EATER

SASTHI BRATA

PENGUIN BOOKS
An imprint of Penguin Random House

PENGUIN BOOKS

USA | Canada | UK | Ireland | Australia
New Zealand | India | South Africa | China | Singapore

Penguin Books is part of the Penguin Random House group of companies whose addresses can be found at global.penguinrandomhouse.com

Published by Penguin Random House India Pvt. Ltd
4th Floor, Capital Tower 1, MG Road,
Gurugram 122 002, Haryana, India

Penguin
Random House
India

First published in the UK by Hutchinson & Co. 1971
First published in India by Sterling Publishers 1792
This edition published by Penguin Books India 2006

10 9 8 7 6 5 4 3 2

ISBN 9780143061878

For sale in the Indian Subcontinent and Singapore only

Typeset in Sabon by S.R. Enterprises, New Delhi
Printed at Repro India Limited

www.penguin.co.in

FSC
www.fsc.org
MIX
Paper from
responsible sources
FSC® C047271

This is a legitimate digitally printed version of the book and therefore might not have certain extra finishing on the cover.

For

Angela, Anita, Ann, Barbara, Brenda, Caroline, Connie, Cynthia, Deborah, Doreen, Eileen, Elsebeth, Emy, Fatima, Gail, Ginnie, Helen, Irene, Iris, Jane, Janet, Judy, Kathy, Kristina, Laura, Leona, Linda, Lorna, Lynn, Margaret, Mary, Meg, Moira, Natalie, Nancy, Pat, Penelope, Phyllis, Raina, Rona, Rosalie, Rose, Sally, Santa, Susan, Tanya, Ursula, Vimala, Wendy and K.

for

Angela, Anna, Anne, Barbara, Belinda, Caroline, Connie, Cynthia, Deborah, Doreen, Eileen, Elizabeth, Emily, Fiona, Gail, Ginnie, Helen, Irene, Iris, Jane, Janet, Judy, Kathy, Kristina, Laura, Leona, Linda, Lorna, Lynn, Margaret, Mary, Meg, Moira, Natalie, Nancy, Pat, Penelope, Phyllis, Paula, Rona, Rosalie, Ruth, Sally, Serena, Susan, Tanya, Ursula, Vimala, Wendy and [illegible]

No character described in this book exists in total congruence with real life. In fiction, as against professed autobiography, real persons and events are used as launching pads for a flight of the imagination. People who figure in the following pages often display personality traits which would not meet with the moral, metaphysical and aesthetic approval of the right-thinking citizen. All such characteristics are fruits of the author's contorted imagination and must on no account be attributed to any member of the human race, living, dead, or yet unborn.

—S.B.
London

CONTENTS

ONE

~

NAYA DILLI

I now realize that leaving home was a gesture, like goodbye notes from failed suicides. It was the first of many crucial decisions I have taken on impulse. And looking back on all those kinks in the curve, I see they form a pattern. But at the time I had no idea of any such pattern; I did not know where I was going, or what I wanted to do. It would be pleasing but fanciful to interpret those defiant gestures in a heroic light, for on the outside it does look as if there was an inexorable motivating force, more than a suggestion of evangelical fervour.

I think the difference between pure histrionics and what I did lay in the absence of let-out clauses in my contract. Once I had put those books in my bag, written that note to my sister-in-law and climbed into a third-class railway compartment at Howrah station, Calcutta, there was no way I could return to the servant-studded halls of my father's house. In more than just the nominal sense I had begun my journey into . . . Life . . . with less than a hundred rupees in my pocket.

I was hoping to shock some people, influence events by that single symbolic gesture. In effect I succeeded in jerking my life out of its predestined grooves. I could no longer rely on father or family to help me build a future. By leaving home I broke down the sheltering fantasies of adolescence and forced myself to learn to become a man for I was determined not to return as a repentant Prodigal.

But before I describe that twenty-six-hour journey from Calcutta to Delhi I must list all the material possessions I carried with me. I was wearing the sacred thread of the Brahmins slung over my shoulders, covered by a brown, half-sleeved, nylon bush shirt; a pair of grey gaberdine trousers; a small gold talisman containing a holy text on palm leaves, tied by a black string round my right arm; shoes and socks. There was a handkerchief, some loose change and seven crisp ten-rupee notes in my trouser pocket. In my haversack there was a face towel, a toothbrush, a bundle of white paper and nine books:

Death by Maurice Maeterlinck

The Communist Manifesto by Karl Marx and Friedrick Engels

The Sacred Wood by T. S. Eliot (inscribed by the girl I loved)

My Philosophical Development by Bertrand Russell

A Collection of New York Herald Tribune Articles on India by Karl Marx

Discovery of India by Jawaharlal Nehru

Enemies of Promise by Cyril Connolly (borrowed from the British Council Library in Calcutta and never returned)

Materialism and Empirio-Criticism by V. I. Lenin

Monist View of History by Plekhanov.

(There was one other book I wanted to take with me but it was rather heavy and since I knew most of the important sections by heart, I left it behind. It was written by an odd collection of men, some of whom were illiterate fishermen.)

I don't remember much of the physical details of the episode except that I sweated heavily all day long. Most of the men in the compartment were bare above their waists, the women took off their blouses, leaving only the filmy cover of cotton saris over their bodies, the children scuttled about in the nude. But both my nylon shirt and anglicized schooling clung close to my skin. I did not sleep that night.

When morning came we were in northern India. The fields were no longer green but parched and brown. Every so often a telegraph pole whizzed past; the meshes of wire seemed to undulate in gentle waves, looping towards the ground in the middle and then tautening to a crest as the next pole came by. Cows with cavernous sides sauntered about near the tracks. The landscape was potted with little huts thatched with hay, men and women squatted near puddles, with their backs to the train, performing their morning ablutions. Inside the carriage, babies clung to pendulous brown breasts, the men chewed neem twigs and so cleaned their teeth, a thin layer of bronze desert dust covered my books, while I sat hunched up in the bunk, overlooking this mobile miniature of an India I had never seen before.

That whole journey was rather unreal, though. Certain scenes impinged upon me like stills from an instamatic. But they remained unconnected, they failed to evoke any response. I was rejecting a secure and ordered future with nothing to put in its place. As the train sped through the flat barren wastes, and the sound of the wheels jug-jugged an insistent rhythm in my brain, my thoughts spun round the same unalterable centre with increasing frenzy. What I had done was futile, it would lead nowhere, it symbolized nothing but a pointless adolescent defiance. The result of my action, however, would be ineradicable in my own life. The way to change society was not to opt out; evil was never expunged by turning one's back to it. If I wanted to show my feelings for the girl I loved, I should have stayed on in Calcutta, not run away. But now I had cut all ties, I was alone. Like a meteor spearing the dark, I would blaze for an instant and then turn into cold lightless ash. As the train lumbered into Delhi station, I was afraid.

I must now explain why I chose Delhi instead of Bombay or Madras or even a small village near Calcutta. Obviously I could not stay on in the same city in which my family lived as I would then be tracked down with ease and showered with consolation and advice. Nor could I go to a place totally foreign to me as I had not learnt to rely on myself and had no faith in my ability to find a job and acquire the other essentials for physical subsistence. But I had visited Delhi before, and Kamal, whom I had known at college, lived there with his mother. This was not to be the last time I had leaned on other people to avoid working out things for myself, alone.

Kamal was three years senior to me and we had both read at the same faculty in college. He had got a first in post-graduate nuclear physics and was waiting for a reply to his application to Princeton. I had sat the four theoretical papers for my honours degree in physics and left town without completing the practicals. Thus I was about to fulfil the prediction of the family astrologer who said that I would never hold a graduate degree nor be admitted to Oxford, where I had been promised a place. And though I was to learn later that I had high first-class marks in the theory papers, it was at this point that I put a stop to what had till then been a brilliant academic career. I arrived on Kamal's doorstep, having thrown away the last crutch on which I could conceivably hobble towards a viable future. Or so I thought at the time.

Kamal asked me into the house without a query. He knew my exam schedules and must have guessed that I had decided to abandon them. But his face showed no censure. My feelings of apprehension and guilt vanished. He took the bag off my shoulder, led me into the kitchen and introduced me to this mother. And just as suddenly my hands started to tremble, beads of sweat formed on my brow, as I noticed the disapproving grimace on the old woman's face. I realize now that she was provoked by my appearance, not by what I had done. I was unshaven, unwashed, my trousers were rumpled, with generous blotches of mud, and dust was all over my shirt. Kamal's mother was reacting to the incidental results of my action, not to the deed itself. But my antennae were out to receive hostile messages, identifying all response in terms of my own feverish rebellion. And I conceived an instant antipathy for the woman who was churning a curry on a coal oven in that soot-coated kitchen.

'Take him to the washhouse,' Kamal's mother said. 'Food will be ready in a minute.'

I went through the motions of having a bath as if I was soaping someone else's body. The lukewarm water poured down my back but I felt nothing. Suddenly I was a stranger to myself, watching the movements of my limbs from afar. Hurt, loss, guilt and fear, in fact all feeling, had vanished. I had become disembodied.

Kamal and I sat on the floor, with the rice and curry laid out on brass dishes before us. I should have been hungry, I hadn't had a meal for a day and a half. But my hands refused to move. 'Come on, start,' Kamal said. 'What are you waiting for?' His mother went on waving a bamboo fan over our heads to keep the flies away.

After lunch I went to the washhouse and brought up the whole meal.

Kamal was squint-eyed and short. He wore thick horn-rimmed spectacles with bulging lenses; his voice was low and bass, with the ponderous diction of a pendant. In most things he was very unlike me. He would never lose his temper nor make an impulsive gesture with his hands. The syntax in each sentence was always correct, he would choose his words with care and seldom displayed any emotion. When he had returned to college with a clean-shaven head after one summer vacation, he had dismissed all queries with two words: 'Father died.' There was nothing further to be said. Whatever other bond there might have been between us, it was not one of temperamental affinity.

So his first question wasn't unexpected. 'What are you going to do now?' he asked, as I joined him in his room.

I peered out of the door to see if his mother was within earshot. 'Don't really know,' I replied nervously, 'but I wondered if you could...'

'Yes, of course,' Kamal interrupted. 'But you must have made some plans?'

'None, I am afraid. I just . . .'

'I see,' he said looking philosophically out of the window. 'Well don't imagine you're going to have an easy time. As far as the job market is concerned, you're a cipher. You don't even begin to exist.' He took off his glasses and wiped them clean with a spotless white handkerchief. 'And, of course, you do realize that Oxford and M.I.T. are definitely out.'

Now that it was being spelt out for me, my old defiance rose up again. I wasn't going to give up so easily. Of course I could get a job. I was intelligent, alert, swift with my tongue. There must be lots of things I could do, lots of employers on the lookout for just my kind of talent. *I'd show them.*

Kamal heard his mother's footsteps before I did. 'Look, she is going to give you a lot of motherly advice, like going back home and all that. But don't take her too seriously. You have made a decision and you've got to work this one out for yourself. But it is best to know your co-ordinates at the start.'

The interview with the widow made me angry. I resented her assumption that she was fit to instruct me in the way I should live my life, merely because she was older. If I hadn't taken this kind of thing from my own mother, I wasn't going to take it from an illiterate old hag who had barely known me for a couple of hours.

As I lay down on the string bed on the verandah that night, I decided that I did not like Kamal's mother. The initial friction that afternoon would produce a few sparks and ultimately an explosion. Most fortunately for me, as it turned out. But of that later.

I did not even know how to start looking for a job.

New Delhi is a non-residential capital, like Washington or Canberra, with few commercial houses or business centres. The biggest employer in the city is the Central Government and to get a job even as a Grade IV clerk you have to sit for exams. Most successful applicants—for this the lowest rung of the clerical ladder—hold university degrees and are happy to take home a wage packet of less than a hundred rupees. The process of selection takes months and having an uncle or two on the examining board does not hinder your chances.

I gleaned all this information on my first day of job-hunting through an accidental encounter near the Rivoli Cinema in Connaught Circus.

I was having a snack meal from a stall on the road when a man on a bicycle bumped into me. The food I held on a dried leaf in my hand fell on the pavement, while the man started to apologize profusely in Hindi. 'It's quite all right,' I replied in English.

'You *parfect* gentleman,' the man persisted.

'Thank you,' I replied, walking towards the stall to get another helping.

'No, no, must not eat food on roadside. Get cholera,' my strange acquaintance advised. 'We go to restaurant.'

I was surprised to be showered with such excessive bonhomie and my first reaction was to suspect a trap. Nevertheless I found myself being jostled into a steaming cafe, where curry fumes and sweaty bodies combined to produce a most noxious odour. We sat down at a grease-coated, marbled-topped table, while my pick-up guide shouted an order to the waiter.

'You *parfect* gentleman,' the man repeated, looking unnecessarily pleased with himself. 'You give woman your seat in train.'

I couldn't help wondering if the man was clairvoyant, for I had in fact given up my seat in the train to a woman who was carrying an infant in her arms. It was a gesture I had regretted all through the journey, as I had had to climb to the top bunk, where I could neither sit with my back straight nor lie down. But my speculations were soon resolved by my garrulous companion.

'I wondering all the time what *parfect* gentleman do in third class.' There was a glint in his eye as he said this, as if he was about to discover a millionaire travelling incognito.

I explained as briefly as I could that I had very little money and had come to Delhi looking for a job. There was a fleeting look of surprise on his face and then he burst into a deep, gutty laugh. 'You have education, father, mother. What for looking for job and going third class?'

I was beginning to feel uncomfortable under his interrogation, as I realized that this would be the question that prospective employers were most likely to ask. And my story would sound a trifle too unrealistic to be believed. Sons of rich parents in India *never* leave home, not without family blessings and a fat bank account for support. My companion must have noticed my unease, for he suddenly switched his ploy.

'You eat now and we come friends and talk later,' he said, putting his hand on my shoulder. 'I must return to office in much quick time.'

The mutton cutlets arrived shortly after and, though bathed in oil, they tasted better than the curry at Kamal's place. My stomach made strange noises as I washed down the meat with weak tea. I remember the bill came to a little over three rupees and my friend insisted on paying. When we came out into the dry, sizzling heat of the pavement once again, I felt strangely elated, as if the Gods were on my side and what I had done was not quite so ludicrous after all.

'My name Ram Singh,' the little man said, smiling, and I realized that the meal was by way of introducing himself. 'I work in South Block with telephone number . . . . You speak with me and take you home to see family after office.'

'My name is Amit Ray,' I said, 'but I'm afraid I don't know what I shall be doing this evening. You see, I really am looking for a job and I haven't got much money.'

It took a good deal of broken Hindi, laced with an English phrase or two, to convince Ram Singh that I was indeed near destitute and couldn't expect help from home. He was rather taken aback, but his camaraderie didn't vanish as he explained how difficult it would be to find a job in a Government office in a few days.

'I am I.A. (Intermediate Arts) and my salary only eighty-five rupees,' he said with despair. 'But we make some way.'

With this he clapped me on the shoulder and rode off on his bicycle. I thought of all the stories I had heard and read of Indian hospitality and poverty and belief in Fate. It was obvious that Kamal wasn't going to help, even if he could. I knew no one in this strange city, where even the language was not my own. Heat and hunger would soon become the two most obsessive features of my world. What I had learnt at college was of no use as I had not earned the graduate label. I had not even brought my School Certificate and Intermediate Science papers with me. My talents, such as they were, could only be utilized in a given context, propped up by a letter of commendation from my Head of Department, a telephone call from my father or at a meeting of the Rotary Club in Calcutta. On my own I was a dud cheque.

I went round all the newspaper offices in the city (five national dailies are published in Delhi, along with a host of weeklies and periodicals), but I seldom got past the man at the foyer. Invariably I was handed a sheaf of forms to fill in—qualifications, experience, testimonials. Each page an added blow to my dwindling self-confidence. I was a non-starter in the race, the book of rules excluded me, I was never ever granted an interview.

The word 'lonely' had not figured in my vocabulary till then. I had grown up in a large joint family, and though I had a room of my own, there were always a lot of people flitting in and out—no one in our house ever shut the door on entering or leaving a room. If there was anything I missed at home it was privacy, not company. Brothers, nephews, sisters-in-law, aunts—there was always someone I could talk to. But in that first week in Delhi I discovered loneliness, just common physical loneliness, the ache and the longing to be with a person I knew, even for a little while.

I would leave Kamal's place early in the morning, having barely exchanged a sentence. All day long I would meet strangers, walk the hot crowded streets, from one spot of buried hope to the death rattle of another; sit in restaurants and eat rice and mutton curry in silence, and plod back to my grudging hosts for the night. Kamal wasn't unfriendly, he was merely disgusted with my clumsy way of going about things. There was nothing coherent or logical in what I was doing; no point, therefore, in offering to pay the fare if I didn't know where I was going.

It is easy in retrospect to explain my motives, to make some sort of sense out of a strong but imprecise urge to break down barriers. It wasn't so then. I had neither the intellectual apparatus nor the vocabulary to justify my actions even to myself. In a society where the 'drop-out' is held to be either insane or criminal it is hard for an adolescent to devise an imperative for himself which defies the accepted ethos. I went around looking for a job yet I couldn't give myself an adequate enough reason for doing so. The gulf between having and not having a job or a home or a degree was bridged by a foolish and pointless act which made no sense even to me, let alone to anyone else. I understood why I wanted to leave home but not the manner in which I had done so. I could sympathize with that half of me which wanted to register a protest provided it produced results, but what I had done affected no one else except me and possibly my mother—and she was not the target of my attack.

The more time I had to brood, the more angry and impotent I felt. My desire to be a rational human being was obviously not matched by my actions. And this inconsistency was underlined by a strong inner conviction that what I had done was right even though I could find no logical framework for support. Older and wiser men would have found the correct label 'intuition', and let it go at that. For me it created a state of nervous mental confusion, the like of which I had never experienced before. The only obvious result of all this was that I became more stubborn and desperate. I was needlessly offensive to Kamal and his mother; with prospective employers who looked as if they were about to turn me down, I was jumpy and rude even before they had said the word. Doors were rapidly closing shut on all sides;

the small inner chamber of my mind was growing steadily darker; even hope was about to die.

But during those dry friendless days in Delhi, as I turned one futile door handle after another, I discovered something about my country which unnerved me. Not only were the best jobs parcelled out to the 'old boys', but there wasn't a single job going for anyone without connections. Walking out of the office of the personnel manager of a large oil firm, I asked the peon who was sitting in the corridor if I could get work as an orderly or messenger boy. He explained that such vacancies did occur from time to time but a 'young gentleman' like myself couldn't possibly think of 'obtaining such post'.

'Why not?' I asked in Hindi.

'Oh, sahib,' the man replied in English, 'we look after little sons. Old man dies, then I telegraph beta in village, tell boss and son works in office. Your father no peon, you no get peon's job.'

The same was true of waiters in restaurants, clerks in private firms, chauffeurs, gardeners, cloakroom attendants, et al. It is easier for a rich man's son to enter the Gaylords Restaurant in Delhi than to get a job as a lift boy at the Imperial Hotel. Here was the caste system all over again, tarted up in new clothes, but preserving the status quo as effectively as ever. A rich man gets his son a rich job, a poor man a poor one. No poaching, gentlemen, please! And woe to the son, wherever he came from, who shied away from using the old man's credit card.

On the tenth day of my stay in Delhi my eldest brother came to visit me at Kamal's place. It was a Sunday and we were having lunch in the kitchen. The door bell rang and Kamal's mother went out to answer it.

'I think I ought to tell you,' Kamal said, 'that your people at home know that you are here.'

The words stung my bleeding ego. Two feature articles I had sent to the *Statesman* newspaper had been rejected, there was no job in sight, I had pawned my gold talisman and Kamal's mother was becoming more intolerable every day.

'But how . . . ?' I shouted. 'You didn't . . . ?'

'No', Kamal replied sternly, 'I didn't write, but your brother wrote to me. I couldn't tell him a lie and if I hadn't replied, he would have known anyway.'

At this point the widow came back to announce, 'Your brother is here to see you,' with a self-satisfied grin on her face.

I walked into the sitting room, nervous enough to faint. I had always respected my eldest brother as a father-figure. To defy him face to face would require more courage than buying a railway ticket and dropping my exams, especially as I had no obvious justification for my actions.

'Hullo, Amit,' my brother said, embracing me. 'How are you?'

'All right, thank you,' I replied, my voice low and tremulous. 'But why did you come all the way to Delhi?'

'Well, I had some business here and thought I'd drop in and see you.'

'But I said in my note that I didn't want to be followed around . . . like a criminal.'

'Yes, but who says you are a criminal?' My brother put his arm around me and I was shaking and cold.

'No one . . . no one,' I burst out hysterically. 'Just your attitude . . . writing to Kamal, flying up to Delhi, as if I was some kind of moronic infant.'

'Of course you are not an infant and far from being a moron . . . but . . .'

'There are no buts,' I shouted, and within a sharp second I had snapped the umbilical tie and become a new man: this was the first time I had raised my voice to an elder. 'I am sorry,' I added limply, 'but I want to live my own life.'

'No one wants to stop you from doing that, least of all me.'

'Yes, I know, dada,' I said, sad and touched, 'but I don't want any support either. I want to be left alone to fend for myself.'

My brother smiled and squeezed my shoulder. 'When you grow up . . .'

'That's just it, I want to grow up now and do it my own way.' I was surprised at the tone of confidence in my voice, as if I had discovered something new in myself. There was no more need for apologies; uncertainty had vanished. I seemed to have discovered a creed for myself, towards which I had been groping. Things had suddenly become very simple, the pieces in the puzzle had inexplicably fallen into place. Whatever the obstacles, I knew now that I would win through.

My brother produced all the good conventional objections to my course of action—if there was a course, that is. If I wanted to give up physics, it was all right by him. But writers have to live too—eat meals, bring up a family and so on. But without a degree . . . ? In any case there wasn't much future for an Indian writing in English. The British don't accept foreigners writing in their language; at best, they patronize. I could never hope to make a mark other than in my mother tongue. Look at Madhusudhan Dutt!

There was genius, if ever there was one. And he even got published in England. I could scarcely hope to achieve even that kind of partial success. But what had he been forced to do in the end? Return to India, the land of his birth, relearn Bengali and write the immortal *Amritakkhar Chanda* (the first poem to be written in blank verse in Bengali). And *he* died a pauper. Fortunately for me I would inherit enough from my father so as not to have to worry about money. But really, without a degree in this modern age, what respect could I ever hope to command?

'But, dada, I didn't leave home to command respect or to become a writer,' I said impatiently. 'I left home because . . . '

'Yes, I understand . . . it was hard on you . . . When one is young . . . . '

'It has nothing to do with being young,' I interrupted.

The pleading went on, hand in hand with threatening descriptions of squalor and poverty and untimely death. What could I possibly *do* without a degree? How could I possibly earn enough to live on, let alone maintain a decent enough standard so as not to disgrace the family? Now that I had made my protest, why didn't I return home and carry on with my studies?

At the end of two hours, when none of his pleas had had any obvious effect, my brother played his trump card.

'Mother is very ill,' be said, in a low subdued voice. 'Since the day you left home she has hardly eaten any food.'

'But why didn't you tell me that all this time?' I shrieked.

'I didn't want to upset you,' he replied, 'but if I return home without you, I cannot guarantee that you will ever see her again.'

It was good old blackmail, but I didn't see it like that at the time. That my brother could be lying was inconceivable to me. In fact my mother *was* ill, but not as seriously as he had made out. But it posed the hardest choice I have ever had to make in my life. Do I defend a nebulous principle at the expense of my mother's life? Or do I swallow my pride, return home and nurse her back to life? I ought to be ashamed to say that pride and principle won. But in retrospect I seem to have justified myself. Mother didn't die, nor did poverty and squalor engulf me for all time.

My brother left me weary and dejected. Then Kamal's mother came into the room to tell me what a silly, stubborn boy I was to have rejected such a kind and forgiving reconciliation. Kamal handed me an envelope, given to him by my brother, which contained two hundred-rupee notes. I smiled, picked up my book from the shelf and put them in the bag. 'Post that money back to him,' I said to Kamal, 'and thank you very much for putting me up all this time,' to his mother: 'I am leaving.'

When you are at the bottom of the well, you cannot descend any further and you gain a strange, desperate confidence.

There was much less reason to hope, fewer possibilities left unexplored, than when I had boarded that train at Howrah station. But my walk was more firm, there was less confusion in my mind. From somewhere outside myself I had drawn a certain strength which urged me to go on. I can't explain this rationally but I felt that even leaving Kamal's place, the only sure shelter I had, was a step in the right direction.

I arrived at Ram Singh's just as the family was sitting down to dinner. 'You are so kind to come,' Ram Singh said, as he rushed towards me with outstretched arms. 'You sleep here tonight definitely. Too late for going home back.' I wondered where the thanks were due—God, my friend or my impulsive madness?

'Thank you very much,' I replied, 'but I must tell you . . . '

'You tell me later,' Ram Singh said, cutting me short. 'I now show you my wife and my mother and you eat a little food at a poor man's house.'

I was introduced to each member of the family, including three bumptious kids, with a great deal of ceremony. Then Ram Singh added, addressing the entire household, 'Mr Ray *parfect* educated gentleman. Very honour to us for him visiting here so far away.' (Every day Ram Singh cycled eleven miles to work and back—it was a choice between missing a meal a day or taking the bus.)

Food had already been served for the kids and the male members of the family: chapatis, vegetable curry and some lentil soup, laid out on brass dishes. As a guest of honour, I was provided with a glass plate and a plastic tumbler. I should have felt uneasy with all the fuss but in fact it was the first time I lost all self-consciousness and ate the meal as if I were at home. Ram Singh's wife was very flattered when I asked for a second helping.

After dinner my host explained hesitantly that before going to bed we would have to take a walk in the fields—there were no lavatories in the house. So Ram Singh, his little brother and myself, set off in the dark, with a kerosene lamp for a torch, each of us carrying a jugful of water. Perhaps Brecht might have found a symbol or two in the sinuous mud track we had to trudge. My only concern at the time, however, was to suppress a laugh which was bubbling within me.

Finally we set foot on consecrated ground and the three of us squatted at a distance of about ten feet from each other—the kerosene lamp being placed at almost the geometric centre of the line connecting the three points. Grunts, groans, and ultimately the sound of water splashing against flesh, brought the ceremony to a satisfactory conclusion.

On the way back home, being lighter both in body and spirit, I told Ram Singh of my predicament and accepted his offer of hospitality the moment it was offered. He asked me only one question: Why hadn't I come earlier? Rather than pollute such a splendid evening with a lie, I kept silent.

It was on the third night that it happened.

Ram Singh put me on a string bed on the flat roof of his one-storeyed house; the rest of the family slept in the open courtyard below. This was a privilege since the light breeze that blew over the rooftops of these rows of houses made a difference in the sweltering heat of a Delhi summer. But it also gave me an added bonus of which my host was unaware.

Two houses away there was another string bed on the rooftop. I had seen an unturbaned Sikh yawn awake at dawn after that first night. On the second night I was too tired to wake early the following day. By the time I got up the bed across the way was empty. But it was on the third night, as I lay staring up at a budding moon, that it happened.

It must have been about an hour after the neighbourhood had fallen asleep that I heard a creaking noise, as if someone was climbing wooden stairs. There was a film of light all around and I saw the Sikh rise up in bed. Someone was obviously climbing to his rooftop, as he turned his head towards the point where the ladder was placed. Within seconds a silhouetted figure had placed a foot over the low wall around the roof. I held my breath for fear of disturbing the scene.

The Sikh didn't move but the silhouette did. By now I could see the outline of her sari and a fan of hair across her back. She tiptoed to the bed and started unwinding her sari. The man stretched out a hand to touch her but the woman dipped a pointed finger at him and instantly his hand fell back on the bed. It took a few minutes before she had taken off her sari, folded it neatly and placed it at the edge of the bed. She was less fussy about her petticoat and blouse, which lay on the roof floor, as far as I could see.

By this time every nerve in my body was sharp and alive, my eyes hungry. I had not yet made love to a woman, nor had I ever seen a couple copulating. As in a thriller I was aching to see the next move.

The nude woman sat next to the Sikh and gently pushed his head back on the bed. Then her hand moved over the whole length of his body, stroking him. With an impatient frenzy I started counting the number of times she did this. I had reached seven when her hand halted and the gliding horizontal motion was replaced by a brisk vertical one.

I must have *imagined* that I could hear the sound of heavy breathing, for the breeze was blowing the other way and our two houses were at least thirty feet apart, but I had read enough to be able to fill in the blanks of this silent tableau.

When she lay down on the bed beside him, however, my imagination gave way, as I could see no further movement. And since it was at this point that I craved most for a demonstration, I was left with a longing which strained every blood vessel in my body. But within minutes I was put out of my misery. The Sikh turned sideways and arched his back; I knew (though I couldn't actually see) that he was lying over her. The convex curve of his buttocks was now sharply outlined as it rose and fell with a slow, irregular motion. My mouth went dry, my hand was firmly clasped round my own penis. Then as the oscillations increased in speed, I too followed the lead. On and on it went, rougher and faster, the unoiled bamboo joints of the bed creaking with each new attack. The woman was twisting and turning her head, the Sikh's mass of hair obscuring her from view every time he descended. Then suddenly they were both very still and he fell back on the bed, like a sated leech dropping off a man's leg.

I masturbated three times before falling asleep that night.

That incident was my christening in sex. It *aroused* me far more intensely than any love-play I had had with women. Outside the act of sex, the actual emission, voyeurism is far more erotically *stimulating* than digital manipulation. I think several things added to the excitement—the fact that it was dark and I couldn't see the faces of the copulating pair, that they were not aware that I was watching, that there was a certain amount of stealth and secrecy in what they did. To watch a woman masturbating in her bathroom across the street with a pair of binoculars from your window is more exciting than to see a couple make love in front of you in a lighted room. The instinct is the precise opposite of rape, i.e. necrophilia. You participate in the act without even the possibility of rejection. In my mind I was the Sikh doing it to that woman. But as she didn't know of me, she had no choice.

Of course, the most obvious reason for my violent response was the breaking of a taboo. I was doing what I wasn't supposed to do—prying into the sacred and private world of 'sexual intercourse' without permission. Apart from being bad-mannered, it was immoral and degrading. And judging from the sex books I had read till then, it was also something of a perversion. To find greater erotic thrill in *watching* than doing it oneself was sign of decadence. This somehow made me feel adult. For adolsecence, by definition, is an innocent rather than a jaded state.

I woke up next morning feeling proud and manly.

Money was running out. For though I was having my evening meals with Ram Singh's family, I had to pay for the bus fare into town and back, several glasses of ice-cold water (yes, you have to pay for that in Delhi) and the occasional roadside snack during the day.

There wasn't any office left to visit, I began to see that Kamal had been right about the job market. I walked around the city in a state of anaesthesia, not even daring to hope that any of my applications would turn out fruitful. I thought of Orwell with envy; to be down and out was all right provided you chose the right place to do it in. And in a way I had been quite lucky too. So far I had at least managed to find a bed for the night and one free meal a day. If there had been no Kamal or Ram Singh, would I have gone back home? I wonder. Perhaps there would have been a different set of people, another pair of helping hands. But supposing no such help turned up? How far can one try oneself? What is the breaking point of a human personality beyond which one cannot stretch? I don't know. I do know, however, that over the years I have come near enough to that point several times and these experiences have shaped my personality more than the routine of day-to-day living. In retrospect they also make good stories, for nothing is more romantic than having survived to tell the tale. At the time, however, if a choice were offered, I am sure I would have opted for the easier alternative. Heroism is for the past, for other people and Hollywood movies; not for me, not in the present.

I was standing outside the Tea House in Connaught Circus, idly watching the traffic and wondering if I could afford a cup of coffee and a plate of crisps, when a shoeshine walked up and put down his box in front of me. 'Cream and polish, sir?' he asked.

I smiled back at him, pondering on the irony of a *parfect* gentleman sporting mud-stained shoes. 'No thank you,' I replied.

'Your shoes do need a polish, sir,' the boy persisted in earnest Hindi.

'Yes, I know,' I said, still smiling, 'but I can't afford it.'

'Can't afford it?' the shoeshine retorted, joining me with a smile. 'Only four annas, sir.'

'I haven't got four annas for a shoe polish,' I said, walking away. But there was a puzzled and hurt expression on his face, as if I was making fun of him. 'You see, I am looking for a job.'

The boy picked up his box and started walking with me. 'Can't get a job with dirty shoes like that, sir. The boss sahibs won't like it.'

'The boss sahibs don't seem to like me in any case,' I answered, beginning to get irritated. 'Polished shoes won't make things any better.' I wanted to get rid of the boy, but he persisted in walking with me.

'You don't live in Delhi,' he said after a while.

'No,' I replied firmly. 'I come from Calcutta and I don't want my shoes polished.'

'I have an uncle who works in Calcutta,' he went on, ignoring my curt reply. 'Earns a lot of money in the house of a Bengali babu.'

Instantly the thought seized me. 'And how much money do *you* earn?' I queried.

'Oh, it all depends. On a bad day about three rupees, on a good day when there are lots of tourists, about five. Sometimes more.'

I did a spot of quick calculation in my mind; the answer sent a shiver through me. The shoeshine earned more than Ram Singh, a clerk in a Government office. Here at last was salvation!

'Do you think I could . . . ?' I asked hesitantly.

'What sir?'

'Polish shoes? Like you, I mean?'

'Polish shoes?' the boy asked drawing to a rigid halt. 'On the pavement, like me?' I didn't anticipate the loud mirthful laugh that followed.

It took a lot of persuading. Shovan Lal, for that was his name, refused to believe that I wasn't making fun of him. He had had to leave school two years before his matriculation; why should I want to do his job when I had been to university? If he could speak English he certainly wouldn't be polishing other people's shoes. He would sit in an office and be a sahib himself, earning a regular monthly salary. But he hadn't been born under a lucky star; his father had died of smallpox about three years ago. No, shoeshining was no job for an educated man like myself. What would my friends say?

I explained that I had no friends in Delhi, that I had left home without sitting through my exams. And most important, that even if I did apply for a clerk's job, it would be weeks before I could start and even then I would be earning less than himself.

'But think of the status of working in an office, with an electric fan over your head,' Shovan Lal argued.

'There is that, I suppose,' I replied, smiling, 'but I have to get a job straightaway.'

'Well,' my friend said, reluctantly giving in, 'if you really want to . . . I mean I don't know how the others will take it. There is a Shoeshines' Union, you know. And Connaught Circus is a very good beat. It is easier in the Old City, but there the fellows are very jealous. If there is an extra shoeshine, it means that everyone else earns a little bit less.'

I hadn't thought of it like that and Shovan Lal opened up a whole new world for me. For a moment I lost the feeling of hopelessness and despair which had possessed me ever since I arrived in Delhi. To work as a shoeshine became the most important goal in my life.

'But if I can persuade the others,' Shovan Lal said, breaking into my thoughts, 'you will need to get all the stuff. A box like this one, brushes, cream and polish and some rag cloth.'

'Yes, of course,' I replied, drawn back to reality once again, 'and how much will all that cost?'

'About ten or twelve rupees,' Shovan Lal answered. 'Shouldn't be much more than that.'

'Really!' I said and started laughing.

'Why, what's the matter? Don't you believe me?'

'Of course I believe you. But the simple fact is that I only have five rupees and some loose change.'

This time Shovan Lal was truly stumped. His mouth fell open and his eyes shot up in shocked surprise. 'You mean, you really mean . . . ?'

'I am afraid I do,' I replied, controlling myself. 'You see, I could never have an electric fan over my head.'

He drew his eyes close and his face became thoughtful while he put his hand inside the pockets of his half-pants several times. 'Well,' he said, 'we shall have to find a way.' It was nearly six o'clock and we walked a few yards in silence towards the Rivoli Cinema where a show had just ended. Shovan Lal quickened his steps. 'I must work now. But you come to see me at eleven o'clock after the last show. Then I shall talk with my friends and see what they say.'

'All right,' I nodded, as I watched him walk away.

'And don't worry,' he shouted, just before he turned the corner, 'if they let you work here, we'll find the money somehow.'

Night comes on in Delhi with the sharp stroke of saffron across the sky. There is a sudden breeze and the dust whirls up in the air like speckled smoke, before it is dark and peaceful once again. Streams of cyclists pour down the pavements, the three-wheeler motor-scooters honk their way through the mesh of cars at crossroads. For about an hour or so there is a spurt of extra life on the streets. Then the lights come on, the fevered rush of home-bound traffic slackens, other than a persistent few the beggars vanish from sight. Later, long American limousines slide down the wide streets, cigar-smoking men in evening dress escort bejewelled ladies into banqueting halls, and the city starts to change into the smooth effortless speed of a top-gear drive.

I walked along the long, tree-lined avenues, past statues of our erstwhile rulers, past fountains and lush lawns. I could almost feel the slow throb of ease and luxury around me; never the impatient flutter of the low, not a step taken in haste. Cars purred softly by, music across the pebbled drives wafted over in gentle soothing tones. Was this the city where Ram Singh went for a walk in the fields every night and Shovan Lal lived?

The British Embassy was aglitter. The bland face of the Rolls-Royce swerved past me. And I remembered my professor of physics, yellow chalk in hand, held between knarled fingers: '. . . water-cooled radiators are comparatively inefficient. Cooling by air, on the other hand, is inexpensive but can only be conducted in cooler climates. The Germans produced a car called the Volkswagen which . . . But there is a special system which the manufacturers of the Rolls-Royce engine use . . . One cannot say that it is the most efficient, but it is certainly the most effective. Unfortunately the use of the motor-car would have to be restricted to a very small percentage of the world's population if every single engine was to be fitted with a Rolls-Royce radiator.'

Fatehpur Sikri, Qutab Minar, the Red Fort—I wondered what the history of my country meant to me. There were such stupendous contrasts. Here was a land where human achievement had excelled on every plane. Astronomy, algebra, architecture, even poetry, music and art, every single avenue of Man's aesthetic quest had been explored with skill and care. Yet in this very city, where seven empires had come and gone, where Akbar and Ashoka ruled, I could not get a job, Shovan Lal had not been able to finish his schooling, hospital beds had to be bought by graft and no one could eat at a decent restaurant without a jacket and a tie. Could we blame it all on the British?

By eleven o'clock I had walked eight miles. When I met Shovan Lal, Connaught Circus was nearly deserted. A couple of drunks richocheted from lamp post to lamp post, a solitary policeman stood in front of the Tea House and two neon signs on the side of a tall house began to blink their adieux.

'Hullo,' Shovan Lal said, greeting me in Hindi.

'Hullo,' I replied, as a few men around him moved aside to let me through.

'These are my friends,' Shovan Lal added, waving his hand over the group.

'What do they have to say about my working with them here in Connaught Circus?'

'Well,' Shovan Lal replied, pulling a face.

Just then one of the younger men started speaking very fast in a strange dialect I could not easily follow. This was taken up by an older man and in a few minutes four others joined in. When they had simmered down a bit, Shovan Lal, who had been quiet all this time, translated for me.

The Union was having trouble with the authorities, who had refused to grant a licence to the shoeshines, although hawkers and vendors could apply for one. So, in effect, polishing shoes on the pavement was illegal, like begging, and one had to depend on the goodwill of the policeman on the beat and the Deputy Superintendent of the area. The head of the Shoeshines' Union knew some English but obviously someone with superior knowledge of the language would be of great help. So, though most of the group was against letting me in, they had reluctantly agreed to give me a chance provided I helped out with the correspondence.

I literally jumped for joy and gave Shovan Lal a close hug.

'They also say,' he added, 'that we will take a collection for you to buy the box and the rest of the materials. So you can keep the five rupees to buy food and other things till you begin to earn a little. And after a few weeks you can pay back the money for the box.'

A toffee tin was passed around and a little over seven rupees was collected that evening.

'We will get more tomorrow,' Shovan Lal said, somewhat apologetically, 'when the rest are here. You know, there are thirty of us who work in Connaught Circus.'

The group dispersed and I went home with Shovan Lal that night.

It was a bustee, a shanty village, within walking distance from the centre of the city. Most of the other shoeshines lived there too. When the particular plot of land on which the little huts squatted like flies was 'requisitioned for development', the whole community simply moved to another spot.

There was one communal tube well and no lavatories anywhere near the place. Nor were there any large fields. But there *was* a wide trench with fern and bushes on either side. When the wind blew away from the trench, towards the bustee, the stench was noxious.

Shovan Lal lived in an improvised tent held up by bamboo sticks and small planks of wood, covered by canvas and cloth. In it there were two string beds, one slightly larger than the other. The mother and two younger children—a sister and a brother—slept in one; Shovan Lal, as head of the family at sixteen, had the other one to himself. The younger sister, Mukti, was twelve and already a full-blown woman.

'I send this one to school,' Shovan Lal said, pulling the girl's long hair, 'but she is a dullard . . . ' This obviously embarrassed her, for she drew the sari tight over her face, while the smaller boy started giggling at her discomfiture.

Just then Shovan Lal's mother walked in, carrying a bucket of water.

'Excuse me,' I said, 'let me help.'

'And who is he?' she answered in reply, looking at Shovan Lal with a frown on her face.

'Amit Ray, my friend,' the son replied, 'and this is my mother.'

I didn't know what to say so I merely smiled back at her.

'Mr Ray is going to help me to learn English,' Shovan Lal added, by way of introduction.

'Well, he shouldn't expect any fees,' the woman retorted. 'If he goes to college, his parents must be rich enough. If he wants to teach you English, he must do it for free. We can't afford any fees.'

'Mr Ray is not asking for any fees, Mother,' Shovan Lal pleaded, acutely embarrassed. 'He is going to stay with us.'

'Stay with us,' the woman shrieked, letting go her hold of the bucket. 'Knew there was a catch in it somewhere. And at this time of night too.'

'Mother,' Shovan Lal said.

'Yes, Mother,' the younger girl's voice added.

The woman looked at her two children and then at me. 'Ah well, I suppose he could sleep in the small bed there with you.'

I nodded again and smiled, inwardly mumbling thanks to whoever it was up there for helping me over another hurdle. 'There are some chapatis for you, Shovan,' the woman said, turning up the wick in the kerosene lamp. 'And if your friend hasn't eaten . . . '

'I have, thank you,' I replied.

'Well then, let's get ready for bed, little ones,' the mother said to her children. 'And, Mukti, come on, get along.' My stay at Ram Singh's had told me just what this meant and I couldn't help wondering how women manage to perform in such an open and populated area, and I even tucked away a secret plan at the back of my mind to spy on Mukti one unsuspected evening.

Shovan Lal finished eating his chapatis, the small boy had a pee just outside the tent and Mukti walked off with a jug of water in her hand. The older woman sat at the edge of her bed chewing a betel-nut leaf.

'Shall I put out the kerosene lamp?' Shovan Lal asked, and got a vigorous nod in reply. 'Well,' he said, turning to me, 'if you will please lie down on the bed, there Mr Ray, I can sleep on the floor.'

'Yes, yes, Shovan can sleep on the floor,' the mother added in agreement. 'The ground is not wet at all.'

I protested vehemently for a while, but when I finally shut my eyes in the dark, I thanked my guardian angel once again: the bed was three feet wide and creaked every time I turned.

By the time I got up next morning, the whole place was astir. There was a long line of women queuing in front of the tube well, Shovan Lal's mother was baking chapatis on the portable coal oven just outside the hut, Mukti was combing her hair and the youngest boy was hitting a stone with a stick.

'Mr Ray, sir,' Shovan Lal said hesitantly, 'we have to go very quickly before the babus get to their offices.'

'Why don't you call me Amit?' I asked. 'After all, I am going to work with you.'

'Yes, but that is just unfortunate,' he replied. 'You are going to be my tutor and teach me English. I can't call my tutor by his name.'

I realized that it would be pointless to argue; Shovan Lal had decided my role.

Mukti had finished plaiting her hair and looked up at me with a smile. Ma brought over the cooked chapatis and handed them to her son and Shovan Lal flung his box over his shoulders: 'Come on, let's go.'

There was no such thing as having a wash in this quarter of town.

As we walked down the road with the other shoeshines, Shovan Lal explained that I would have to sit next to him till eleven in the morning, when business would slacken a bit. We would then take the remainder of the collection from those who hadn't been there last night, then go to the Old City, buy a box there and return to Connaught Circus just in time to catch the afternoon trade.

Shovan Lal was a good tutor too; at the end of the first day I had earned over two rupees and polished eight pairs of shoes. 'Good start, Mr Ray,' Shovan Lal commended, as he put out the flame in the kerosene lamp that night.

Over the next three weeks the routine remained almost identical. I began to earn about three to four rupees a day; some of the customers were so amused to hear a shoeshine talk English that they became regulars. I was reticent about the 'history of my life' and this made them even more curious. Shovan Lal bought *The New English Reader* and the lessons lasted for an hour at night; both Ma and Mukti sat reverently silent while I tried to make sense out of the perversity of Anglo-Saxon pronunciation—P-U-T, put, and B-U-T, but—to Shovan Lal. I wrote several letters to the Deputy Commissioner on behalf of the Shoeshines' Union, none of which was answered. Each of us in the Circus had to pay our 'dues' to the 'law' and so keep our berths.

My gaberdine trousers had become glazed and shorn on the seat, the nylon shirt had been burnt at several places and there was uneven growth round my chin. But I was earning enough to feed myself. I was paying for my lodging by giving nightly tuitions and I could even afford to give Ma a couple of rupees every so often to help her with her 'housekeeping'. Once when I returned to the hut earlier than usual and Ma was out gossiping with the women, I gave Mukti a small present—some glass bangles—and manged to sneak a glimpse of her tight, small breasts under the sari as she was taking off her blouse.

I dropped in to see Ram Singh at his office in South Block and was treated to sermons on 'degradation of *parfect* gentleman'. I saw no point in keeping up contact with Kamal, as I didn't want the story of my present occupation to be relayed back home in Calcutta. I kept writing the odd feature and sending it on to the *Statesman* newspaper and kept getting rejection slips addressed to me 'care of The Tea House, Connaught Circus'. I had averted complete disaster, I was my own boss and had settled into a groove.

Then one morning the papers announced that a foreign dignitary was about to descend on the capital. It was also 'collection day' for our policeman friend. But at about two in the afternoon, instead of the friendly cop coming round with an extended hand, there was a sudden screeching of brakes outside the cinema and a squad of helmeted policemen charged at us with batons. Shovan Lal slung his box over his shoulder and dragged me off with him to the narrow alleyway leading to the latrines.

'Arrests,' he whispered, 'there will be arrests.'

When we emerged from our hideout an hour later we learnt that five shoeshines had been bundled into the police van and taken to the station. The Deputy Commissioner had sent out instructions to 'clear the streets of beggars, vendors, shoeshines and all such nuisances' in view of the impending visit. Overnight all thirty of us lost our means of livelihood. And for Shovan Lal, with three other mouths to feed, 'starvation' was no longer a copywriter's word—it was about to become as stark reality.

That afternoon I wrote an irate piece, describing the whole episode, pointing out the hypocrisy of 'clearing the streets' just when foreign dignitaries visit the capital, and took it along to Ram Singh's office to have it typed. Then I telephoned the regular weekly columnist of the *Statesman* and asked for an appointment. I told him that I had been to the same college as he had attended in Calcutta, hoping that the alma mater might have some effect. It did. He asked me to come and see him at the Gymkhana Club that evening. My concern for the shoeshines—at the moment I was one of them—must have shown on my face, for the interview proved successful and the man appeared impressed.

'Eleven o'clock tomorrow morning,' he said, as I shook his hand again. 'I shall have a word with the editor before you come.'

Hope began to bubble up again; not only had I been able to do some good for my colleagues, I seem to have done myself a favour too.

I went to the barber's next morning and had a shave. There wasn't much I could do about my clothes but Shovan Lal gave my shoes a cream polish. I presented myself to the receptionist at the *Statesman* office at five to eleven. A secretary came down to meet me within minutes. As if in a dream, I was sitting opposite the columnist in an air-conditioned room, being offered a cigarette, precisely at eleven o'clock.

'I've given the acting editor your article,' the man said. 'Perhaps he would want to see you.'

'Thank you, sir,' I replied, 'I am very grateful to you, sir.'

'You have nothing to be grateful to me for.' he answered, lighting his cigarette. 'I have merely passed you on. Unfortunately the decision is not mine.' He picked up a gallery-proof and started going through it with a pencil. I stared silently at him, not knowing what was expected of me. 'The acting editor is in conference at the moment,' the man added, by way of information, head still bowed over the proof.

'Yes, sir,' I replied.

'And you can cut that "sir" out, you know. This isn't a military camp.'

'I understand,' I answered meekly.

The silence was irksome; perhaps it lasted for no more than ten minutes but it seemed like hours.

'What did you think of the article yourself?' I asked finally.

'As I said,' the man replied, looking up at me, 'it's not my decision, so it's best for me not to comment. If I say I liked it and the editor doesn't, you still won't have it printed. On the other hand if I say it was rather laboriously written but the editor likes it, you would get into the paper.' I must have shown my reactions on my face, for he added: 'Obviously it has some interest.'

Just then his secretary walked in. 'Yes,' he said, 'if you will go along now, the editor will see you.'

Several rooms, sounds of typewriters, orderlies, clerks and jacketless men later, I entered a large carpeted room which was even cooler than the one from which I had just emerged. A tall, gaunt man, with a receding hairline and silver-rimmed spectacles, came forward and shook my hand.

'Sit down, Mr Ray, sit down,' he said, in his bluff English voice. I could see the man loved horses by the way he walked. 'I am Stuart, John Stuart. I am filling-in for the editor at the moment . . . er . . . er he is away on home leave.'

'Yes, I see,' I replied in a weak frightened voice, while John Stuart walked round his desk to the window, with his back to me.

He had my article in his right hand, his spectacles in his left, and there was a long sharpened pencil dangling from the corner of his lips.

'Well now, you have been working as a shoeshine!' he exclaimed, suddenly turning round to face me.

'Yes, sir,' I replied, 'for three weeks.'

'Hm . . .' he grunted, smiling. 'Interesting. Well, what shall we do with this?' he queried, as he held out the sheets of papers in his hand.

'I thought you might like to . . .'

'Of course we can't publish it. You realize that, don't you?'

'As a matter of fact I hadn't,' I retorted pertly, my hopes dashed to bits. 'I thought the whole point of . . .'

'Yes, of course. But you obviously haven't heard of a thing called libel . . . . ' Mr Stuart returned to his desk and started lighting a pipe. 'Hm . . . ?'

'No, I must say I didn't think . . .'

'Even if we did take out the names,' the huge ruddy man continued in between puffs on his pipe, 'it simply wouldn't stand up in a court of law.' He started nodding his head as if he was reading the piece over again. 'I don't say I don't believe you but . . . You are attacking an institution of the state. Now, if one of the Indian-owned papers were to print this . . . But for us, we would land ourselves in a right royal soup.'

'Well, in that case I don't see much point in your calling me here.' I said heatedly. 'If a newspaper isn't prepared to expose things like this, then what damn purpose does it serve?'

My little speech was received with convulsive laughter and I started to get up from my seat.

'Sit down, young man, sit down,' John Stuart commanded. 'Don't get so hot under your collar. We can't all be crusaders, you know. But I'll tell you what I shall do. I'll send your article, with a covering letter, to the Commissioner himself and see what he has to say.'

'Thank you, thank you very much, sir,' I replied, rather subdued, with the wind taken out of my sails.

'Meanwhile, since we cannot pay you for an article we are not going to use, what shall we do about your board and lodging? Hm . . . ?'

'I don't really know,' I stammered, now completely taken aback.

'Perhaps you would care to work for us, hm?' John Stuart said, and before I had had a chance to speak another word, he added: 'And it wouldn't be a bad idea if you went along to my tailor and fitted yourself up with a new suit of clothes.'

He jotted down the address of the tailor and handed me the note. 'See you on Monday, ten-thirty sharp,' the Englishman said, as I as I came out of this room.

So I became the youngest and most inexperienced reporter the *Statesman* has ever employed. And it helped me to see Shovan Lal through the next few weeks, until civic fervour had simmered down and he was back on the pavement again.

When I went to Ram Singh's office to tell him the good news his reaction surprised me: 'Only to be expected,' he said, 'educated gentleman like yourself . . . ' And he was not slow to take me around and introduce me to his colleagues as 'a reporter in the *Statesman* newspaper'. I got a few unbelieving looks, as my clothes did not match the exalted status into which I had suddenly catapulted.

Talking of status, it is important to explain here that working for the *Statesman* in those days meant a lot more than merely holding a job in a national daily. It was the only British-owned paper in the country; given the obsequiousness with which almost all Indians look up to things British, a reporter with the *Statesman* automatically occupied an elite position both within the journalistic world as well as the larger social one around. The politics and tone of the paper were—then—a punch between the *Guardian* and the *Times*, a dose of radicalism, rendered innocuous by the sedate piety of a neo-Victorian style. Financially, a new recruit in the *Statesman* earned more than his opposite number on any of the other papers. And although the monthly cheque was smaller than that of a newly covenanted officer in a firm like Shell or Unilever, it was the only paper which carried enough kudos to attract graduates freshly out of Oxford and Cambridge. Journalism in general was a quasi-menial profession; journalists per se were near-illiterates. But the *Statesman* managed to produce in its 'leaders' some of the best English prose written by Indians, and its influence in political and artistic circles was quite out of proportion to its comparatively small circulation.

Ram Singh was, of course, unaware of these nuances. To him every man who had been to university and spoke grammatical English fell into a general mosaic of '*parfect* gentleman' and could expect to join the *Statesman*, become Chairman of I.C.I., and be elected as Prime Minister. But by now I had had some experience of the machinery which selected candidates for the juicer jobs and John Stuart's dramatic gesture left me in a state of euphoria I had rarely felt before. I went to the tailor and asked for a pair of trousers and a shirt. The man brought out some readymade pieces, asked me to try them on and insisted that he measure me for a fitted suit: 'Mr Stuart said that you should have one tailor-made suit.' The phone call had preceded me and my bill was put on a charge account, to be cleared in monthly instalments. As I listened to the man, I took a few minutes off to wonder if I was dreaming.

My first day at the *Statesman* was anticlimactic. I walked into the reporters' room and was cordially met by the chief reporter, a burly man with small slit eyes and a fat cigar precariously wedged between his lips. Although he was approaching complete baldness, his head was generously splattered with hair cream, defiantly maintaining the illusion of a younger and more verdant era. The effect, however, bordered on vaudeville, especially as he had a habit of taking out his comb every so often, in full public view, and weaving it through the surviving strands. I put him in his late forties and, watching the other faces in the room, realized that Mr Stuart had plonked me into a den of hard, weather-beaten men who had been at the game for a long time.

We trooped along to 'conference', in the news editor's room, which lasted for half an hour. Assignments for the day were handed out and at the end of it all I was given an escort who would take me round the magistrates' courts. I was not to write any copy for a week, just follow my colleague and watch him at work. 'After that,' said Mr Stuart, 'well . . . we shall have to see, won't we?' Scarcely the start to a career of crusading zeal and burning idealism, I told myself.

In a while I began to write copy under the by-line of 'A Staff Reporter', and was given the pompous-sounding title of 'Crime Reporter of the *Statesman*'. I became an 'equal', though some were always more equal than others. I noticed hierarchies and rivalries between people from different communal backgrounds—racial antipathy at work in real life. They make no sense now, the intensity has vanished, but then it was in earnest—Punjabi versus Marathi, Bengali versus Kashmiri, etc. I kept clear of these intrigues, but they affected me indirectly, exposed me to a way of treating and thinking about other human beings that I had not known before.

I came to know a South Indian called Rangaswami rather well. He took an indulgent, quasi-paternal interest in me from the start and would drop his nuggets of advice in odd and rather endearing ways. One afternoon, when we were both lunching late, he lifted his fork in the air, whirled it around like a sword and announced fiercely: 'This is a jungle, dear boy. Got to sharpen your claws if you want to survive.' Then he made some comment about the pudding being indigestible, wiped his mouth and left the table with the words: 'Never drown your sorrows, boy, for in the end they'll always manage to drown you.' It was not until I became a member of the Press Club that I realized the significance of Rangaswami's remark—the man was fond of bending his elbow.

He was in his late thirties and a confirmed bachelor. There was an odour of decadence about him; he walked with a slouch and wore loose, ill-fitting clothes. He would smoke furiously when he was at the typewriter, stubbing out each cigarette halfway through. In his cups he was always wildly funny, never morose or broody. Rangaswami was the most experienced reporter in the office and he felt he had been denied promotion because he was South Indian. That might have had something to do with it, of course, but his lifelong courtship with the bottle was probably the greater deterrent.

Assigned to cover the royal visit of her Britannic Majesty, Queen Elizabeth II, he had turned in a brilliant copy at the end of the first day of the tour. But some frustrated private eye had spotted him in a corner of the Press Club bar for most of the day and wondered how he could have seen the Queen's dress or heard her speech when he had not attended the reception nor gone to the airport on her arrival. 'What the hell?' Rangaswami had replied. 'The Queen's dress isn't a classified secret, you can get her bloody speech on any of the agency ticker tapes and you don't need a sixth sense to figure out that the Duke is going to have his hands clasped firmly behind his back as he trudges on after her like a lap-dog.' Of all the reports, his had been the most authentic sounding eye-witness account, but in fact it was pure induction, with a touch of the short-story writer thrown in. The British editor, however, did not relish such imaginative reporting, especially about his beloved Queen.

Rangaswami got me out of several scrapes, once when I had misnamed a cabinet minister, on another occasion when I had used my own words in a speech—within quotes—as I knew no shorthand and had to improvise. I felt I owed him a return and suggested that I take him out for a meal. 'Meal, boy, you mean food?' he had laughed out loud. 'Liquid diet, that's what I am on. But what do you say to half-a-dozen bottles, eh? That's more in my line of business, you know.'

So I agreed to take the afternoon off on his free day and bought a dozen bottles of beer and carried them back to my flat. I had had a sip or two of liquor before then but had never gone 'on a binge'. And I felt adult and daring in being invited to lift a glass with such an ardent devotee of Lord

Bacchus. Rangaswami arrived late and it was obvious that he had had a few on his way down. Without any ceremony we settled down to the serious business at hand, but not before I had drawn the curtains to keep prying neighbourly eyes from discovering the decadent side of my nature.

By the end of the third bottle the table began to blur at the edges and Rangaswami became fidgety and started to pace about the room. 'What about some juiced-up pussy, huh?' he shouted. 'Well, er . . . er . . .' I replied, dry-throated and nervous. Drinking was adult and wrong all right, but it was not entirely taboo. My mother would never approve of what I was doing just then, but my brother would probably raise only a censorious smile. What Rangaswami was suggesting however . . . I mean, it belonged to the tradition of Baudelaire and Rimbaud. I had no clear idea of what he had in mind, but my thoughts leapt riotously ahead, clutching at images of Restoration licentiousness and Paris bohemianism. Of course, a 'writer' had to experience 'life' not the strait-laced variety of routine chores in suburbs and 'happy homes' either. If there was anything morally wrong in going to a prostitute, then because of the writer's special mission, the wrongness would be neutralized in the name of 'art' and 'experience'.

'Sure,' I added, 'let's get some juiced-up pussy.'

I felt a thrill in uttering these words, as they sounded harsh and disconnected, coming from my lips. I don't think I had ever heard them before let alone . . . So I kept on repeating 'juiced-up pussy', just to make sure that I had got it right and convince myself that I had at last become an emancipated adult, a man of the world.

Rangaswami started laughing, in a raucous, unartistic voice. 'And the next thing I know, I'll be had up for corrupting the innocent.'

'I am not innocent,' I shouted, 'and you can't corrupt me! I've had juiced-up pussy many times. In Calcutta I used to go to Pleasure Alley every Friday night . . . and here in Delhi I . . . '

Of course, the sterilized truth was that I was the most uncorrupted virgin in the northern hemisphere, as starchy and uncreased as they come. I had kissed a girl or two, but my greatest sexual adventure befell me quite accidentally in the dark room of my college laboratory when my elbow had bumped into a girl's bosom. But that was it, the entire bulk of confessional material in my sexual bag. And faced with the prospect of having to carry out in deed what I had often pondered in my mind, I experienced the oft-quoted sensations of weakening of the knees, dry throat, rising pulse beat and frosting of the palms.

But as I was determined to be a writer with a boundless imagination, I was able to string together a number of convincing anecdotes (which I had picked up from books and more advanced friends), names of people and places. At the end of my modest monologue Rangaswami appeared satisfied with my bona fides and said, 'All right, but not a word of this to any of the boys in the office. Not even to your friend, the Bengali babu. Understand?'

'Of course I understand,' I said, histrionic talent competing with imminent nervous collapse. 'What do you take me for? A breast-sucking infant or something?'

Rangaswami went off in a taxi to fetch the booty, I stayed behind. It wouldn't do for both of us to go to G.B. Road (the red-light district of Delhi), too risky. Besides, it was far more comfortable here in this flat. And with a bottle or more, never know what might happen . . . I agreed. Anything Baudelaire might suggest. Of course! With a bottle or more, never know what might happen . . . (What would? What could happen? What did he mean by that? Some really adult thing like taking off all our clothes or perhaps . . . No, I don't think he could have meant that. I mean, there *are* limits! I wasn't a prude but . . . I couldn't really be party to gross animal behaviour.)

I spent the next hour visiting and revisiting the lavatory. I took off my trousers, rubbed my penis with soap under the cold tap, dried it, put some talc on it, then went to the bathroom again and washed off the white powder. Then I had a shave, daubed my cheeks with cologne, changed into a freshly laundered shirt, tidied up the bed, gave my shoes a fresh polish, stood in front of the mirror with my flies unzipped, inspecting every little spot or pimple on or around my genitalia.

And still Rangaswami had not returned. Time crept on, a slow, sneaking thought started to grow inside me. Perhaps he had abandoned me, perhaps what would happen with a bottle or more had already begun to happen, perhaps . . . I met this thought with an appropriate mixture of adult outrage and adolescent relief. Yes, perhaps I was off the hook, perhaps he hadn't really believed my stories, confound him! What right did he have to take me for a ninny? I wasn't any worse than . . . I mean a man must start sometime.

A taxi snorted to a halt outside the flat. I peered through the curtains to see Rangaswami jump out of the cab, as if he was about to commit a burglary. Following him was a woman, dressed in the North Indian dress of loose pyjamas and a long overhanging shirt. I let the two of them in and Rangaswami went to the window and shut it. 'Bolt the door too, will you?' he commanded.

After serving my guests some fresh beer, I had a chance to observe Venus. (And no exaggeration either!) She had a noticeable protuberance about her middle, which extended from the top of her groins to well into the chest region. He breasts hung low and loose under the shirt, and a rolled-gold necklace swung pendulously each time she broke into our conversation with a laugh. Yes, her laugh, that was the most memorable feature of her personality! Like timber over-dried in the sun, the laugh was splintered and warped, a cross between a jackal's cry and a crow's. But her face took the prize for all that is desirable and seductive in a female—a lump of plaster yet to be moulded, wrinkled, brown, not quite dead but with no good reason for staying alive. I cannot now praise this woman enough. Then she held the key to all Puritan virtue. If to suffer was to be pleasured, then here was Epicurus incarnate. She was chewing betel-nut leaf and the scarlet juice trickled down the numerous sharp ravines on her chapped lips.

And then she came over and kissed me, with her tongue inside my mouth.

'Go to it, bitch,' Ragaswami shouted at her in Hindi. 'Work on the boy, come on. You're being paid, aren't you? Prick-sucking whore!'

The delicate balance of discernment was upset for a moment. I didn't know which moved me more, the explosive

Baudelairian language or the clawing fingers which were attempting to unbutton my shirt. But there was no doubt in my mind that something terribly exciting and wicked was happening, right there in my room at that very instant.

'Perhaps we should have some more beer,' I said, clumsily extricating myself. 'With a bottle or more, never know what might happen . . . . ' I did try to carry a smile on my lips as I said these words but I am not sure if I succeeded.

Venus got up from the divan, walked out of the room and I heard the sound of a flushing toilet. But she wasn't exactly dilatory at her job either. Even before I had finished pouring three glasses of beer, she returned, nude, inviting, her massive rolls of flesh rocking thickly with laughter.

'There,' Rangaswami said, in a voice too hoarse to be called a whisper. 'That's the way. Go to it! Come on, go to it!'

I had not time to sort out my reactions. The bombardment of stimuli left me numb. But I finally caught on to the fact that that phrase was a mutually agreed signal. For Venus sat down on the chair, parted her legs wide and began rubbing herself, removing her hand every minute or so to expose a dark encrusted valley, with thin streams of foam streaking down her thighs.

I wanted to look away but dared not. With a bottle or more, I kept repeating to myself, never know what might happen . . . Rangaswami looked as if he was about to explode, his eyes had turned red with the beer, his tongue darted in and out, covering his lips with saliva, his cheeks were puffed.

Did I start praying? No, I was beyond all that. Like a man peering over the edge of a sheer gorge, then taking the jump, clinging fiercely to grasses and shingle for a while and then fascinated by the horror of his descent and plunging forward.

Venus wanted to 'go to it' with Rangaswami, right there in the sitting room. But my friend and mentor had not lost all sense of mystery yet. They retired to the bedroom, squeals and grunts following minutes later. It's not as if I didn't know that a woman's private parts would look like that, I told myself. I mean, I had attended physiology classes in college. There is the labia majora. Then there is the vaginal canal and, of course, the clitoris, the counterpart of a male penis. Yes, I knew all that. In a state of erotic stimulation, the vaginal walls secrete juices to facilitate entry . . . . Entry? Right now, Rangaswami was actually *entering* her. That's right, he was putting his thing into her 'juiced-up pussy'. Oh my God! And he is going to discharge inside her, make her all soggy and wet. And then I . . . No, no, it couldn't be. He wouldn't do that to me. Rangaswami was a dear friend of mine, he wouldn't put all that white stuff into her, not when I was supposed to . . .

I started thinking of the Binomial theorem.

The two of them emerged from the bedroom, interrupting my meditations, Venus as nude and obese as ever, Rangaswami tousle-haired, shirt-tails hanging out of his trousers. 'Your turn,' he said, as he flopped down on the chair.

I accompanied Venus into the inner chamber, with thoughts of Cupid and Krishna screeching fruitlessly in my brain. The moment of truth, I told myself, a time of trial. A man had to win his spurs sometime, and here was the colt, all hot and ready for a gallop.

My clothes fell off my body with remarkable alacrity, and I found myself lying on my back, legs spread-eagled, with chapped, grating lips encompassing the tenderest region of my anatomy. I looked up at the ceiling with mystical thoughts flitting through my mind and wondered about the exact dimensions of my bedclothes. It was autumn you see, or at least the time of year when green leaves turn brown and start to blow away.

I looked down at the hunched-up figure at the foot of the bed, the arched curve of her back and buttocks, brown breasts dangling over my thighs, while the tin-plate necklace grazed my innocent skin. Venus performed feats of contortion, sat on me with her legs forking over my groins and very nearly crushed my breath away. She started massaging my calves, then my thighs, and then suddenly grabbed hold of my penis, twisting it between her fingers.

But after fifteen minutes of hectic activity, when she had run through her whole repertoire, she started giggling, spitting out bits of chewed betel-nut leaf from her mouth. I couldn't quite understand what provoked the amusement and asked hesitantly: 'What's the matter? Why are you laughing?' in broken Hindi.

'Little man won't wake up, that's what's the matter,' she replied, adding the obligatory giggle.

'Doesn't matter,' I said, paternally forgiving both the little man and her. 'I don't mind.'

She went back to the sitting room, with a final flick of farewell to my little man, while I dressed. When I followed her in next door, I found Rangaswami panting furiously over her on the divan. Not having developed a taste for mobile sculpture till then, I sharply retraced my steps to the bedroom and remained immersed in less viscid thoughts. When the operation was completed, to the mutual satisfaction of both parties, Rangaswami shouted, 'Come on boy, we're through.'

A little later Rangaswami went out to fetch a taxi and Venus put on my silk dressing gown. And not content with feeling the smooth cloth against her raw skin, she got into her own clothes and donned the gown like a coat. When Rangaswami returned, Venus gave me a farewell kiss with her red lips. Just then my thoughts were so confused that I could not bring myself to ask her to take off my dressing gown. Thus the Scarlet Woman left with Rangaswami in the taxi, with a bit of me still clinging to her. And I sighed as I went back into the flat.

My friend and colleague did not mention the incident ever again. Neither did I. But I was not to forget that first time I saw a whole nude woman.

In the first two months at the *Statesman* I made no friends outside the office. I was still aching for the girl at college in Calcutta, who had been forced to marry another man by her parents. At odd moments, in between assignments, in the early hours of the morning when I had just finished reading a book by Camus or while watching the Delhi college girls bicycle past my flat, I would begin thinking of her and old familiar dreams would come crowding in. I missed her voice, the soft, unexpected touch of her hand on my eyes, our daring sexual adventures (which went as far as a kiss and an embrace). I wanted to talk with her, share the exploding new world of artists and writers I had recently discovered. Her absence oppressed me; I read and re-read her letters— the ones she had written during the holidays. The memory of our three years together was still too raw for any other female to supplant her.

Then one day I want to Broadcasting House, the headquarters of All India Radio (A.I.R.), and saw a tall, sharp-boned girl walk into one of the studios. I had come on business, as a representative of the *Statesman* newspaper, and the person I had to see was, by accident, an anglicized Indian lady. So after we had finished talking shop, I ventured to ask if she knew 'a tall, rather fair-skinned girl who works here, what's her name?'

'Not you too,' the lady replied, smiling. 'Of course I know her. In fact the whole of A.I.R. knows her, if not the whole of Delhi. And if I might give a small warning, there's a waiting list running from here to Hyderabad.'

'I am not particularly interested.' I said, trying to effect nonchalance (and not succeeding very well). 'Just wondered who she was, that's all.'

'She is an announcer. In fact if you want to hear what she sounds like, tune in your radio at four this afternoon, she'll be on the air.'

'What did you say her name was?' I asked, as I was getting up to leave.

'I didn't say her name was anything,' the woman answered, stubbing out her cigarette. 'But I'll tell you if you ask me sweetly. But I would still advise . . . . '

'Oh come on,' I said, 'I told you I wasn't all that interested. But I'll take pot luck all the same.'

'Well, it'll be your funeral,' the woman said, 'but if you really are serious, I could go one better. I could even introduce you to her.'

'That sounds very generous of you,' I replied, my heart beating marginally faster than before. 'I shall be most grateful.'

'On condition, of course, that you put our story on the first page.'

I stared at her for a minute, and then smiled. 'It's a hard bargain. But since you are obviously in the practice of what is commonly called "wheeling and dealing", I accept.'

'Well, turn up here this evening at five, sharp. Her name is Mimi and she sits in the next room.'

'Thank you very much,' I said, taking her hand and kissing it with a slight bow. 'I'll be here.'

'Enough of that,' the lady countered, adding with a sigh, 'I still don't see why I should help a bright young boy like you to ruin yourself.'

The build-up was impressive and exciting. A woman with a waiting list running from here to Hyderabad was more intriguing than a woman with a waiting list approaching the differential zero. And I had never been the one to under-appreciate my own prowess and powers, taking on all comers, excluding Tolstoy and Bernard Shaw. So I put myself in top gear and revved up for the encounter.

The introduction ceremony was perfunctory and bathetic. Mimi rushed in, shook hands with me, not even bothering to sit down, and addressed herself solely to my anglicized Indian lady friend. She had arranged to meet someone that evening and was going to be late. Did they always have to keep her so long in the studio? Sorry she couldn't stay on and chat. Bye . . . ee . . . ee!

No impact. Amit Ray had not even flickered on the screen.

Fortunately, Osborne's *Look Back in Anger* had just come out in paperback from Faber & Faber. I bought a copy and inscribed the following lines from Eliot in Chinese ink:

'... to lead you
to an overwhelming question. Do not ask
What is it?'

I wrapped the book in ordinary brown paper and sent it to Mimi at Broadcasting House, not signing my name.

The next time I went round to see my anglicized Indian lady-friend there was the expected response: 'Mimi wants to talk to you.'

It was winter in Delhi and I was wearing my suit. So I adjusted my tie, pulled out the breast-pocket handkerchief, so it would show more than a whisper of white above the brown gaberdine, and lit a cigarette.

Mimi walked sedately into the room, with the measured gait of a supplicant. The calculated disengaged frenzy had vanished. And commitment wasn't only in the eye of the beholder.

'Have you read a play by John Osborne called *Look Back in Anger*?'

'Yes, it came out about a year ago.'

'Do you like it? I mean, are you impressed with his work?'

'I couldn't really say. I think it is a play which is meant to be performed, not read, unlike Shaw's huge lectures which he chose to call drama ... And as I haven't seen a performance of *Look Back in Anger* I couldn't give an opinion. But why do you ask?'

'Well, I was sent a copy of the book, but it wasn't signed. And there was a quotation from T. S. Eliot .... '

'I can assure you that I didn't sent it,' I said, smiling, 'if that's what you are getting at.'

'Well, I heard you worked for the *Statesman* and I don't know anyone who would . . . '

'I am sorry to disappoint you but I wouldn't ever send a book to a girl without signing my name . . . . Besides, I don't think you'd be the kind to like *Look Back in Anger*.'

'Why do you say that?'

'Well, you are a butterfly, aren't you?'

'How dare you . . . ? I am sure you're the one. You even talk like Jimmy Porter.'

'My dear girl . . . I don't even know you.'

'Don't "dear girl" me! Didn't they teach you manners at school?'

Mimi stormed out of the room, leaving an unrehearsed grin hovering across my lips. The anglicized lady who had introduced us clapped her hands and shouted, 'Fireworks!' I got up leisurely and walked out into the cool air of a Delhi December. I had bowled well for a first over.

Time, I reckoned, was on my side, and so was . . . 'Life'. I was young, bright and idealistic. I worked for the *Statesman*; there was a glittering future ahead of me in the world of journalism. Besides, I had literary talents and my ambitions were sure to be fulfilled. In any social gathering I could outshine the best of them. Waiting list or not. Mimi knew no one who would send her *Look Back in Anger*. That was my winning card, and I decided I would have to play it right. So I waited.

But first let me describe her to you, physically I mean. She was tall for an Indian girl, a good five foot eight or nine. But she did not slouch or stoop, carrying herself erect, with the chin tilted slightly forward, giving a hint of defiance. Her walk was usually slow and measured, one foot preceding directly before the other, instead of the lateral step most Western women have (which is why they look so comical in a sari). She had long arms with slender fingers to match. You could see the outline of her figure through the sari, as she wore it tight around her. In summer there was a wide band of exposed flesh between the top of her sari, tied round her waist, and the bottom of the cotton blouse, which fitted close to her bosom. If the wind blew off the end-lap of the sari, which went up from the waist, across the front and over the shoulder, you could see two aggressive peaks trapped under her blouse. The band of exposed flesh showed her real complexion, a tropical sky at dusk, smooth, clear, with a hint of saffron. By Western standards she was not fair but by Indian standards she was pale-skinned, just slightly ruddy and bronze. Her face was darker, with two large brown eyes shaped by long natural eyelashes of the deepest black. So was the colour of her hair, fanning out across her back in thick masses. There could have been nothing particular about her nose, for I don't remember its shape. But I do remember her lips, soft, pouting, both upper and lower turned slightly out, always parted a little, showing a set of blazing white teeth. Yes, she was beautiful, the kind of beauty that cross-fertilization always produces, for her father was a North Indian, with a rough-leather face and her mother a sturdy Scotswoman: Mimi had collected the best features of both the Aryan and the Celt.

When you add to her looks, a quick tongue, a flashing temper and a certain engaging flamboyance, you can see the reason for the particular length of the waiting list. For in addition to being an announcer on All India Radio she modelled for one of the deluxe sari shops in town and occasionally worked as a tourist guide for the Royal Dutch Airlines. This brought her in contact with many people, and she was always vigorously sought after at Embassy cocktail parties and Presidential receptions. And her fluent command of English coupled with a quasi-British accent, inherited from an anglicized father and Celtic mother, made her the most desirable as well as the least accessible single girl in New Delhi.

And to make things even brighter for me, Rangaswami sketched in the details of her numerous liaisons when I told him of my encounter. Mimi was nineteen then, I twenty, aching to be twenty-one. No, it didn't look very hopeful.

After having listed the credits in my favour, I was forced to ponder the debits as well. I was shorter than she, I did not have a car, on my salary I could not afford to take her to expensive restaurants nor give her impressive presents. She was not particularly literary, so that after the initial spark of curiosity there would be nothing in my talents, such as they were, which could possibly stoke a flaming fire. By Indian standards I was neither handsome nor particularly attractive. I was dark, she was fair; I was small, she was large (and very well proportioned too); I had a snub nose and narrow, slightly stooping—what I chose to call 'intellectual'—shoulders. I did not excel at any sport, I had no experience with women.

The list was too long and depressing. Less daring men would have surrendered even before the battle had begun. But not I. Remember, I had promised myself to take on all comers, excluding Tolstoy and Shaw. And of the two, the first was dead, and the second too old and weak to be able to make the journey to India for the purpose of meeting Mimi. So I decide to take the plunge.

The first time we met in company outside Broadcasting House was in a play-reading group at Mimi's sister's place. This was a stroke of luck—her sister was married to a journalist whom I knew. So I was invited to the group on what looked like legitimate grounds—Mimi couldn't possibly think I was chasing her.

The play we were to read was an added bonus too, Shaw's *You Never Can Tell*. And because of our ages I was chosen to play Philip and Mimi for Dolly—twin brother and sister to the heroine. We had to sit next to each other, as there weren't many copies of the book, and the physical proximity certainly produced the expected tension in me. Also, it gave me a chance to display a talent which I knew I possessed, an opportunity which would have been hard to find in any other situation.

During breaks we were polite to each other, indulging in pleasantries which revealed neither hostility nor intimacy to the others in the group. As the evening was drawing to a close, however, the spectre of 'confrontation' (or its absence, which would be equally debilitating) loomed larger. And I thought I would throw in a test line during the last break.

'Have you found your mystery man yet?' I asked.

'What makes you think I've been hunting round for him?'

'You seemed pretty obsessed the last time we met,' I replied. 'Of course, women's curiosities are not always tenacious.'

'Well it's none of your damn business anyway! Whether I've found him or not, whether my curiosity is tenacious or not.'

I smiled. 'I suppose you think that a pretty girl has the right to be rude in answer to a perfectly civil remark.'

She stared back. 'And I suppose you think that you are a paragon of politeness yourself.'

Just then the leader of the group motioned that we should start reading again.

'Look,' I said to Mimi in a whisper, 'what do you say to talking this over a coffee?'

'Sh . . . sh . . . sh,' came the stern reprimand from the man who was directing us. But I persisted. 'What do you say? After we finish here?'

The eyes of the whole group were on us now. Mimi was embarrassed.

'All right,' she said, biting out the words.

We took a taxi and went to La Bohème, the only coffee-bar-cum-restaurant in Delhi with a reputation for flamboyance and elan. In those days it had an Indian Room, with cave architecture, flowery fountains and incense; a Chinese Room with reproductions of the famous 'horse', low-hanging balloon lanterns and an appetite-whetting menu; and then, of course, there was the European Room, soft wax candles in the manner of a continental bistro, low piped music, separate intimate tables for two and 'milk shakes' for the cognoscenti. It was expensive and chic. I hoped it would impress Mimi. For this was where film stars came when they were on a flying visit to Delhi; artists who were known in Detroit and Tokyo could be seen sipping iced coffee, and, of course, the usual complement of emancipated Delhi belles on the make, extras on a Hollywood set, Playgirls of the Month, with reputations shrieking to a crescendo for a week and then blasting into silence as a newer face came along.

But I mustn't give the impression that Delhi was a 'swinging' westernized town, where men and women moved around as freely as they do in London or New York. It was less aristocratic than Calcutta and therefore more ostentatious. Girls who 'dated' men did so at the expense of knowing that they would never find a 'respectable' Indian husband. The noveau riche dominated the scene, there were fewer restraints and a certain amount of public exhibition of defiance did take place. But society, Indian society, did not approve. The people who came to the La Bohème were on the fringe, they had never been within the hallowed sanctum of Indian prudery and aristocratic hauteur, so they did not know or acknowledge the feeling of exclusion. Men, some men, got away with it, as they managed to create the impression that they were slumming, mixing with the 'low' on a night out. But women were doomed. If you date a man as a single girl, you lose your chastity, and no man, however emancipated and groomed in Oxbridge permissiveness, could possibly take you as his wife.

Being seen with Mimi created the appropriate flutter. There were two men from a rival paper and one senior correspondent of the *Statesman*, who saw us come in. We were not holding hands; in fact, when we sat down in one of the 'intimate' booths in the European Room there was no exchange of dialogue for the first quarter-hour. But Mimi, the inaccessible, devouring, hungrily sought-after goddess of all frustrated males in Delhi, had been seen with me in La Bohème. That was enough. My stock as a lady-killer rocketed.

This is the perversely exciting thing about India. Because no toothpaste professes to increase your 'sex appeal', because couples are not seen kissing in the street and indulging in pre-copulative shuffles on the dance floor, the least sexual gesture has an intensity quite unimaginable in the West. This is why talk about 'intrinsics' in sex falls so flat, for different societies have different mores and what in one is natural and acceptable might, in another, be taboo. And it is always the breaking of taboo that is the spur to eroticism.

Mimi had sat with numerous other men in any number of these 'booths'. This was my first experience. And I thrilled in it precisely because there was an added excitement, outside what was happening between her and me. This gave me confidence and I managed to carry off the evening with a certain amount of savoir faire which, had we been by ourselves unknown to the rest of the world, would have been quite impossible.

We arranged to meet again.

When I came into the office the next day it was already humming with the story of my conquest. Rangaswami, who was so well versed in the bawdy and voluptuous world of the female, was mesmerized by the news that Mimi and I had coffee together. He accused me of pretending innocence when all the time I had been a potential Farouk. How could I have so deceived him? Mimi simply never went out with Indians, so what was my secret? How was she, as juicy and soft as she looked or as hard as a coconut shell? And the more I disavowed any knowledge of the intimate details of Mimi's physiological and erotic life, the more the impression was confirmed that I had perpetrated the most daring sexual seduction of the twentieth century.

Indians are devious about sex. If you want to deceive them just tell them the truth.

Another thing I learnt from that evening's encounter concerned the 'half-caste' phenomenon. No offspring from a mixed marriage—Indo-European—could ever be respectable. Especially women. If they weren't actually tarts, plying their wares on the street, they were always lewd, lascivious and thoroughly disreputable. They had no standards of decency, no morals. They were good for a rough and tumble in the hay but never good enough to bring into your house. So what I had imagined to be the glittering social life that Mimi lived was in fact little more than polished tinsel: the Negro crooner who sits at your table in the restaurant, the 'untouchable' who stands beside the President at the formal Republic Day Parade—condescended to, taken out for a 'good time', but never accepted.

There is always an a priori judgement against any violation of the status quo. Europeans are fine—they are white-skinned, rich and progressive—provided they stick to themselves. Indians should 'mix' with them, drink their liquor, sleep with their women if possible, but to go any further would show lack of pedigree. I was to see the same basic belief in many Indian undergraduates at Oxford and Cambridge a few years later.

Mimi and I started 'going out'. This in itself was quite daring, for 'dates' did not take place in Delhi. If a boy and girl were seen together outside their homes more than twice, it was assumed that they were about to get married. And even such couples were thought to belong to 'progressive and westernized' families. Rangaswami warned that my association with Mimi would cost me my marriage—to a 'respectable Indian girl', that is. But there was envy all round. I had managed to land the most delectable of all female treasures in the capital. What caused dismay was my obvious infatuation with the girl. If I had made it clear that I was 'just out for a good time', then all would be forgiven. But to introduce words like 'love' and 'feeling', especially about an Anglo-Indian girl, was somehow in bad taste and rather juvenile. (None of my unmarried colleagues had ever slept with a 'proper Indian girl', although they were all over thirty, and the ones who had had any sexual experience were like Rangaswami, subscribers to Venus or some Anglo-Saxon girl out on a philanthropic mission to India.)

But I did not feel any restraints. My three-year-long association with a proper Brahmin girl in Calcutta had left me badly bruised. I needed the ego-boost that Mimi's status in Delhi society offered me. And after the first few encounters I felt at ease and enjoyed her company. No, not in the way one would enjoy a man's company, no. I liked to feel the sides of her thighs rub against mine in a taxi, I like the smell of her perfume when she came close to me, I enjoyed sitting opposite her at a restaurant. But none of these things incited me to go any further.

This state of platonic bliss lasted three months. Mimi was my girlfriend, we went to the pictures together, I took her to a charity ball at the Ashoka Hotel, visited her frequently at Broadcasting House, bought her occasional presents and even wrote a poem about her. Everyone in Delhi acknowledged my status as 'her man'. If she could be seen flirting with the new French attaché or that handsome young Arab at the Egyptian Embassy, why, it was only to be expected! 'Her professional life, you know . . . . ' This didn't bother me; I was getting all I wanted from her. If there were others who got other things, well, so long as I didn't have to see it with my own eyes and so long as her 'professional life' did not conflict with the private life she lived with me, I didn't really mind.

Then one evening the 'private life' exploded in my face.

But before I go on to describe what happened, I must tell you of an incident that occurred during those three months, which concerns Mimi only marginally but which was to leave an important impression on me and affect my future life.

The Indian Council for Cultural Relations had invited a group of British authors and artists to deliver a series of lectures on the occasion of an anniversary of Tolstoy's—his birth, death, marriage or some such. Since I was supposed to be the 'literary one' at the *Statesman* office, I was sent to cover the inaugural session. Of course, it made no sense at all. I didn't know shorthand and there were five long speeches, all of them delivered extempore without written texts. The fact that I was familiar with the works of some of these writers did not necessarily mean I could reproduce what the speakers said on a public platform. But as I had realized by now 'journalism' and 'logic' were not blood-brothers, and I went along, hoping that I might chance to meet one of the authors personally.

I took Mimi with me, knowing that she would be impressed with the literary ambience.

One of the speakers was Luke Varme, the novelist and critic, who was the first of the Angry Young Men to be published. I had read his book *Tarry Yet A While*, which described the experiences of a young, provincial working-class lad with a university education, who suddenly found himself in the screaming competitive world of London. I had identified with the choking, incoherent anger of the hero, I enjoyed the terse colloquial style. I brought to Mr Varme a certain adulation, mixed with a feeling of pride—I was pretty certain that no one in the audience would have read his work.

So, later in the evening when the guests were treated to a 'reception' at the Imperial Hotel, I went along, hoping to catch Mr Varme alone for a few minutes. Of course, the situation was ludicrous and comic. There were these four white-skinned faces—bobbing up and down, like cork on a wild sea of some five hundred Indian males—looking frantic and caught, sweating profusely, and being inundated with questions by a myriad aspirant writers. Clearly, I was out of luck. But curiosity and zeal got the better of me and I decided to follow Mr Varme from group to group, as he extricated himself from one earnest young fanatic and landed in the lap of another.

'Water is really marvellous, you know,' Mr Varme was saying, trying desperately hard to be non-literary and casual, and holding a glass of clear liquid in his right hand. 'This is the first party I've ever attended where they didn't serve liquor.'

'Yes, sir, in our country we do not commit alcoholic degeneration,' one young man replied.

'Quite, quite,' Mr Varme went on, 'could be quite the thing. Even fruit juices don't stand a chance, against water I mean, You know the genuine *aqua* stuff is an absolute killer.'

His voice had a disturbing nasal grounding, like a soprano's attempt to sing in bass. His face was a cross between a zoo keeper's and an astronaut's, intent and accessible, pleasant and inconspicuous. The nervous twitch on his lips seemed exaggerated when you thought of the twenty pair of eyes scrutinizing his every gesture.

Then one man, with a bald pate and an adenoidal neck, intervened. 'I want to ask a serious question, Mr Varme, if I may be so bold as to venture upon your invaluable time which you have kindly spared for us this evening in the benign hope that you will bring enlightenment into the clouded skies of Indian literature . . . . '

'I hope so too, but what is your question?'

'You see, Mr Varme, in these days of grave apprehensions and momentous thunders, when the world is but a speck of dust in the cosmic universe of Man's happiness and fulfilment, we are indeed very gratefully humble that your genius has chosen to visit this ancient city, and if I may speak for the whole of Delhi, not only the present but the past and the future as well, we are indeed most deeply . . . '

The attention of the group was now entirely focussed on our bald intruder who produced in the audience a mixture of envy and awe. Mr Varme's genius was so exalted that the man who had come not to bury Caesar but to extol him, caught the communal fancy. 'Yes, Mr Varme, I have a question,' the man went on, in his sonorous Welsh voice, 'and the question is of the utmost seriousness since it is directly concerning you and your noble vocation which myself and all my countrymen hav deeply revered . . . . '

'Excuse me,' Varme said, extending his hand, 'I don't know your name but it's nice to have met you. And I really must . . . ' The genuine aqua stuff in the glass was being twisted round and round in both hands by now and an attentive observer might have deduced that Mr Varme was looking quite deeply and reverently trapped. (He was actually physically surrounded, being at the centre of a circle.)

'Yes thank you, Mr Varme,' our bald sage continued, putting out his own hand and shaking Varme's heartily. 'My name is Hakim. Hakim Singh is my name and I belong to that community which worships the saint and master Guru Nanak, who was a warrior and a prophet . . . . '

'Mr Hakim Singh, I thought you had a question,' Luke Vamre interjected in the voice of a supplicant. 'I would really be very interested to hear it.'

'Yes, Mr Varme, my question is the following,' Hakim Singh said, Adam's apple bobbing up and down at a higher frequency than before. The whole group was now frozen into awestruck silence. Varme removed one of his hands from the glass and delved into the recesses of his trouser pocket, and Hakim Singh wiped his forehead with an ash-coloured handkerchief. 'This is my question and it concerns your noble vocation, Mr Varme,' bald pate repeated, as if he was not quite convinced that his audience was yet purged of philistine and flippant thoughts. Varme stifled a sigh.

'How do you write a novel, Mr Varme?'

Silence . . . . Seconds, minutes, or was it hours? All eyes on Varme, not a giggle or a smile, eager intense faces waiting for the revelatory answer, Hakim Singh resembling John the Baptist, leading the way to the great master 'whose shoes he was not worthy to unloose', but doing well enough as a literary guide and probing interviewer.

Varme looked around, words forming noiselessly on his lips and vanishing into immobile silence. 'I mean . . . ' he started once and gave up.

'Yes, Mr Varme,' Hakim Singh's sombre voice prodded—the guru must not disappoint his shishyas, especially as he was lucky enough to have such an able lieutenant.

'What am I supposed to say?' Varme finally answered. 'I mean I don't know how I write a novel.'

'You mean you are really not in the possession of the knowledge of executing the writing of a novel?' Hakim Singh insisted, a smile of triumph and victory beginning to flicker across his eyes. 'Mr Varme, you must not be under the impression that these boys have no wisdom because they are young. All of them are graduates holding BA degrees and I belong in humbleness to a noble profession also, namely teaching. So you can be intimately frank with us.'

'Yes I know and I didn't mean to say that either you or these young men are not wise but . . . '

At this point I pushed myself forward. 'Excuse me, Mr Varme, I don't mean to interrupt, but I think you will remember that you have an appointment for an interview with the *Statesman* newspaper.'

'Oh yes, of course,' Varme replied effusively, picking up the cue, relief flooding in on his face. 'I very nearly forgot . . . er . . . er . . . shall we go to my room? It's somewhere in this hotel, I understand.'

'If you like.' I said, as the circle parted to let us out.

'But, Mr Varme, you have not yet answered my question,' Hakim Singh bellowed, panting hotfoot after us.

'Sorry, Mr Singh, but I promised this young man that I would give him an interview, and I have another date later tonight.'

'Then perhaps I can accompany your company down to your chamber . . . .'

'I am afraid,' I said, cutting in, 'the *Statesman* interview is not conducted in public.'

'But I am not public . . . I am an ardent devotee of the English literature, having spent my whole life in the noble vocation of imparting my humble knowledge to my students.'

'I am sorry,' I replied firmly, 'it's one of the house rules of the paper. We don't allow outsiders listening in on interviews.'

'And what about her then?' Hakim Singh shouted, pointing at Mimi.

'She is one of our sub-editors,' I replied, smiling.

Varme had sneaked into the men's cloakroom while this interchange was taking place. And Hakim Singh, furious at having let go of his prey, started to follow the noble genius into the ignoble surroundings of the pee house.

'Mustn't do that,' I said, holding him by the arm. 'Westerners don't like being followed in there.'

'You are in the right,' Hakim Singh said, resolved not to surrender. 'I shall just wait here then for Mr Varme to emerge.'

'You do that,' I replied, 'while I go and make a telephone call to the office.'

I knew that Hakim Singh had never been to the Imperial Hotel before and had certainly not visited the men's room.

There was in fact another exit leading out on to the lawn. Varme was obviously securely ensconced in his room by now, pouring himself some beer and wiping his face.

I went to the foyer and asked for Varme's room at the reception desk.

'Mr Varme has instructed that no one should be given his room number.'

'I am from the *Statesman* and I have an appointment with Mr Varme. So if you will please get him on the phone and tell him that the reporter from the *Statesman* is down here at the foyer . . . '

'Oh please excuse me, I did not realize,' the receptionist said. 'I shall get Mr Varme for you.'

It took a few minutes for the man to get through. Obviously Varme was in no mood to answer the telephone either. Mimi and I looked at each other, while my heart jumped about with irregular abandon. To come so close and then to miss out . . . Damn that bald adenoidal moron!

I was handed the receiver across the desk. 'Hullo,' Varme said, 'I'm sorry to have skipped out on you like that but . . . '

'I understand, Mr Varme,' I replied gravely, 'but I really am from the *Statesman* and I wondered if you would spare the time . . . '

'Of course,' Varme said, 'as I told you, I do have a dinner date, but there is a little time between now and then. So if you would care to come up to Room——. And look, just make sure that the crazy old man isn't following you.'

'He is waiting outside the men's room,' I replied, 'for you to "emerge".'

Varme laughed. 'What does he think I've got? A case of the trots or something?'

Mimi and I entered Varme's room to see a pretty white girl sitting on the sofa and sipping beer. I introduced myself and apologized for bringing Mimi along with me. 'Not at all,' Varme replied, pouring out some beer for the two of us and introducing his American lady-friend. 'A pretty woman is always welcome to my house . . . wherever that may be.' Mimi blushed, I shook hands with the girl sitting on the sofa and felt a thrill to be amongst such sophisticated adult company.

'Cheers,' Varme said, holding up his glass, as he stood in the corner of the room next to the window.

'Cheers,' the three of us echoed.

'Now if you really do want an interview, I suggest we skip the births, deaths, marriages and so forth. It's all down in the *Who's Who*, all you've got to do is to go to the library and look it up.'

'I wasn't going to ask you any of those things,' I replied.

'Oh good, then you're an exception. I meet hundreds of people everywhere I go and they've all heard of me but none of them has read my book.'

'I have read your book, Mr Varme,' I retorted.

'Really?' Varme queried, quizzically, 'Well then, fire away.'

I crossed my legs, took out my notebook and held my pencil poised over it.

'You are identified as an important member of a new movement in English literature . . . '

'Oh not that Angry Young Man stuff again, please. Look, it has already become a bloody cliché in England and I don't see why you people make such a song and dance about it.' The American girl held a bored disengaged smile on her lips.

'If you had let me finish, Mr Varme,' I continued, firm and a little angry, 'I was going to ask whether you think that the idea of a "movement" in literature has any validity as far as the work of an individual artist is concerned.'

'Well, that's an entirely different point . . . .'

Varme said that the label 'Angry Young Man' had been invented by journalists, and not very literate ones either, for the purpose of making a sensation. It had little relevance to his own writing. He was not angry and not so young either. He had nothing in common with Osborne, he did not scream. He had been up at Oxford, had taught there after coming down with a degree, had married early and unwisely. He was interested in literary criticism and poetry.

I asked about Wilson.

'Which one?' he retorted. 'There are several of them, you know. Edmund Wilson, Angus Wilson . . . '

'Colin Wilson, of course.'

'Don't see why it should be so "of course". That young man wrote a book which sold very well and made a lot of money for him. But if he was one of my students I'd advise him to take a course in elementary logic.'

Every time I asked a literary question it was converted into a personal one. I realize now that I should have sent the script to *Playboy* magazine and earned a fat fee. As it was, I could only offer it to John Stuart and, horse-loving man that he was, literary gossip didn't seem to titillate him. Besides, it wasn't *assigned* to me. Apparently, I hadn't yet qualified to do an interview, special techniques had to be learnt for these things, what readers wanted to know, what makes a good headline. No, the *Statesman* couldn't print 'this stuff'.

But Varme and I got on well enough for him to give me his address. I corresponded with him twice before I met him at his home in London.

Through Varme and a little luck, I met the other visiting dignitaries. I was introduced to Helen Lumme, the poetess who had edited a 'little' literary magazine in the twenties, and whose only claim—as far as I could gather—to be a member of the artistic troupe was her beautiful silver hair, crushed in static curls over her head. Even in her advanced physical condition she had not lost all love of 'life' or young boys and had proceeded to give me a very close hug when I had daringly entered her hotel room unchaperoned.

She was one of those 'professional' writers who have long given up writing but who, because of a superabundance of energy and enthusiasm, are always asked to sit on committees, sign petitions and letters to the *Times*. They are invited to visit faraway places like India and Japan, judge poetry contests, become 'author in residence' in Midwestern American universities, in short to live up to the image of the 'writer' in public because the genuine writer is far too busy doing his stuff to spare time for such frolics.

At the time, however, I was not aware of the intricate mechanics that operate the literary world and I had heard of Helen Lumme's name, by courtesy of the publicity machine, more often than W. H. Auden's or Quasimodo's. So I went to her with a devotee's heart and left a bunch of my poems on her desk, as soon as I could politely extricate myself from her unpoetical advances. Four months later when I still had not heard from her, I wrote asking if she had managed to take a look at my offering and if she had, what did she think of it? A very legible scribble on an aerogram came back in ten days: 'Sorry to have lost your poems in transit. Could you send me another set, please?'

I could not, and said so in reply. And thus ended the story of Helen Lumme's association with Amit Ray.

I have often wondered who the loser was. For I do fancy curly silver hair, even at the best of times, especially on women advanced in years and experience.

The third member of the delegation was Tobias Darnley, the well-known critic and short-story writer. Meeting him was the most fortunate experience for me and it came about through a series of improbable accidents. I had gone to see Mimi at Broadcasting House round about midday, only to learn that she had been put on the air and would not be free till two. I decided to hang around and dropped in to see my anglicized Indian lady-friend next door. Bad luck again, not at her desk. So I finally strolled out of the place and was sauntering down Parliament Street when I heard someone shout my name. I turned round to see Hakim Singh approaching me with rapid strides. There were no men's rooms nearby, alas, and he caught up with me.

'My young friend,' he said, placing his hand on my shoulder, as older people do in India, 'you are very clever. But mistake not that one day that very cleverness will be your most extreme undoing.'

'Well,' I stammered, uncomfortably pinned down by his arm, 'I suppose we shall have to wait and see, won't we?'

'Yes, yes, we shall certainly do that . . . . ' And then suddenly, without any warning, Hakim Singh started running. I started at first and then was faintly amused.

'What's the matter?' I yelled.

'I shall get them this time,' he shouted back. And I looked down the road to see Helen Lummè and Tobias Darnley enter Broadcasting House in a taxi.

It was one o'clock, I was curious, Mimi would be free in an hour. So I decided to go back and see what was happening. Poor Hakim Singh was not much of a sprinter and had not been able to stop the taxi in time, and the armed guard would not let him enter Broadcasting House without a pass. His angry eyes would have spewed fire if they could when he saw me walk in without a word of obstruction from anyone at the gate.

I went to find my anglicized Indian lady-friend, as I was sure that she would know. And I found her screaming in frenzy on the phone. As I sat down in the chair across her desk, she turned and saw me. Her eyes dilated, her face switched from violet to brown and she banged down the receivér. 'Thank God you're here,' she said, in a voice low with exhaustion and relief.

'What have I done?' I asked, interested.

'What you are about to do, you mean?' she replied, 'Come on, be a good boy. You've been on the air before. You can do it.'

'What?'

'The interview . . . you know. They are both here at the same time. There has been some awful bungle.'

She was not very coherent but I finally managed to piece the story together. Both Helen Lumme and Tobias Darnley had been invited to Broadcasting House for an interview. But due to someone's ineptitude somewhere they had both turned up at the same time, unexpectedly. So there was one interviewer on the premises and two interviewees. Wanted: Second interviewer! And that was precisely what she was trying to get on the phone, just before I turned up—a second interviewer. But now that I had arrived, there was no further problem, was there? I could do it, I had debated in college, remember.

And when was this thing supposed to be? In fifteen minutes, of course. You know how the English hate to be kept waiting. Just now the two of them were having coffee with the Director General, but as soon as they finish . . . .

I like a challenge, but not when there is no chance of victory at all. The woman assured me that the interview would be taped, so if I came out badly it need not be broadcast at all. They wouldn't know. Whether it would or would not be broadcast was of no concern to me however. What would my interviewee think? What could I ask? How would I follow up my questions?

I decided to take the chance and asked to do Tobias Darnley (whom I had not met before). I had not read any of his books or his short stories at the time. My sole acquaintance with his work was through the *New Statesman* where he used to write every week in those days. I knew he had a formidably analytical mind and a facility for the sharp telling image. So I thought it would be best to stick to what I knew rather than foray into uncharted waters.

We were introduced by our lady producer just outside the studio. Then the two of us walked in, Darnley slightly stooped, bespectacled and leather-faced, and I, cold, hungry, and determined to be brave.

They tested the voice levels, the distance of the microphones from our mouths, warned us about the creaking of the chairs every time we moved in our seats, and then we were all set.

The interview lasted for half an hour. Darnley shook my hand afterwards and said, 'Good luck and hope to see you in England sometime soon.' The lady producer did not feel hesitant to broadcast what was on the tape (it was not edited). The reviewers in the newspapers made complimentary noises, one of them even taking time off to remark that my voice sounded more British than the Britisher who was being interviewed. When Darnley returned to London he wrote a piece on his visit to India in the *New Statesman*, in which he referred to me as 'a brilliant young man'.

In India this sort of testimonial is not the best way to win friends.

Mimi's father was a writer too. On the surface of it he had had an exciting career. He had left India at sixteen—long before Independence—and arrived in England, working as a cook's boy on a ship. Then he had taught himself English, put in time with numerous local papers and had learnt the journalist's craft from the stone to the editorial chair, the hard way up. There weren't too many Indians floating around in Britian in those days; those who were there were mostly students from upper-class families and were treated with respect and awe—'Never know, he might be the son of a maharajah'—by the populace. Mimi's father climbed the social ladder fast; his burning eyes set in a dark handsome face more than endeared him to hostesses at elite dinner parties. By the time he was in his mid-twenties, Mimi's father was well known in London as a crusading journalist and engaging raconteur. Then *Time* magazine offered him the post of 'European Correspondent'. He accepted, fervent patriotic feelings about his 'dear India' notwithstanding. He had arrived.

Publishers hunted him. He wrote several monographs on 'Socialism', 'Nationalism' and all the other innocuous *isms* that sold in the market place in those days. (He must have stayed away from the only viable *ism* going, i.e. Fabianism, for he once confessed to me that he had never read Shaw. 'Never follow fashion, boy,' he had said. 'Let it follow you.' I was too awed by his flamboyant career to point out that the old man was hardly in the vanguard of current fads.) He also wrote travel books, having made several forays into dangerous and unheard of terrain—Greenland one winter, the Black Forest in the following summer. Expenses paid and photographer provided by *Time* magazine, of course.

He had married a Scottish singer, produced two lovely girls with alacrity and was about to settle down and enjoy the fruits of his labours when demon politics caught up with him. The war came foolishly to an end, the Labour Party got into power and gave India her Independence. Having fought so valiantly for the 'cause' in self-imposed exile, Mimi's father rightly expected to be showered with medals and trophies on his return to 'dear India'. But the Goddess of Fortune had developed a taste for flirting with this Man of Destiny. More than ten years after the return of the exile, when I met him, he still had not found a job. His wife worked as a manageress in a small restaurant and Mimi's wages provided an important prop to the family finances.

It was all too bewildering for Papa. 'What happened? I came back to serve my country, to help build a "new India". Why don't they lay out the red carpet for me, provide me with an air-conditioned room from which I can direct the affairs of the nation? Delhi is too hot in the summer.' So he slept for most of the day, took the dog out for a walk in the afternoon and corrected and re-corrected the manuscript of his 'opus' through the rest of the evening.

In fact there was a genuine odour of tragedy about this man. He was still handsome, no wrinkles on his face, no paunch or double chin to destroy the illusion of a tiger about to leap into action. The girls adored him, the missus sulked sullenly while doing the dishes. And Papa went on living an illusion, apparelled in dreams which all artists must know.

His last book came out some two months after I met Mimi. I got hold of a copy, read it and was appalled. The style was lumbering and leaden, the anecdotes as flat as unleavened bread. I could not understand why a British publisher had chosen to bring it out. There was something wrong somewhere. If the story of his life was true, if he had really made it from the ship's kitchen to the *Time* office, then it just couldn't be the same man who had sired this dismal tract. Of course, I was young then, impatient as only innocence can be. I had not yet learnt that people do change, even writers; inspirations dry up, idealism and courage wither away.

The book created a problem. I had promised Mimi to review it in a weekly magazine in which I had begun to write. Yet I could not genuinely utter a single word of praise for a work which in my opinion should never have smelt the printer's ink. I knew too that it was important to Mimi; she was hoping that it would revive the family fortunes, pull Papa out of his well of depression and self-pity. What do you do in a situation like that? Refuse to review the book? Or tell lies? Or worse still, say nothing at all, padding your comments with homilies and 'on-the-one-hand, on-the-other' phrases of puerile banality?

I began my review by saying that it was a readable book, if you were interested in the subject-matter, that is. The author had a lust for travel; the book was an attempt to record the sinuous track along which that lust had had to be guided. I qualified every single statement I made, neutralizing each phrase that might sound even vaguely complimentary with a thrust at the author's 'inability to capture mood, report dialogue which sounded authentic', etc.

The Friday on which the issue came out, I was nervous and taut. I did not want to lose Mimi and I knew that her father had a lot of influence over her. All morning I roamed around in the *Statesman* office, tense and touchy. In the afternoon Mimi was on the phone. She had just spoken to Papa; would I care to come over for dinner at their house that evening?

'Er . . . er . . . what does he think of the review?'

'Daddy said that you write very well and that it was a thoughtful analysis of the book. He is very pleased.'

From that day on, I have never doubted my capacity to deceive, to say one thing and mean another. Words can wear many masks—you can always keep a straight face and come out with the most outrageous things—if you know how to use them. Dinner that night established me firmly with Mimi. Her father approved.

After I had presented my credentials to Mimi's father with the review, I followed up my debut with a profile of our hero in the *New Delhi Notebook*. Here I could really wax eloquent. For there were no qualifications to be made about such a startling career. If it looked as if it was about to end with a whimper, then it was all the more romantic to dwell on the furious bangs with which it had been launched. I showed the proofs to Mimi on Sunday night, Monday morning brought Papa to my door.

'Splendid, young man, simply splendid,' the crusading warrior remarked, as he slapped down a copy of the paper on my coffee table. 'You'll go far. There is a genuine flair in your style.'

Mimi came round a while later.

'Why don't the two of you go out and have an evening on me?'

I would love to. So would Mimi. Yes, she had an 'engagement' tonight but she could cancel that, 'Daddy, it's lovely of you to do this.'

'Out of the royalties, you know,' the old man replied, slapping me on the shoulder.

I bought a bottle of Indian whisky (Black Knight), Mimi came round to my flat at six, looking radiant and voluptuous. She wore a blue silk sari and a velvet blouse; my fingers grazed the smooth skin above her waist as I helped her off with the cape. The neckline of the blouse swept down low, I could see the cleft between her breasts as she drew one deep breath after another.

'What's the matter? Have you been running?' I asked.

'No, Amit,' she replied, 'I am just so excited. You did a marvellous thing for Daddy. He looks so happy.'

'I am glad,' I said, avoiding her eyes. 'Do you want a drink?'

'You mean you have some?'

I poured two large whiskies, put some ice cubes (which I had bought from the shop down the road) in the glasses and opened a bottle of soda.

'Neat for me, please,' Mimi said. 'I don't want any fizz in my drink.'

'To your father,' I toasted, raising my glass.

'To my father,' she replied.

She had never looked so sparkling before, not with me anyway. I had seen her once at a party and she had had the same eager expression in her eyes. But never when we had been alone with each other. Tonight she was radiating sparks all over, I could feel them darting at me, over my thighs, my face, even my hands. Every time I touched her I felt a swift charge run through my whole body.

'Daddy likes you very much,' she continued. 'He thinks you will become a very good writer: and he knows.'

'Of course he does,' I agreed. 'He's been at it all his life, hasn't he?'

Mimi handed me an envelope which contained four ten-rupee notes. We decided to go to the Volga. In the taxi she leaned over and put her head on my shoulder. I breathed in her perfume, felt her thigh rub against mine, and the small inner voice whispered, 'Caution'. A vague undefined fear began to well up within me, as if I was no longer free to move, the stark stare of the hunter on the prey.

We ate in silence. Then the band started to play a soft, lilting number. I took Mimi on to the floor and her body seemed to melt into mine, yielding, soft, full of promise. I had never experienced this sensation before, both hard and pliant, charged yet mellow. My whole body was awake, hairs stood on end, my hands were cold. Mimi's face was close to mine, her lips grazing my cheeks. The smell of her hair, the nude skin above her waist, the feel of her velvet blouse against my palms, they were all speaking to me, inviting. And I was afraid.

We came off the floor. I paid the bill and asked the doorman to fetch a taxi. On the ride back home, Mimi took my hand on her lap and began stroking the back of my palm. Each stroke was so full of pleasure that it verged on pain, like thin long pieces of skin being ripped off one's back. I could not move, I could neither respond nor draw away. 'I feel so happy with you,' she sighed. And just before the car was about to turn into her street, Mimi said, 'Let's go back to your place for a night-cap.'

'Isn't it a bit late?' I replied. It was midnight.

'Just this once, please,' she pleaded. 'Daddy won't mind.'

I told the driver to take us to my flat and I felt trapped and frightened. Some deep black hole yawned in front of me, I was about to hurtle down a depthless well. Feelings froze. I did not want to think about the future. My hand lay listless on Mimi's lap, unable to stir. Tears were ready to burst into my eyes.

'It's full moon tonight,' she said, as we got out of the cab.

We sat on opposite ends of the table, drinks at hand. Minutes went by loaded with silence. Every now and again Mimi looked up at me, soft, pleading, offering the key to a world of uncertainty. I did not know what was in that world; I did not have the courage to open the door. I would think about it often, but in real life . . . The time has not yet come, I told myself. I am a writer, Mimi is a woman, there is whisky in the glass. I can see her bosom heave, she is breathing hard, there are beads of sweat on her brow. We are four feet apart, there is a divan next to the window, it's full moon tonight. Her eyes are burning, I can feel their heat on my bare arms, I am sweating. I want to get up and walk over to her, hold her in my arms just as I did on the dance floor. There is no one else in the room. I want to rub my naked skin against hers. Yes, I want to feel those lips with mine. I am a writer, Mimi is a woman, it's full moon tonight. There is whisky in the glass . . . .

I woke up with an ache, the clock said three, and there was still some whisky in the glass, though the ice had melted. The note on the table read:

> The night cap wasn't such a good idea, was it? Hope you don't walk around with a monstrous hangover all day. We shouldn't meet here like this and we won't in the future. The intimacy of your four walls frightens me. I look into your eyes and feel a warm glow inside. I can't help it. Sometimes when I am walking down a street, I hear all those hard voices in my ear, and I think of you. And a small unwilling drop of my soul falls to the ground.
>
> Sweet dreams. Mimi

I undressed and went to bed, feeling as if some roots had been plucked out of the ground. I was free, yet not entirely my own master. Mimi had scissored some cords which were holding me down. 'I love you,' I whispered, before I fell asleep.

I woke up in the morning soaked in sweat. There is no spring in Delhi. It was March, hot, dry and windless. I drew all the curtains to keep out the sun and stood under the cold shower for a long while. Images began bubbling up in my mind: the dance floor of the Volga, Mimi's head on my shoulder in the taxi, pouring out large shots of whisky after midnight. I could see myself sitting in the chair, glass in hand, staring emptily at Mimi across the table, adult thoughts racing through my head. I couldn't remember how or when she left. Had I . . . ? No, I couldn't have done. Not really kissed her! I remembered trying to get up once. Then the floor had begun to spin under my feet and I had slumped back in the chair, steadying my hand to reach the glass and taking another sip of the whisky. No, obviously I had no capacity for alcohol, shouldn't touch the stuff really. But then again, if we hadn't been drinking, would Mimi have come back to the flat after dinner? Not that anything had happened. But it could have done. Didn't she say, 'The intimacy of your four walls frightens me'?

In a way, the day that began with the cold shower was the most important watershed in my life. I walked into the office to find the chief frantically screaming down the phone. Rangaswami had rung in to say that he was ill. Two other reporters were away on holiday, another one had been sent on a special out-of-town assignment the previous day. What was so frantic about all that?

'Just that the Prime Minister is speaking at the National Science Institute this evening,' the chief replied. 'That's all.'

The four of us—including my Bengali friend—who were in the office, walked into John Stuart's room for 'conference' precisely at eleven.

'Good morning, all,' bellowed John Stuart, pulling his silver-rimmed spectacles down to the tip of his nose. 'What's on the agenda, Chief?'

'The Prime Minister . . . '

'Yes, I saw that,' Mr Stuart said, cutting him short. 'At the Science Institute, isn't it ?'

'Yes, it is the closing day of the International Conference on the Peaceful Uses of Atomic Energy,' the chief explained.

'Hm,' the boss replied, creasing his brow. 'Has Ray got over his teething troubles yet? Hm?'

'Well, sir, he has been turning in some good copy recently, but . . . er . . . '

'The wind . . . or was it the rain, isn't "lingering" any more, is it?' Mr Stuart said, staring hard at me.

'No, sir, it has stopped blowing "whither it will" too,' I replied, smiling.

'You did science at college, didn't you?'

'Yes, sir, physics.'

'Well, it's all settled then,' Mr Stuart announced, looking at the chief. 'See you get him a press card before he goes. We wouldn't like the *Statesman* man to be barred at the door, would we now?'

My heart missed several beats, my palms turned moist and my mouth went dry.

'Thank you, sir,' I stammered, 'thank you very much.'

'That's all right. Don't botch it up, will you? I'll have some explaining to do if . . . '

'Conference' ended after less momentous matters had been discussed. It must have been the combination of a whisky hangover, the evening with Mimi and John Stuart's munificent gesture, that lifted me off the ground and sent me reeling into a world of fantasy. 'Who did that *Statesman* report?' I heard Mr Nehru asking his press secretary. 'It was brilliant. I would like to see the man sometime.'

'The Prime Minister's Secretariat on the line for you, Mr Ray,' the girl at the switchboard whispered.

'Hullo, this is Ray here.'

'The Prime Minister wishes to see you, Mr Ray . . . '

'It's a senior assignment,' the chief barked, pulling me firmly back to the reporters' room. 'You realize that, don't you?'

'Yes, of course, I should think that . . . '

'Don't think. Just put down what he says. And don't add any of your own flowery words either.'

With Mimi's note in one pocket and the press card in the other, I walked out of the *Statesman* building after lunch, wondering if the gods had really picked me out as their special messenger on earth. I had phoned Mimi at Broadcasting House, but she was on the air and would not be free till five. Nehru was due to speak at seven. That gave me two hours, plenty of time to placate my darling girl, tell her the good news and . . . perhaps I could even take her along with me. That would impress her! Oh, but she didn't have a press card. Never mind, she would see my report tomorrow. And, of course, we could meet later in the day and I could tell her about my appointment with the Prime Minister. Yes, of course it was bound to happen. John Stuart had spotted my talents, hadn't he? And Nehru was a thousand times more perceptive. 'There's a long glittering career ahead of you, young man. Are you really committed to journalism? What about External Affairs, does that interest you any? How about taking over the Cultural Affairs Section of the Embassy in London?'

Twenty past five. 'Do you know if Mimi has left for the day?'

'She was on the air till five, so I don't think . . .'

Two cigarettes and lots of exercise, sitting down and getting up from the chair at two-minute intervals. 'She usually comes straight back to her desk from the studio, doesn't she?'

'Unless she had an appointment and flew off in a hurry.'

Twenty to six. Rising pulse beat, palms moist, mouth dry, as in the morning. For different reasons.

'What are you doing here?'

'Look, we've got to go. I am in a God-awful hurry.'

'So am I,' Mimi snapped back.

'Please, let's not fight. Nehru. I mean the Science Institute . . . a senior assignment, don't you see?'

'What are you talking about? And you are lighting the filter of your cigarette.'

'Please . . .'

It is rush hour, all the taxis with their flags down. Even the three-wheeler motor-scooters were scarce. Nearly six o'clock. 'Well, I am *not* going to La Bohème or anywhere else,' Mimi had insisted. 'I look an absolute mess. If you want to talk, let's go back to your flat.' Which was only twenty minutes from the centre of town and a good half-hour from the Science Institute. Talk of women being contrary! 'You don't have to talk to me this evening, you know. There's next week, next month, perhaps never.' Very ominous. Threats, invitations, promises, showdowns. Anyhow, nothing adolescent about a single line of this script, all very suave and sophisticated and adult.

The clock ticks away as we get into the motor-scooter. I try to speak but the spluttering of a silencer-less engine drowns my voice. We sit silent, tense and hostile. Mimi looks away from me, unyielding. But I feel a strange new confidence which I did not have the night before. Uncertainty has vanished, I don't feel trapped any more. 'The intimacy of your four walls frightens me.' Is that why she suggested that we go back to my flat, to be frightened some more? If I could handle Nehru's speech, I could handle Mimi.

The motor-scooter refuses to wait. 'You'll just have to ring for a taxi,' Mimi says, walking into the sitting room. The curtains are still drawn, it is dark inside. 'Do you have to have the light on?' she asks, as I walk towards the switch.

'No really,' I reply, picking up the bottle of whisky from the table. 'I think I should keep myself sober for Mr Nehru. But I'll pour you one, if you like.'

'No thanks,' Mimi answers. 'Let's just hear what you want to say and then I'll be off and you can do your senior assignment to your heart's content.'

'Well . . . '

'Well?'

'Er . . . er . . . I mean your note.'

'Yes?'

'I don't know . . . What did you mean?'

'Exactly what I said.'

'The business of the four walls frightening you, Why should they?'

'You have a fantastic imagination, don't you?' Mimi says, walking over to the window.

'I mean . . . I am sorry I . . . Drink affects me. I didn't mean to pass out like that,' I plead, my earlier confidence in the motor-scooter sharply dwindling away. Mimi has her back turned to me, she is standing next to the divan, I am sitting in the chair, wondering if I should have that drink, after all.

'You know, for someone who wants to be a writer . . . ' She doesn't finish her sentence, I can't think of anything to say. Do I go up and . . . ? Is she angry with me? Doesn't she admire me any more? Is she making fun of me perhaps? I can't think of all these things at once. Thoughts are tumbling about in my mind, my ideas about myself, the image I project to others, my obligations as a writer. Above all, decency and sin and good conduct, the voice of my Methodist Principal droning in my head.

'You are an attractive woman. It's only natural that I . . . ' The words come tumbling out, incoherent, unforeseen. 'When I am with you . . . Like last night, when you were stroking the back of my palm. And when we were dancing. You have such smooth skin. Your lips were rubbing against my cheeks. When we got back to the flat, I didn't want to take advantage. The whisky . . . I know I shouldn't have drunk so much. But I was so scared. I wanted to get up and kiss you.'

'So why didn't you?' Mimi asks, turning round to face me.

A huge thud against my chest. I feel dizzy, speechless.

'I didn't know if you would . . . '

Mimi is staring at me, her lips slightly parted, her knees resting against the edge of the divan. My hands are trembling, a drop of sweat hangs at the tip of my nose. I try to speak but can't get the words out of my mouth. The radio next door is on full blast, some slushy Hindi song. I don't even hear the words. The thudding against my chest is too loud and fast. Yes, I want that drink. I need it desperately. I cast a quick glance at the bottle, but before I can reach for it, Mimi puts her hands up to the back of her head and draws out two long pins. Her hair falls down in thick mane-like masses and she shakes her head. She doesn't take her eyes off me; the drop of sweat at the tip of my nose falls to the floor.

I get up from the chair, in slow motion, under hypnosis. My knees are weak; I can hear my own breathing. I am standing in front of her, she remains perfectly still. Her lips have parted a little more, her nostrils flare up for a second. I am going to kiss her. Yes, now!

She holds me very tight, almost suffocating me. I weave my hands round her back and press her closer, against the whole of me. I have a hard aching erection under my trousers. It is throbbing, very fast, I can feel it and it hurts. Her tongue is searching for mine inside my mouth, she is breathing hard too. Her breasts are crushed against my chest. I try to pull her closer, my knees give way and we tumble on to the divan, she on top of me.

We lie like that, my tongue inside her mouth now, her thighs wedged between mine. My erection is hurting me, the tight underpants holding my penis down when it wants to stand up. Mimi rolls away, lying on her back, her sari scaling up her thighs. Her hands are groping for the zip on my trousers. She touches me, presses it down and I feel I am about to explode. It hurts.

Mimi gets up from the divan and unwinds the sari from her body. Petticoat falls to the floor. I get up and unbutton her blouse, then unclip her bra. She is nude. It is like a vision, not quite distinct, not quite real, her eyes burning into me. I take off my shirt, she unzips my trousers and pulls them down, along with my underpants. We are both nude. My hands are cold, my penis is hard and throbbing. She feels it, pulling the skin back. I move her hand away, I am ready to burst.

There are no thoughts in my head, no feeling of sin.

Mimi lies on the divan, leg spread wide apart, the brown nipples on her small tight breasts hard and erect. I come over her and she pushes my face down to her bosom. I take her right nipple between my teeth and bite it. She screams, softly. I begin sucking with my lips. Mimi is feeling my penis, pressing it against herself. I thrust my waist forward. No entry! Won't go in. Try again. Same result. I take it in my hand and try to push it in. No, I don't know where the hole is. Do I feel her with my fingers? Would she mind? I can't hold myself much longer. Oh yes, she is very wet. There is a lot of slippery liquid around. Then why won't it go in? Push again. No!

Mimi lifts her legs in the air, holds my penis in her hand and pushes it into her cunt.

Warm, soft, liquid. I shut my eyes. Aching. Mimi moves. 'No, don't . . . ' Bang, whuff, phoosh . . . h. h. h. There are no words to describe what I feel, this has never happened to me before. No, never when I masturbated. A slight ache remains in my balls. My penis becomes limp, I can feel her muscles squeezing it. I lie over her, inert and weak.

When we finally get up, the floor refuses to remain firm. It slips away with every step I take, it is trying to run away from me, I am floating in the air. When I shut my eyes, the walls begin to spin. I cannot hold anything with my hands, the cigarette falls from my fingers. I cannot stoop down and pick up my trousers. I open my eyes but Mimi looks blurred, fuzzy at the edges. I see several faces, great masses of black hair all round her head.

I flop down on the divan and shut my eyes. I can hear Mimi getting dressed, the swish-swish of her sari. I hear her footsteps pattering out of the room, the sound of running water from the wash-house. I have to get up, put on my trousers, ring for a taxi. 'It's a senior assignment. You realize that, don't you?'

Mimi comes back into the room and switches on the light. I blink open my eyes and look at my watch. Eight o'clock!

Nehru's speech has come and gone.

'Don't botch it up, will you?' John Stuart had said. 'I'll have a lot of explaining to do if . . . ' What excuse could I possibly give? If I couldn't make it, if I had been struck down by the bubonic plague, if a thousand unforeseen calamities had descended on me, why hadn't I phoned the office? And it was the Prime Minister too, no less, talking at an International Conference on the Peaceful Uses of Atomic Energy. Perhaps he had made a policy statement, perhaps in a fit of irony he had announced that India had started making her own bomb. In any case, Mr Nehru's speeches were always reported on the front page, with a two-column spread at the least. 'The long glittering career ahead' of me looked as if it was about to suffer an abrupt eclipse.

Which was the better bargain, a rendezvous with the Prime Minister or making love to Mimi? I wasn't sure. I felt light and confident. I had whispered, 'I love you,' just before she had left the flat. Mimi had smiled and kissed me again. I was happy, boundlessly and ecstatically happy. 'Today I am a man, a real man,' I kept repeating to myself. If the actual performance had not been all that efficient, at least it symbolized something. She was now 'my girl' not only in name but in deed. I would no longer hang my head in embarrassment when Rangaswami teased me. Not that I would give out any details; that would be sacrilege. But I could hold my head up high. Now I know. It was no longer a secret.

Why couldn't Nehru have spoken some other day? Why couldn't it have been later in the evening? What would I do now? Should I ring up the chief and tell him . . . ? Well, if they gave me the sack, I could always go back to shoeshining. (I wonder how Mimi would take that?) I had met Shovan Lal the other day and he said that business was good in the summer. At least that was a 'trade' I had learnt. Or perhaps I could go to another paper, now that I had 'qualifications'. No, there was no use in being so pessimistic. I would have to do something.

Rangaswami was an old hand at this; he must have been in hundreds of similar scrapes. I dialled his number and his mother answered the phone. 'No, you can't speak to him. He is very ill and sleeping. I can't wake him.' Her voice was too strident, the words too firm.

'Mrs Rangaswami,' I pleaded, 'I am a close friend of your son's. And I am in very bad trouble. So if you could possibly tell me how I could get in touch with him, I should be very grateful. It won't get back to the office, I promise.'

'Well, he decided to take the day off,' the woman's voice answered. 'He has been working so hard recently, you see.'

'Yes, I understand,' I replied.

She gave me a number, a 'friend's place', where Rangaswami had gone to spend the evening. I replaced the receiver and thanked Jehovah for a woman who kept such efficient track of her son's whereabouts.

'And how come you didn't go?' Rangaswami asked, after I had explained my predicament three times over.

'I told you I was held up . . . '

'Fucking that Anglo-girl, I bet . . . . I don't know what the world is coming to these days. Hardly out of half-pants and scratching around for pussy while . . . Rome burns.'

'Look Rangaswami, I am in a jam . . . '

'You sure are!'

'What am I going to do?'

'You didn't think of that when you were poking your prick into her, did you? Did you now?'

'Please . . . '

Rangaswami was silent for a while and then I knew he was going to help me.

'Look, I can't do the story for you,' he said. 'I am half a bottle down and . . . Besides, even if I was in a fit state, I wouldn't . . . . You've got to get out of this by yourself. But I tell you what . . . ' He paused again, taking a swig from the bottle. 'I'll ring up my friend at the *Times of India*. He is a good chap and he likes you. And Nehru's speech isn't such a glory either. Most of the time he just rambles on. So if my friend shows you his copy and you go to the Press Club and get the text of the speech from the agency tape you should be all set . . . . '

'But do you think he would . . . ?'

'I don't see why not. It isn't a scoop. Just an ordinary bloody speech. But use your own style, get the names right. Who presided, the people who were there, you know, that kind of thing. And try and keep it short. Avoid quotes as much as possible; unless there's some special gem which sounds great, I'd say don't use quotes at all. Get the main point, you know, the kind of thing you do in school for precis writing. And then add the other stuff at the end, a couple of paras.'

'Yes, but don't you think they'll have noticed that I wasn't there?' I asked, hope beginning to revive.

'Well, that'll happen tomorrow. And I'll see about it. Just say you weren't in the Press section, came in late. You can be sure that the meeting didn't start on time either.'

'What if . . . ?' I began, still nervous and empty in the stomach.

'No ifs,' Rangaswami shouted. 'This is not the first time such a thing has happened to a journalist. And you can be damn sure that it won't be the last either. But don't do the story in the office. Pick up my friend's copy and the speech text from the Press Club and go back home and do it there. And hand it in to the chief sub himself, just about half past eleven, not before that. So he won't get a chance to bugger around if he smells something fishy.'

Nehru had spoken for half an hour, about the need for co-operation among the scientifically advanced nations of the world. How Man's mastery over nature had placed him in an unique position for bringing about total human good and so on. Homilies, platitudes, high-sounding moral bombast, in loose, often uncompleted, sentences. Could do with a speech-writer, I thought, or even a written text. But the Prime Minister of India, the executive head of the biggest democracy in the world, had never stooped to such menial devices. He had always spoken extempore, a habit picked up at the debating union during his days at Cambridge. The result was stale cliché-ridden sentiments. Stripped of the magnetism of his personality and voice, the words on the printed page were flat and uninspiring, hardly a spur to creative reporting.

My guilt and fear made me cautious. I followed Rangaswami's advice to the letter. I got the names right, using a flat deadpan style, direct and without embroidery. I avoided quotes altogether and condensed the speech to its essentials. I did not feel any excitement in doing the story; some of the paragraphs for the *New Delhi Notebook* had given me a much greater thrill.

Next morning I walked sheepishly into the office and the chief said, 'I had some doubts at first. But you've done a good job. You seem to be getting the hang of it at last.' At 'conference' John Stuart came over and patted me on the back. 'Splendid, Ray, splendid.'

Rangaswami smiled.

Mimi and I did not meet for nearly a week after that evening in my flat. There was a whole row of 'engagements', fashion shows, Embassy cocktail parties, rehearsals, special film sessions at the President's house, etc. She couldn't come out to lunch either, as she seemed to be incessantly on the air. This didn't upset me very much as I was glad to be alone for a while, to sort out my reactions. It gave me time to analyse my feelings for Mimi and attempt to resolve the conflict of loyalties—to the girl in Calcutta and to Mimi. I knew I was still in love with the other girl. I wanted her back and hoped for a miracle which would break up her marriage, so she could return to me. Making love to Mimi had been wonderful and ecstatic, but it created a feeling of queasy uncertainty. After all, we were not married and . . . The more I thought about the incident, the more I began to realize that she had engineered the whole thing, that I had in fact been *seduced*. It was an unflattering thought to ponder, it did nothing for my sprouting adolescent ego, and it fed the ideas with which I was being constantly bombarded by the likes of Rangaswami. Anglo-Indian girls were cheap, they'll do anything for . . .

Even if I was not in love with Mimi it was important to tell myself that I was. Love-making could not be justified in any other way. And I was too full of puritanical reflexes to be able to live at peace unless I could find some justification for an act which, I still believed, was sinful and degenerate. A week's absence reinforced my feelings for her, of course. At the end of six days, when we were finally to meet, I was trembling with anticipation and excitement. I wanted to talk to her, hold her in my arms, kiss her again. I was not so sure that she would want to . . . . And I dared not allow myself to think that it might ever happen again.

We met at the La Bohème at six in the evening. I had been waiting there for a while and Mimi came in dressed in a saffron sari streaked with blue. She looked ravishing, And the waiters winked at me when I got up to help her off with the cape. I could think of nothing to say and a good fifteen minutes went by before Mimi spoke: 'I thought you wanted to see me.'

'Yes of course I do, I mean . . . '

The waiter appeared just then and I ordered two iced coffees.

'I love you, Mimi,' I said, leaning over to hold her hand. It was cold, unresponsive, and static. I felt stung. 'I love you so much,' I repeated, hoping to unfreeze her. What had I done? Why was she so distant?

'I like you,' she replied. 'I think you are very clever and very nice.'

'Do you want to have dinner and go back to my place afterwards?'

'I am afraid I can't,' Mimi said. 'I have a cocktail party to go to at eight.'

The shattering of porcelain, the blast of an air gun; my heart went thumpety-thumpety-thump, hectic, hysteric, on the verge of collapse. 'But why? We haven't seen each other for a whole week.'

'I have things to do you know, obligations to meet,' Mimi answered, taking out her compact and powdering her nose. 'Besides, a week isn't eternity and tonight isn't the only night.'

'Can't you miss the party? Can't you ring up and say that you are ill or something?'

'Absolutely out of the question. The hostess is a very close friend of mine. I couldn't let her down.'

The dialogue seesawed between pleas on my side and refusals and excuses on hers. I couldn't make it out. What had come over her? What had I done? Was she feeling guilty about having made love to me?

An hour went by and Mimi was fidgeting in her seat.

'I don't want you to go to the party,' I said, raising my voice.

'Huh?' Mimi retorted, sharply. '*You* don't want me to go to the party. And who do you think you are? My lord and master or something?'

'I am the man who made love to you, that's who I am. I love you, Mimi, I love you so very much,' I tried to take her hand but she drew it away.

'If you think that gives you a right to order me about, well . . .'

'I didn't mean to shout, please, Mimi. I want to kiss you, take you in my arms, I want . . .'

'Want away,' Mimi said firmly. 'But I am leaving. And thank you for the coffee.'

Mimi got up and put on her cape. I could not believe what was happening. It was all so sudden. What caused this volte-face? Was she flirting with me, trying me out? It was only when she reached the door that I realized that she meant what she had said. I ran after her, barring the door, 'Mimi, you can't leave me, you can't go like this. I want to know what happened, what made you change? I want to know.'

'You want so many things, don't you?' Mimi replied, her voice sharp and metallic.

'Please, Mimi, please!' Tears were beginning to well into my eyes, my voice was low, hoarse and broken.

'Don't be such a slob, Amit,' Mimi said. 'I thought you had some self-respect.'

'No, no, Mimi, you can't. You can't leave me tonight. I love you, I want you.'

The waiters were whispering and giggling to each other, some of the customers raised arched eyebrows. I had created a 'scene'.

'If you want to talk, can we leave this place, do you think? You have made enough of an exhibition as it is.'

'Yes of course,' I replied, sniffing back my tears. 'I am sorry, I didn't mean to.'

'The trouble with you is you never do mean to.'

We walked out into the street and Mimi said in a firm but conciliatory voice that she would see me tomorrow but tonight was out of the question. She *had* to go to the party. Couldn't I come with her? Of course not, where did I think I was, in a jungle or something? How could I suggest going to a party to which I had not been invited? Would she come over to my place afterwards, after the party was over I mean? No, how could I be so inconsiderate? Didn't I know she had been working the whole day and now this and then the party. She would be ready to flop into bed by the time the party ended. She would see me tomorrow. Bye . . . ee . . . ee!

I bought half a dozen bottles of beer, took them home, got drunk and cried myself to sleep.

Next day in the office Rangaswami didn't stop winking at me for a good fifteen minutes. 'What's the matter?' I asked. 'Something wrong with your eyes?'

'No, no, nothing. Just a slight twitch. Anything wrong with yours?'

I kept sullenly silent.

'I didn't know that Anglo-girls liked tandoori chicken,' Rangaswami said after a while, stalking round to my desk. 'I thought they went in for the European stuff like caviar and champagne and that sort of thing.'

'All right, what is it?' I asked, exhausted and exasperated.

'Nothing, nothing at all,' Rangaswami replied, adding another wink to the conversation. 'Just found it kind of strange to see an Anglo-girl eating tandoori chicken at the Taj Mahal restaurant last night.'

I heaved a sigh. He was not referring to the La Bohème episode.

'What's so strange at out that? Is there a law against eating at the Taj Mahal?'

'Not at all,' Rangaswami replied, now in full gallop. 'Only the combination was a bit exotic, that's all. A blonde-haired German and a dark-haired Anglo-girl eating Indian food with bare hands.'

'What do you mean?' I queried, my curiosity aroused.

Mimi and the First Secretary of the German Embassy were seen eating at the Taj Mahal restaurant last night. Rangaswami was not there but he had been told about it by 'reliable sources'.

'When?' I asked, hands starting to go cold and the throat about to be held by a pair of pincers. 'What time?'

'Well,' Rangaswami answered, relishing his little game, 'I met my friend, the "source" you know, at about ten o'clock in the Press Club and he had just come from there. So it couldn't have been much before nine.'

Snap, click, thunder in my brain. Cocktail parties which begin at eight don't end by nine. It wasn't an after-drinks dinner.

'You mean to say you didn't know?' Rangaswami prodded. 'I would have thought that she would tell you about little things like that.'

He hasn't heard about La Bohème yet, thank God, I told myself. I wanted to ring up Mimi and ask her then and there. I am sure there was a good reason, she couldn't be telling lies. She is not that sort of girl.

Mimi was upset with me, for some reason, but it was just a lovers' quarrel. I was 'her man' all right. I mean I had proved it, hadn't I? Yes, Rangaswami would have to eat his fun-poking words when he saw us together again, walking hand in hand, me looking into her deep dark eyes, she whispering soft cooing words in my ear . . . . Yes, of course, it would all work out right. Damn these nosy parkers! Why couldn't they mind their own goddamn business? She must have had a good reason for eating tandoori chicken with the German at the Taj Mahal.

Mimi couldn't speak to me on the phone, she was busy. She couldn't see me this evening either, something unexpected had turned up. Sorry, but would I ring tomorrow? We could fix up something then. Sorry, but she had to go. On the air in ten minutes.

I walked around in a daze, as if a hundred ceaseless blows had landed on my face and I had not regained balance. What had gone wrong? Was it something I had done? Perhaps I was exaggerating the whole thing, something unexpected *had* turned up. After all, unexpected things do turn up, don't they?

It took a lot of doing, trying to believe my own excuses for Mimi. We did not meet for a whole week. And then her holidays began. I couldn't get her at Broadcasting House. She was never at home when I rang. I went round to see her father and he told me that Mimi had gone to Bombay to spend a fortnight with her aunt. Three days later I saw her driving down in a big Mercedes near the Ashoka Hotel. Something was definitely wrong. I phoned her father again and he swallowed his word before replying: 'Look, why don't the two of you meet and talk things over? I don't make a good middleman.'

Then her letter arrived in the post:

Dear Amit,

I do wish you would stop pestering me. I thought you were a little more sensitive. But you just don't seem to be able to take a hint. I liked being with you while it lasted. But I've found someone else. And I am in love with him. But even if I weren't, there could be nothing between us. You are a small man and there are things which are very important for me without which I cannot go on. I don't think you could ever satisfy a woman in that way.

Intellect is not everything. Mimi

I was twenty, a near-virgin, full of grandiose notions about myself, convinced that I was in love, I read the letter once over and it made no impact. I did not believe it. After several cups of coffee, and on the twelfth reading, I got the message: 'You are a small man . . . . I don't think you could ever satisfy a woman in that way . . . . ' She was talking about my ineptitude in love-making and the size of my penis. Even I could get that. And it very nearly broke me up.

Of course, I congratulate myself in retrospect. This is the stuff out of which homosexuals, rapists and perverts are made. The letter gave me a deep feeling of inadequacy, sexually, and that's all that counted at the time. Intellect be damned! It took me three long years to get over this feeling, sufficiently that is to make some kind of a viable life for myself. I remind myself now, whenever I am faced with a debacle, that no man's attitude towards the size of his genitals is ever neutral. Either it is too thin or too short or too something or another. Just as women are obsessed with breasts, men are with their penises. They may not admit it, sometimes not even to themselves. But buried deep within the doubts are always there. The Jew is embarrassed about his circumcised prick, the goy about his crinkly drooping balls. I knew a man whose penis was eleven inches long when erect and he was intensely self-conscious and shy about its size. He could never get the whole thing in, women were hurt and sore and would never come back after the first session. There was another man who apologized to every girl before be entered her: 'I am sorry I am not very big. But . . . the way it's done is what counts, you know.' In the normal instance I would probably have had the usual slight complex about my penis, but Mimi's letter produced a tumult: anger, frustration and impotence—for there was no way I could get back at her.

So my 'affair' with Mimi was over. And Rangaswami, to his eternal credit, stopped teasing me about it when he realized that we had broken up. I began working harder at the office, read later into the night. There was a gap, a feeling of nothingness, in the evenings. But I became a member of the Max Müller Bhavan and began reading the German and French philosophers. I was doing well at the *Statesman*, no one sneered at my lack of expertise in 'journalism' any more. I wrote two 'leaders', one on 'Student Unrest' and the other on 'Indo-Anglian Writing'. The resident editor in Delhi liked both the pieces and sent them down to the head office in Calcutta on the telex machine. The answer was prompt and positive. I had really made the grade. In another year or so I would be made a Special Correspondent, the next step up from the reporters' room.

Shovan Lal and Ram Singh were nearly a year away, Mimi and the tandoori chicken were only a few weeks old, and my heart was as heavy as Time itself. Then one afternoon John Stuart came into the lunch room and sat down at my table. 'Look, Ray, the old man has come down with flu. And there is an art exhibition opening this evening. It wouldn't be all that important if the sponsors weren't big advertisers as well. Normally, I would not mind if the opening of an exhibition was not covered. But in this case . . .'

'So what do you want me to do?'

'Well, I thought that since you know about these things, art and literature and all that stuff, perhaps you could . . .'

The 'old man' was the art critic of the *Statesman* and he covered not only painting exhibitions, but drama, European classical music, sculpture shows, English films, in short any and every thing even remotely connected with art. And to give him his due the man was an extremely versatile character, one of the old kind, an expatriate Hungarian Jew who had married an Indian woman and lived in India for over a quarter century.

'You know, Mr Stuart,' I answered hesitantly, 'I might know something about literature but I really have no idea about paintings.'

'It's all the same thing,' the boss insisted, 'if you know one, you can generally say a few things about the others. And that is all we need. You know, who opened the exhibition, the name of the painter and the gallery, how long it will be open, the sort of average price of the exhibits, and then a few words about the paintings. That shouldn't be difficult. You can do it.'

It was a challenge again and I decided to accept. I made up my mind to look at the paintings with an open eye and say 'frankly' what I thought of them.

It was something like the party at the Czechoslovak secretary's—the exhibition I mean. Only no vodka or Scotch was being served and there were not that many European women in ankle-deep dresses either. The girl who wore a short black dress was looking intensely at a painting when I came up to her from behind. She turned round and smiled. 'Hi,' she said.

'Hi,' I replied.

She had dark curly hair covering her ears, a slender neck and a sharp-boned face. 'I am Diana,' she continued, carrying the monosyllabic conversation into words. 'Diana DeRouche.'

'My name is Amit Ray,' I responded, putting out my hand. 'How do you do?'

We shook hands and she turned towards the painting again. 'The man has talent, don't you think? But someone should tell him that he is barking up a wrong tree.'

'What do you mean?' I asked, interested, hoping to pick up something that I could use in my piece.

'He has a sharp eye for colour, especially these lighter shades of blue and green. And he is a very good craftsman. But he isn't a real painter yet. All this,' and she waved her hand over the whole room, 'is just imitation. He wants to be Western. And he can't, you see.'

'I don't know that I do, but I'll take your word for it.'

'Why must you take my word for it? Aren't you a painter?' I shook my head morosely. 'I thought you were. That beard . . . '

'I have been carrying this thing around on my chin ever since I was sixteen,' I said, trying to be witty. 'But tell me, are you a painter, yourself?'

'Of sorts,' Diana answered, still with her back to me. 'Not really,' she cried an instant later, wheeling round, 'I am a fashion designer by profession. But I studied art in college.'

'Then you are just the girl for me . . . .'

Diana was a freelance fashion designer from New York. She was in her late twenties and the ring on her finger said she was married. 'No, I was. But not any more.' She had been divorced about six months ago and then she had decided to take a year off and travel around. India was first on her itinerary, next was Europe.

I got enough material from her to fill a whole page of newsprint. So I managed to produce six inches of art criticism, mentioning names of European painters whose influence was 'clearly detectable' in the paintings on show, and so on. Everyone in the office was impressed. I had done it again. The ever-spreading ripples of my fame disturbed the still waters of 'journalism' once more.

Diana and I had dinner together on that first evening. Next day I picked her up at the Ashoka Hotel, hired a car and drove out to see the Qutab Minar. The third day I took her to the museum. On the fourth day . . . A whole week passed. She came back to my flat once, I was constantly in the hotel room alone with her. But I had made up my mind that nothing would happen, I would not let anything happen. I could not afford to face another fiasco. So we kissed a little and held hands. She was much older than I and took a quasi-indulgent interest in me. But walking down the Delhi streets with her made me feel proud and manly. The poison from Mimi's letter was being neutralized. I felt I could rise again, even if it was a long time after the third day.

Then Diana said, 'I am leaving in a week. Why don't you come to Europe with me?'

Did I say that leaving home was the first of many crucial decisions I have taken on *impulse*? Well, leaving India was the second. I replied. 'All right, I have always wanted to go to England. Perhaps I'll get to Oxford yet.'

I got one of the magistrates to sign my passport forms, Rangaswami agreed to act as guarantor, John Stuart reluctantly granted a three-month leave of absence from the *Statesman*. I rang my mother at home and asked if I could borrow four thousand rupees. It didn't seem wrong to do so any more. I had made my point. I had established myself and I said I would pay back the money. (Which was never expected and which I never did.) I arranged to meet Diana in Bombay three days later. Then I flew down to Calcutta to say goodbye to my family. Mother said, 'You must be careful about those Western women. They are like witches. Once they get their paws on you . . . Never stay in a room alone with a white girl.'

I promised her that I wouldn't.

By the time Diana arrived in Bombay, she had changed her mind about flying out with me. She had too much luggage, she would have to travel by ship to Genoa and start out from there. We could meet somewhere in France. And what would I do for money? (I had already bought my plane ticket.) Government regulations did not allow Indian rupees to be officially changed into any foreign currency without special permission from the Reserve Bank. Diana had dollars in traveller's cheques. Since she would have to spend a lot more money in India while waiting for her ship, I could give her the rupees and she could give me the cheques. Seemed simple enough. I gave her two thousand rupees and she countersigned ten fifty-dollar cheques. (In other words, each cheque carried two signatures, one at the top and one at the bottom.) I had never seen traveller's cheques before. I had no idea what this would lead to.

Anyway, I was too excited to be suspicious. A strong gale seemed to be blowing me forward. The girl in Calcutta, Ram Singh and Shovan Lal, John Stuart and Rangaswami, even Mimi, lay behind. At 12.15 a.m., as the plane rushed into the sky, I looked out of the window and saw the twinkling lights of Bombay harbour receding into the past. A dark night lay ahead.

TWO

~

ROME EN PASSANT

It was a little different from that train ride in a third-class railway carriage from Calcutta to Delhi, when I had sat hunched-up in the bunk, looking down on the mobile miniature of an India I had never seen before. Now I was reclining on a foam-rubber seat in an Air India Boeing, with stewardesses in saris swishing down the aisle, tinkling drinks on trays, soft sitar music on the speaker. Destination: Europe.

My birthday was six weeks away, soon I would be an 'adult', enter my twenty-second year. I would be able to look *anyone* in the face, insist on my rights, turn the handle of the door which opens on to *real* life. I would create international sensations, write great and brilliant novels, speak to audiences running into thousands. Women would be falling frantically in love with me, Mimi would beg me to make love to her again, the *New Statesman* would print a profile of 'A Brahmin Youth from India'. (Reader, please, don't condemn me for living in a world of fantasy. Most of these things did in fact happen, only several years later, not then, not in the way I thought they would.)

How do I describe the feelings of an Indian—an educated Indian youth—who is about to visit Europe, England? It is like the Muslim's lifelong ambition to say a prayer at the mosque in Mecca, the Jew's obsession with Israel, the Irish-American's dream of visiting the Lakes of Killarney. London to me was the source of life, where all the glorious and wonderful things had happened, the place which held the key to the future and the past and where I longed to be in the present. If there was a place where judgements were made, it was London; if there was a balance on which I would want to be weighed, it was the intellectual-literary gauge of English critical opinion. I had not written anything yet, but I was sure I would; I had not done anything yet, but I knew that I would not fail to deliver. As a man, as a writer, as an intellectual, I was heading for the laboratory where my mettle would be tested and analysed. I sat back in my seat with confident anticipation, knowing what the results would show. (In some sharp contrast to the uncertainty I had felt on leaving home.)

I was on the aisle seat; on my left was a Swede, loaned by his Government to a community development project in India; on *his* left, next to the window, was a Norwegian woman who had worked as a nurse in a village near Bombay, and was now returning home. Our first stop was Rome and it was to be a ten-hour flight. The Swede and the Norwegian had met at the airport in Bombay for the first time and, discovering their common Scandinavian background, had asked the stewardess to seat them next to each other. I had been talking to the Swede while waiting to have my passport stamped, so I asked if I could sit next to him. All this had been arranged with no bother at all, and the three of us soon introduced ourselves and fell into first-name conversation while a midnight snack was being served.

I had changed seventy-five rupees (the legally permissible amount) into fifteen dollars and thought I could afford a drink. After all, I was going to Europe and people drink there all the time. So I might as well get started and accustom myself to doing the things that Romans do in Rome. I asked for a Scotch, the Swede ordered a dry Vermouth and the Norwegian lady wanted a glass of wine. We had some cold chicken and salad; the Scotch made me slightly garrulous and I started talking about 'the new novel'. Neither of my two companions seemed very interested—a fact I noticed only when they began to converse in an unintelligible language. I wanted to point out that this was very bad manners, considering there was a third party around, but I decided to order a second Scotch instead.

By the time I was halfway through the new drink, the trays had been cleared and the captain was wishing us goodnight and pleasant dreams. I had sat silent for over fifteen minutes and felt the need for some stimulating conversation—in which, of course, I would take the leading part. So I turned my head in the direction of my Swedish friend and observed that his left hand was on the Norwegian's right knee. *This* was not only bad manners but positively obscene. The gesture could not be called ambiguous, it could not be explained as a 'friendly pat'. For the dialogue in the foreign tongue had ceased and the hand was not remaining stationary on the knee but was freely reconnoitering further up the incline of the woman's thighs, an act which produced the undesirable side-effect or drawing up the hemline of her skirt to well above civilized levels.

Morals were being violated and I felt obliged to step in and attempt to protect the lady's honour.

'Mr Sorensen,' I said, 'Steen, I mean . . .'

'Yeah . . . es,' came the answer, in a thick Swedish accent, the face not bothering to turn in my direction.

I felt impelled to look again, since unitary word replies are not known to encourage further discourse. And this time the situation was truly critical. The hand had progressed much further up, in fact to a region of the woman's anatomy which only doctors and midwives should explore or feel. 'Mr Sorensen, what are you doing?'

'Huh, huh,' was the only response I received, which I translated as the broken laughter of a guilty man. Of course, I could not take my eyes away at this stage; a lady's honour was at stake. He did not even know her, they had only met two hours ago. Yes, a rescue operation would have to be launched. Even if she was looking intensely at his face (which was advancing closer to hers every passing second), she was defenceless, stuck as she was against the window, she needed help. Yes, I must do something. Soon!

And then the two pairs of lips met.

'Mr Sorensen!' I gasped. And before I had time to admonish any further, the lights went out. 'Good night, ladies and gentlemen,' a soft feminine voice announced on the speaker. 'Hope you sleep well and soundly.'

Well and soundly indeed! When the most grotesque bestiality was going on right here next to me? Sounds of over-activated lungs, sucking noises, lip against lip (I surmised this, for I couldn't see clearly any more), and then hands rubbing against clothing, snapping apart of buttons, unzipping of zips. What's going on here? 'Mr Sorensen,' I repeated, louder and firmer. 'Sh . . . sh . . . sh,' came the stern reprimand from the fat man in the row up front. What the devil!

I was trembling with consternation and outrage. Right here in public, in a crowded plane, with a woman he had never seen before? Really!

The Norwegian woman half got up, turned round to face the Swede, lifted the hand-rest between the seats out of its socket and then sat on him, with legs akimbo and her skirt scaling way up her hips.

I couldn't stand this any more. I was speechless.

And then she started moving, slowly and silently at first, then more vigorously, breathing sounds becoming louder with the increase of speed.

I turned round to see if there were any stewardesses around. No, the three of them were at the back of the plane. None of the other passengers could see what was going on (most of them were asleep anyway), only hear the sounds, and even those were drowned by the loud intermittent snore of the man across the aisle.

And I was disgusted with myself. Morally I was outraged. Yet I couldn't help watching. I had an erection under my trousers. I wanted to feel my penis and make myself come. How hideous! How obscene!

I got up and walked down the aisle.

'Look,' I said to the stewardess, who was putting away the plastic trays. 'There is a man up there who is doing all sorts of things to the woman sitting next to him. Could you perhaps . . . ?'

She started giggling and looked at the other stewardess. 'You mean the Swedish gentleman sitting next to you, sir?'

'Yes, that's the chap. You must go and stop him. I mean . . . '

'Is the gentleman disturbing you, sir?'

'Disturbing me?' I shrieked. 'Do you mean . . . ? What is this, some kind of a brothel or something? Of course he is disturbing me.'

'I am sorry, sir. But perhaps you would care to sit here for a few minutes and have a drink with the compliments of Air India.'

'Do you mean to say that you're going to let this beastly thing go on? And soften me up with a drink, while a woman's honour is being violated? He is not married to her, you know.'

'It won't be long now, sir,' the girl said, in a soft conciliatory voice, exchanging giggles and glances with her colleague. 'Another five minutes and I am sure you will be able to return to your seat without any fear of being disturbed.'

I glared at her for a full minute, with eyes bursting out of their sockets. I couldn't believe it. I simply couldn't believe it. And in an Air India plane too! 'Yes, I'll have that drink. Scotch, with some ice in it.'

'Pleased to oblige you, sir,' she said, turning away to pour the drink.

'Does this sort of thing happen often?' I asked, taking a sip of the Scotch. 'I mean have you seen this . . . this before on a plane?'

'We are not here to *see*, sir,' she replied, smiling innocently. 'We are here to serve our passengers.'

When I returned to my seat both the Norwegian nurse and the Swede had reverted to their original positions. 'Mr Sorensen,' I whispered. But there was no answer. His hand hung limply down beside him, the sound of his breathing was deep and regular, he was sleeping 'well and soundly'.

That was my introduction to the sexual mores of the Western world and it disturbed me profoundly. But none of my friends believe my story. They say it is the product of a fevered imagination, the projection of my mind, the way I would have wanted it to be. One of them says, 'I have travelled on a plane countless number of times, but I've never seen anything like that. A little kissing and petting perhaps, but not two people actually *doing* it, not in a plane. You must have dreamt the whole thing. Those two Scotches . . . '

My reply, alas, can only be a superior supercilious smile. I can't prove that it happened. But I know it did. And I also know that this was only one of a long chain of episodes and encounters, which appear bizarre to the point of disbelief, which I have experienced. Unusual people and strange situations continually crop up. I don't know if I search for them or whether they hunt me out. I do know however that the weird and exotic have never been strangers in my life.

I slept very little in the next five hours. I kept seeing visions of the woman horse-riding on the man's lap. The picture of Mimi in the nude, with her legs in the air, rose up again and again in my mind.

I was hard and erect, with an aching, throbbing penis, aggressively rising up under my tight pants. I was ashamed of myself. I dared not go to the toilet and masturbate. What would people say? I mean, if I went in there now the stewardess would know what I was going to do. Then she would laugh and giggle with her friend. And I couldn't let that happen, couldn't let them make fun of me. Could I?

When the lights came on the captain announced that we were flying over Malta. Sorensen woke up, rubbed his eyes and leaned over to kiss the girl next to him, saying something softly to her in Swedish. I avoided looking at him, with memories of the night flooding in. It was light outside, grey fluffs of cloud swam past us, the sky was a gentle blue and shafts of sunlight sparked on the wing-tip of the plane.

'Mr Sorensen,' I began, looking straight ahead, and then could think of nothing further to add.

'Yes, huh, huh,' he replied, 'we had a little play last night. I hope we didn't disturb you.'

'Not at all,' I retorted sharply, 'but aren't you ashamed?'

'Ashamed!' Sorensen said, rippling with laughter (which was complemented by the Norwegian's feminine giggle). 'Why be ashamed? I did not murder anyone. Or make rape with a young boy.'

'But,' I insisted, turning to face him, 'you are not married to her.'

'No, I am not. That is true. But it is no reason to feel ashamed.'

'Do you love her, then?'

'Love?' Sorensen queried, creased brow, eyes drawn close together. 'What is to do with love? We only met eight hours ago. She liked me, I liked her, so . . . huh . . . huh . . . we make a little intercourse.'

'You are disgusting,' I said vehemently. 'An animal.'

Sorensen laughed, but did not bother to answer. We remained silent for the rest of the journey.

Rome!

The thing that hit me hardest on my first encounter with

'Western civilization' was legs. It seemed to me that everyone everywhere had bare brown legs. Long ones and slim ones and fat stumpy ones. A veritable avalanche of legs. I don't think my that eyes had feasted on so many legs all at once ever before. Women in India wear saris. One can see some bare waist now and again, exposed ear-lobes, ungloved hands, faces without make-up, an occasional toe or even a full nude foot in sandals. But never legs. At the terminal building in Rome I kept banging into people as I walked because my eyes were focussed firmly on the floor, at a sharp gradient to normal horizontal vision. One girl had a seam on her stockings, another had, what I later learnt was called a 'ladder'. Of course, I had seen women in stockings before, but never such vast numbers assembled in one place. If there was nothing else in Europe, I felt I could spend the rest of my life simply gazing at all these fantastic cylindrical props of flesh which, in addition to other things, carried heads, breasts and even some well-constructed behinds.

Rome was not built in a day and neither was my obsession with female podia. It took twenty years of leg-starvation to produce the delirium I experienced in being presented with an abundant supply of this particular commodity. Let me add at once that all these legs—hairy, depilated, brown, silken or elephantine—did not inspire the slightest feeling of carnal longing. On the contrary, I was entranced merely to witness the walking glories, those small dainty things which click-clacked down the stone floors on pointed, high-heeled shoes. Aesthetic pleasure, moral rectitude and a curious sensation in my brain (when my eyes following the curves vertically up were abruptly halted by the hemline of the skirt) were reactions which jostled within me for supremacy. (As I said, 'The Phenomenon of Legs' caused the first frantic flutter of intellectual consciousness on my initial encounter with 'Western civilization'.)

While my luggage was being inspected at the Customs deck, I felt a strong disinclination to leave this building, to forsake this paradise, this leg Valhalla, where women were incessantly on the click-clack (and where my eyes were being treated to a rich abundance of slim smooth curves which led to the forest of Heaven).

But earthier decisions had to be made. And I remained myself that there would be other times and other places. The terminal building in Rome was not the only surviving leg post of the Western world. There were in fact streets, roads, and avenues where similar treats could surely be obtained, parks, cafeterias, hotel lobbies . . . . No, life here was too full and rich to be true. I decided to board into a fairly decent hotel for a day or two, before making further concrete plans and laying out my itinerary. I had five hundred dollars in traveller's cheques and I had been told that I could spend a comfortable month in Europe on that before going on to London.

The hotel was not far from the terminal building, although the taxi ride lasted for an interminable half-hour. (It was in fact a five-minute walk.) I paid the cabbie out of the dollars I had changed into lire at the airport. (I had about twelve dollars left in cash and I thought I would wait till I got to my hotel before changing a fifty-dollar cheque.) I checked into the Hotel King George, which was a bath. It had massive swing doors, a large foyer and liveried doormen. The clerk at the reception desk spoke fluent, if accented, English. I had never lived in an expensive hotel before and I went up the stairs to my room on the second floor with feelings of adulthood and manly pride thickly filling my heart.

I paid the pageboy a handsome tip, shut the door behind him and looked around. Yes, this really was living. Scandinavian bestiality on the plane, legs at the terminal building and now a room in a three-star hotel in Rome. Somehow it all seemed to fit. All these things were an integral part of the writer's material. How many non-writing mortals could speak of having 'experienced' as much within such a short time? The sign on the road said, 'To the Hall of Fame'. I could see myself attired in ancient Roman costume, leaning back on a large feathered pillow and passing sentence on the Swede: 'Yes, give him fifty lashes of the whip and then throw him to the lions. A Christian heretic, a Scandinavian sub-homo sapien!' Then all those long rows of stockinged legs, daintily, reverently, walking down the aisle, with wine and meat and fruit in their hands: 'A little more thigh, my lovely,' to one; 'Swing that delicious bum of yours, my darling, yes, do,' to another; 'Must you hobble so?' in stern reprimand to a third. Yes, I was on the way to literary canonization. For to an artist 'experience' is all, the actual execution in paint or print, a mere triviality. And so, first to the field!

I picked up the phone and asked for room service. 'Yes, sir,' the voice replied. 'Room service, please,' I repeated. 'Yes, sir,' came the obstinate answer. Well, if the switchboard operator was going to insist on serving as my valet I had no objections, provided the service was efficient. 'A glass of wine, please,' I said. I had been told that they drink wine in Rome—a spiritous liquor which I had never tasted—and so I wanted to conform to native custom. 'What kind of wine would you like, sir?' the voice inquired.

'Well, er . . . er . . . you know, the good kind, the best you've got.'

Twenty minutes later there was a knock on the door and a man in a red waistcoat came in with a bottle and two glasses on a tray. 'This is our best wine, sir,' he announced proudly. 'It is a rich lovely wine from Frascati.' He cradled the bottle in the crook of his arm as if he was holding a new-born infant. 'Forty-seven, that was one of the best years we have had for a long time.'

What was the man talking about? First I ask for a glass of wine and he brings me a bottle. Then he starts talking about 'Fruscadhi', whatever that might mean, and then this business about forty-seven. What has forty-seven got to do with it? All I wanted was a glass of wine.

'Do you want me to open it for you now, sir?'

'No, not really. I mean I don't think I could drink a whole bottle. I'd much rather just have a glass please.'

The man's face shrivelled, his eyes drew sharply together and creased his brow and he put the bottle back on the tray. 'You can't get the best wine in a glass. There is a bar downstairs.' There was an unnecessary abruptness with which he left the room and banged the door loudly behind him.

I changed into a new suit of clothes and decided to go downstairs to the bar and insist on my glass of wine. I took one fifty-dollar cheque and the spare cash I had in lire and walked to the reception desk. 'You change American Express traveller's cheques, don't you?' I asked.

'Yes of course we do, sir,' the man replied.

I took out the cheque and handed it to him across the counter. A minute, two minutes, carrying on to three . . . .

The man looked at the paper, turned it round to inspect the blank side at the back. Then he took out his glasses and held the cheque close to his face. 'You are Mr Ray, aren't you?' he said finally.

'Yes I am. You have my passport to show that.'

'Yes, sir, but this cheque is signed by Dia . . . De . . . '

'That's right. Diana DeRouche, a friend of mine, an American. At the top and bottom. Isn't that how it's done?'

'Yes, sir, of course,' the man answered, taking off his glasses. 'But you are not DeRouche.'

'I never said I was.'

'Well, sir, we cannot cash a cheque which has been already signed.'

'What do you mean? A cheque *has* to be signed. That's the whole point of carrying a cheque instead of cash.'

'But we don't know DeRouche. If you bring one of your own cheques, then we shall be very happy to cash it for you, sir. But this one we can't.'

'Oh,' I exclaimed, losing patience, 'this is absurd. It is a perfectly valid cheque. American Express dollars. It's been counter-signed and everything.'

'Yes, sir, but I am sorry . . . '

'You don't look it, but never mind. Do you think I could speak to someone, the manager or something?'

'Of course, sir.'

The man went into a room behind his desk and I picked up the cheque from the counter. If these people wouldn't cash it, obviously a bank would. A traveller's cheque was like cash. The onus was on American Express, not on the drawer. If the signature on the top and bottom matched, then there could be no reason for not honouring the cheque.

The manager was an older man with grey hair, who stooped slightly as he walked. His voice too was mellow: 'Mr Ray, I am sorry you have been inconvenienced. But you see,' he continued, holding out his hand for the cheque, 'this lady has not signed the cheque in front of us, we haven't seen her passport, nothing. If she is in Rome, perhaps you can go and . . . If not, perhaps a bank might cash it, but I am afraid we can't. Sorry!'

'Well, what time do the banks shut here?' I asked, a little less confident.

'They have closed for the day. You will have to go tomorrow,' the manager said. 'But in the meantime you have your own traveller's cheques, Mr Ray? If you want to cash any of those I should be most happy to . . . '

I knew what he was getting at and it did not make me feel comfortable at all. He wanted to know if I had any *real* money. As far as he was concerned, the cheques were dud. 'I am afraid I don't have any cheques of my own. All my money is in cheques like this.' Of course, it was a foolish thing to admit, I could have pretended. But it turned out to be a blessing in disguise. The manager insisted that I pay him in advance for the time I was going to stay. 'Ridiculous,' I said, 'I have never heard of such a thing. Just because *you* won't cash this cheque doesn't mean it will never be cashed.'

'Sorry, sir, but we have to insist that you pay us in advance.'

'In that case I'd like to move out,' I shouted.

'Very well, sir, I'll make out the bill for you right away,' the manager said.

'Bill, what bill? Whatever for?'

'For one day's board and lodging, sir.'

'But I haven't spent a day here. In fact I've hardly been here for an hour.'

I was beginning to feel more and more throttled. And worse, I was getting that cold cramp in my stomach, as if disaster was just round the corner.

'Yes, sir,' the grey-haired man agreed, 'but you have checked in with us. And that means we have to charge you for a day, however short a time you stay.'

'You mean if I pay for a day, I can stay for a day?'

'Till noon tomorrow, sir. If you stay after 12 p.m. then we have to charge you for another day.'

The mechanics of hotel boarding were becoming more clear. The bill was made out and came to a little less than seven dollars. 'This does not include any wine you might have with your meals, sir. That will be extra and you will have to pay for it in cash at the restaurant.'

I paid, abandoning the idea of visiting the bar. What if . . . ?

Anyway, the next thing to do was have a bath, get some sleep and then start looking for a cheaper place to stay. 'Pensiones', they called them here. Yes, the three-star hotel would have to wait till after I had got the Nobel Prize. Meanwhile, not a whisper to the manager of the pensione that I was carrying cheques of questionable character.

I found a pensione easily enough. Further down the same street as the Hotel King George, there was a working men's bar and next to it. 'Pensione Roma'—an original enough name for any establishment in the city. The owner of the pensione—which was three flights up from street level—was a short dark Neapolitan called Pietro, who prided himself on being able to converse in English (not the King's version, of course, but it passed off as an intelligible language with a goodly spattering of G.I. Americanese, German and French). And he had every reason to boast of his accomplishment. Most of his 'guests' came from other parts of Italy, on holiday or on 'business', his pensione not being listed at the tourist office. And since English-speaking visitors were mostly fixed up before they arrived in Rome, a modest little place like Pietro's did not attract 'foreigners', so there was no call for him to use his knowledge of the exotic tongue.

We struck a mutually responsive chord within the first ten minutes of our meeting. Pietro seemed to me to be an angel of benevolence when he mentioned the price of a day's board and lodging: 'Breakfast, lunch and dinner for 1500 lire' (which was then a little less than two dollars) 'and I give you room with bidet, hot and cold water. Add vino, you have vino with food for no price.'

I didn't care if the food was made of decomposing leather, if the mattress on the bed harboured rodents and lizards or whether the vino was the toughest vinegar in southern Europe. The price, for all the luxury Pietro had to offer, was the acme of seduction, given the condition of my purse. I put out my hand and shook his. 'I'll move in this evening after dinner,' I said. Pietro said that he would send his cousin down to my hotel at eight to fetch my luggage. He then poured out two glasses of wine and we toasted to 'Speaking English, you and me.'

There had been no talk of any advance payment. He hadn't asked to see my passport—which was not with me anyway. He did not want to know how long I was going to stay, nothing. I, on the other hand, hadn't asked to see the room, I did not wish to inspect his 'loo' or the rest of his pensione either. Perhaps we should have to take a chance—I had nothing to lose. And neither did Pietro. And it worked out well for both of us. Pietro had been impressed with the fact that I was staying at the King George, spoke English and mentioned dollars with the casualness with which the Aga Khan talks of diamonds. He had never had many customers who paid in dollars, I was an exotic and like Ram Singh's '*parfect* gentleman' I was an 'educated signor'.

I got up early the next day, had a sparse Italian breakfast with large mugs of hot coffee thrown in, and set out into Rome. I had very little money left and deliberately suppressed thoughts about the non-cashability of the cheques. The banks opened at ten, there was an hour to go and I walked into a cafe and asked for a glass of red wine. After some initial non-communication I pointed to a bottle and a small carafe was placed in front of me on the table. I had wanted a glass, I was given a carafe: the old battle over again. But I was quickly soothed when the bill was presented to me—eighty lire (which came to about fifteen cents of American money). Yes, I could afford that.

But three glasses of rough red wine did more than allay my nervousness about the cheques. I walked into the first bank, Banquo de Roma, confident and self-righteous. After being shunted from counter to counter, I was finally ushered into a small room and asked to take a seat.

'I understand you have a little problem, sir,' the man said, from the other side of the desk.

'Yes, I would like to cash these cheques, please,' I replied, throwing the whole bunch down on the table. 'Or at least some of them.'

The man inspected all ten cheques carefully and individually. 'You have five hundred dollars here,' he finally remarked, lifting his chin to look into my face.

'That's right,' I said, marvelling at the quick mathematical mind of a banker. 'And perhaps you would care to cash a hundred dollars. They're perfectly all right as you see, the two signatures match and everything.'

'Yes, but this is not your signature?'

'No, but how does that matter?'

The man leaned forward to pick up my passport. 'Well, Mr Ray, it matters like this. These cheques have been countersigned, yes, and if the lady Diana DeRouche was here now I would be very happy to give her the money. But you . . . '

'Look, she gave me those cheques. So why can't you give me the money?'

'That is just the problem, Mr Ray. We don't know if she *did* give you these cheques.'

'What do you mean?' I shouted, beginning to get an idea of what he was hinting at. 'Look, I am a journalist. My passport says so and I have a letter from my paper to show that I am on a reporting tour of Europe. And you can ring up the Indian Embassy to find out what prestige the *Statesman* commands in India. I am a respectable man.'

'Yes, Mr Ray, I am sorry but we can't do it. If you had a letter from this lady or something to show . . . '

I roared out of his office, furious. The three glasses of wine were beginning to assert their belligerent rights within my stomach. I began cursing and shouting to myself, not without providing free entertainment to a number of people who passed me on the street. This was the first time anyone had accused me of being a thief. How dare he? I mean . . .

After a coffee and several glasses of cold water I began to observe that my condition could not be described as hopeful. Because what that man had said would be what any reasonable banker would say too. And unless I chanced by luck to meet a 'trusting man', these ten leaves of paper were as good as soiled napkins here in Rome. I could write to Diana in Bombay, but she might have left by the time my letter got to her. Anyway, what would I do in the meantime . . . ?

I decided to try my luck and hope for that 'trusting' man. By about my fourth attempt, it was lunchtime in Rome, and the banks were to close for three hours. I trudged back to Pietro, unable to conceal my dejection yet apprehensive lest he discover my plight. I felt that he would be sympathetic if I did tell him, he might even decide to help me. On the other hand he might not. And if *he* insisted on advance payment I would be well and properly grounded. So I brooded at lunch, drank his 'vino for no price' and went out again at four o'clock.

This time the man suggested that I go to American Express directly: 'They might decide to take a chance. If not, they could advise you on what to do.' When I arrived at the American Express office it was closed for the day. The weekend loomed ahead. I would have to wait till Monday, with a little over a dollar in my pocket to keep me between now and then.

For the next two days I ate at Pietro's table, drank his vino and slept most of the time. My host and friend expressed some surprise. But when I told him I was a writer, corroborating my assertion with the clacketing of the typewriter in my room, Pietro was amused, excited and abundantly proud to have me as one of his 'guests'. I would occasionally go out for a walk into the great world outside the Pensione Roma. On two of these forays Pietro accompanied me.

'You are young,' he said once, 'you like Italian girls, no?' I nodded, smiling. 'My woman not so young no more,' Pietro added, sighing. He was in his mid-thirties, stocky, tough, with the look of a man who could lift a few weights, roll some stones over and around. 'I show you good, real good Italian girls, yes? Not plenty money, only good time, no?' I threw back a disapproving glance, more at his mention of money than moral vandalism. But the ambiguity of my look was well taken. He did not venture on the topic again. We drank a few glasses of wine (I was beginning to like the taste of the stuff) for which he always insisted on paying, a feature of our relationship to which I did not specifically object. He offered to take me to some 'interesting places', but I turned him down, firmly but politely, enhancing the mysterious and unapproachable aspect of a writer's personality. Thus Pietro's attitude to me was always marginally docile, touched with awe and respect. Which suited me fine.

The officer at American Express repeated what I had been told already by several Italian bank managers. 'You see, this Diana DeRouche could write to the American Express, saying that her cheques had been stolen.'

'But then why should she sign five hundred dollars' worth all at once? I thought that was the precise point of carrying around money in traveller's cheques, that they can't get pinched?'

'There is that, yes. But if she did instruct our branch to stop payment, her instructions would have to be followed.

Which means that if I decided to cash these cheques for you, the money wouldn't be coming from Miss DeRouche. It would be coming from us. And since we are not a charity institution . . . ' He left the sentence in mid-air, finishing it off with a smile on his lips.

My lips were in a very different shape. Here I was in Rome with five hundred dollars' worth of dud cheques, with not a single solitary soul I knew, not even a dollar in cash in my pocket. I didn't speak the language so I couldn't get a job. I couldn't write home for money, because Indian rupees cannot be sent out of the country without Government permission, and the reasons for Exchange Allowance Grants would have to be very special indeed. In any case, it would take weeks, if not months, even if it did come through. There was no branch office of the *Statesman* in Rome, the man in London would hardly be aware of the existence of a junior reporter like myself. I could go to the Indian Embassy and ask to be repatriated, and Rangaswami, as my guarantor, would be forced to bear the cost at the other end. It would be an ignominious epilogue to an odyssey which had been launched with such regnant declarations.

The American Express man cut into my thoughts: 'Of course, we could do one thing Mr Ray . . . . '

'Yes,' I replied, panting back to hope.

'We could send these cheques to our New York office, have them wire back an OK. And then we could issue fresh cheques in your name here at this office.'

Didn't I say everything works out right in the end? Yes, of course, naturally. The gods were always on my side. 'Why don't you do that then?' I answered, trembling.

'All right, Mr Ray,' the man said, rising from his chair. 'I shall make out an order and the girl at the counter will tell you how much it will cost.'

'Cost?' I barked. 'What cost? What for?'

'Well, Mr Ray, you don't expect . . . We shall have to send these cheques by express air mail. Then there is the cost of the cable from this end and the answer back.'

'Oh I see,' I said, finally beginning to see black, dead endless black. 'And how much will all that cost, do you think?'

'About five dollars I'd guess,' the American answered, 'a quarter more or less.'

'I don't have five dollars.'

'In that case, Mr Ray, I am sorry we can't help you.' Five dollars, five dollars, five dollars! How on earth . . . ? I knew Pietro would lend me the money, in fact he would be glad to do so, even proud. But how could I explain? And if he suspected that I might not be able to pay his bill would he continue to be as generous and friendly? Besides, the air mail and telegram stuff would take time. And if Diana had really done the dirty on me, if she had wired New York to say that her cheques had been stolen, then I wouldn't get any of the money.

'I suggest, then, that you go to the Indian Embassy and try for a loan. If you are certain that these cheques are valid and the lady would not stop payment, then you could return the money once we . . . '

The man wrote a 'TO WHOM IT MAY CONCERN' letter, saying that he had seen the cheques, but due to a technical hitch he could not cash them for two weeks. I walked the three miles to the Indian Embassy and after a two-hour wrangle with the Second Secretary of the Mission, managed to extract 10,000 lire. My trump card was John Stuart's letter in which he said that I was on a roving mission in Europe on behalf of the *Statesman*. The stodgy Indian bureaucrat was impressed and he authorized the loan instantly. The money was not a fortune but it left me with about 6000 lire (about twelve dollars) after paying American Express.

I took the receipt from the girl at the counter, thanked the officer of American Express who had so benevolently suggested the whole plan, and trudged back to Pietro's. I hoped and prayed that human nature would not turn out to be as evil as the Bible makes it out to be, that Diana was a sweet honest girl, that everything would work out all right in the end.

But while the prayers were shooting up to Heaven there was nothing I could do but wait.

For the next sixteen days I spent most of my time with Pietro. We would go drinking in bars, shoot down narrow Roman alleys in his little Fiat, visit the Trevi Fountain at least once a day. He took me to the Vatican, the Colosseum and the superb stone monuments built by Mussolini. One evening we went to see *The Millionairess*—dubbed in Italian—and I remember every time Sophia Loren showed more than an ounce of bosom the audience whistled and booed. In the last scene, when Peter Sellers allowed himself to be embraced by the heroine and finally met her lips with his, nearly the whole audience stood up on its feet and the dialogue on the screen was drowned by piercing cat-calls.

'You like Italian girls, no?' Pietro would keep repeating, as if it was a matter of national honour that I should be entranced by the native product.

'I like their legs,' I would reply with a smile.

Oblique suggestions of 'a night of good time' intruded continually into our conversations. But I warded them off by pretending incomprehension. The idea in fact attracted me because I was quite sure that any Italian girl would be better than Rangaswami's Venus and Pietro would be a more sympathetic guide. Besides, I was no longer a virgin. I might not have had a lot of experience, no, but I now knew what it was all about. I mean, I was going to become an 'adult' very soon. But the critical deterrent, of course, was cash. We could go to bars and I could accept Pietro paying for my drinks. With a woman it was different. No self-respecting adult male could accept another man paying for his whore. Obviously!

So we didn't follow that one up.

But female-kind apart, Pietro kept me amused. One day he announced at breakfast: 'We make little trip to Napoli.' His father-in-law had a vineyard which provided Pensione Roma with its house vino. It was about a hundred kilometres from Rome, just north of Naples. Pietro made a trip every month, collecting fresh barrels of wine and returning the empty ones. It was a delightful drive; the weather was mild enough to leave the roof of the car open. Pietro, like all Italians, drove very fast and with, what seemed to me to be, pure intuition. He would never signal his intention to turn right or left, always deciding in the last ten seconds before a turn that he really wanted to take it. So did all the other drivers. That most of them did survive seemed to me a minor Roman miracle.

At the vineyard the old man and his wife were 'very honoured' to have a foreigner visit their humble abode. I was taken down to the cellar and asked to taste the best wines in a very small glass—just about the size of a thimble. All this was very exciting for me, being treated like minor royalty, being fussed over and showered with offers of hospitality: Would I like to stay here for a week? Did I like Italian food, could I stay for dinner and spend the night here, then return to Rome the following day?

I declined, expressing my gratitude. The purse dictated my decisions with rigid authority. If I did decide to accept, who would pay for the train or bus fare back, who would pay for an occasional visit to a bar, etc.?

So the two weeks passed swiftly. My apprehensions about Diana and her cheques were like a toothache which is persistent but never acute. I could not drive the fear completely out of my mind, but Pietro's vino ensured that it never gripped me firmly enough to cause agony.

When I rang American Express on Monday morning I decided it would be best not to have any breakfast beforehand in case . . . . But Lady Fortune had chosen to supervise my destiny at that point: 'Yes, we have the money, Mr Ray. If you care to drop in we would be very pleased to issue the cheques in your name. Or if you prefer cash . . . '

'No, cheques will do fine, thank you.'

I collected five hundred dollars' worth of traveller's cheques, one hundred in tens and the rest in fifties, from American Express. Then I went to the Indian Embassy and repayed the loan. After that I went to the Tourist Office—taking taxis everywhere, just to balance the milage I had done on foot before—and bought a round-trip train ticket for Venice, Florence and Milan. I would have to return to Rome to catch the plane to wherever I wanted to go next.

I asked Pietro out for a drink and stood him two brandies. 'I am going to a nightclub tonight. And I leave for Venice tomorrow afternoon.'

'Good, good,' Pietro said, rubbing his hands. 'Good Italian girls, no?' There was a smirk on his lips, he had won his point at last. I may be a writer but I was human after all. 'I go with you and show you nice place, beautiful girls.'

'All right,' I said, 'it's a deal. After dinner tonight.'

'Yes, good. I tell my woman I show you Roma at night.'

After dinner I changed into my suit. Pietro whispered to me at table that he was having trouble with his wife, so would I wait for him in the bar next door? 'Not take much money,'he said, when we finally met a little while later. 'Only fifty thousand lire.'

'As much as that?' I queried, raising my eyebrows.

'For two people, money to get in and drinking,' he replied.

'What do you mean by two people?' I asked, not quite following his logic.

'You pay for me to get in and to drink,' Pietro answered, 'I show you nice places. Young boy like you . . . '

'I most certainly won't,' I retorted sharply. 'Young boy or no, if you want to come with me, you will have to pay for yourself.'

His point was that he would be acting as my guide, ensuring that I wouldn't be taken for a ride. In return I should have to stand him the night. No, he wasn't asking me to pay for any girls he might care to pick up, no. But the admission fee and the drinks I would have to pay for. Why should he pay for himself when he was doing me a favour? The drinks in the bars, for which he had paid, those were different. They were tokens of hospitality. But this, this was no hospitality. Nightclubs in Rome were expensive. He knew the good ones, he knew some of the managers personally, he would make sure that we got value for money. If I wanted a girl he would see that I paid the right price. So naturally, in exchange for his services, I would have to carry him.

'Most definitely not,' I said, starting to leave.

Well, in that case, would I settle my bill with him before I went out.

'What do you mean? Are you asking me to leave the pensione?' I shouted, incensed.

'No, no, not like that. Better you pay before going.'

If he thought I was that silly, well . . . I paid the bill after a slight wrangle about the exchange rate (since I was paying in traveller's cheques, i.e. dollars). Who does he think I am? A ten-year-old infant or something? I can look after myself, thank you. Protect me indeed!

I got into a taxi and asked to be taken to a 'good nightclub'. The man spoke broken English and I explained that I wanted a 'juiced-up Italian pussy'. I had never been to a nightclub before; I had no clear idea as to what went on in such places. I had read of them in books. I knew that near-nude women flounced around. I also knew that something called a 'cabaret' happened there. But I did not know what exactly this was. I mean, did they actually show men and women copulating? A friend of mine who was in England had written to me describing his experiences in London. 'And then one naked woman came and sat on my lap,' he had said in his letter. Evil, the dark enchanting deeds of moral degradation, took place in nightclubs. The worms of carnal lust wriggled about in the open, taboos were broken, the ten commandments were recklessly violated. Yes, this is what a writer must observe, he must get inside the belly of 'real life', watch men and women with their masks ripped off.

The taxi stopped in front of a large neon-lit establishment. The driver opened the door to let me out and asked me to accompany him. I walked in, my eyes taken unawares by the sudden dark inside. My guide spoke a few words with a man wearing a dinner-jacket and a bow tie. 'Yes, sir,' the man said, coming up to me. 'Very honoured to have you here, sir.'

'Thank you,' I replied, looking round in the dark, my eyes not yet accustomed to the fall in luminosity. 'I would like to . . . '

'Yes, sir, which table would you like?' It was a large room with a round empty space in the middle (obviously the dance floor). Most of the tables were empty, but those that were occupied had single girls sitting at them. There was only one couple in a corner booth, an elderly man with a pretty young girl dressed rather less fully than would a lady.

'Any table would do actually,' I replied. 'But I would really like a girl.'

'Which one would you like, sir?' the manager asked, waving his hand over the whole room. 'Any of these young ladies would be happy to sit at your table.'

'You mean I can choose? Anyone here, any one of them?

'Of course, sir,' the man answered, smiling. 'Just point her out to me and she will come over to your table.'

'Yes,' I said, a little confused. The taxi driver had told me that I could get a girl here, I mean *get* a girl, you know, to do

. . . I mean, who wants to just . . . ? 'But I want a girl for . . . Not just to sit at my table.'

'I understand of course, sir,' the man assured me, leaning over to whisper in my ear. 'You just pay for her drinks and she takes you home with her.'

This boosted my temporarily flagging enthusiasm for the establishment. 'All right then,' I said, 'that one,' pointing to the prettiest exhibit on show.

I was shown to a table by a waiter and the girl came over and sat with me. She wore tight black pantyhose and I could see the cleavage between her breasts which bulged out under her close-fitting blouse. 'You give me drink?' she asked, putting her hand halfway up my thighs. A high-voltage charge shot through me and I replied, 'Yes, of course.'

Two glasses were placed on the table, wide, flat-bottomed, supported on thin long stems. (I didn't know that they were to hold the elixir of alcoholic beverages, champagne.) The drink duly arrived, in a bulbous bottle, wrapped up to the neck in a spotless white serviette. The glasses were filled to the brim, sparkling bubbles of gold fizzed into a thin foam on the surface and my table companion stirred her container with long sticks provided at no extra charge. The bottle then disappeared with the same sharp alacrity with which it had shot on to the scene in the hands of the waiter. Conversation was limited to cryptic remarks, 'Good, hm . . . mm . . . mm, no?' from the enchanting female in the next chair, and replies from me which were equally monosyllabic. The hand in the middle of my thigh did not remain idle meanwhile. A swift yet gentle movement up and down from my knee to the nether regions of my groins produced an immobility which I find difficult to describe. I was transfixed.

This went on for three more glasses each. You might well ask, wasn't I worried about the money angle? No, I was not. A carafe of wine in a bar cost a hundred lire, a hundred and fifty at the most. In a nightclub, where things were obviously more expensive, it could cost twice, thrice or even four times as much. And I was prepared for that. I had over four hundred dollars on me (in traveller's cheques) and even at the most exorbitant rate of alcoholic consumption this would last endless weeks. No, there was no need to be worried about money. I had an attractive—devastatingly so—female sitting at my table, her hand was on my thigh, there was an inexhaustible smile on her lips, and all I had to do was stand her a few drinks and she would 'go home with me', as the manager had said. Why grumble about a few drinks then? I was young, I was a writer, and this was life. What the hell!

After I had consumed the third glass the bubbly liquid had begun to weave through my veins and there were gentle knocks in my brain, my eyes were not quite as open as they had been before. 'Can we go home now?' I suggested to my companion.

'Go home?' she exclaimed, bursting into a ripple of laughter. 'No go home now,' she added, 'very early night, not twelve o'clock. I do cabaret first, you like, no? Then you and me, we go home. Yes? You like me?'

I was consoled but I couldn't quite follow her questions. I mean, why should she want to know if liked her? I thought that had been settled long ago. I had already stood her three drinks. That should have been proof enough, surely. 'OK,' I said, 'but when will you be ready to go home?'

'Not very long,' she answered, looking around and playing with her empty glass. 'I no speak good English. My cousin know English. You like, no?' She pointed out a girl sitting by herself at a table. 'She come here sit, no?'

I looked at her and smiled. 'All right,' I said, 'but you and I must go home after you do your cabaret. All right?'

'O.K.,' she said, waving her hand to the girl. Her other hand moved away from my thigh and lifted the empty glass to her lips. The other girl came over and smiled at me. I rose from my seat and helped her into the chair on my right. I now had two females at my table, one on either side of me. The newcomer had a maxi-bosom, spilling out of her bra. And her smile was more intense, somehow a little more desperate. She was older than 'my girl'.

'Could I have a drink?' she asked.

'Of course,' I replied, summoning the waiter. 'Your friend says you know English?'

'Yes, I was in England many months. I learn English very much.' Hearing was believing. I smiled.

A fresh empty glass appeared in front of my new guest, another bottle masked by a white kerchief disgorged its contents into our three glasses and disappeared from sight. And I said, 'Cheers.'

'Cheers,' the two girls echoed, smiling at each other and me. The room had begun to fill up now, there were fewer girls sitting alone. Several couples occupied the booths. One table not far from ours housed four rumbustious males who were raising glasses and talking loud fast Italian. The band had started playing, there were couples dancing in the empty space in the middle of the room. The wine was making me feel mellow and happy. This was life, really. Two girls at my table, music in the air, sharp swift curves of breasts and thighs all around me.

And soft flickering candlelight, accenting a profile here and a stem-like neck there.

'Shall we dance?' I said to the girl who knew no English.

'Dancing not now, after cabaret. You like, no?'

What was this 'cabaret' she keeps talking about, what would she be doing?

'I have no drink,' the girl on my right said, interrupting my thoughts.

'I am sorry,' I replied, embarrassed both with my lack of savoir faire in keeping a lady thirsty, and with her crude insistence. 'Waiter,' I shouted, 'another round, please.'

This was my fifth glass. My head was beginning to buzz, I could not hold the cigarette with a steady hand. But my words were still coherent, my mind obsessed with the thought of 'taking this girl home'. And I realized that the drinks were being consumed at a much faster pace than at any of the tables around.

'We go have dinner now,' the English-oriented lady announced. 'Then we do cabaret and come back here. You like, no?'

'Yes, I'd like that,' I replied. 'But I really would like to take your friend home very soon. I don't think I'd like to drink any more.'

'Yes, after cabaret you take her home,' she said. 'But now you give money for dinner.'

'What?' I asked, slightly disconcerted.

'Money for dinner,' she repeated. The other girl was watching. 'Two thousand lire to me, two thousand lire to her.'

'But why should I do that? I only agreed to pay for the drinks.'

'Then we not come back to your table after cabaret,' she said flatly, rising from her seat.

'Wait, wait,' I pleaded, 'all right. But your friend *will* go home with me, yes?'

'Yes,' replied the girl who had her hand on my thigh. 'I promise by the Mother of Jesus.' An inappropriate oath, I would have thought, considering . . . . But I let it go and took out my traveller's cheques (the whole lot was in one book) and signed a ten-dollar bill. The manager wanted to see my passport to check the signature and the money—in lire—was brought to the table by the waiter. I gave the two girls four thousand-lira notes and sat back to sip my drink.

The two of them gulped down theirs and got up from the table.

'Ciao,' they said.

'Ciao,' I replied. As I lighted a cigarette and looked around the room, I noticed that most of the other tables had red wine or what looked like spirits (with ice in the glass), while ours was white and bubbly. Also the bottles remained on the table, they were not wrapped up in white cloth. I deduced from this that the wine I had been served was probably a more expensive brand and thought it would be just as well to determine at this point how much the evening was costing me. I asked the waiter for the bill and the manager walked over to my table.

'You are not leaving, sir, are you? You haven't seen the show yet.'

'No, I am not going yet,' I replied, 'but I'd just like to look at the bill.'

'Very well, sir, I shall make it out for you.'

I have never been more surprised, furious and speechless than when I looked at what he 'made out': Six bottles of champagne, at a little less than thirty dollars each, plus a cover charge.

'What's the meaning of this?' I shouted, after recovering from the shock.

'The bill, sir,' the man replied blandly.

'What's the price of . . . ? Six bottles! I mean, we only had six drinks. Those bottles must hold . . . '

'You had six bottles, sir. And each bottle of champagne costs . . . '

'Well, I didn't ask for champagne in the first place. Look at them, just look at that table, are they drinking champagne?'

'The young ladies can only drink champagne, sir. If you want any other kind of wine we would be very happy to serve you, sir, but the ladies will not be able to sit at your table.'

'You mean when you said that all I had to do was pay for a few drinks you meant a clean sweep of two hundred dollars?'

'That is our price, sir, for champagne. If you would like to look at the wine list . . . '

'Yes, I would. I most certainly would.'

And sure enough the price of a bottle of champagne, printed on the wine list, was exactly what he had put down on the bill. I was trapped. 'But we didn't have six bottles. First of all, the second girl only joined us on the fifth glass, so altogether we had . . . '

'You had six bottles, sir,' the man calmly insisted. It was his word against mine. He was the manager, I was a customer—a foreigner at that—and I was drunk.

'How many glasses does each bottle fill?' I asked, weakening at the thought that I would in fact have to pay the bill.

'You had six bottles, sir,' the man repeated. 'I don't know how many drinks. We don't serve champagne by the glass, sir, only by the bottle.'

There was no point in pursuing the conversation. I had been taken, that was all there was to it. Now I had to make a decision. Should I pay and leave, without waiting for the girls to come back? Or should I wait and take one of them home, and recover some of my lost investment?

I decided on the latter course. 'Thanks,' I said to the manager, 'that'll be all right.'

'Are you going to wait for the show, sir?'

'Yes, I think I will,' I replied.

'Then would you like another drink?'

'No thank you, I am all right for the moment.'

'As you please, sir,' the manager said, bowing to me. Then he walked away.

I looked at the bill, wondering if Shovan Lal would be able to imagine spending two hundred dollars in a single evening—six months' earnings swilled down in six large gulps. There was something wrong somewhere. 'But at least I am going to get a "juiced-up Italian pussy" out of this,' I said to myself, consoling a bruised ego for not being adult enough to have smelt smoke before the fire had consumed two hundred virgin dollars.

The cabaret began. The girl who knew no English was the first to perform. She smiled at me as she started swinging her hips and came close to my table when she undid her bra. Her breasts were tight and full; under the strange glow of the arc lamp the nipple took on a deep violet colour. Then she took off the other pieces of clothing, leaving only a brief triangular patch covering her 'pussy'.

I was reminded of my friend's letter. 'And then a naked woman came and sat on my lap.' No, he hadn't made it up. This sort of thing happened in the West, it was happening to me. At some cost, of course. But it was happening all the same. You wouldn't get any of this in India even if you spent a million. And what was two hundred dollars, after all? Just money. But think of the 'experience', what that means to an artist!

I was stirred. I forgot the bill, the money I had been forced to pay out for their dinners. Only a fierce insistent urge to hold her very tight in my arms and rip off her last cover. And penetrate her. Yes, 'fuck her', as Rangaswami would say. She was mine, after all. She had promised by 'the Mother of Jesus', and she was Italian, Catholic most likely. Catholics take their Virgin Mary very seriously. Of course she wouldn't let me down. And I had paid—was about to pay—heavily enough, God knows. Yes, it was worth it; it would be worth it. I was aching for the show to end. I did not want anyone else to see what was by rights only for my eyes. At least for tonight. The four Italians had brought their chairs closer to the dais to have a better view. I resented this. That 'juiced-up pussy', I felt like shouting, is mine, stay off her, will you?

But the 'thing' went on and on. In between performances, each of which lasted for about ten minutes, there would be breaks and the dance floor would fill up with couples from the audience. I sat by myself at the table, empty glass in hand, nervous, aching, feeling a gnawing pain in my stomach, my eyes rolling around without corresponding dictations from the brain. It was two o'clock when the girls returned to my table, fully and properly dressed this time.

'You give us drink, no?' the English-knowing lady asked, settling herself in a chair.

'No,' I replied, 'I would like to go home with you now,' I said, turning to the other girl.

'I cannot go now,' she answered, smiling, 'one more little drink.'

I looked at her, not knowing how to take this. Was she just asking for another drink? Or was she putting me off? 'You like me, no?' she continued, putting her hand on my thigh again. The same high-voltage pulse shot through me, my penis throbbed under my pants and her hand wove up my trousers and felt the tip of its risen head. 'You want go home with me, no?'

'Yes, yes, I do,' I replied hoarsely. 'Waiter, bring a bottle of champagne and open it here.' The other girl's face clouded for an instant, but I ignored her. The bottle arrived, the cork erupted with gunpowder violence and the foam spilled over on the table. The waiter filled the three glasses and was about to whisk the bottle away when I said, 'Hang on, leave it here.' I took it from his hand and removed the white cloth. Yes, it was champagne all right. But there was half a bottle of the precious stuff still left inside. 'Thank you,' I said, 'I'll be able to pour the drinks myself.'

I took 'my girl' on the dance floor. She was soft and close against my body, the tight bare breasts I had seen a little while ago were now covered. But they pressed hard against me. So did her thighs. I knew she could feel my 'little man' aching to pierce her. My balls hurt. They wanted to burst. And all the while we moved in tune with the music, her hand caressed my face and my ear and down the arch of my back.

It was worth it, I kept telling myself, what is money after all. She is the most beautiful girl in the world!

We went back to the table, the other girl had poured herself a fresh drink. 'My girl' swilled hers down in a gulp. I refilled her glass, topped up mine, the bottle was empty. 'You like me or you like her?' the English pedant asked.

'I like both of you,' I replied, 'but I would rather go home with her.'

'You don't want go home with two girls?'

'Yes,' I replied, sharply taken aback. 'I would like that very much. If you like that . . . '

'All right, we two go home with you,' she said, settling the issue. 'Then you buy another drink for me and her.'

'Oh no,' I said, 'she said she only wanted one more drink. We are going home right now, after I have paid the bill.'

The girls looked at each other, sipping their drinks, while I signed the cheques. I thought I would cash three hundred dollars and keep the spare cash in case . . . . The manager picked up the bill and the cheques, the girls' eyes followed the cheque book from the table to my breast-pocket.

'We cannot go before closing,' one of them said. 'We work here. You wait up to three o'clock and then we come home with you.'

'Well, if that's the case, fine. But not a minute after three.' I had found out that the establishment did close at three. They could not put me off after that.

'Then you ask for one more drink, no?'

'No,' I replied firmly. 'Enough is enough.'

'Then we sit at other table. We not allowed to sit with you with no drink.'

This was blackmail. But what the hell! The hand on my thigh was not idle, the champagne swam in my stomach and I ordered another bottle. Then I had another dance, then I drank another glass of the inebriating fluid.

Three o'clock. The lights came on, harsh, discordant and blinding. The band stopped playing.

'You pay money first before we go.'

'What money?'

'One hundred dollars.' That was the exact amount I had left in traveller's cheques.

'One hundred dollars for what?'

'To go and do . . . ' The girls giggled.

'But you said you would . . . The manager said that all I had to do was stand you a few drinks.'

'That only to sit at table and dance with you. Not for going home.'

I went up to the manager. 'What arrangements the girls make is none of my business. I only employ them here.'

'But you said . . . ?'

The soft, tight-breasted girl came up and started stroking my face. 'One hundred *dollares*, no? You no like me? No?'

'No, no, no,' I shouted hysterically. 'Damn bastard! Bloody bitches!'

A big burly man came over, caught me by the collar and dragged me to the door. 'Bye, bye,' the two girls said, giggling at each other. And then I found myself on a Roman street with my face down on the pavement. It was four o'clock in the morning.

I picked myself up, put some spit on my face and rubbed it off with a handkerchief. My nose was bruised and it stung.

I felt weak at the knees, there was a sharp throbbing pain in my head, I could not focus with my eyes. There was a faint film of light around, not quite dawn. The stars in the sky were pale and fading. Even the moon wore an exhausted look on her beamless face.

I walked down the street, turned into a cafe and ordered cognac and coffee. The woman sitting at the next table smiled at me. I swilled down the cognac and started sipping the coffee. The woman eased her chair closer to me and whispered, 'Want a little good time?'

I said, 'Yes,' without turning to look at her. 'How much?'

'We go out and talk,' she replied, in a whisper.

I left the coffee and walked out. She followed me. At this point I could not afford to think. My feet plodded on without any conscious willing from my brain. My walk could not have been firm for the woman linked her arm in mine and held me in a firm grasp. 'How much?' I repeated.

'Ten thousand lire,' she answered, 'and I give you very good time. You pay hotel.'

I did not have the money, most of the remainder of the three hundred dollars I had cashed had gone on the last bottle of champagne. 'Do you know any place which would cash traveller's cheques?'

'Yes, hotel,' she replied.

We got into a taxi and made a tour of five 'hotels' before we found one which would cash cheques. Obviously, my lady companion could not go to a 'respectable' establishment, they wouldn't let her in. So when we finally alighted upon a kindly soul, who was willing to provide a roof and a bed for the two of us for 'a little time' and also cash a fifty-dollar traveller's cheque, it was nearly six o'clock and the sun, though shy, was about to hold court over a Roman sky. After the ten per cent commission to the pimp, the price of the room and the pay-off to my darling Madonna, there was very little of the fifty dollars left. My purse felt considerably lighter than it did the evening before, and my soul, or what I had left of it, as heavy as a Hollywood hangover.

We climbed a flight of dark wooden stairs, the man ahead kept 'Sh . . . sh . . . sh . . . ing' every time the planks creaked under our feet and the woman whispered, '*Politsia*'. The door of the room groaned open, the man handed us two towels, switched on the light and withdrew. I looked at the face of my Madonna for the first time.

She was not in the spring of life, the make-up on her face had cracked along lines etched out by nature. Her lips were deep red from an over-generous application of scarlet wax. A crucifix dangled between the two minor mounds which used to be her breasts. Her hands must have started on their pilgrimage to unscrubbed floors and dirty dishes before Madison Avenue got around to inventing soap flakes. But she could smile, open, without cunning, grateful. 'Business no good this night,' she said, as she started undressing.

I looked around the room, not quite sure where I was and how I came to be there. There was an enamel basin in a corner on the floor, a cube of red soap by its side. A large jug was filled with water. The bed cover was shorn at the edges, there were patches of mild rust-stains all over. The walls were an ashen white and bare. There were no windows, no vents. A small stool by the side of the bed, carrying an ash tray, one solitary chair on the other side. The light bulb hung from the centre of the ceiling, harsh, unshaded.

She was nude. Her breasts were small and shrivelled with two bulbous nipples which were almost black. The crucifix, suspended by a thin gold chain, swung slowly as she approached me.

'You take off coat and shirt and do fucki-fucki, no?'

'Yes,' I replied, unable to muster a smile.

Madonna helped me off with my clothes and I lay down on the bed. She started fondling my penis, stroking my thighs. After a while she hunched over me at the foot of the bed and took my prick in her mouth. The crucifix dangled over my navel. I looked down at her, with images of another Madonna at another time flashing through my champagne-soaked brain. She sucked furiously, moving her face up and down, her tongue licking the tip of my reluctant phallus.

'Wait,' she said, getting up from the bed. I watched her sitting over the basin, splashing water in the crevice between her legs, working up a lather with the soap and covering the bushy black fern with white foam.

'You get inside and come hard, no?'

She sat astride me, as someone else had done before, squeezing, shoving, pushing, in a fruitless attempt to get the thing inside her dark cavern. 'Little man sleepy, sleepy,' she said, smiling, as she took him in her mouth again. 'Much drink in night, no good.'

Then it started. Without warning, without my willing, I began sobbing. First in small embarrassed spurts, then as she put my head in her lap, whispering, 'Oh me bambino, oh me bambino,' I could no longer control myself. Tears gushed down my eyes, I took my breath in sharp jerks like under a hiccup. 'He threw me on the street. And she said . . . said she would come home with me. She promised by the Mother of Jesus. She promised.'

Madonna punctuated my sentences with, 'Oh me bambino, oh me bambino,' gently rocking me in her lap all the while.

'I am a writer . . . I have to see life . . . . I know I can do it, I know. I am not impotent, I can . . . I can satisfy a woman in that way. Mimi is a bitch. They are all bitches. He threw me on the street. I didn't do anything wrong. I only wanted to . . . '

I must have been asleep for nearly two hours. I woke with an ache in the head, as if there were steel springs being tightened round my forehead. Madonna was still cradling me in her lap, her hand stroking my back, gently, almost like my mother. Yes, I thought of my mother, how she had rocked me to sleep on countless nights, stroking my back, her soft smooth hands weaving through my hair and grazing over my eyes. 'Now feel better, bambino?' Madonna asked, as I opened my eyes.

I nodded.

She leaned over and touched my prick. And, wonder of wonders, it woke up with a sudden vehemence, hard, erect and ready for action. Madonna came over me, took my 'little man' in her hand, pushing him inside herself with a sharp swing of her loins. It hurt. And I almost came. 'No move,' she whispered, 'wait little time.' She sat there, perfectly still, smiling down at me. Her crucifix, with its small slender arms, swung like the pendulum of a clock which was about to stop.

It didn't last long. Madonna swooned and gasped, 'Oh . . . oh . . . oh,' and 'Good . . . good,' as she moved, slowly at first, then in swift gyrations. I held on as long as I could and then spurted out my seed with a cry. It hurt again. But there was pleasure in this hurt, a thin piercing pleasure. 'You fucki-fucki good,' Madonna said, as she moved away. 'All Indian fucki-fucki good like you?'

I had no answer.

'You go now? Want one more little good time, no?'

I smiled through my sleep-sodden eyes. 'Yes,' I said, 'one more little good time.'

'Me you like or other girl?' She knocked on the wall, there was an answering tap from the other side. A girl with a Mongoloid face, wearing a tight dress, came in. 'My friend, you like?' Madonna asked.

'Yes, I like,' I replied. She was younger, wore very little make-up and carried a soft smile on her lips. My prick raised its head in salutation to the newcomer. 'Twenty thousand lire?' Madonna asked. 'She speak no English, Japanese.'

'All right,' I answered.

The woman undressed quickly and lay down on the bed. She had firm breasts and a smooth slender body. She was worth twenty thousand lire all right. I entered her without ceremony. She let out a small scream and cried, 'No, no, suck, suck.' I put my arms round her and began nibbling her nipples. 'Oh . . . oh . . . oh,' the Japanese gasped. Madonna came over to the bed and started stroking my buttocks. And then she pushed her soapy finger into my podex. I screamed, hurt, yet there was a sudden tightening of my balls. The finger withdrew, I began moving very fast, the Japanese continued gasping.

It was all over in two minutes.

'One more time for me?' Madonna asked, as I rolled off the tight silken body. 'Not plenty money. Only seven thousand lire.'

'Yes,' I replied, 'one more time, in a little while.'

The Japanese soaked a towel, washed my penis and wiped it dry. Then she started sucking it, while Madonna fingered my anus. My 'little man' didn't feel sleepy for very long. 'You good fucki-fucki,' Madonna said, as I came inside her again. The Japanese nodded with a smile. 'All Indian good fucki-fucki like you?'

Again I had no answer.

When I walked out of that 'hotel' it was ten-thirty. And I had signed away the last of the fifty-dollar cheques. All I had left was a couple of thousand-lira notes. But it was worth it, I told myself. The cars honked, the sun blazed, my loins ached. I kept hearing Madonna's voice: 'You good fucki-fucki.' Did she mean it? Who cares? It was enough that she said so. Between the two of them they had breathed fire into my dormant balls. And I would never forget waking up in Madonna's lap, with her hand stroking my back and her voice whispering in my ear, 'Now feel better, bambino?'

I didn't want Pietro to know of the catastrophe which befell me for not taking up his offer. But the tell-tale marks on my face induced the expected smirk: 'Good time in night, no? Italian girls plenty money, no?'

'No,' I replied firmly.

I surrendered the round-trip train ticket for Venice, Florence and Milan. The Tourist Office returned the fare, less ten per cent. Rome had been costly but instructive. And there were other expenses still to be met: Pietro's maid, the taxi and the airport tax. On board the Air India Viscount I had two drinks. There were no Swedes or Norwegians this time. And I could do with some sleep.

At Heathrow Airport, London, the lire I changed into English money came to five pounds (sterling) and a few odd shillings.

The battle had begun!

THREE

~

LONDON STOP ONE

Those were the days when they hadn't tightened up on the immigration laws in Britain and an Indian passport did not provoke the look of animosity that it does now on the face of officials. I got through Customs and Immigration with no trouble at all. And then there was the hour-long bus ride from Heathrow airport to the centre of town. I had imagined that London would be pretty. Indeed, that is how it had looked from the plane. The houses were grey and brown, each one identical to the other, small boxes of stone, with tall black chimneys jutting out of their conical roofs. The cars were like millions of duty-bound centipedes, a slow ceaseless procession threading its way through acres of grass. But as we descended lower, Surrey and Middlesex had come into view, an occasional house set apart, lawns and golf courses, motionless automobiles waiting patiently on pebbled drives. And then those large patches of green, the parks, iridescent with the summer sun, and the grey-green waters of the Thames, languidly weaving through stone and glass and domes of black smoke puffing out of factory chimneys.

On the ground, from the bus, London was not pretty. At first the houses backed on to the road, clothes drying out in the yard, garbage bins, children scuttling about on the pavement, broken window-panes, vacant lots, tricycles, fat mamas screaming against the wind, grey men in bowler hats wearily emerging from pubs. Somehow it did not seem very lively. The other cars didn't rocket past our bus, the driver maintained a monotonous speed. I got the feeling that everything was controlled, inert, almost static.

Then we approached town, and the houses began to face us. There were more people on foot, the traffic was denser, there were even a few jarring hoots from impatient horns. The stop-go lights became more frequent, the sun milder and Earls Court, London, came into view.

I met Stanley Brown in a pub on that first evening.

I had just booked into a guest-house which charged twenty-five shillings per day for bed and breakfast. The landlady was reluctant at first (all the others had turned me down with various kind replies: 'Sorry, but we're full up', when there was a big 'Vacancy' sign hanging in front of the window; or 'We only take recommended guests', or even 'You know, I would if I could but sorry, no'). But after I had used my large adolescent eyes on her and explained that I had just arrived from Rome and had been walking for four hours, carrying two suitcases in my hands, she agreed, 'but only for tonight'. Tomorrow I would have to find another place. The room was small but there were clean sheets on the bed and a long mirror on the wall. The landlady—bless her Polish soul—made me some tea and toasted two buns. I thanked her, and strode out into the street with the keys to the house and my room jangling in my pocket. Here I was in London at last, rooming in a guest-house (what if it was just for one night) in Earls Court, with nearly five pounds on me and a 'high tea' in my belly.

It was nine-thirty, the sun had set, but it was not yet dark. I had been told that pubs shut at eleven in London. There was an hour and a half to go. I entered the Dragon's Head. The sign on the door said, 'Saloon', and I didn't know what exactly this meant. Obviously it couldn't be a hairdressing saloon because . . . because, well, because it was a pub! Obviously! I mean, with a name like Dragon's Head . . . . Besides, I had seen men come in and go out, I had a glimpse of what was going on inside. 'Saloon' must be an English adaptation of 'salon', you know, the French 'salons', where intellectuals and writers met and talked. Strange, though, that I should not have come across 'saloon' in any English book I had read, however . . .

I looked around, pondering my next move. Yes, this was a great moment in a writer's life, I mean much greater than the rather lengthy moments I had had at the nightclub in Rome. This was the writer's world, the 'saloon' in a London pub. Here I would meet fellow writers and intellectuals, discuss philosophy and art and literature, here I would enter the kind of company after which I had hankered all my life. Several men were standing by themselves, a few others were at the counter. One table was occupied by three men and a woman. Most of the men carried large mugs of a brown liquid in their hands. Obviously Scotch. 'You don't drink anything but Scotch in England,' Rangaswami had said. 'The elixir of elixirs, the Queen of inebriating fluids.'

I walked up to the counter with a mild flutter in my heart.

'Yes, sir,' said the barman, 'what would you like?'

'A pint,' I replied, firm, confident, about to be initiated. I had heard the two previous customers—intellectuals obviously—order 'pints'.

'A pint of what, sir?' the barman queried. 'Red Barrel or the ordinary?'

I remembered the size of my purse and thought I would deny myself deluxe treatment at this stage. 'No, just the ordinary Scotch will do fine, thank you.'

The bartender looked up sharply. 'Thought you was having a pint?'

'Yes, just a pint of ordinary Scotch, thank you.'

'What?'

'A pint,' I replied, beginning to hear the familiar thumping against my chest. What was this, some kind of inquisition or something? He didn't throw all these questions at any of the others. So why was he doing it to me? Must be some kind of initiation ceremony. 'A pint of ordinary Scotch,' I repeated, more firmly.

'You must be joking!' He turned to one of the customers at the bar. 'Here, get this, man here wants a pint of ordinary Scotch.' Laughter rippled down the line, my hands began to go moist.

'Why don't you serve him then?' one patron remarked. 'No skin off your nose, is it?'

'May I know why there is such a commotion about serving me a pint?'

'Commotion and all, get him,' the bartender retorted, dragging out the last word, quite contrary to the elocution rules laid down by my teacher at school.

At this point Stanley Brown, who had been listening in for the past two minutes, walked up to me. 'You're new here, aren't you?'

'Yes,' I replied, grateful to find support in his voice. 'I just arrived today.'

'I thought as much. Give him a pint of Red Barrel and take it from here.' He put down a pound note, the barman went on laughing while drawing out the beer and I said, 'Thank you, thank you very much.'

My rescuer was wearing a loose-fitting corduroy suit and smoked a pipe. His words came out chewed; I found it difficult to follow, what I later learnt was a Midlands accent. He had been born in Shakespeare country, in fact only about ten miles from Stratford. His parents still lived there. Stanley Brown was a farmer's son, and even after six years in the city, urban life still grated on him. He was an artist and he wore a painter's beard, full-face, bushy, untrimmed and streaked with strands of flaming red. He had a perpetual smile on his lips. 'No nonsense, laddie,' it seemed to say, 'I see you.' His stint with the National Service had taken him to Malaya, and he wondered if I came from there.

'No, I am from Calcutta.'

'Calcutta eh?' he queried. 'Stopped in there on our way back. Bloody beastly place, isn't it? All those beggars and the dirt on the streets?'

'Well, there is more to a city than what you see from a taxi window,' I replied, becoming defensive about my birthplace.

'Oh sure, but doesn't it get you down, all those helpless miserable creatures living out their lives on pavements and railway stations? Accepting, accepting, accepting all the time?'

I kept silent. My first night in London, and memories of that horrendous city in which I had grown up being revived.

'Yes, I see what you mean,' Stanley said, smiling. 'Let's get out from here. I know a place where we might land a couple or birds with a bit of luck. You need some female company.'

We came out into Earls Court Road and it was dark now. The pavements on either side of the street were thick with people. Mostly women, young, full-bodied, everyone in a frantic rush. I kept banging against them. My eyes strayed from the brightly lit shop windows to those sturdy legs, then up to the pointed breasts and shining waxen lips. There was nothing inert here. Little groups of three and four, laughing, poking each other in the ribs, flitting in and out of pubs, couples holding up traffic—human traffic—in the middle of the pavement, arms around each other and kissing, yes, kissing, right there in the middle of everywhere for everyone to see.

'I thought this sort of thing only happened in Paris,' I said to Stanley, as we navigated around one erotically entwined pair.

'On the contrary,' my friend replied, 'the French are far more discreet and dignified. Exhibitionism was invented by Anglo-Saxons. It's a natural outcome of Puritan repression. It would be one thing if they really wanted to kiss. Look, look at that one there. She isn't kissing. Just showing off to the other girls, that's all. A bit of roadside theatre on the free.' Stanley smiled and puffed at his pipe.

'Where are we going?'

'Another fifty yards or so. It's called the Overseas Visitors' Club and all the birds come there. There's a shortage of males round here. So you can really take your pick. In a pub they don't often come by themselves, but here it's sort of respectable. Being a club and all that, you know.'

I wasn't too sure if I really did want to have my pick. How much would it cost? Remember what happened when

I had my 'pick' in Rome? And where could we go? I didn't have enough money for a hotel. Besides, I was in London now, there would be plenty of time. No hurry!

'How much is it going to cost?'

'What?'

'I mean, "the birds"?'

'Oh that. I don't know. Depends how you get them. Sometimes . . . sometimes you get them for nothing. Pay for a few drinks . . .'

I didn't follow the rest of the sentence. Hadn't I heard that somewhere before? 'Pay for a few drinks and . . .' 'Look, if you don't mind, I . . . I mean I really don't have much money and I would like to . . .'

'Don't be bloody silly. You're not going to spend your fortune,' Stanley insisted. 'And if you are stuck for a few bob I have some cash. Come on, what have you got to lose?'

We entered the Overseas Visitors' Club, walked through the hall and into the bar. Yes, this was paradise. There were girls everywhere, standing up, sitting down, reclining in chairs, foot up on the window-sill, chattering, laughing, swilling drinks, every discernible sign of Epicurean and erotic living. Several 'birds' threw me a glance and turned away. I walked up to the bar counter with Stanley.

'It's my turn to pay for the drinks,' I said, delving into my pocket.

'Go ahead,' Stanley replied.

I waited till the bartender had finished serving the other man. Then he came towards my end of the counter and walked past me to a man who had come after us. Then there were two girls, then a group at the other end. The man walked past me three times; on each occasion when I tried to catch his eye he looked away.

'What's the matter, how about the drinks?' Stanley said, turning to me. He had been surveying the scene, giving 'a couple of birds the once-over'. 'You haven't asked for a pint of Scotch again, have you?'

'I haven't had a chance.'

'Hey,' Stanley hollered, 'bring us a couple of pints, will you?'

The bartender walked towards us and leant over to Stanley. I couldn't hear what he whispered. 'What do you mean you can't serve me if I am with him?' Stanley shouted. 'Of course I am bloody well with him and he is a friend of mine.'

At this point a man in a velvet jacket and a tie came into the bar and walked up to me. 'Sorry, but you'll have to leave.'

'What the devil!' Stanley roared, banging his fist on the counter.

'We don't allow non-members. This a club, you see,' the man continued, talking in a soft conciliatory voice.

'I am bloody well not a member and I have always been served here,' Stanley persisted.

'I am sorry about that, you shouldn't have been,'

I did not understand why Stanley was so upset. It seemed understandable that non-members were not allowed to use the facilities of a club.

'Sorry, but you'll have to leave.'

For a moment it looked as if my friend was about to throw his fists around. But after a short glaring minute he looked away from the man. The noise in the bar had subsided, everyone was staring at the two of us. 'Come on,' Stanley shouted, and strode out. I followed meekly behind, escorted by a host of glances.

'What was all that about?' I asked, after Stanley had begun to breathe normally once more.

'Bloody bastards, mustn't take any notice of them. A bunch of plebs, that's what they are, scum. Bloody foreigners.'

I learnt later that Stanley's current girlfriend was a Rhodesian and a member of the Overseas Visitors' Club. But at that time I was puzzled by his violent reaction. The manager of the club had seemed to me a reasonable and pleasant man. The only thing I could not explain was how the bartender had known that I wasn't a member.

London to me was a collection of names, each with a precise literary connotation: Hampstead, from Forster's *Passage to India*, Soho, Chelsea, Bloomsbury, Thames, Tower of London, Bond Street, Piccadilly Circus, Trafalgar Square, British Museum, Covent Garden. Earls Court was not one of them. And I had actually imagined that it was a place where earls held court. I was prepared for the most unexpected things to happen, the most glorious sagas to unfold themselves before my eyes. My 'real' life was about to begin, my head hummed with all the stories I had read about all the wonderful people who lived in this city.

It was a hard and bitter thing to have to unlearn so much, to discover that Bloomsbury was not an area of town but a state of mind and at least forty years out of date; that the Tower of London housed no prisoners and the Thames was a sluggish old river, redeemed only by one or two splendid bridges that span it. I had thought of Soho as the den of Mephistopheles and the Muse, the place where poets and prostitutes lived. I was to discover that hardly anyone ever *lived* in Soho, not even the girls who stand in doorways, luring in trade for strip shows, that Dylan Thomas or the likes of him no longer drank in the pubs there. It was far better known for its bookshops which sell dirty pictures, the offices of the major film companies which are located there and some of the best restaurants in London. Covent Garden was not only where the Royal Ballet performed, it was a tangle of streets which harboured the biggest fresh-vegetable market in Europe and the only neighbourhood in the British Isles where the pubs opened at five in the morning.

Any great city which is alive changes with each new soul which enters or leaves it, with each fresh pen which tries to trap it down in words. We create as we observe; every look, each sigh, all the laughter and tears that we see or hear, makes the place uniquely our own. Eliot's London was precisely that—it belonged to one Thomas Stearns Eliot, who worked as a bank clerk and lived in digs. Now that man no longer exists, neither does his city. Neither does Isherwood's Berlin, Henry Miller's Greece, nor Gide's Alexandria. They are all literary conceptions, juxtaposing the impermanence of life itself with eternal monuments, figures of stone, 'an aimless smile that hovers in the air and vanishes along the level of the roofs'.

Earls Court had inherited no such literary mystique; there were no preconceptions I could fall back on. It was a specifically mid-fifties phenomenon. Literature had not caught up with it, Doris Lessing had yet to write her opus. It was in a sense the most daring as well as the most dead place one could find in London. The average age of the Earls Court population was not a statistical abstraction; there were hardly any old people and no children at all. The women were all in their twenties, the men slightly older. The Earls Court Road was a long narrow isthmus connecting the debutante world of Kensington with the lower reaches of 'artistic' Chelsea on Fulham Road. On that narrow strip, someone once estimated, there were more skirts per unit area than anywhere else in Europe or perhaps even the world. The female-male ratio was approximately nine to one; with a good face and a bad reputation any male could get 'free bed and breakfast'.

Any male except me, that is.

No one has any trouble finding a place to stay in Earls Court. It took me four hours and a great deal of plaintive pleading to discover a Polish landlady who would rent a room for bed and breakfast for 'one night only'. I had yet to accept a feature of my personality which I had not observed with any attention at all till then. And only the mirror, a 100-watt bulb and glances and remarks from passers-by brought it to focus: the colour of my skin.

I was to learn in the weeks and months ahead that Earls Court was the capital of a new imperialistic power which had invaded London. Hordes of 'tourists' had poured in from what was euphemistically called 'the older members of the Commonwealth'. Translated into Everyman's language this meant that a large influx of *white* immigrants had established a firm hegemony over this area of town.

So it was an incestuous cabal. The white colonials screamed and scratched at each other, helplessly revolving in doomed gravitational orbits, because they had neither the escape velocity nor the means to break out into the outer space of mainstream London life. For a South African girl to have a 'real English date' was the prize of battle. Most of the women, aiming at a career in holy matrimony rather than in any other sphere, were able to leave home unentangled and carefree. While the men, having to 'make a success', of their lives, remained behind. The women were on the hunt, for husbands, lovers, even 'one-night stands'. If they managed to land the first of these things they would stay on in London, move to another area of town and proceed to become 'English'. The unlucky would return to Sydney or Johannesburg; having 'done Europe' and acquired the veneer of an English accent, they would have raised their prices in their native marriage markets.

An Indian did not fit into this scheme.

The colour thing struck me with such sudden vehemence precisely because I had not anticipated it. Both my brothers had been to England before me and neither of them had had cause to notice any discrimination. But that was before the white 'tourists' from South Africa, Rhodesia, Australia and Canada had brought with them instinctive rejection devices which the British public *at large* had not *yet* developed. Perhaps I overemphasize. Earls Court was, of course, an artefact, a simulated hothouse where things did feel a lot more congested than perhaps anywhere else in London.

Having no prototype against which to compare, Earls Court remained elusive and intimidating. If I had landed in Hampstead or Chelsea I could begin to find my bearings by judging my experiences against norm. Although the definitions I used were arch, literary, mostly out of date, they still would have helped. But I started London life in a place which was fluid, ephemeral and totally un-English. (I must add, however, that Earls Court could not happen anywhere else but in London.) The people who lived there were just as isolated, uncertain and alien to the native population as I was. Except for one thing: they were white and I was brown.

I started work as a kitchen porter in a restaurant on my third day in London. There was a big burly chef who drank chilled beer all day (nominally my boss), a pretty young manageress, heaps of waitresses and my 'mate'. He was Irish, with one foot shorter than the other, a twisted arm and frothed at the sides of his mouth whenever he spoke. We earned the same wages: seven pounds sixteen shillings a week, before tax.

The chef's favourite game during the post-lunch recess was to tease my 'mate' about the secret affair that was *not* going on between him (the Irishman) and the manageress. When I joined the staff I usurped the role of the 'beast' in this faintly surrealistic drama of *La Belle et la Bête*. Exactly a week after my arrival on the scene my 'mate' knocked me down in the scullery with a huge saucepan. He was spitting with rage at the audacity of a black man dating a white girl: I have never witnessed more venom or prejudice before or since than I did that afternoon. The man won the contest, however, as I could neither hit him back nor call him a deluded spastic.

Years later I was reminded of that knock on the head just after the Commonwealth Immigrants Act was passed (the Act legislated against unrestricted entry of Commonwealth citizens who had been issued with British passports outside Britain, in effect stopping the influx of 'coloured' immigration) when I eavesdropped on a conversation in a pub between two City gentlemen.

'What do you think of this new bill?' one of them asked. 'Three years too late,' the other replied. 'Of course I am not colour prejudiced myself . . .'

'Aren't you?' I found myself asking, a strange new vehemence in my voice.

'No . . . I mean . . . I am not in favour of discrimination and that sort of thing . . . . But the trouble with these people is that they don't *integrate*.'

The man was more embarrassed about my lack of manners than his opinions. Amused, I persisted without apology. 'Why do you think they come here then?' I queried, in a more subdued tone.

'To make money, I suppose,' the man replied, with a hunted look on his face.

'But the British went to India for precisely the same reason. And *they* didn't integrate for over two hundred years . . . .'

I must have gone on speaking for another minute or so, repeating the stale old arguments, when his companion intervened. 'Yes, well, if you want a soapbox, there's always Hyde Park Corner, you know.'

With this remark the two gentlemen walked to the other end of the bar, the publican threw me a reproving glance, and the other customers around me shifted uneasily on their feet, trying to edge away. I gulped down my drink and left, wondering which of the two knocks was harder, the saucepan or Hyde Park Corner.

The word 'integrate' hummed in my head as I remembered that it was a good five years after my arrival in Britain that I realized, try however I may, I would never be one of 'them'. I had started off by accepting the image my British friends had of me. I looked carefully in the mirror every morning to see if 'the chip on the shoulder' was wearing off. I let down the turn-ups of my India-tailored trousers, started ordering pints of bitter instead of Scotch in pubs and even took to carrying an umbrella. But all to no avail. The genes had done their work and I would for ever remain a 'foreigner', and, worse, an Indian.

I discovered that I would be far more acceptable in London society if I sported a genuine Indian accent instead of what approximated to an Oxford one. Editors were far more receptive if I wrote about *India* than on subjects over which the Anglo-Saxon seemed to have acquired unique prerogatives. A publisher (who had never visited India) wrote back to say that I was 'authentic' when I talked of Indian customs and social life but was 'most unconvincing' when I tried to think and react like an Englishman. At Knightsbridge dinner parties I was always invited the second time round, provided I fulfilled the exotic role.

It was a hard lesson to learn and I took a long time in learning it. With each new incident the shock was less intense, the pain milder. I began to interpret glances, inflexions of tone, the thrusts of silence. A slow wall of distrust and suspicion began to grow around me. There was a sentry at the gate checking the credentials of every visitor, at first casually, then with greater and greater scrutiny. Instant responses of warmth were to recede into the past, reactions become guarded. I was to travel along that long road which leads to a fortress, circled by moats of antipathy, with cannons of revulsion posted at strategic points, within which resides that vulnerable monarch Ego, and who, but for these protections, would have been vanquished long ago. But once I entered that fortress, it was difficult to emerge again, walk around without bodyguards, take other beings on trust. The monarch was as much a prisoner as a ruler. In England I lost my freedom for the first time. And it was not till ten years later that I was to regain it in New York.

Stanley had found me a room in the house in which he lived. It was in the basement and had been used as a storeroom. But the housekeeper had put in a basin and a gas ring, so it was habitable. 'If you stay till the winter I'll get you an electric heater,' he had told me, as I handed him two pounds ten for my first week's rent.

It was a small room, about ten feet square, with a bed in one corner and a broken-down chest of drawers in another. The floorboards creaked, one wall was permanently damp, with plaster peeling off near the top. The basin was next to the window, and the gas ring on a wooden shelf near it. There was to be no 'service' as the rent was so low (the other rooms in the house had 'service' once a week; the floors were vacuumed, waste baskets emptied and clean linen supplied). I had to clean the two bed-sheets, which were part of the effects in the room, myself. The pillow did not have a case.

The lavatory was on the ground floor, up one flight of stairs, and the bath on the third floor (there was only one in the whole house). You had to put in six single pennies to light the Ascot heater to get enough hot water for a bath.

(As my brother had told me that 'The English are a very dirty people, you know, they never bathe, why do you think they complain about the cold all the time?' my habit of taking a bath every day proved to be a mild drain on the purse.) I had to boil water on the gas ring for my morning shave.

I thanked Stanley and the housekeeper for providing me with this accommodation. It was not until I got to know my friend rather well did he tell me that the housekeeper had done me no favour at all. My room could not have been rented to anyone else and the housekeeper had said, 'Well, if he is an Indian, I don't suppose he could grumble. They live in mud huts out there, you know.'

There was one other man who lived in the basement, though his room was much larger than mine. He was a World War I veteran and lived on a pension. There was some trouble with his back and an equally elderly widow came to cook his meals for him occasionally. But as she was rather fond of the bottle and entertained the notion that she was an actress of repute, their meals were not without historic garnishments; 'a bit of theatre on the free', as Stanley had remarked about that kissing couple on Earls Court Road.

To find a job was a lot more difficult than I had supposed it would be. I visited several offices and was told that I was 'ineligible' as I had no clerical experience in Britain. I pointed out that if no one gave me a first chance it was rather unlikely that I would ever gain such experience by myself. But the logic of my argument did not convince prospective employers. Newspaper editors were equally impervious for the same reason, though they phrased it differently. 'You've got to be a member of N.U.J. (National Union of Journalists),' they all said, 'before I can think of taking you on.' And the N.U.J. office replied that I would have to have an offer of a job first before they could consider my application. Vicious circle, closed shop.

I had three shillings left and had to turn down Stanley's offer to accompany him to the pub. 'Look,' he said, 'it's money, isn't it?' I nodded.

'Well, why the hell don't you take any kind of job that comes along? Then you can start looking around.'

'Nothing seems to be coming along at all,' I replied.

'Don't be silly. You can always get a job, cleaning lavatories, washing dishes, anything. And if you don't have to go on too long, I can tell you it'll be a lot of fun.'

I agreed to try.

Stanley took me to the restaurant, introduced me to the manageress and explained that I was looking for a job immediately. She hired me on the spot. Next day I went to the National Insurance office, took out a set of cards, returned to the restaurant and started work. After tax and rent I was left with four pounds ten shillings per week. Subsistence wage, I suppose, but not exactly a princely sum. I was given one free meal a day and a piece of cake for tea. As I walked to work, there was no charge for transport. Five and a half days a week, nine to six on weekdays, till noon on Saturdays, an hour and a half's break for lunch from Monday to Friday. The restaurant was part of a departmental store; after working there for two months I would get a twenty-five per cent discount for any goods I might wish to purchase for myself, which was a generous offer, except that I had no money with which to buy anything.

I had to help my 'mate' in the scullery every morning, clean three large soup vats in the afternoon and do the dishes the rest of the time. Once a week the deep freeze, which was about two-thirds the size of my room, had to be washed and swept. As the temperature was such as to preserve food, and even with the door open and the machine turned off it did not warm up all that quickly, I developed a nasty bronchial cough, had to stay home for ten days and was given a week's wages and the sack when I returned to work.

This was two months after my arrival in London. And a few things happened in that time.

I had written to Luke Varme from India and when I spoke to him on the phone, he invited me to come over to his house in Blackheath. The Arts Council was organizing a poetry festival and Varne had been asked to direct the show. Would I care to read some of my poems, as a representative of Indian poets writing in English?

Would I . . . ? Of course I would. I was ecstatic. There was a ten-pound fee, which Varme paid me from his own pocket in advance. Then there was an offer from the BBC to read two poems on the Third Programme. That was seven guineas. The money, as much as the prestige, helped.

One afternoon before D-Day, Varme invited a few of the participants to a snack lunch in a pub near the Arts Council's office. There were several eminent poets and a bunch of photographers. My picture—in dark glasses and a polo-necked sweater—appeared in *Town* magazine and the *Daily Telegraph*. On the day of the reading I had dinner with Ted Hughes and Sylvia Plath just before going on stage at the Mermaid Theatre.

I had entered literary London.

Varme was a kind and sympathetic man. He listened to short stories I read aloud to him, his wife made helpful comments and I felt elated and proud to have been taken up so readily by someone whose first book I had admired so much. The trouble was of course that I had not learnt the unwritten rules of the game. You must never express a hostile opinion about an author's work to the author himself. Honesty was not the best policy. A certain diplomatic deviousness was more desirable. What I failed to realize was the tenderness of a writer's ego. I could not imagine that my opinion would make any difference to an established writer's estimate of himself. But it did. And my habit of saying whatever came into my mind at the moment, articulating opinions as and when they were formed, was not received kindly.

Varme threw a party shortly after the poetry festival. A book of his had just been published and his position in literary London then was more established than it is now. He invited me to the party to 'meet some people who might be of help to you, if you want to make a career in writing'. And it would have been, if I had more tact, known how to drink better and keep my voice under control.

The party was to start at eight; I arrived at nine-thirty in dark glasses, having had three Scotches on the road. Varme's wife introduced me to some of her guests and each name fell on my ears with a loud gong. Here was literary London in full force. Even more exciting was the fact that most of these people seemed to have heard of me. Varme had done a thorough job of advance introductions. I met Tobias Darnley again: 'Oh yes I remember you. How could I forget? Mustn't be so modest, you know.' There was no danger of that, as he was to discover as the evening progressed.

The lights were low, there were flagons of wine on the table, a roomful of literary men. And women, very pretty women. Yes, this was why I had come to London: sparkling intellectual conversation, delicious wine and women; rubbing shoulders with celebrities, tossing off epigrams, making 'passes'. Yes, thank you, I would love another glass of wine.

'Stop playing with your beard,' Alvarez said. 'It's a kind of auto-eroticism. Rather distracting too.' I wanted to make a devastating retort, but by the time I had taken in his remark the man had disappeared from view. A lost opportunity.

'This is Eileen,' Varme's wife said, introducing a small dark-haired girl. 'She is from America and her work has appeared in several avant-garde magazines. This is Amit, he writes poetry and short stories. Some of them are damn good, he is from India.'

'The trouble with avant-garde writing is that it is childish . . . . I mean . . . . ' I announced.

'What have you read?'

'Yes, well, you see, most of the stuff has no structure, no plot, a sense of vacant incoherence . . . '

'You mean a poem should have plot?'

'No, I don't mean that but a certain organic validity like Eliot's poetry which is lucid and coherent and . . . '

'Do you think that all of Eliot's poetry is lucid and coherent?'

'No, not all. But if you take these modern writers you find a kind of emptiness. I mean, take Luke Varme's book. I liked *Tarry Yet a While*; in fact I liked it very much . . . '

'Excuse me, I'll go get another glass of wine.'

'I think I will too.' We approached the table and there were several people around. I broke through the group, filled my glass and in the process of pouring out another, spilt some wine on the girl's dress. 'Now Varme's book is vacuous . . .'

At this point our host approached us. 'Are you two enjoying yourselves?'

'Yes,' I replied. 'In fact, I was just saying that this last book of yours is vacuous. It is nothing like your best. And it certainly shows that the fund of raw experience, on which you drew in your first book, has been exhausted.'

Varme withdrew hastily and so did the American girl. I was left there, standing all by myself. I swilled down my wine and refilled the glass. Then I caught sight of Tobias Darnley in a corner of the room. 'Mr Darnley, do you really think that the short story is a more efficient literary vehicle than the novel in the middle of the twentieth century?'

'Well, I . . . I mean I wouldn't make a flat statement like that.'

'That's just it,' I continued, 'the novel you see can involve itself in a panoramic effort while the short story is pointillist. You can develop character many-facetedly in a novel while in a short story you have to be sharp, provide an instant glimpse. Totally inadequate.'

This to the author of The Novel and the People and some of the best modern short stories in the English language.

As I was filling my glass again, Varme's wife came up and tapped me on the shoulder. 'Do you think you should drink any more, Amit?'

'Of course,' I replied. 'I have hardly had anything at all.'

'Well, you should try and control yourself. Luke was very hurt by what you said. He has gone up to his room and . . . '

'But I meant it. I mean, writers should be honest with each other, don't you think?'

'Yes but . . . '

At this point Muriel Spark came up to us. Varme's wife did the introductions.

'Are you an avant-garde writer too?' I asked. I had not heard of Muriel Spark.

'Who is that rude young man?' the woman asked the hostess, as she was escorted away from me. I could not figure out what rude thing I had said.

I don't remember much of what followed, except that I filled and refilled my glass several times. My words remained coherent, unslurred, my walk straight. I cornered many of the guests, treated them to lectures on aesthetic theory, poetic insight, etc. Towards the end of the evening Luke Varme's wife followed me about incessantly, steering me away at awkward moments, cutting me off in mid-sentence, relieving me of a half-filled glass when both hands became necessary to demonstrate a point. I don't think I could have made a great impression on the people who met me at that party. Yet I harboured the feeling that I was being witty and clever and scintillating while they were being dull and unresponsive.

I stayed overnight at Varme's place. Next day, polite as ever, his wife made me breakfast without saying a word about the previous night. The only thing she did say was, 'Pity you didn't get on with Eileen. She is such a bright girl. I was hoping that you two might shack up for the night.'

Varme saw me to the bus-stop, I thanked him and waved goodbye. After that I spoke to him several times on the phone but he did not invite me to a party ever again. Nor have I seen his wife since then.

Literary London came within my grasp and in one short evening I let it go.

In all those weeks I had a chance to glimpse another facet of London literary life. My obsession with pubs, and my belief that this was where 'things happened', led me to spend every weekend and my whole weekly allowance in the 'arty' pubs on Fulham Road. I visited Finch's and the Angelsea and the Queen's Elm every Friday night, Saturday evening and, if I had any money left, a good part of Sunday too. By Monday morning I was always down to two or three shillings, waiting for Friday afternoon and a heavier purse to start on the rounds once again.

I met and talked with many aspirant writers, poets, painters, sculptors, film producers, actresses, et al. I remember one man who introduced himself to me as George Barker. The name made no impact, as I did not know who George Barker was. He said he had just returned from Morocco and was carrying 'a bagful of shit'. In my own arch way I took this to mean sheets of priceless manuscript and was naturally impressed. I had been calling myself a writer for a while now but the total result of my endeavours amounted to two short stories and seven poems.

'A bagful of shit' was a good deal more than that, I presumed. It was a shock when he explained the jargon to me. 'Shit' meant marijuana, a word as esoteric to me then as 'psychedelic' or 'ectoplasm'. It turned out that he was not

George Barker nor was his 'shit' the passport to a timeless haven.

Another 'writer' talked to me about a story he was writing for *Partisan Review*. It was all about an elephant who woke up one morning feeling rather dissatisfied with his long trunk. This sent him into a deep depression and he thought of various ways he could rid himself of his abnormal appendage. Finally, with these thoughts spinning in his mind, the giant beast fell asleep. Only to wake up next morning to find himself transformed into a butterfly. I listened patiently to the story and innocently remarked at the end of the narration that it bore resemblance to a fable by Franz Kafka called 'Metamorphosis'. The man gulped down his beer and left the pub. I saw him several times after that but he never deigned to speak to me.

There were others. A painter called Sean who said he specialized in 'mixed media'. His flat in Earls Court Road was strewn with wax works, painted in different shades, with clippings from the glossy magazines pasted all over them. Sean's pièce de résistance was a wax penis, about twelve inches long, in crimson red, with batteries and a small bulb inside: the tip lighted up on pressing a button. His conversation consisted mainly of a string of names, celebrities he had met, fucked, had drinks with, introduced girls to, etc. Sean seemed to know everyone worth knowing, all writers worth reading. Amongst his professed acquaintances there were such famous and diverse personalities as Francis Bacon, Colquhoun, Dom Moraes, Brendan Behan, George Macbeth, etc. I became his disciple without much prodding.

There was another man who figures conspicuously in this glorious firmament—the landlord of the Queen's Elm.

He was tall, athletic, mustachioed and Irish. At that time it was difficult for me to discern between the vulgar and the merely pompous. I took his favours seriously. If the 'guv'nor' condescended to have a drink with you it was considered an honour. The great man normally drank only with persons of renown: poets who had been to tea with Her Majesty the Queen, actors who had won several Oscars, painters who exhibited at the Tate, etc.

To have three pounds in your pocket—as I did one evening—and for the guv'nor to come up and say hullo to you, was to be given the key to paradise. But to be allowed to order a drink for him—'yes, I'll have a double'—was to frolic with the gods, swing in the hammock of celestial bliss.

My stock rose several points with Sean after that evening.

Yes, they were all 'artists' at the Queen's Elm. And because I had these feelings of uncertainty about my 'true' worth and doubts about whether I was really any kind of an artist at all, I felt privileged to be allowed into such august company. For the first two or three months in London, I got the feeling that the city had been extraordinarily kind to me. Despite the kitchen and my Irish 'mate' and the low wages, I had been received with open arms by men of distinction and calibre. The milieu on Fulham Road was exactly what I longed for, the artistic world about which I had read and dreamt so much. It took me a long time to discover the meaning of words: '"A writer" is one who writes, not someone who *has* written or is *going to* write.'

Those same faces are still leaning over the bar counter at the Queen's Elm, the same stories are being retailed to a new bunch of innocent recruits, the same delusions, those old crutches are still being used. I, meanwhile, am somewhere else.

Everyone had a girl. There were couples everywhere, in the parks, on the streets, at the bar counters. I would watch girls kiss and fondle their men in public and feel outraged. But the motivating force was envy. In Kensington Gardens, under the green summer trees, I would steal up to a couple lying on the grass, stare hard into their faces with an intense look of disapproval and walk on, hoping that they would stop enjoying themselves. But I did not ever dare to turn back and look to see if my stare had had the desired effect. In the pubs I resented the calm air of possession that the men displayed over their women. The girls on Earls Court Road were a perpetual threat to my psychic well-being. There they were, in skirts and tennis shorts, with ripe round breasts and taut calves, skipping down the street, rushing into coffee bars, chattering and laughing, grabbing hold of a friend, kissing him smack on the lips and hurrying on. And all I could do was watch, think up schemes in my mind which always disintegrated into amorphous daydreams on actual encounter. 'Excuse me', or 'Thank you very much', or even 'See you sometime', was about the most I could muster.

The extent of physical love-play that went on in public disgusted me. And the feeling of indignant impotence was intensified as I could neither emulate the couples nor make them stop. Once when I came upon a pair in the park, I was shocked to find that the boy was actually lying *over* the girl. Her eyes were closed, he had his arms round her, under her back. They were kissing and I could hear the sounds of hoarse breathing. An impulsive shriek of horrified disgust escaped my lips. The man turned his head, then rolled away from the girl and sat up. 'Don't you have anything better to do?' he said sharply. I put my heels to good use and ran till I was out of the park and on the street. When I recovered my breath, the thought struck me that soon it would be dark and the two of them would still be lying there, with no one watching them. I tortured myself for hours, thinking that they might actually 'do it'—they had been near enough anyway, for God's sake—and that I had somehow lapsed in my duty to the world for not stopping the perpetration of such a venal sin. I blamed my cowardice for this—I should really have stayed on instead of running away—and determined to reform myself.

Of such stern stuff are Billy Grahams and Joe McCarthys made.

The trouble was that I did not know how to 'meet' girls. Physically they existed all right, I saw them all the time. In singles, in pairs, or even in groups of three and four. I could pass close to them, in a crowded bus or Tube, I could smell their perfume or the musky odour of under-arm sweat, bump into them on escalators, feel their soft tight behinds rub against me; sometimes I even managed to dig an elbow or two into their bosoms. My prick would rise into an aching erection and I would feel guilty and embarrassed. Then the girl would walk away or get down from the bus without even a last look back at me. Or else the Tube would suddenly empty out, she would walk over to a seat and become unapproachable once again. Instant encounters kept my nerves in perpetual tension. I was not allowed to forget that sex existed; the atmosphere was suffused with it. Whatever I saw, the conversations I overheard, the scenes that were acted out in front of me, were all a reminder that I was the misfit, the loner, the deviant. And since I was in this condition not through choice, I was forced to rationalize my inadequacy by recalling the dicta of St Paul and Calvin and work up an adequate fund of moral indignation. (A propensity, I might add, from which I have not totally recovered. For overtly outrageous sexual behaviour, which I often display in public, is the other side of the coin of puritan repression.)

Well, the question was, how does one acquire a girlfriend? Stanley was 'going with' a girl who lived across the hallway from his room. I knew she often spent the night with him, as she would make the Sunday morning breakfast—to which I was often invited—in her dressing gown. When he 'picked up a girl', he would go to her place and spend a good part of the night there. I was always entertained to the grotesque details of each of his encounters and they did not make me yearn for Nirvana or the Himalayan mountains. He would often remark, with puzzled wonderment, about my single condition, never pausing long enough to hear me explain or respond to a plea for help that I might have made to more sympathetic ears.

Sean too had a girlfriend—he would refer to her as 'my woman'. Her name was Sally and she always sat in a corner of the Queen's Elm, nursing a gin and tonic for endless hours, while Sean made the rounds from the top room back down again across the thickening crowd of stationary men, distributing his 'hullos' and handshakes with generous abandon and frequency. Sally was a lumpy red-faced girl, with two enormous breasts mutinously spilling out of her bra. I would talk to her sometimes, sit at the table while she waited for her man to notice her and bring back a refill from the bar. But I was always aware that she belonged to someone else and this desexualized her for me. Months later I was to discover that she had been very attracted to me and it was only because of my apparent disinterest that she had restrained her impulse to make concrete overtures.

Of course there were other women in the pubs. None of them was quite single, though they changed partners often. I would watch these couplings and uncouplings with interest and curiosity. But it never did occur to me that I could be a candidate for m'lady's favours. I was an outsider, it was enough that I was allowed in here. To think that I could compete as an equal was simply ludicrous. What did I have to offer? I was not an artist, I had not met any famous people (I chose to cover the Luke Varme episode in a curtain of discreet silence), I had no money and I was not good-looking. Besides, I could not talk, I had no ability to impress a girl with my conversation. And I was shy and guilty, to the point of crusty impotence, about my lack of sexual experience.

There was a woman called Jeanette who looked quite different from what her name would lead you to expect. Jeanette was somehow a young girl's name, pert, vivacious, and endearingly reckless. At least that was how I thought of the name. But the real Jeanette was a woman of thirty-five, puffing out like leavened bread, creases on her face, always slightly drunk, and exuding a permanent aroma of stale gin (if you approached her close enough). She didn't look right in slacks, though she wore one pair more frequently than any other costume. Her behind stuck out with massive asymmetry and her small breasts did nothing to balance the fleshy cantilever which protruded in front. And Jeanette talked incessantly. She would often go through three men in one evening. You knew that she was with someone the moment she would put her arm round his back, draw him close to her disproportionate frame and bellow out her favourite words: 'Come on, luv, be a sweetie. You wouldn't want me to die of thirst, would you?' The male hand would dutifully disappear into the recesses of the right-hand pocket, the bartender would be called to attention, and soon, very soon, Jeanette would be raising another glass of gin and tonic to her lips.

But it was hard for her to keep them. An unwary newcomer would often stick it out for a couple of hours, an older man in philosophic resignation with his low price in the market might chance a whole evening. The 'regulars' were good for one drink and a quick dip into her huge pool of words. Then out! But she never bore a grudge, didn't sulk at a refusal. If it's a no, it's a no, oh well. Can't score every time, you know. On to the next, for bigger and better things. Jeanette had a good philosophy, she never lost.

Of course, Jeanette went home with men. If they paid for her drinks, they deserved her cunt. It was a fair exchange. I don't think she ever asked for money.

She worked as a receptionist, earned enough to keep herself in food and clothes and give any man the boot if he became too meddlesome and bossy and wanted 'to change her'. I think she was a kind woman and if anyone was in trouble, her steady stream of words dried up and she would play mother with genuine feeling. Her one cardinal principle was that pubs were for drinking, not the place in which to sit around and hold hands. And you should never leave the premises before the law and the guv'nor forced you to. Many a man would suggest that she had had enough by the middle of the evening and 'we could have a couple back at my place'.

'Yes, luv, of course we could. But your place is open night and day while this one shuts at eleven. Can't leave a baby crying, can I? And you wouldn't want to run them out of business, would you now? Where would they get their wee little pennies if we all stopped drinking at nine?'

So one benefactor after another would leave or else accept her terms, stay till closing time and walk out of the Finch's or the Queen's Elm with the considerable bulk of Jeanette's weight on his arm. She never showed up with the same man the next day, not even on Sunday mornings. At some stage between Saturday night and Sunday lunchtime the adieus would be made and Jeanette would be all set for a new encounter.

There are, of course, women like Jeanette in bars in every major city of the Western world. Perhaps they are not all as overt as she was nor so unflinchingly committed to their ways. But she *is* a type, a representative of that vast urban community of dislocated, disenchanted souls who have lost the key to a prosaic happiness somewhere along the road and cannot find the courage to retrace their steps and undertake a search. The path ahead is slippery, demanding no conscious willing other than the involuntary response to inertia, as final and inexorable as a fused bulb or a dagger in the heart.

But Jeanette intrigued me. I had never seen anyone like her before; if she did not play out her role before me I would never have been able to imagine her. I connected her to the 'artistic world' only tangentially. I did not see her as a direct offshoot of the creative pursuit. For she professed no such ambitions. Perhaps she would not exist in any other environment but she was not created by the one in which she lived.

I was never properly introduced to Jeanette. I knew her name—just as everyone else in the pub knew her name—and I would nod to her if she ever looked my way. It was the kind of relationship I had with most members of that community. They knew I existed—'that young Indian with a beard'—but nobody was quite sure who I was or what I did. The few people who did speak to me invariably mispronounced my name when there was my occasion to use it. I was never introduced to anyone even when I was part of a group. I was on the outer fringe (it seems that I have been on the outer fringe of most things all my life) of a small cabal which pivoted around Sean, with Jeanette as a visiting member. I would stand a foot or so away from them, with half a bitter in my hand, listening in, interjecting a word or two, discreetly respectful to the devotees of 'art'. No one would shout my name—as they did for Sean and Jeanette and many others— when I entered the pub. I would have to wait longer to be served at the bar and edge my way towards one cluster of people or another, if I wanted to enter a conversation, due to my marginal status of a nodding acquaintance. Sean spoke to me only when the pub was half-empty—early evening on a weekday—or else when all his other friends were in some other pub. And I always responded with an adequate recognition of the privilege he conferred upon me on such occasions. I was grateful that he once called me his friend.

It was Friday evening, ten to eleven. They had called 'last orders' at the Finch's, I was at the bar waiting for my half a bitter (ordinary this time, not Red Barrel). It was not very crowded that night, the 'group' had gone off to a party of which I had heard but to which I had not been invited. Jeanette was alone, she had just lost a man. 'No dice, old girl,' he had said, when she asked for one last drink.

'Wasn't my type, anyway,' she said, sidling up to me at the bar. 'Dice? Hmph!'

I preserved a respectful silence, aware that it wasn't my turn either to comment or console.

'What's your name, luv? You're from India, aren't you?'

'Yes, from Calcutta. My name is Amit.'

'That's a funny one, Am-et.' Jeanette began to laugh and the rising tide of resentment and nervousness began to grow within me. 'You'll buy me a drink, won't you, luv? I am thirsty. Haven't had a proper one all night.'

'Of course,' I replied, 'it will be my pleasure.'

'Jack, I'll have the usual,' Jeanette shouted to the barman. 'And make it a double.'

I had just been paid and had spent only ten shillings out of the four pounds ten. I could afford to stand Jeanette a double gin and tonic. In fact it was rather a privilege to be asked to do so.

'Cheers,' she said, rising her glass.

'Cheers,' I replied, flushed and excited. Would she come home with me perhaps? Or was it just . . . ? Wasn't likely, was it? Not with me. What would she think of my little room if she did? Besides, I wasn't sure if I could . . . There's no use thinking that far ahead, just wouldn't happen anyway.

'Wouldn't like to have a few back at your place, would you luv?'

'Well . . . er . . . er.' My mouth was half full of beer and I started to choke as I tried to gulp it down fast. Jeanette patted my back and I recovered my breath. 'I don't . . . I mean I haven't . . . '

'Don't you have a place? Not a student, are you?'

'No, no, not that. I am not a student. I mean I have no . . . I don't have any drink in the room.'

'That's no problem,' Jeanette persisted. 'Why don't we get a bottle here and take it back?'

'Yes,' I replied, a full blast of arctic air rushing up my lungs. My hands had turned cold. 'Yes, let's do that. I mean if you would like to . . . '

'Of course I would,' she said, waving her hand to Jack again. The bottle of gin was two pounds ten, Jeanette's drink was another six shillings. I had less than a pound in my pocket as I left the pub, and this was to last till next Friday.

'You do have some tonic water at your place, don't you, luv?' Jeanette asked, as we started walking.

'I am afraid not,' I replied, deflated again.

'Oh well, we'll just have to use the tap then,' she said.

Would she? I mean, what should I do? I had seen men kissing her on the street, holding her tight in their arms. Should I do that? But we weren't standing still, in fact she was walking quite fast, her left arm slung around me. Should I stop, turn her round and . . . ? No, it was better to walk on. I mean, she might decide not come back with me if I did that. It isn't as if she had kissed every man with whom I had seen her. Perhaps she didn't 'do it' with everyone either. Anyway, she was coming back with me. A girl was coming back with me on a Friday night. That was quite something, wasn't it?

'The landlord doesn't live in the house, does he?'

'No,' I replied, suddenly reminded of Harry the housekeeper.

'No stupid rules about "guests out by eleven" and all that?'

'No, not that I know of.'

'I mean, you haven't got into hot water about girls in your room before, have you?'

'No, no, I haven't.' Yes, well, we were on the right track anyway. If she thought that I had girls in my room, she couldn't expect to go away without . . . No, obviously not. 'I live in the basement which has a separate entrance. There's no one else around except an old army man who lives on a pension. They wouldn't know that you were there.' And then I remembered. 'Unless you wanted to go to the bathroom. The toilet is on the . . . '

'That's easy,' Jeanette whispered, as I turned the key in the lock. 'You have a sink in your room, don't you?'

I was too embarrassed and shocked to answer yes.

I switched on the light and Jeanette came in. The bed was undone. I had not washed the sheets in six weeks. There was a pot, a frying pan and some crockery in the sink, the electric cooker was lined with grease. As I always kept the window closed, there was thick smell of fat and stale food in the room.

'Gosh! What have you got in here, a dead rat or something?' She rushed to the window and threw it open. Then she looked around, surveying the dismal scene. 'And when did you last take those sheets to the wash?' The linen was ripped off the bed, bundled up and thrown into a corner.

'Got some clean ones, haven't you? I can't sleep on sheets with come all over them.'

'There's no . . . I mean . . . '

'Stop playing the satin. Come on, let's have the clean sheets. And while I'm making the bed you can get me a little drinkie.'

'I am afraid I haven't got any clean sheets,' I said, dragging out the words. My doubts oscillated like random sparks of thunder across a charged sky. Would the smell put her off? No, she wouldn't have bothered to open the window in that case. Would she spend the night here? Of course, otherwise she wouldn't comment about the sheets. But without clean linen . . .

Jeanette looked at me in the same way as a teacher at school used to do, exasperated and forbearing. 'Oh well, we'll just have to sleep on the mattress then. And use the blankets for cover. It'll probably get quite cold in the night. And this room is damp.'

She picked up one blanket, held the two adjacent corners in her hands and whipped it in the air. The room was filled with dust and she started coughing. 'You've got enough germs in here to start an epidemic.'

'I am sorry,' I said meekly, still standing and holding the bottle of gin in my hand.

'Come on, we can have the apologies later. Just pour out the drinks.'

'Yes, of course.'

I went to the sink, washed out a cup and started unwrapping the cover on the bottle.

'Make it a tall one for me, will you? I'll need it.'

'How much water would you like?'

'Half and half,' Jeanette answered.

I took a few minutes opening the bottle, drying the outside of the cup, half filling it with gin and the rest with water. When I turned round with the drink in my hand, Jeanette was lying on the bed, completely nude. Her blouse and slacks were lying on the floor, the blankets were neatly folded back at the foot of the bed.

I stood there staring.

'What's the matter? Haven't you seen a cunt before?' Jeanette said, with an expression poised between a smile and a frown. 'Might be a little fat but I've got all the bits and pieces. And I can use them too.'

'Yes of course. I mean . . . yes . . .' I stammered, holding the cup and motionless as ever.

'Come on, luv, this isn't a party. No point in fucking around. Bring me the drink.'

I walked to the bed, slow, caught and trembling. Jeanette took the cup from my hand, raised herself on an elbow and took a large gulp. 'That's better,' she said, licking her lips. 'Now, come on, take off your clothes. Aren't going to do it with your trousers on, are you?'

'No, I mean . . . yes, of course.'

I stood over the bed, looking at her. There were long parallel lines on her belly, thin long ridges of curved fat. Her thighs were wide and loose and streaked with wrinkles. The turf of hair between her legs was mouse-brown in colour. The breasts were small, about the diameter of a tennis ball, with stubby pink nipples surrounded by a ring of darker flesh.

I took off my shirt, then my shoes and socks and started unzipping my trousers.

'Yes, take them off and come and sit here,' Jeanette said, taking another swig of the gin.

'Can we switch off the light first?'

'Why? Don't you want me to see your little John?'

'No, I don't mean that. But I mean . . . '

'Come on, I won't eat you,' she assured me, smiling a little.

Gingerly, I took off my trousers, then my underpants and sat down on the bed next to her.

Jeanette finished her drink in one final gulp and handed me the cup. Then she put her left hand on my prick and started playing with it.

I felt disembodied and distant, as if the whole thing was happening to someone else. I was no longer nervous, my heart wasn't beating loud, my hands were not cold. I began stroking her belly, almost as if I was feeling a soft warm animal. I couldn't think of anything and I even felt a slow glowing urge of tenderness. I looked at her face and bent over and kissed her lips. It wasn't a feeling for her so much as a sudden release born of exhaustion, a long string of plasticine stretched and stretched till now it was thin as gossamer, far away from the force which was pulling it apart.

'Let me switch off the light,' I said.

'All right,' Jeanette replied. 'You're nice and hard now.'

I came back to bed and lay beside her. She took my face in her hands and put her tongue inside my mouth. A sharp sizzling sensation ran down my spine. My prick gave a sudden kick against her thigh. I felt I was ready to burst. So I took it in my hand, jumped over her and tried to push it in between her legs.

'Not so fast,' Jeanette said, almost in a whisper. 'Play with me a little.'

Oh yes, I remembered. 'The woman's clitoris has to be stimulated to produce the lubricants which facilitate entry.' That's right. I must stimulate her clitoris—the female counterpart of the male penis.

I put my hand over her cunt and my fingers began investigating a female anatomy for the first time in my life. First, there was hair, lots of it, in thick wiry masses. But I got through that easily enough. Then there were folds and folds of flesh, but I managed to open up the petals too. After that obviously the next thing to do was to push my finger in. And as I did just that, Jeanette shrieked, 'Oh . . . oh . . . oh.' I withdrew my finger with a sharp reflex jerk. 'That hurt,' she hissed. 'Why are you in such a goddamn hurry? Can't you play with me for a while?'

How could I play with her? Never mind women are not always logical. I decided to continue the peripheral tour with my fingers, hoping that would do the trick. After a while Jeanette uttered what sounded like a low groan. 'No, not there.'

Well, here was a problem. She wanted me to feel her, yet she wouldn't let my finger inside. And external manipulation was obviously having no stimulating effects whatsoever. These thick folds of flesh—and there was a rich abundance—were not provided with sufficiently sensitive nerves. But the mound must be. And yet . . . ?

A sudden thought struck me. Could it be that it was not *inside* the vagina but somewhere outside it? Well . . . if that was the case, I should have found it by now. I had covered the ground pretty thoroughly. And all I had encountered were these . . . these lips . . . yes, the labia majora. No, there was something wrong somewhere. If the light was on, I could go down and have a look. But in the dark . . .

As a student of science I reasoned that it was better to ask and be told than remain ignorant and bumble around. So I popped the question: 'Where is your clitoris?'

'What?' the woman said, in a tone holding the balance between a shout and a threat.

'Your clitoris, where is it? I can't find it.'

Jeanette jumped out of bed in the dark. 'And you fucking well never will, will you, my little Indian?' she barked, as she ran towards the switch.

'Please, Jeanette, I only wanted to do what you asked me to. Just that I couldn't find your clitoris.'

The light came on and she rushed for her clothes.

'Please, Jeanette, I didn't mean to . . . ' I pleaded, going up to her.

'Don't you dare touch me, you dirty black wog,' she shrieked. 'What do you think I am, deformed or something?'

'No, no, no, I didn't mean that, please. I just didn't know.'

'You can take your little Indian prick and shove it into a rotting corpse for all I care. No room here, sonny.' In less than a minute she was dressed. 'I should have known better than to come back with a nigger.'

All I could say was 'Please . . . please,' as the tears started rolling down my face.

'And I am taking this,' Jeanette said, picking up the bottle of gin. 'And don't you fucking dare to talk to me again.'

The door banged shut behind her. I heard her steps thumping down the corridor and then the sound of the front door closing. I looked round the room and it was empty—no clit, no Jeanette, no gin.

The silent tears turned into sobs as I threw myself back on the sheetless bed.

Then I lost my job.

It was nearly three months since I had arrived in London. I had read poetry at the Mermaid, broadcast on the Third Programme of the BBC, attended a literary party at Luke Varme's house. My picture had appeared in *Town* magazine and the *Daily Telegraph*. These were my achievements. On the debit side was the ghoulish impression I had made on literary London, and Varme's disenchantment with me. Also, I had no money, had not slept with a woman, and didn't have a girlfriend. And then the sack.

Stanley said I could get unemployment benefit, so I went along. 'No, your cards have to be stamped for six months. In any case, how long have you been in this country?'

I didn't think that this was a fruitful line of enquiry as I was not quite sure if I could be deported for having no money and no job. So I left the office without further ceremony. I wrote a piece for the *Statesman* and got five pounds for it. But there was nothing regular they could offer, a correspondent was permanently stationed in London. I had not been writing so I had nothing to show prospective publishers. I tried all the restaurants on Earls Court Road and Kensington High Street, but they had no vacancies. Winter was approaching, the Tories faced a steady barrage of criticism from the Labourites for the rising unemployment figures. The man who interviewed me at London Transport said, 'Why should an educated boy like you want to work as a porter? Obviously, you don't mean to stick with us. And we don't want any drifters. We are a family here.'

Finally after scrounging meals from Stanley for two weeks and owing my rent for the same period, I got a job as a 'lavatory attendant' at the Blue Long John in Studs Farm. Formally, I was to wash and polish the linoelum floor of the car showcase, but as that took only three hours of each day, my main job was to clean the shit off the commodes in the two lavatories. The pay was lower than what I had been getting as a kitchen porter, but the manager said, 'There are prospects for promotion here. If you do a good job . . . '

The ride from Earls Court Road to Studs Farm took half an hour, the bus fare came to over a shilling per day. There were no free meals and by the time I returned to my room at six-thirty every evening my literary ambition stood a weak chance in a fight against fatigue. Sausages and baked beans and occasionally some bacon were my staple diet.

There was a glutinous quality about those days, each one identical to the other, the whole period one viscous mass. I remembered my earlier romanticism about poverty and my contempt for wealth and material possessions. Now I discovered that the poor were just as despicable as the rich and they had cruder ways of showing it. There was nothing noble about 'the working class', they were as greedy, selfish, mean and vicious as any group of human beings could be. To look down from above with all options open and then to glorify a condition from which, for some people, there is no escape, is to commit the worst sin of all—myth-making. And to construct myths about real people suffering real pain is not only to fall into the error of innocence, it is a crime. Marx had a private income—a small but steady one—all his life, Orwell was never short of a fiver and Caudwell did not starve. Hope is the critical determinant. All of us have reserves on which we can draw for limited periods of time in crisis. But there must be a door in the wall, a chance of escape, the possibility of life. The condemned man, Camus's *Etranger*, is not free without food in his stomach.

One afternoon stands out, vividly sketched in the flaming colours of a final despair against the muted grey of endless days, one following the other in mindless succession. I had just finished cleaning the floor and it was time for a coffee break. Normally, I would sit in the office reading a book or chatting with one of the mechanics. That particular afternoon I decided to go over to the cafe across the road and have a steak-and-kidney pie. No one saw me leave the garage and I did not see any reason to tell the cashier—the petrol pump attendants were always going out for a beer in the pub next door. After all it was my break and I was entitled to spend the time wherever I pleased.

I ate the pie and asked for a coffee. I was reading *Ape and Essence* and had come to the seduction scene. It was a long time since I had read anything as stirring as this and I allowed the coffee to get cold. By the time I had finished the section, I had exceeded my time by ten minutes. But I didn't rush back as there was no one who could tell how long I had been away.

When I did return to the garage, the pump attendant made a face at me and pointed to the office. A bulbous man in a bowler hat was sitting at the wheel of the car he was filling. I had a premonitory feeling that this red-veined face was the harbinger of ill-tidings. His eyes swivelled in their sockets with that malicious curiosity which one associates with health inspectors and private dicks.

I entered the office to find the manager pacing furiously up to the cashier's desk and back to the window, an atmosphere of strained silence pervading the room. 'Where have you been, Ray?' he asked, in a barely audible voice.

'I went across the street for my coffee break, sir.'

'And since when have you started taking your coffee break at two in the afternoon?' He looked at his watch, then at the clock on the wall and then at the watch again. 'Five past two,' he said, his voice rising. 'Five past two . . . it's . . . it's . . . what do you think this is, a private club or something?'

'No, sir, but since I didn't go out for lunch . . . '

'And whose bloody fault is that?' the manager shouted, at full pitch this time. I heard the car drive out of the garage. 'Just go and come when you bloody well please . . . you're supposed to be working here, you know, not having a jaunt.'

The man in the car was the executive manager of Long John Garages Ltd (Studs Farm garage was a branch of a large chain). And he had gone to the gents' room for an innocent pee. Re-emerging rather abruptly, he had entered the office and given the manager—my boss—a sharp dressing down in front of all his subordinates. The commode was splattered with diarrhoeic outpourings, the seat was caked and the executive manager had estimated—with years of long experience in such matters—that 'it must have been a good two hours since . . . since . . , for it to get like that'. The point being that someone—someone definitely other than himself—had perpetrated the deed a while ago, and the natural propensity of human excreta had combined with environmental conditions to produce a certain 'at home' appearance. I mean, shit and commodes—least of all commode seats— don't become good friends in a hurry. So it must have been at least . . .

I was taken on an inspection tour of the site. And yes, it was one of the most violent scenes I have ever witnessed in my life. Shit was everywhere, on the floor, against the wall, on the seat and, most ingenious of all, on the cover of the cistern. Caked, smelly and certainly very much at home. It was floating inside the commode too. (Why the fellow did not have the elementary courtesy to flush the toilet I shall never know.) The manager did not enter the room but held the door open for me to gaze at the spectacle. I could have retched instantly—might have made an interesting chromatic contrast—if there hadn't been a certain intimidating quality in the man's voice. Fear conquereth all things.

Studs Farm garage had won the contest for the Best Garage Award for two years running. This was the third year, and if he managed to score a hat trick my boss was sure to be given a desk at the head office. And now, with this, I had gone and spoilt everything. Serious situation, I had to agree. But could I be directly blamed? Was I expected to inspect the loo every time someone came out of it? Or would it have been different if the shit had looked less enshrined, was more fluid, so to speak? My boss was in no mood for humour. Next time this happened I would be given my cards and told to take a running jump into the Thames. He was a lenient man, was my boss, or so he told me. Any other man would have . . .

The actual business of cleaning up the place was not as funny as listening to my boss. I had to tie a handkerchief over my face and use twice the dose of disinfectant to kill the smell. And while I went to work with broom and swab, I wondered what my mother would think if she saw me then. This was the sort of job that was done by 'untouchables' in my country. Yet here I was in London, the son of a wealthy Brahmin who had been called 'a brilliant young man' in the *New Statesman*, confronting caked liquid shit in the gents' room of the Long John garage in Studs Farm. I mean, turds I could take. (In fact I had once seen a splendid one, about two inches in diameter and some five inches long, floating carelessly on the water and had taken time off to wonder about the anal aperture of the man who had produced it.) But this attempt at action painting, using biological apparatus, was a bit more than even my artist's craving for 'experience' could endure. To be threatened with the sack for not having cleaned the loo in two hours, was that 'real' life?

What was I doing here? Should I go back home? What was so glorious about cleaning shit, especially other people's shit? The slow throb of doubt began to make itself felt. I was alone and there was no one to tell me if I was doing right. I could not take the present as a transient state, there was no proper goal ahead, certainly no clear road to take me there. I could bend, I had resilience. But that afternoon stretched it hard.

That was the nearest I ever came to throwing in my hand.

One morning the alarm rang, I turned it off and went back to sleep again. Next time I woke up it was three o'clock. I turned over in bed several times and then decided against getting up. The curtains were drawn, it was dark inside the room. And damp. Winter had come on. It was cold. I had no money to put into the meter for the electric heater, no overcoat, and my shoes had holes in them. I felt warm under the blankets and it was easier to bear hunger if one was asleep. I slept for two whole days.

On the third day I went back to the garage, collected the two days' pay they owed me and my cards. I was jobless again. But this time my cards had the necessary six months' stamps that I needed to qualify for unemployment benefit. Also, the officer said that I could ask for National Assistance if I had no money for food and rent. So a man came to see me in my room, looked around, examined my rent book and decided that four pounds a week would be enough to keep body and soul together. 'We aren't going to support you for ever, you know. Just till you get another job. An educated man like you shouldn't have to beg the State for help.'

I agreed. Hadn't Ram Singh said just about the same thing?

It snowed, that first Christmas in London. I had collected the dole three days before. After rent and heating up my room for four hours, I had a pound left. I was hungry and decided to go out and have a meal. That cost eight shillings. In the next two days I spent six shillings more on sausages and newspapers. On Christmas eve I had exactly four shillings left.

The snow was heavy on the roads. My feet squelched with every step I took, the socks were wet, even the leather seemed to have absorbed moisture. I could feel the cold slush through my tattered soles. I had put the newspapers under my jacket to keep warm, but paper didn't do any good inside the shoes.

I had a pint of bitter at the Queen's Elm at eight o'clock, firmly resolved not to spend the remainder of the money till midnight. (Pubs remain open till after midnight on Christmas

Eve.) I stood next to Sean and tried to join the conversation. But I could think of nothing to say. They were all drinking Scotch and one man turned to me and said, 'How about a Christmas drink?' But before I could nod my grateful acceptance of his offer, he had turned away and was walking towards the bar. When he returned, with hands full of tumblers and jugs, the others in the group grabbed their drinks from him. There was none for me.

Then they decided to walk over to the Angelsea. I went along with them. The bottom of my trousers got wet, my shoes were heavy with water. The wind blew through the jacket and the newspapers. I felt I was about to faint, I had not eaten for a day and a half. When we finally arrived at the pub it was too crowded to get in, so the 'group' decided to go to the Finch's. Sally walked next to me and started singing 'Silent Night'. I joined her in a strained bass.

'You have a lovely voice,' she said.

'So do you,' I replied, slipping in the snow. She put out her hand and helped me up. When we started walking again she didn't let go of my hand for a while. That was sweet of her, I thought.

They were all singing at the Finch's, loud, throaty Irish voices, well liquored and merry. The mirth was infectious. I started singing too, standing round in a ring, holding hands. Every so often someone would break into a carol with a dirty limerick. Laughter. Falling over tables, kisses galore. Friendships remade, jugs of beer spilt, breasts squeezed, other people's girlfriends felt up. There were too many people, too much motion. The streamers and the balloons and the twinkling lights burping on and off. The road to the gents' lined with bursting bladders.

Sean said, 'Christmas is a fucking idiocy. The other day I met . . .'

Jeanette said, 'What's he doing here, the heathen?'

Sally said, 'Where did you learn Christmas carols?'

They all said, 'Star of wonder, star of light . . .'

At midnight I had my beer, kissed Sally on the cheek and left the pub. It was a long walk through the snow. There were lots of people on the road, 'Happy Christmas', and 'Happy Christmas', and 'Happy Christmas'.

'Happy Christmas.'

Next day I came down with fever.

Sally shared a flat in Hammersmith with a girl. 'You must come over and meet Celia someday,' she said.

'I would love to.'

'Well, why don't you come for a meal on Thursday then?' Sally looked around to see if Sean was within earshot, her 'man' was one of the possessive kind. 'There would be no point in asking Sean, Celia doesn't get along with him.'

'Just as you wish,' I replied.

'We could all meet in a pub at about six and go home afterwards,' Sally continued. 'Celia works in the library at Notting Hill Gate, so we could get together round there somewhere.'

'I shall have to take the evening off in that case,' I said, apologetically.

'Why, what sort of work do you do?' Sally queried. 'Funny, I've known you all this time but I've never . . .'

'It's not really my work, you know. I mean, that's not what I really do . . .'

I had started work as a barman in the newly opened London Steak House on Kensington High Street. The manager had insisted that 'We don't have a policy of discrimination here. If you can do the job, that's all that counts.' My starting wage was nine pounds sixteen shillings a week and I would be given all my meals. 'You're well spoken and intelligent. Shouldn't have much trouble in picking up the business.' I was sent on training for three weeks to the restaurant at the corner of Oxford Street. There I learnt the names of various brands of whisky, the way to pour a beer and the techniques of being a barman. Money-wise I was doing better than ever before.

I agreed to meet Sally at the Bull's Head at six on Thursday.

It isn't really a 'date', is it? I said to myself. But it is the first time . . . . I wonder what she looks like. I mean, if she is pretty, really pretty, she must have a lot of boyfriends. Even Sally had a boyfriend and she was no beauty. So Celia was probably . . . Not that I mind. I really had no right to expect anything. She is doing me a big enough favour as it is. Imagine, being asked over for dinner with two girls in a flat. I would be the only man there. That's something, isn't it?

Celia was a dark-haired girl with blue eyes. Her breasts stuck out sharply under her tight sweater and her skirt was a good six inches above her knee, at a time when the mini had not yet hit the scene.

'Why do you play with your beard all the time?' she asked, a mischievous twinkle lighting up her eyes. 'Are you nervous or something?'

I had bought a round of drinks, gin and tonic for Sally, neat whisky with ice for Celia and a beer for me. We said

'Cheers', sat down at a table, and I was frantically searching for words to start a conversation.

'Sally tells me you work in a bar.'

'Yes, well, I mean, I work as a barman, not in a bar really. It's a restaurant.'

'Slumming, I suppose. Gathering "experience"?' She emphasised 'experience', a smile flickering at the edge of her lips.

'No, not that. I mean I want to write but . . . I just couldn't get any other job.'

'Hmph!' Celia exclaimed. 'You Indians are all the same.'

'Do you know many Indians?'

'A few,' Celia replied, her face clouding for an instant.

Silence intervened.

'We'll have another round and then we'll go home,' Celia announced, gulping down her Scotch. My mug was still half full of beer. 'Come on, drink up.'

She went to the counter and ordered the drinks, bought a packet of cigarettes, looked round the bar impatiently and started humming a song. 'She is a strange girl,' Sally said.

'What? Yes, oh yes,' I replied. My eyes were on Celia's legs.

'Here you are,' Celia said, returning to the table with the three drinks in her hands. 'Sally, you've got to get the wine. Amit bought the first round, I got this one, so it's your turn this time.'

'All right, I'll get it.'

'Well, just don't sit there then. There is an Off Licence next door, go on.'

Sally obediently rose from her seat and left the table. Both of us watched her walk out of the door before returning to our drinks. 'That girl,' Celia sighed, 'she is always half asleep.'

'I understand you are a painter,' I ventured, after a while.

'Who told you that?' Celia retorted sharply. 'No, I am *not* a painter. There are too many of those things around. So-called artists. I am not an artist. I work in a library and one day I am going to be a full-fledged librarian.'

'You are very pretty,' I said softly, staring into my beer.

'What? What did you say?'

'Nothing, nothing. I am sorry.'

'Come on, don't be embarrassed about paying a compliment. Especially if you meant it.' I looked up at her and the smiling eyes made my palms moist. 'Are you really shy or is that just a front?'

'No, really. I mean I didn't expect that . . . I thought you would be like . . . '

'Like Sally?' Celia burst out laughing. 'Just because we share a flat we've got to look alike? Well, you know there's room for all kinds. Some men like it that way, plenty of stuff to hold on to. But you should see her without her bra. They spread out like pancakes.'

I had never heard a woman talk like this before. The monosyllabic words, yes. But they were not very expressive. While Celia's language was graphic, they did not leave any doubts about what she meant. 'I think you need a Scotch,' she said, getting up from the chair.

'No, I mean really . . . '

Did she like me? Or was she just teasing? Every time I looked at her my eyes ran down her face and focussed on her breasts. Two conical peaks in slow horizontal oscillation, in tune with her lungs. When she was at the bar, my eyes started their journey near her ankles, then up her calves and . . . I could see the beginnings of her thighs.

'You can look at me if you like,' Celia said, putting the whisky on the table. 'I won't eat you.'

Her eyes shot out points of fire like a sparkler. They came at me sharp and piercing. My nerves stretched, hairs stood on end. 'Thank you,' I croaked, as Sally returned to the table with the bottle of wine.

We walked from Notting Hill Gate to Hammersmith, with the two girls on either side of me. Celia carried on an unceasing monologue, about the latest film in the Odeon cinema, the John Osborne play at the Phoenix Theatre, the new club called The Establishment which the 'Beyond the Fringe' crowd had opened, etc. It was fascinating to hear her talk, that urgent tone in her voice, an occasional joke, derisive, slightly cynical, and a torrent of raw energy cascading out of that small dainty frame. I was mesmerized.

It was a basement flat and by the time we got there it was dark. Sally put on all the lights and Celia came sharply at her. 'This isn't a television studio, we don't have to have the arc lamps on, you know.' She switched off two lights, then lit some candles and placed them in different parts of the room. Yes, it did feel cozier. While Sally retired to the kitchen, Celia put on a record. 'Shall we dance?' she asked, after it had been playing for a while.

'I am afraid I don't know how to,' I replied.

'Oh . . . ' she sighed, getting up from the sofa. Just then Sally walked in. 'Oh . . . ' Celia repeated, flopping back again.

I said little throughout dinner. The two girls talked, mostly about mutual friends, parties, and other topics equally incomprehensible to me. When it was time to say good night, Sally came up and kissed me on the cheek. Celia shook my hand at the door and walked back to the living room. 'I'll walk you to the Tube station,' Sally said. I wished Celia had made the offer.

Lying in bed that night, I turned over a myriad schemes in my mind. Finally, I had been introduced to a girl. And I hadn't done too much on first exposure. But if I had a second chance I was sure I would. Well, perhaps she had a boyfriend, a pretty girl like her . . . She seemed to like me though. And she had known Indians before, so she wouldn't call me a nigger or anything like that. More intense than my desire to have a girlfriend was my fear of rejection. But I felt, without being able to put words to the feeling, that Celia would not reject me. She was alive, almost too alive for me. Celia knew how to use words and this impressed and attracted me more than her breasts and her thighs. There was a sexual undercurrent in her talk, oblique references, tightly corked sensual energy. I felt it, not quite sure what it meant and to what it was directed. I think that was my first contact with overt sex as an adult. With Mimi it had been stolen sweets; with the tart in Rome, a variation on the Oedipal theme; with Jeanette, sex had been stripped of sensuality and dressed in the barren neutral garb of mechanics and utility. Celia was different.

I decided to visit her in the library during my lunch-break the next day.

'What a surprise!' she exclaimed. 'Fancy seeing you here.'

'Well, I was just passing, so I thought . . . '

'You thought right. But listen, what are you doing tomorrow night? Sally and I are going to a party. Would you like to come?'

'I . . . I . . . yes, of course. It's my day off tomorrow.'

'Well, that's all settled then. We'll come over to your place at about six. Then we can have a few drinks and go on to the party.'

'Do you think that Sally . . . ? I mean my room is very small.'

'Look, I am very busy just now. So cut out the Indian crap. Just put down your address here and we'll see you tomorrow evening.'

I did what I was told and she said, 'Bye, see you tomorrow.'

All Saturday morning I paced up and down my room, nervous, cold, haunted. I cleaned the electric cooker, aired the room, washed the bed-sheets in the launderette and dusted the blankets (I had no bed-cover). Then I had a long bath and put on my suit. Then I waited. It was only three o'clock.

The intensity of an experience is proportional to the quantum of surprise it contains, the rawness of receiving nerves and the lack of preconception. I did not know what Celia was doing or intended to do with me. I was not sure if she would turn up, if she had really meant to take me to the party. The three-hour wait exhausted me as my mind leapt from possibility to possibility, from the bathetic to the ecstatic. Could she have fallen in love with me? She had sounded eager enough. Or was it just a game she was playing? Perhaps to prove a point? (I had discerned a certain rivalry between the two girls.) Do I have to take this event—of my being invited to a party and two girls visiting me in my room—as unique in the history of intra-sexual relationships? Or was it quite simply a prosaic everyday thing which would lead to nothing more than going to a party with two girls?

By half past six I had explored all alternatives, my mind had been battered down to near-insensitivity, and I was thinking of taking off my clothes and going to bed, when the doorbell rang. Celia walked in by herself.

'Hullo, I hope I am not intruding,' she said, smiling that old sly smile through her eyes.

'No, no, not at all,' I replied, slightly dazed. 'I mean I was just thinking of going to bed.'

'What?' Celia cried, arching up her eyebrows. 'Isn't that a bit premature? Especially as I said that Sally would be coming along too.'

'No, I don't mean . . . ' I said, taking her seriously. 'I meant I thought you weren't going to come so . . . '

'So . . . ?'

'So . . . so I thought I'd go to bed.'

'On a Saturday night? Are you just a wee bit crazy perhaps? A girl lets you down—and I wasn't all that late anyway—and you decide to retire to bed for the night?'

'What else could I do?'

Celia nodded her head, her face drawn in fierce concentration. 'That's right, I suppose. What else *could* you do?' Then suddenly she burst out laughing. 'Come on,' she said, holding my hand and pulling me up from the bed. 'I think you are the sweetest, innocentest man I have ever met.'

'I am sorry.'

'Oh, don't be sorry, men like you don't come along every day. And when they do, they don't stay that way for long either.'

We went to the Dragon's Head and Celia said she preferred to stand at the bar rather than sit at a table. I bought the drinks and said, 'Cheers.'

'Cheers,' Celia replied. 'Hope you didn't mind my turning up at your place all by myself.'

'No, as a matter of fact . . . '

'Yes, I know, you don't have to tell me. Sally is moping about that bastard Sean, and I didn't think she would be much fun in a threesome. So I didn't tell her I was meeting you at six-thirty.'

'Actually, you said six,' I corrected hesitantly.

'Did I . . . ? Well, I think that half-hour wait was good for you. It made you think of going to bed and that's always good.'

I raised my glass again to tide over the silence.

'Look,' Celia said, abruptly changing her tone, 'have you ever been drunk? Really drunk, I mean?'

'No,' I answered. 'I mean yes, once. But I wasn't really drunk. I got sick and passed out.'

'Oh, you poor thing . . .'

'It was quite an experience,' I continued, shedding some of the starch. 'I upchucked on the hostess's dress. A gold-laced, ankle-deep effort, it was.'

Both of us laughed. Celia smiled through her eyes.

'I am your girl tonight. So let's both get drunk, while you pay for the drinks. Have you got any money?'

'A little,' I replied, nervous.

'Good,' Celia said, 'and we'll go Dutch on the dinner. Something cheap like chow mein and sweet-sour pork. All right?'

'All right.'

I couldn't believe it. I had had no time to get adjusted. Celia really liked me. It was Saturday night, we were drinking at the Dragon's Head, we would be having dinner later and then there was the party. Nirvana? Not quite, but near enough.

The party was in Belsize Park. After dinner we took a bus to Swiss Cottage. Celia was pleasantly merry and so was I. We sat close together and my hand brushed her bare thigh. 'You've never had a girlfriend, have you?'

'Not in England, no,' I replied. 'My mother warned me about the wicked white women who lure the unsuspecting solitary male into all kinds of wily traps.'

She laughed. 'And you've strenuously kept away from them ever since?'

'Not through choice, I can assure you.'

'Your mother might have had a point though.'

'I am sure she did. But there are certain things one should experience oneself rather than be warned off from by others. However "wise" it might be to listen to them.'

'Right,' Celia warned, squeezing my hand. 'Live dangerously. And if you can't do that, at least have fun.'

'But I am not much fun, am I?' I said softly.

'Not yet. But you will be. By the time I finish with you.'

'Are you going to be my girlfriend, then?'

'I'll give you a try . . . .'

The party was in full swing by the time we got there. Eleven o'clock, familiar faces from the Fulham Road pubs.

'There are lots of people from Chelsea,' I remarked, not quite knowing what I should do or say.

'Chelsea? What Chelsea? Fulham Road is no bloody Chelsea. It's the Irish bum colony. A brotherhood of would-bes.'

'What do you have against would-bes?' I asked. 'Everyone has to start off that way. Joyce was a would-be writer for years, so was Henry Miller and Hemingway . . . . As a matter of fact I am a would-be writer too.'

'Unh, unh,' Celia countered. 'Not you. You are going to be a real writer. At least I hope you will. You're allowed to gestate only for so long. And then, if you don't produce, you've got to be dumped.'

I saw Sean dancing with a small blonde girl.

'I thought Sally was Sean's girlfriend,' I inquired, changing the subject.

'He has one at every port. Or party, as the case might be,' Celia answered, looking round the half-lit room. There were couples in various semi-recumbent positions, plenty of half-filled wine glasses. The music was low and dripping. 'That's what the trouble was about. But I bet she'll turn up. Just to torture herself.'

'You mean . . . ?'

'Yes, I mean . . . . But we don't have to worry about Sean and Sally, do we? Won't you dance?'

'I told you I can't. I don't know how to.'

'Look, with this music you don't even have to know how to walk. Just hold me and let yourself go. Unless you would rather follow your mother's advice?'

'No, not really . . . '

I remembered Mimi and Volga, the band-leader chewing betel-nut leaf. Seven thousand miles and many moons away, this was Celia, blue-eyed and dark-haired, with her taut breasts pressing against my chest, a record on the turntable, the room trembling on the edge of life and drawing away again. 'You *could* kiss me, but I really prefer that sort of thing in private.' Celia said, drawing me closer.

'What do you see in me?' I said, helplessly.

'Your innocence,' she replied, halting abruptly. The music stopped a few seconds later. 'And I think you are probably very bright. But that's just a feeling. I am not quite sure yet.'

Just then Sally walked in through the door. Celia went over to her, I followed. 'Is he here?' Sally asked sniffing. Her eyes were red, she had been crying.

'Of course he is. Told you he would be. Why do you torture yourself like this?'

'You never loved him, Celia,' Sally replied, 'but I do. I can't help loving him in spite of all he does to me.'

'Well, it's your birthday party in that case. But don't tell me I didn't warn you,' Celia said sternly. 'Amit, dance with Sally. She can do with a dance.'

Celia left the room, my eyes followed her. Sally was sniffing back her tears all through the dance, looking over my shoulder, trying to spot Sean. The other side of the room was quite dark, the candles had spluttered out, and there were several couples lying on the long sofa. Wasn't much dancing going on, sounds of deep breathing, an occasional low whisper, 'Don't . . . ' or 'Not here . . . ' or even 'Please . . . '

'Celia was Sean's girlfriend, you know,' Sally said, breaking in. 'Once when she was in hospital, he came over to the flat and asked me out for a drink. I had nothing better to do, so I went. And then . . . . She hasn't forgiven me for that.'

The course of instruction was rapid. I had trouble keeping pace with it.

'Sean is married, you know,' Sally added.

'Why are you telling me this?' I asked.

'Just to let you know the kind of girl she is,' Sally replied. 'She wants to get married so badly.'

'But if Sean is already married . . . ?'

'Yes, she was trying to get him to divorce his wife. That's why he dumped her.'

Then suddenly, without warning, Sally flung her arms round me and put her lips on mine. It must have lasted a minute or more, for I did not see Celia come back into the room.

'How was that for a starter?' Celia said, as Sally and I drew away.

'Amit is quite passionate,' Sally answered, picking up her glass of wine.

'So I noticed,' Celia snapped back. 'And you don't lose much time, do you, my little seductress?'

'Look, I am sorry,' I stammered. 'I had better go.'

'You had better do nothing of the kind,' Celia cut in, firmly holding my hand. 'Don't you think you had better try and retrieve your darling lover, instead of . . . ?'

'Oh, what the hell are you on about? It was just a kiss, nothing more . . . . '

Then Sally started crying.

'All right, all right,' Celia said, softening her tone. 'Baby-time now.'

The girls got their coats, I thanked the hostess and gulped down a last glass of wine. We left the party, Celia hailed a cab, and the three of us got in. Sally sobbed all through the journey to Hammersmith. 'I am sorry,' she kept repeating, while Celia and I remained silent. 'I don't want to see him again, ever.' When we got down from the cab I hunted around in my pocket but there were no pound notes left. Celia paid the fare.

It was one o'clock in the morning, I didn't know if I was expected to go back into the flat. 'Well, thanks a lot for taking me to the party . . . ' I said to Celia.

'What's the "thank you" for?' she replied, holding my hand. Sally had walked on and was turning the key in the door.

'You are not getting away so easily. Go into the living room and play Uncle to Sally, while I fix some coffee in the kitchen.'

I did as I was told, following the tearful girl. Celia shouted, 'No seductions, mind,' from the door and vanished.

This was turning out to be much more complex than I had anticipated. It was all right to have two girls on your arms in theory but in practice . . . I mean, wouldn't I get a kiss from Celia? But where, this was the only room and she had said quite emphatically that she preferred to kiss in private. Perhaps her disappearing into the kitchen was a hint . . . . Perhaps I should follow her there.

'Excuse me,' I said to Sally. 'I had better go and give Celia a hand with the coffee.'

'She doesn't need any help to make coffee,' Sally replied, pulling me on to the divan. 'Amit, why are you being so beastly to me? What have I done to you?'

'Nothing, nothing, it's just that . . . '

'It's just that you are abandoning me, everyone is abandoning me.' Sally started sobbing again. 'I don't understand. Why?'

'No one is abandoning you, Sally,' I said firmly, a sudden resolve gushing into my system. 'Celia asked me to the party and I would like to be alone with her for a little while.'

I got up and walked out of the room.

'Looking for the loo?' Celia asked, as I entered the kitchen.

'No,' I replied, 'I was looking for you.'

'Really?'

'You remember you said I *could* kiss you if I liked, but you preferred it in private?'

'But not in the kitchen, with all these herbs and spices staring at you.'

I went up and put my arms around her.

'Unh, unh,' she shouted, extricating herself brusquely. 'For someone who was about to go to bed at six-thirty on a Saturday night you are pretty forward, aren't you?'

I looked at her, silent.

'And then the hurt wounded look to boot!' she cried. 'Really!'

'I am sorry.'

'There's nothing to be sorry about,' Celia announced, pouring out the coffee from the percolator. 'It's just that there is a time and place for everything. Come on, I told you to play Uncle to Sally, and that's what you should have been doing, instead of trying to seduce me on the kitchen floor.'

'I am sorry.'

'I said there's nothing to be sorry about! The girl's been given a runaround and a few words of male sympathy wouldn't cost you a penny. Just hold her and cuddle her a bit. She is not very sexy, really. And you will be quite safe sipping coffee in her company, while I go and have a bath.'

Celia walked in with the tray, I followed sheepishly after her. Sally was in bed, with the sheets drawn up to her chin. The bed lamp was on and she was still crying.

'That was fast work,' Celia said, putting the tray on the coffee table. 'Don't you want any coffee?'

'No thanks,' came the nasal answer, punctuated by jerky sobs.

'Come on, Sally, you don't want to be a crybaby, especially with a man around the place,' Celia said, softening her tone. 'Come on, I'll put on a record and you can dance in your slip. You don't mind, do you Amit?'

'Er . . . er . . . no, of course not, not at all.'

'You two go on,' Sally replied. 'I am tired.'

I looked at the other bed, Celia's, and thought of 'time and place for everything'. When? Where?

'Come on, Sally,' Celia insisted. 'Amit dances beautifully, as you've had reason to find out.'

Sally, who was waiting to be coaxed, came out of bed, braless, her slip as short as Celia's skirt, her fat stumpy legs matching her leaden walk. Reluctance gave way to panting abandon as a smile floated up above her tears and her arms clamped firmly round me.

'There . . . ' Celia exclaimed, as we started moving in time with the music. 'Such a divine-looking couple, as my aunt would say.'

She went out of the room and Sally drew me tight against her ample bosom. 'Kiss me, Amit, kiss me,' she whispered.

'Sally . . . '

'Please . . . You know I wanted you from the day I first saw you. I love your eyes, they're so soft and dark . . . '

'Celia will be back in a minute . . . ' I pleaded, as Sally's lips pressed against mine, her tongue searing into my mouth.

'Celia can go to hell,' Sally shouted. 'You're *my* friend, aren't you?'

'Yes, but you are Sean's girlfriend, not mine.'

'Oh . . . oh . . . oh.' The sobs came back again, her arms tightened round me. 'Sean is a bastard. I hate him. I don't want to see him again, ever. I want you, I don't want to be alone. Sleep with me tonight, Amit. Please . . . '

Panic seized me. I unentangled myself and ran out of the room without uttering another word. Sally didn't follow. On my way to the kitchen I passed the bathroom. It had a frosted-glass door and I saw the outline of Celia's body against the light. She was nude, or at least I assumed she was. Celia was rubbing herself with a towel, her body moving in slow liquid curves. I was caught. I abandoned the idea of seeking refuge in the kitchen, as the chase seemed to be over. I waited in the corridor like a nervous poacher enticed by the sight of fresh game.

Celia emerged, wrapped up in a huge bath towel. 'What are you doing here?' she cried, sternly.

'I . . . I . . .'

' . . . was spying through the keyhole.'

'No, not really. I just saw you against the light and so I thought . . . '

'But you were supposed to be dancing with Sally, bringing her back to life,' Celia said, walking into the kitchen.

'Yes, but she . . . '

'She tried to seduce you, is that it?'

'No, but . . . '

Celia suddenly changed her tone, turned her face to me and smiled, beckoning me with her finger. 'I am supposed to be your girlfriend, remember?' she said, holding my face in both her hands. 'So if you will wait here and ponder the mysteries of the universe, I'll get dressed and be with you in a minute.'

'Yes, but . . . '

'No buts,' Celia retorted, walking away. 'There's beer in the fridge. Pour yourself one and leave some for me.'

Ten minutes later she returned to the kitchen with a small bag in her hand. 'All right, I'm ready.'

'Ready for what?' I queried, completely thrown off balance.

'To go for a walk, you silly fool,' she replied. 'Come on.'

I didn't say good night to Sally, as she was asleep. 'Don't take any notice of what she says when she is in one of these moods. Sally can't hold her liquor, sometimes in the morning she can't remember what she's said or done the previous night.'

I nodded. Then we walked silently for a while.

'Do I have to explain that I am coming back to your place to spend the night with you?'

As our affair progressed, I gained confidence. Celia spent a lot of time in my room; when she stayed overnight at my place she would cook breakfast in the morning. Lying in bed I would watch her slim taut body bent over the basin or the stove, and I would feel excited. I would creep out of bed, grab her from behind and kiss her. Often we would land up in bed.

'Best way to start the day I know,' she would say.

I didn't know much about all this, but I was learning. The little things that make up sex, the small unspoken gestures that the books never tell you about. By the look in her eye I would know when she wanted to be taken, fast, without preliminaries. By the way she held me in her arms I could tell that it was to be a slow languorous session, silk fingers caressing my face, a long winding kiss and the ritual of undressing. How, just before she came, she would want me to bite her nipples, hard. When she wanted to romp around the room, half-nude, pretending to ward me off and then falling back on the chair, looking exhausted, wet between her thighs. At night when she thought I was asleep how she would stroke my thighs and all round my balls till I was erect, and then sit on me, as if it was a game she was playing, taking me against my will.

I think she began to love me a little in those first weeks. Though she never said so.

I became daring and proud, full of a heady confidence in my new-found prowess. One night I asked one of the waitresses in the restaurant out for a drink. She said, 'But by the time we get off, the pubs will all be shut.'

'That's no problem,' I replied, 'we could take a bottle back and drink it at my place.'

She agreed. And I couldn't believe my luck.

I pinched a bottle from the bar, hid it in my bag and met Sarah in front of the Tube station. She was Irish with auburn hair and a naughty tongue. I remember her wit, very un-British, slightly barbed, very feminine and full of puns. By the time we got to my room, I was laughing at every third sentence she spoke. We were walking arm in arm, stopping every ten feet or so to hug and kiss each other.

'Holy mother of Jhesus,' she said, after rather a lengthy one, 'a good lick's what I got that both man and beast be proud to give.'

We stayed up half the night and finished the bottle between us. Then she asked me to switch off the light. 'There'll be plenty of time in the morning,' Sarah said, as she got into bed. 'Whisky is one kind of fire that don't agree with the other.'

She was soft, shy and very tender in the morning. 'That's a real stick of fire you got between your legs,' she observed, when we finished making love. 'Not to make a habit of it you know,' Sarah said, smiling, as she kissed me goodbye. Her husband was a truck driver and was away for two days. 'You've got a girl too, haven't you?' I nodded. She had spotted an eyebrow pencil on the window-sill.

I saw Sarah several times after that but I never told Celia about it. The illicitness of our rendezvous made them more exciting. Especially as there was an added spur of guilt from my side. 'But it's all grist in the writer's mill,' I told myself. And so, in a way, it must have been.

It was all Celia's doing. Since I knew I was attractive to one woman, it gave me confidence with others. I began to flirt with the girls at the Queen's Elm and the Finch's. I was invited to parties, Sean asked me back to his place one evening after the pubs had shut. I bought a red corduroy jacket and started taking an interest in my looks. My conversation improved, I now knew when to order Scotch. Slowly, very slowly, the man who was struggling to get out of the regressive adolescent began to make his appearance. I no longer searched for an irony when a woman called me attractive. And I learnt how to dare.

One Thursday night I was walking down Earls Court Road and a woman fell into step with me. 'Do you want to come with me?' she whispered. I looked at her and smiled, intrigued by the idea of fucking an English whore, with visions of Roman and Indian Venuses flashing through my mind.

'How much?' I asked, still smiling.

'Four pounds for an hour.'

'Sorry, I would love to, but I haven't got the money.'

'We'll make it three pounds then,' she said.

I shook my head and quickened my pace.

'Two pounds and that's my final offer,' she pleaded, trying to sound haughty.

'No go, I'm afraid. Better luck elsewhere. I only have a pound on me.'

'Oh . . . you!' she cried, exasperated. 'You people are all the same. All right then, just a quick throw.'

'Done,' I replied, putting out my hand.

'Keep that for the West End,' she retorted sharply.

I followed her down one side street, climbed two flights of dark wooden stairs and entered a room. It was better furnished than mine, a long mirror on the wall, hot and cold water in the basin, chest of drawers and one large bed.

She took off her shoes, then her skirt and pants, leaving her suspender on as well as her stockings. Waist up she was fully clothed. 'Put this on,' she said, throwing me one prophylactic sheath from a packet of three. Then she lay down on the bed, raised her knees and parted them wide. 'Do you want to come in or not?'

I wanted to laugh but feared that it might not be taken in the right spirit.

She wouldn't let me either kiss her or fondle her breasts. After I had been going for about five minutes, she cried, 'Come on, luv, I 'aven't got all night!' Then fiercely under her breath, 'And for one lousy quid too.' My erection went down and I withdrew. 'That'll be two pounds then,' she announced, hopping out of bed.

'You can search me if you like, but a pound is all I've got.'

'Should set the cops on the likes of you,' she spat out, as I handed her the money and came out of the room.

I laughed all the way back to my basement abode, congratulating myself on having won the first bargain with a scarlet woman. When I told Celia of this encounter she said, 'You didn't do that because you wanted to. Oh no! It's this image you've got of yourself as a writer. But if you go on long enough at this rate, that's all it will be. An image.'

That was when I started writing my autobiography, *Goodbye to India*.

The street on which Celia lived was all white and mostly Irish. I would get looks and rude words whenever I walked down to her flat. This frightened me and I never turned back to confront anyone. When I was with Celia, there would be catcalls and words as well. But I was never man enough to grab the kid by the collar and provoke a fight. I pretended, we both pretended, that these things didn't happen. If someone shouted, 'Prick-sucking whore', we would walk by him, looking straight ahead, as if we hadn't heard. Celia and I never talked about the colour thing. I was still too raw and I think she was just a little bit embarrassed about it.

One weekend when Sally was away at her mother's, Celia cooked a meal at her flat and I went out and got a bottle of wine. The lights were low, there was music on the record player and we finished eating in silence. 'I had better draw the curtains,' Celia whispered, after she had taken the dishes away. I kissed her and held her very tight against me. 'And while you do that I'll change the record,' I said in her ear.

Thirty seconds later Celia screamed, running back to me from the window.

'What is it?' I cried, holding her trembling body in my arms.

'That hand. I saw a hand . . .'

I thought for a few rapid seconds.

'Oh come on, you don't believe in things like that? Ghosts and fairies and all that sort of thing?'

'It wasn't a ghost, Amit,' Celia insisted, in a steadier voice. 'It was a real hand, a real live hand. There was someone outside the window just now.'

I am not brave, I have never been brave, I do not claim to be brave. Fear of physical violence is a primary factor of my personality. A man outside the window of a basement flat in Hammersmith, an Indian and an English girl in the room, ten o'clock on a Saturday night, drunken Irishmen all around. How did I feel? Scared! My knees were weak, my forehead wet with beads of sudden sweat, my pulse beat shot up. Yet I was the man, Celia the woman. And she needed, demanded, my protection.

I went out of the door with Celia crying, 'Don't, Amit, be careful,' climbed the flight of stairs up to the street and looked around. There was no one in sight. Celia waved to me from the window, I waved back. Perhaps she had imagined the whole thing, we would have heard footsteps, there would have been some noise. No, there wasn't any danger.

I went back into the flat and said, 'Come on, let's dance.' Celia had drawn the curtains, the music was louder than before. Tension was still in the air but I felt more at ease. Having dared, gone out and looked around in the street gave me courage. In a little while we had half-forgotten that the incident had happened. I started kissing Celia on the sofa, working her up.

When a large brick crashed through the window and landed in the middle of the room!

Celia screamed again and held me tight, with eyes shut and her whole body trembling. This time I was somehow less flustered, more in control. I don't know why. I picked up the brick and there was a piece of paper stuck on it. The message read, 'WOG-SUCKING SLUT'.

'I think we should call the police,' I said.

There was no phone in the basement, so we came out on the street and knocked on the ground floor flat. The police said they would be down 'very shortly'. We returned to the basement and waited. Nothing happened in the next half-hour—which was how long the cops took in coming.

'Your flat, ma'am?' the officer asked.

'Yes,' Celia replied.

'Live here by yourself, do you?'

The other constable was eyeing me, turning over the paper in his hand, reading and re-reading the message.

'Is this your boyfriend then?'

'Yes.'

'You have a lot of boyfriends, do you?'

'What do you mean, officer?' Celia shouted.

The two constables left with the following words: 'Well, we've got all the facts. And we'll make enquiries. Meantime, try not to have too many "guests", will you?'

Five minutes after the police car drove off, a tricycle wheel came tumbling in, breaking some more glass and landing much nearer the sofa. 'I am getting out of here,' Celia said firmly. I could see that she was angry. She packed a suitcase in a hurry, picked up the toiletry from the bathroom and announced, 'Come on, I am moving in with you. I'll come back tomorrow morning and pick up the rest of my stuff. Sally can do what she damn well pleases with this . . . this . . . '

We took a taxi back to Earls Court. And that was how we started living together, Celia and I. Just as 'artists' always do, cohabit with a woman to whom they are not married. I had been initiated.

I learnt a lot about wines at the bar. The wine list carried maps of the different vineyards in France and Germany, showing the place from where each vintage came. I studied the maps carefully, sipped each bottle—there was always some left in a bottle after the customers had finished with it—and learnt to distinguish between a Bordeaux and a Burgundy, between a Hock and a Moselle. I even became pretty good at telling the good years from the bad. Along with sex education, I was learning to become 'sophisticated'.

I followed the newspapers studiously, read the *New Statesman* every week, bought a whole bunch of paperbacks. Once I wrote a long letter—about 1000 words—attacking the 'Angry Young Men' and the *New Statesman* published the whole thing. I was so overjoyed that I had two large brandies at the bar during the lunch-break. Then all through the evening I continued to sneak down a gulp or two behind the counter. One assistant manager suspected something and used a few sharp words.

'Who do you think you are?' I snapped back, with customers in full view. 'I write for the *New Statesman*, I am a genius. Not just a piddly little barman.' And to prove my point I poured the remainder of the bottle of Remy Martin down the drain.

The manager came up and said in a low firm voice: 'Ray, you are drunk. Go down and change into your own clothes and leave by the back door. You can come back tomorrow for your cards. You're fired.'

I went back on the dole again.

Then my parents sent me a plane ticket, London-Calcutta. I had no intention of returning to India, for yet a while anyway. So I wanted to sell it and get the money. But since the fare had been paid at the other end in rupees, that couldn't be done. Then Celia suggested we go to Paris for the summer. She had saved a little money and I could change my ticket to London-Paris-Calcutta. Yes, and I could finish my book in Paris.

Sounded great, especially as all 'artists' have to go to Paris at some stage. What better than to go with a girl? I skipped two weeks' rent and sneaked out of the house in the middle of the night. Celia and I spent the next six hours at the West London Air Terminal.

At ten o'clock we were on a B.E.A. Viscount at Heathrow airport. Destination: Paris. I had five pounds in my pocket, the identical amount to what I had brought into London exactly a year before.

FOUR

~

PARIS APRÈS HELEN

We booked into a pleasant little pension on the Left Bank, eighteen francs a day for a double room. I did not want to visit the Louvre or Notre-Dame, neither did Celia. The days fell into a pattern pretty soon after we arrived in Paris. Breakfast at ten in the cafe across the street, a carafe of vin rouge for me, a large mug of black coffee for Celia, croissant with butter for both of us. Then I would go back to the pension to work on my book, she would go on one of her walking sprees. We would meet again for lunch, and if we were in the mood, splash out on a gourmet meal, three courses and a good bottle of Burgundy. Rest of the day we would make love, stay in bed, drink rough Algerian wine and nibble at cheese and French bread. At night we would go to Montmartre, hop from cafe to cafe, drinking, dancing and kissing. Sometimes we would take a cab back home, at three or four in the morning. It was a good life. I was happy with Celia.

Then, 'I think I am pregnant,' she said one day at breakfast. 'I am a week overdue.'

'But I thought you said you couldn't be . . . ?'

We had not been taking any precautions. Celia had told me that it was impossible for her to get pregnant as she secreted an enormous amount of juice. I didn't know anything about contraception, so I took her word for it. 'Anyway, I've never used anything ever, and if it was going to happen, it would have happened by now. You're not the first man in my life, you know.' That sounded conclusive enough. Who was I to question a woman as wordly-wise as Celia?

I did not know how to react to the news.

'Are you sure?'

'Of course I'm not. I told you I am only a week overdue.'

'What does that mean? I mean, is that natural? How long can a girl be overdue before she . . . '

'How the hell should I know!' Celia shouted. 'I've never been pregnant before.'

We moved out of the pension as money was running short. Three weeks in Paris and we had spent fifty pounds. There were twenty pounds left in the kitty and neither of us had any chance of getting a job. Celia suggested we buy a cheap cardboard suitcase and stuff it with newspapers. This would be our 'baggage' in the next pension, while we stored our real luggage with Perry Smith, an English painter we had come to know, who lived on Saint Michele.

The pension was cheap, six francs for a double room. The toilet was a hole in the ground across the yard, there was no hot water in the room and no fresh linen every week. The concierge did not ask for our passports and we registered under false names. Two weeks after we moved in the man asked to be paid. Celia said we had some traveller's cheques which we could cash the next day. Grumbling a little, the man went away, seemingly satisfied with our promise. After all, we looked a decent enough couple. Leaving our newspaper-filled 'baggage' behind, we went to Montmartre that evening, never to return to that pension again.

We did this four times, not paying a single centime for 'lodging' for the remainder of our stay in Paris. As we became more practised we chose more and more expensive hotels. When they asked for our passports we extended our stay. Celia said, 'By the time the wheels of law start turning, we'll be out of the country. So why worry?'

'And they aren't going to start an international lawsuit just for a few lousy francs, are they?' I replied.

When Celia was overdue for a month, I knew, we both knew, that she was definitely pregnant. She wrote to a girl in London who sent her some quinine tablets. We tried the whole amateur gamut from a bottle of gin and hot bath to poking around with a catheta and jumping about. But nothing worked. And we had no money with which to go back to England.

If I went to the Indian Embassy and told them of my condition I knew they would put me on a plane back to India and my guarantor would have to pay up at the other end. And even apart from the money, it would be too humiliating. What could I say to my parents? What had I done this whole year in Europe? No, the Indian Embassy was positively out.

Celia didn't know anyone from whom she could borrow the money in London. 'I can't ask my parents. What would I say to them? How could I explain? They don't even know that I am here with *you*. Mother thinks I am travelling with a girlfriend. She would throw a fit if she knew.'

Money?

Then Celia hit upon a solution. 'You know I studied art at College?'

'Yes . . . ?'

'Well, I am not much good at it but I *can* draw.'

'And so . . . ?'

'So, we could do the kind of stuff a lot of these bums do in Montmartre at the Place du Tertre.'

I was willing to give it a try—after all I looked exotic enough, even in Paris. I had a full bushy beard, longish hair and a pair of large dark-brown eyes. I wore tight leather trousers—not exactly in vogue in those days—and a full-sleeved red satin shirt. It was summer so the corduroy jacket hung lazily from one shoulder.

The plan was to lure American tourists, especially women (in the mid-forties, early-fifties age group) and Celia would do instant portraits in black and white. So she laid out a few sketches for prospective customers to inspect. I would point at them, use my eyes, smile, sometimes even gently hold the lady's hand. I knew no French but I could put a French accent on English words. My patter was simple and effective: 'Oh, madame, you are so beautiful. *C'est trés jolie, non? Souvenir de Paris, non?*'

'Isn't he charming?' the woman would say to her husband, who would be trying to drag her away. I looked younger than I was, perhaps a late teenager. 'What does he do? Is he a painter too? Ask him, Bob.'

'Do you speak English?'

'*Un peu*, madame, a little bit.'

'Oh, he is cute, isn't he?'

All this time Celia would be furiously sketching away with crayon and charcoal. It took her about ten minutes per portrait, and once she had got started the customer could hardly go away, whatever her man might say. Then while waiting for the show to be over, the gentleman would start eyeing Celia, her sharp angled breasts heaving under the tight sweater, her small red tongue stuck out just a little from the side of her mouth. By the end both husband and wife would seem pleased with our respective performances. We would make anywhere between five to ten francs per portrait, up to fifty francs on a good sunny day. As a couple we were the envy of the square.

It is strange to think of it in retrospect. But during all those weeks we seemed to forget that Celia was pregnant. Or at least I did. And she never brought up the subject. Anyway, we couldn't do anything about it in Paris. Even if we could get hold of an abortionist—which we couldn't, since we knew no French residents—the cost would be murderously prohibitive. So money was the most urgent, immediate necessity. And we had found a way of making it. Enough, that is, to pay for one meal a day, three or four bottles of wine and lots of French bread and cheese.

I think we dismissed the thought of Celia's pregnancy in a gesture of hopelessness. Perhaps we even thought that if we let it go on long enough the whole thing would simply vanish, and we wouldn't have to worry about it any more. But the laws of human physiology had predicted a different course, and it took us some time to face the gruesome reality.

Sitting on the banks of the Seine, Notre Dame in the distance, a long loaf of French bread on our laps and a bottle of cheap Algerian wine at our lips, we would hold hands and kiss. I would recite poetry, Celia would sing, we would laugh. Then something would begin to stir in me, I would eye her breasts, much more filled out than they had ever been before, and I would draw her close, my fingers searching under her skirt. 'Don't be silly, Amit. Not here in public, with all these people watching.' Then she would jump up from the bench, throw the empty bottle in the river and race me back to the pension. Sometimes we stayed in bed for days, rang for the boy to get us some more wine and bread and cheese. We made love incessantly, once, twice, sometimes more than half a dozen times a day.

When the money ran out we would start 'work' again.

I was coming to the end of my book while the summer weeks were rushing past. We had enough money to live in Paris at that time in that way. But there was no room for manoeuvre. If we stepped out of line we would be back on the streets again, starving. Summer doesn't last for ever, tourists don't visit the Place du Tertre all year round. Without the sun and the 'beautiful' American ladies we were done for. Yet we never thought of the future, what we would do about the baby Celia was carrying in her womb, how we would ever get out of Paris, what would happen if the publishers rejected my book. Suspended in a timeless plasma, we lived from moment to moment, packing in as much as we could. We were young and daring. It is a feature of age to look at life as a continuum, with a past, a present and a future. We saw it as instant points of experience, haphazardly connected together. What goes before need not determine what comes after.

But the rains finally came!

The square was deserted, the cafes around the square were packed, it was much more difficult to lure customers for Celia. The few tourists who were hardy enough to climb all those stone steps up to the top were never in the mood for a mild flirtation either with Celia or me. They were younger and more cynical. No one called me 'cute' any more. We were lucky when we earned ten francs in a day.

I finished *Goodbye to India* exactly ten weeks after we arrived in Paris. Celia liked it and so did I. We wrapped it in brown paper and put large blobs of red sealing wax all over the package and posted it to Victor Gollancz, Publishers, Covent Garden, London. I did not realize how symbolic that parcel was. It contained my claims to be considered a *real* writer instead of a 'would-be' one. Of course, we both hoped. But I think my hope was different from Celia's. To me it was not the last word I had spoken, not the final gesture I was capable of making. I wanted the book to be published, but if it wasn't, I wouldn't throw in my hand and take up shoeshining once again. To believe in oneself is difficult enough, but to transmit that belief to another person, who is equally unsure, is a far tougher proposition. Celia was on the razor's edge. She had staked herself on a faith, the faith that I was a writer. And she needed external verification. It wasn't enough that she thought so and that I thought so. For the real truth was that neither of us believed in the book or me.

What would we do while we waited to hear from Gollancz? We were living 'free' but it couldn't go on much longer. They were bound to catch up with us and then we would probably land up in jail. And we had heard of French prisons! Besides, we needed money to eat and there wasn't any coming in. Celia managed to 'work' at least one meal a day. She would sit by herself in one of the cafes on Saint Germain and pick her target with care, usually a foreigner, preferably English or American, single, mid-thirties, early-forties, start a conversation, shake her shoulders so that her breasts bounced around like water-filled balloons. Soon she would be sipping Scotch, her blue eyes intent on the man sitting opposite her. After the third drink or so she would begin to fidget in her seat and announce that she would have to go back to her hotel for dinner. 'I am starving,' she would say. 'Aren't you?' Inevitably, a chivalrous offer would be made and after a few minutes of reluctant parrying Celia would graciously accept. Only after the meal appeared on the table, she would signal me.

'Oh, Suzy, you are eating again,' I would say, rushing up from the other end of the street and giving her a hug. 'And here I am, a poor starving genius, destitute and abandoned.' Celia would continue talking to her man, exchanging a conspiratorial wink, as much as to say, 'These "artists" are all the same, parasites.' But I would go on with my patter, helping myself to her plate. Finally, exasperated beyond patience, and convinced that Celia wanted to get rid of me as much as he did, the man would order for me too. I would immediately adopt an autistic vow and consume my meal in silence. When the bill got paid, I would offer to walk Celia home. She would smile and nod her head. 'See you sometime,' she would say to our mutual benefactor. Leaving him sitting there with the lower jaw detached from the rest of his mouth and eyes glazed with stunned disbelief, we would laugh and dance down the street, buy a bottle of wine and run back to our large double bed.

We never visited the same cafe twice. And only once an American G.I. nearly printed his fists on my face. Being nimble

Standing next to Buster was a blonde Swedish girl, Liza, whom I had never seen before. She was fond of art and literature and had recently arrived in Hampstead to indoctrinate herself in these ponderous matters. 'We always live in a dream, don't we?' she offered, in her heavily accented voice, at the end of one rather longish monologue from Mr Tuffman. His reply to her pronouncement was to weave his heavy hairy arm round her slender waist and attempt contact with her oracular muscles by means of his own. The attempt was unsuccessful as she unwound herself lithely from his arm and looked up at her escort, a habitué of the public bar. He was six foot six and was called Big Bob by his friends. He had blue needle-like eyes under black bushy brows; he loped rather than walked and held the consecrated position of being 'possibly the only genius in Hampstead', an assessment which didn't seem to be shared either by his fellow sculptors or critics.

'I like holes,' Big Bob used to say, lubricated by several pints of cider, 'any kind, anywhere. Just so long as I can get my finger in.' And in this vocation he was remarkably successful. Often he would lift a girl up by the waist and throw her over his shoulder, and thus suitably estranged from Mother Earth (the bare boards of the public bar actually) by six feet and so rendered completely vulnerable, the girl would emit the obligatory scream. At which point Big Bob would go to work on her underpants with his other hand and push his long middle finger into her hole. Mission completed, he would let her down, bring his finger under his nose draw in a deep breath and say, 'Yes, it'll do, smells like fish 'n' chips.' Thus Big Bob was the resident canonized genius of the Bumble-Bee, due principally to his success with 'holes'.

share the spoils. Of course, this restaurant was different from the Left Bank cafes. Nevertheless, when the two of them got into a taxi and drove off, my heart fluttered about madly, as if it was beating within a weightless space, without gravity. I couldn't afford a taxi and give chase. So I returned to the pension, sad and vanquished.

The phone woke me up an hour later. 'Look, Amit, we've got to collect our luggage from Perry. We're leaving Paris tonight.'

'What have you been doing all this time? Where are you? I thought you had left me.'

'Don't be silly. I am at the Hilton. The fellow I picked up at the Métro is a Norwegian architect and lives in Copenhagen. He is here to buy a car, a Citroën, and he is driving back this evening, leaving at midnight.'

'What are you doing in the hotel with him? Are you going to . . . ?'

'Look, Amit, I haven't got much time, he'll be back in the room any minute, so stop being silly and listen to me. Go and collect the stuff and wait for me at the cafe. I should be there in an hour.'

'Celia, are you going to . . . ? Will you let him make love to you?' I started crying.

'Of all the imbecile notions . . . ' Celia shouted into the phone.

'You are a first-class moron, Amit Ray . . . ' And then she changed her tone. ' . . . and I love you for it . . . . Now go and do what I told you. See you in an hour. Bye.'

She rang off. What was happening to us? Did I love this girl? Was I going to marry her? Then why was I jealous?

What if she did sleep with someone else? Did I have any rights over her? She was carrying my baby, yes. But I couldn't afford to support even the two of us, let alone a third party, an innocent infant. She was over two months pregnant. What if we couldn't get an abortion? If she had the baby I would have to marry her, of course. Did she want to marry me, though? She had never said she loved me. '... and I love you for it.' Not the three simple words, 'I love you'. Never. Come to think of it, neither had I. So what was all the fuss about? Perhaps she will get married to this Norwegian architect. Yes, perhaps I should vanish from her life. I had leaned on her long enough. Perhaps I should write her a goodbye note and disappear. But where? Anyway, we could part company in Copenhagen, couldn't we? I had heard it was easy to get jobs there. Yes, that would be the best thing to do. Why indulge in unnecessary melodrama? Goodbye notes and things like that? If she wanted this Norwegian architect she could have him. I wouldn't stand in her way. We could talk it over like two mature adults. No need for histrionic scenes, was there?

Celia was at the cafe dot on the hour. She came running and hugged me tight. 'Oh, it's an absolute godsend. And I'm so happy you're here. I thought you might do something silly and melodramatic like write me a note or something.'

'Why should I ever think of doing that, I wonder.'

'Oh, come on, drop it. That hurt haughty tone doesn't suit you either,' Celia said, sitting down. 'And if you will pour me a glass from your carafe I might think of telling you the whole story.'

'I would have thought that you had consumed enough alcohol to last you a whole month.'

'Amit,' Celia said sternly, 'stop it this minute or I shall really leave you.'

I continued sulking for a while and Celia switched from severe schoolmarm to cajoling mistress. 'And do you know I haven't eaten a thing the whole day,' I said, finally giving in, 'while you've been stuffing yourself silly?'

'Yes, I did feel awful about that,' Celia replied. 'But it was all done for a good cause. Tonight we shall bid goodbye to De Gaulle and tomorrow we shall say *Skol* to the Vikings.'

Celia had got on well with the architect. He had tried to bed her at the Hilton but she had put him off. 'I let him have a feel or two. And I could see he had a hard-on. But the whole point was to keep the bait dangling in front of him.' I resented her kissing that man and being felt up by him. But I managed to conceal my reactions. Or so I thought. 'You're not jealous, are you, Amit?' Celia asked, arching up her eyebrows. 'You didn't think I would run off with him, did you by any chance? Abandon you to a cruel world and leave you pondering about how heartless women can be?'

I remained silent.

'Come on, admit it, or I won't go on with the rest of the story.'

'I admit,' I said timidly. 'And even now I am not convinced that I was wrong.'

'That's better!' Celia exclaimed. 'Now, the plan is this . . . '

The architect would have bought the car and returned to the Hilton by eight in the evening. Celia would get dressed meanwhile, wearing a black low-necked dress and Femme on her bosom. And then they would meet for dinner in a restaurant on Saint Germain. He had suggested meeting at the hotel, but Celia reckoned that the seduction scene would be difficult to avert and if averted might leave such a bad taste in the mouth that the whole plan would be foiled. So she had said, 'I like the Left Bank cafes. They're so much more lively than the stodgy old Hilton. I know one which serves the most delicious snails.' And he had agreed. After all, he had nothing to worry about. He would have the girl to himself all the way to Copenhagen. And once there, who knows?

'And where do I fit into all this?' I queried, feeling cold in the stomach once again.

To be stood a cheap meal was one thing but to be taken on a ride all the way to Denmark was quite another.

'Well, I am counting on one thing. That he has enough of a hard-on for me to stand a little inconvenience. But I must play it right. I mustn't give the impression that I absolutely must have you with me. He is a bright boy and he is bound to suspect something if I did that.'

I would bring the luggage to the cafe. Then Celia and I would talk in French, fast. As he would not follow the conversation, Celia would translate for him. I was a friend of a friend of hers, an Indian painter who was starving in Paris. I had heard that there were plenty of jobs in Copenhagen, especially in the summer. Would he very kindly take me along with him?

'If we spring it like that on him at the last minute,' Celia said, sipping her wine, 'when he is well oiled and amorous, I don't think he will refuse. Especially if he thinks that his kindness and generosity will impress me. But it all depends how badly he wants to get into my panties.'

'And supposing he says no?'

'Well, it's very simple. I'll just have to go with him all by myself, won't I?'

'What?' I cried, shooting up from the chair.

'Come on, Amit, sit down,' Celia said softly. 'When will you stop being a baby?'

She kissed me across the table while her hands crept under the cover and searched for my prick. It was hard, all right.

Celia's plan worked. The architect was annoyed at first but when she gave him a slow soft kiss, he changed his mind. 'He can sit in the back of car. But I have not much room for baggage.'

FIVE

~

KØBENHAVN

We were out of France in a couple of hours, then Belgium and into Germany. We stopped in a village near Hamburg at about five in the morning. The architect decided to kip down for a few hours, waiting for the cafes to open. The seat rests of the Citroën were pushed back and the inside of the car made a narrow double-bed. Our benefactor was obviously irritated by my presence.

'Can go for a little walk,' he suggested to me, frowning.

I pretended incomprehension, Celia translated for me.

'*J'ai sommeil je n' ai ancune envie de ne promener*,' I replied.

Celia shook her head at the architect, 'He says he is tired and wants to go to sleep.'

The man made a wry face and it was agreed that all three of us would lie down in the car, Celia in the middle with a man on either side. The architect tried to fumble with her for a while but soon gave up. Driving had exhausted him and he fell soundly asleep in half an hour, so did Celia. I stayed awake.

After breakfast and a perfunctory face-wash, we set off again. The man drove in a frenzy and we arrived in the German harbour in time to catch the four o'clock ferry which was to take us to Copenhagen.

That first night we spent at the architect's flat. Since there was only one bedroom, Celia and I slept on the floor of the sitting room. 'I can't spend the night with you,' I heard her whisper to the Norwegian, 'not with him around.'

'We will ditch him tomorrow,' Celia whispered to me when the lights were out. 'He has done his good deed for the day.' I squeezed her hand in reply.

Next day we booked into the youth hostel and went along to the Student's Employment Bureau. Within a week Celia got a job in a wine-bottling plant, sticking labels. My physics came in handy and I got a job at a refrigerator manufacturing company, measuring low temperatures with thermocouples. Work permits were easy to get as it was July and many workers were away on holiday; they needed replacements. Three weeks after we arrived in Copenhagen the two of us drew our first week's wage packets, 600 kroner altogether. It was enough to pay the first week's rent for a flat and we moved into a modern apartment, with television set, telephone and garbage dispenser, on Tagensvej, in the centre of Copenhagen. In the youth hostel we had been sleeping in segregated dormitories; for three weeks we could do nothing more than kiss and fondle each other. On the first night in our new flat we got into bed at eight in the evening and did not stop making love until the early hours of the morning.

Celia slept in the nude with her lips slightly open and I could see her belly was noticeably swollen. She had begun to *look* pregnant.

It had to come, of course, the bitterness, the recriminations. You cannot dig your head in the sand for long; reality is insistent. Postponement only hardens the soft seed of pain; surgery then becomes inevitable.

'Do you ever think of anyone but yourself?' Celia screamed one morning.

'What do you mean!' I cried, startled.

'I mean that you are a callous and selfish bastard.'

She was nearing the end of the third month of her pregnancy and we had found no solution. Copenhagen wasn't a permanent state. As aliens we could not go on working in menial and quasi-menial jobs for very much longer. I had not heard from Gollancz, and there was no way we could get back to London. And even if we could, there was no prospect of finding a suitable job for me.

'Do you want to have the baby?' I asked, quivering in apprehension.

'You must be out of your tiny mind,' Celia shouted. 'How do you think you'd go about feeding the two of us, I would like to know.'

'We could think of something,' I answered nervously.

'Yes, something! What?'

'Well, if my book is accepted and if we went back to London . . . '

'If, if, if . . . You are not a man. You are a bloody baby yourself.'

As if in an answer from fate, there was a letter waiting for me at American Express the next day.

Dear Mr Ray,

We have read your book *Goodbye to India* with interest. And though we feel that it raises some interesting questions, and that you haven't been wasting your time, the book does not have a general enough appeal to persuade us to publish it. Regretfully, therefore, I have to return the Mss (under separate cover) to you and hope that you will not hesitate to send us anything you might write in future.

The letter was signed by Victor Gollancz, the doyen of left-wing publishers and champion of minority causes.

For Celia this was the last straw. I was confirmed in her mind as a 'would-be' writer. If a publisher (even just one) thought that the book did not have 'a general enough appeal', well, I must be a layabout, mustn't I? Obviously. From that day on she wouldn't let me touch her in bed.

What would have happened if they had accepted the book? I wonder about that sometimes. Unlike several other points of crisis in my life, where I had made decisions and so directed the course of future events, here was a situation in which external forces took control. If Gollancz had decided to publish my book there would have been a cheque in the post. We would probably have come back to London, Celia would have had the baby. I would be married to her. And by now there would have been a brood of children, we would be owning a house in Notting Hill or N.W.1. And I would become 'a responsible member of the literary profession' (or some profession at any rate) instead of remaining an itinerant bachelor bum. Would I have preferred things to have gone the other way?

At that time, yes. I could have done with an acceptance letter then. I wanted to spare Celia the pain she suffered. I would not have acted logically but out of emotion. But in retrospect it seems that what happened was the best thing for me. Celia rebuffed me, scorned my writing ability, made fun of my social gaucheries. In so doing she was injecting a vaccine into my system. Antibodies started to form, I became much more resilient. A stern, steel determination was born, the dilettante intellectual dabbling in words died. I was going to 'show them'. However long it might take, I would do it. Celia would have to eat her words, Gollancz would be forced to look enviously at the critical notices of a book from a fellow publisher. Yes, on this occasion when, instead of me and my impulse, Fate made the decision, the future turned out to be equally propitious. But only for me, not for Celia. I ponder this sometimes. In encounters with other people I have always come out the winner. There is nothing in my past life which I would like to alter if I were given a second chance. The cost of such victory has been suffering and pain for others. Can this be entirely accidental? Or am I really the 'callous and selfish bastard' Celia described me to be? I wonder.

One evening I went out drinking by myself. Celia and I were drifting further apart every day. Her attacks intensified, she became bitter and venomous. I just didn't know how to get hold of an abortionist. The men at work spoke very little English, the few who did were unsympathetic and distant. I had come to know some students from one of the bars near the university but they all suggested gin and a hot bath or quinine—things we had already tried, unsuccessfully. Besides, she was too far gone for any of that to work. I prayed for a miscarriage, perhaps she could fall down stairs or something. But no, Celia was a sturdy girl. Her body insisted on holding on to the foetus in her womb.

I was unhappy, achingly, miserably unhappy. I cried often in those days; at the most unexpected times tears would come rushing down my face, I would break into sobs. Alcohol only heightened the misery. But sometimes after a few drinks I could forget about Celia and get drawn into the conversation around. I wanted to escape the constant awareness of this load I was carrying. And for limited periods it worked.

I was at the student bar and it was early evening in the middle of the week. There weren't too many people and I sat alone at a table, sipping beer. Thoughts were tumbling about in my mind, incoherent images—Celia carrying a baby in her arms, a weak bony infant about to die for want of food, the Hammersmith Bridge across the Thames with me standing at the edge and then a huge eagle soaring into a blazing white sky. I tried not to let my mind fix on any one idea or image; each time it paused over Celia, I nudged it away, knocking it over into another image, another world.

There was a girl at the other end of the room, also by herself. She smiled at me and I smiled back at her. But I wasn't in that sort of mood. I stared into my beer and those thoughts started droning in my head all over again, till at last they became so insistent that I felt my skull was about to crack and my eyes explode with tears. I rushed out of the bar, relieved to breathe the clean air of the open street again. I started walking very fast, crossed a set of traffic lights, went over to the other side of the pavement, entered a tobacconist's bought a large cigar lighted it and took in a deep lungful of smoke.

'I am sorry I ran. You were walking so fast.' It was the girl from the bar. 'I couldn't bear to lose you.'

I stared at her blankly.

'It was your eyes,' she said softly. 'There was so much pain in them. And so much strength.'

She put her arm through mine and edged me forward. We began walking very slowly. For a long time she was silent.

I didn't know where she was leading me. From the side of my eyes I looked at her long blonde hair grazing my shoulder. She wore a large ear-ring on her right lobe and her face had no make-up. Her lips were soft, pouting, the lower one turned gently outward.

'Let's go and sit in the park,' she said at last.

Silently I obeyed.

'I have been looking for you for a long time. I knew it had to be you the moment you looked up at me. I watched you as you came into the bar, how you sat down, the way you had your hand on your forehead. And then you dug your eyes into your beer. You needed me just then and you need me just now.' She held my hand in her lap. 'Your eyes say so much. I haven't heard your voice but I know what you want to say. I feel I have known you all my life. You are my child my lover and my father. There can be no one else. Only you.'

Was I dreaming all this? Or was she mad? How old could she be? Twenty, twenty-one? Spoke English very well, must have lived in London for a while.

'Names don't matter. Don't tell me yours and I won't tell you mine.' A few drops of rain fell on her face, the sun had turned pale, the light mellow. Birds started to chirp softly in the trees. 'It's not as impossible as you think.'

How does she know what I think? I hadn't uttered a word; for all she knew I could be a deaf-mute. Or French or Arab; I might not have understood a single solitary syllable of what she had said.

'When something like this happens, you don't need to explain. I know, I know what you feel, why you want to cry.

Why you want to hold someone close, someone warm and loving and tender. You need to open yourself, let the tears gush down your façe. There is a way of touching someone that is almost invisible. I am touching you now. Come to me, I want you to come to me.'

Then she leaned over and kissed my eyes.

'You don't have to cry any more, you don't *want* to cry any more. I am with you, don't you see?'

Perhaps there *was* a way of touching people that is almost invisible but I hadn't experienced it for a long time. Not with Celia, anyway. The girl started reciting Eliot, not the ones in anthologies—'Prufrock' or 'Preludes' or even 'The Wasteland'.

'So I would have had him leave

So I would have had her stand and grieve . . . .'

'La Figlia che Piange', and it was my favourite Eliot poem too. I took her in my arms and kissed her. 'You see . . . ?' she said. I nodded.

'When I was young, very young in fact, about ten, there was a boy who lived next door. He was older than I, tall and very strong. We would often walk in the forest, hold hands and kiss . . . . He kissed so well. I wanted to marry him and have his babies. I knew all about sex. Mother had many lovers. I would see them walk about in the kitchen, nude. One morning I saw a man on top of my mother in bed, moving so fast I thought he was trying to strangle her. I screamed and Mother jumped out of bed and hit me on the face and told me to go back to my room. I was six. I cried all day.'

'What happened to your father?' I asked. 'Didn't he ever come to see you?'

She smiled. 'I don't know if Mother was ever married. Anyway, she said that he had been killed in the war.'

I held her close and kissed her again. 'You poor thing,' I whispered.

'No, I am not. Not when you are with me. I love you, I am going to give you all my love till you choke. We'll always be together, every single minute of our lives you and I will be together . . . .'

It was a narcotic haze, the words of the girl pouring over me, as if they came from fairyland, far away, out of the reach of ordinary mortals. The evening had ripened into dusk, about to slip into night. The birds had stopped chirping, there was an instant pulse of cold in the air. Misty.

'This boy took me to the forest one day. It was November. I had my boots on. The ground was hard, snow had caked into ice. He kissed me and held me close in his arms. Then he took my hand and put it on his zip. I looked up at his eyes and felt a sharp quiver run down my spine. He took it out and I gazed at it with a kind of horror. Yet I was curious. I remembered the man on top of my mother. I didn't want that, I didn't want to be strangled. But I wanted to know what would happen . . . . His thing was hard, I was playing with it, he was kissing me. Then suddenly he threw me on the ground and I screamed. He tore down my pants and drew my legs apart and pushed it in. All in one go . . . . I have never felt so much pain. The whole thing was inside me, like a rasp, hurting and burning. It couldn't have been more than a minute. He took it out, stood up and zipped himself and ran.'

Tears were trickling down her face. I wiped them away and kissed her eyes.

'I couldn't scream or shout. Tears, endless tears, just ran, on and on. I must have fallen asleep. Early next morning, the woman from across the street—I used to call her Granny—found me lying there under the tree, unconcicious. A few more hours and . . . There must have been a lot of blood, even my skirt was stained. But I never told them who it was.'

We sat there in the park—I don't know how long—quite silent. Then it got cold, the raindrops heavier.

'You want me, don't you?' she asked.

'Yes,' I replied.

Suddenly the tone of her voice changed. 'Well, we'll have to go to the railway station. I've got my bags there. I was supposed to leave for Helsinki tonight.'

Startled, I asked, 'Don't you live in Copenhagen? Aren't you Danish?'

'No, I am Finnish. I study at the Film School in Helsinki.'

'Then how . . . ?'

'Sh . . . sh . . . No questions.'

We came out of the park and into the street. She hailed a cab, we got in and she asked the driver—in Danish—to drive us to the station. When we got there she insisted on paying. I could see she was carrying a fair amount of money. Things had happened with such speed and in such a dreamlike way that I had lost focus. 'How old are you?' I asked, as we got her bags out of the luggage room.

'Sixteen,' she replied firmly and smiled. 'Shall we have a drink or shall I book into a hotel first?'

'Whichever you prefer,' I answered.

The place was within walking distance of the station, a single room for eighteen kroner a night. Things weren't quite adding up, though. The facts, the words she spoke, buzzed in my head as if I had taken an overdose of asprin. She wanted to spend the rest of her life with me, in fact every minute of it, yet she hadn't asked to come back to my place. Instead, she had booked in at an hotel. And she was carrying a lot of money. She was at school in Helsinki and she was sixteen. Her mother had many lovers, she had been raped at ten and she loved my eyes. Knew Eliot, spoke English fluently and there was a silent air of authority about her. But where was the missing piece in the puzzle?

When we were alone in the room she wouldn't let me feel her breasts or draw her down on the bed. 'I don't want to go back to the student bar. Let's go somewhere near here.'

'As you wish,' I said, following her out of the room.

'Are you unhappy with your wife?' she asked, as we settled down with two large Schnapps.

'I am not married. Why? Do I look as if I am?'

She burst out laughing.

'Look, this has gone far enough. What's the game?'

'No game at all,' the girl answered. 'I am going to marry you that's all.'

'Really?'

'Hm . . . hm . . .'

We drank silently for a while.

'You see, I know all about you. But you don't know a thing about me. Not even my name.'

'That's easily settled. Let's have a look at your passport.'

'No, that would be too easy.'

I got another round of drinks and sighed, 'I give up.'

She smiled and drew me towards her. I was beginning to

feel trapped, the girl had cast a spell and I was moving around as if I was under remote control. I tried to shake myself free, but her eyes unnerved me. She looked hard and long, without a flicker. Her pouting lips led me to think of her nude and in bed. The rape scene, as she had described it, excited me instead of provoking pity. I wanted her. Wanted to ram it inside her just as the boy had done, without preliminaries, without even a kiss.

Just then her left hand moved over my thigh and rested on my groin, pressing down. My prick stood up, aching. 'Can I have another drink?' she said, smiling and moving her hand away.

'Sure, sure,' I replied, nodding vigorously, as if I was the one who had been caught out. 'Anything you like.'

'A brandy this time. I always used to drink brandies in London.'

I went to the bar, fetched two brandies back to the table and waited for her next move.

'What would you want in a wife?'

'Nothing. I mean, I hadn't thought . . . '

'Well, think!'

I was going to get back at her this time. I would even out the score. 'Whatever else it is, I certainly don't want her to be Finnish, studying in the Film School in Helsinki and only sixteen years old. And I don't want her to be so bloody mysterious.'

She broke into a laugh, hoarse, condescending, not at all gentle.

'That's it,' I shouted, getting up. 'I am going.'

'Where?' she asked, calmly, without making the smallest attempt to stop me.

'Home,' I replied, waiting.

We stared at each other for a while.

'All right,' she said at last. 'Let's both go home, to my hotel I mean.'

I had been outdone, she had won. On the way back, the girl put her arm through mine, just as she had done on the street when I had first met her hours ago. 'You are a sweet little baby, aren't you?'

We had to sneak past the porter as she had taken a single room. Once past that hurdle, she relaxed and reverted to her soft gentle self. She helped me off with my coat, took off my shoes and sat me down on the only chair there was in the room. Then she opened her suitcase, took out a bottle of cognac and poured out two large glasses of the burning stuff.

'Cheers,' I said, raising mine.

'Cheers,' she smiled back in reply.

She undressed slowly, watching herself in the mirror. Two small tight breasts appeared in view and then the rest of her sinuous body. I shot up from the chair and tried to take her in my arms, but she drew away. The drinks had to be finished first and then I too would have to undress before the mirror. She was obviously calling the tune, so I obeyed. When the ceremony was completed, she switched on the bed lamp and turned off the main light.

'Be gentle with me,' she whispered, as we slid under the covers.

There was a slow soft warmth in her body which spread to mine. Our skins grazed for a long while before the crack between her thighs was moist enough to let me in. And when it was, the pressure of the warm walls around my stiffened prick was of a kind I had never experienced before. It was tight and hard one moment and all loose and flabby the next.

'Slow, very slow, there is no hurry.'

She would not let me move fast, each stroke had to last several seconds. And when I could no longer hold myself, she sensed it and drew away from me, waiting till I had dropped back to a lower pitch. I don't know how long it was but it was dawn when we finally came, together, with sharp, almost epileptic spasms in her case and a thin searing spurt in mine. We swooned off to sleep, with me still inside her.

I woke up at nine and was late for work. She opened her eyes and said, 'You are beautiful.' I kissed her again, dressed and hurried out of the room, arranging to meet her at six that evening. All through the day I was torn. Guilty about Celia, yet fascinated and drenched with a new hope about this mysterious girl. I had never spent a night away from Celia and she would know. I tried to console myself by ringing her up at work but she refused to answer the phone. Served me right, I thought, for being such a bastard. Yet what should I do? I wasn't happy with Celia, she wasn't happy with me. Should I give up happiness with this delicious, voluptuous Finnish wonder for . . . ? But Celia was carrying my baby. I couldn't abandon her. After the abortion perhaps. But until then . . . ? If this girl really lived in Helsinki, there wasn't a chance in any case, was there?

All my doubts were set to rest that evening when I went back to the hotel. The girl had checked out at midday, leaving no note or forwarding address. The name she had signed in the register was Candy Floss.

By the time I got hold of an abortionist Celia was over four months pregnant. Her breasts were hard and swollen, belly protruding. She was still going to work, still managed to do the household chores and cook a meal in the evening. But she hardly ever spoke, either to me or to any one of our friends who would turn up at the flat. At night she slid away from me to the far side of the bed; she would not let me kiss or caress her body, let alone . . . I did not know how to heal the breach and resented her unspoken censure. I was not alone in this, I had not brought it about all by myself. Why should I take all the blame?

It happened on a Saturday afternoon. I had cleaned the flat, washed out the bathtub. The large dining table had been overlaid with cushions and a rubber cloth. The reading lamp, which swung out of the wall, was poised directly over the makeshift operating table. Celia was obviously nervous, so was I. For the first time in many weeks she came up to me and put her head on my shoulder. I stroked her cheeks and there were tears in her eyes. We cried together for a while.

The man arrived punctually at four in the afternoon. He said he would want a large bowl of boiling water and two clean towels. Celia went into the kitchen to get things ready, the quack and I sat in the drawing room. He carried a large bag of tools in his hand and appeared as nervous as the two of us. He would not sit down but kept darting glances at various objects in the room. Finally his eyes alighted upon the bottle of brandy. Pointing his finger at it, as if it were a rare anthropological specimen, he said he would like a glass and could I give one to the lady too? I responded to the idea with relish, brought out three glasses and poured large doses in each. The man gulped down his share in a single swig; when Celia came into the room I handed her the glass and she did the same, with the same defiant lack of ceremony. I lifted the brandy to my lips and said, 'Skol', and took a sip. The two of them reciprocated the gesture with empty glasses in their hands.

The quack went into the next room, Celia followed. As I was about to enter, he shook his finger at me—I wasn't going to be admitted. The door was bolted from the inside, I stood outside with the glass of brandy in my hand. Suddenly my whole body went very cold; my feet, my hands, even my stomach, gave a turn, as if shivering from a wintry blast. Only my face glowed with heat, my ears burned and there were beads of sweat on my brow. I too swilled the brandy down in a single gulp.

I have never felt so frightened, alone and impotent, as I did just then. There was nothing I could do, could not even be with her when it happened. I had no idea what abortionists do, what the whole thing leads up to. Would she die? I had heard it was dangerous, especially so late in the pregnancy. What could happen? Would it hurt very much? Was it an operation? How did they go about it?

I knelt down and peered into the keyhole. Celia was lying on the table, with her face away from the door. She was fully clothed, only her skirt was drawn up above her waist, her pants lay on the floor. She had raised her knees and the man went up to her and parted them wide. I could scream when he did that. It was such an affront. I did not want to see any more, I was shaking all over. I don't know quite what I expected, perhaps a rape or worse. Perhaps Celia would scream and I would break the door and rush in and rescue her. Slowly I walked back to the next room, mesmerically I poured some more brandy into the glass and stoppered the bottle. But before I had taken a single sip the two of them bustled into the room, Celia smiling and jovial, the quack a bit drawn and creased on the brow.

'What's the matter? Couldn't he . . . ? I mean, isn't he going to do it?' I asked Celia.

'Of course, he's done it. It's finished,' she replied, walking towards the bottle.

'Finished? You mean you've had the abortion?'

'Don't be silly,' Celia said, laughing. 'The man isn't a magician.'

'Then what? How is it finished?'

Celia turned and smiled at the quack. They seemed to have entered into a conspiracy between them. Perhaps he had a quick fuck, perhaps he wasn't a doctor at all. What was going on here? Was I being taken for a ride? I had already paid him the money, couldn't very well take it back from him now, could I? Besides, he was a good deal taller than I and heavier.

The man gave her an envelope, went into the bathroom, washed his hands and was out of the flat in a couple of minutes. I picked up the envelope and there was an address on it along with a stamp.

'What's this for?' I asked.

Celia came up and drew me to her. 'You're a perfect innocent, aren't you, Amit?'

'Well, I don't know about that. But I really would like you to explain what went on in there? Why wouldn't he let me in? Was he being funny with you or something?'

She burst into a laugh, of a kind I had not heard from her for a long time. 'Is that what's been worrying you, poor little darling?'

'As a matter of fact, yes! And I don't see what you're so bouncy about.'

Celia's face clouded, suddenly there were tears in her eyes. 'Take me to bed, Amit, and hold me close.'

Almost instantly we were in each other's arms, all these weeks of separation dropped away, and I kissed her just as I had done on that first night in Earls Court. 'I love you, Amit,' Celia said.

The pains started at about nine in the evening, in short spasms lasting for a couple of minutes at first, separated by intervals of a quarter of an hour. Then the spasms grew longer, the intervals shorter. Celia clung to me, her face twisted with pain and fright, for neither of us knew what was in store. It was as much a fear of the unknown, the exaggerated horror born of ignorance, as the response to those sudden thrusts in her belly, the kicking of an unborn foetus drained of life before its time.

Perhaps it was an hour, perhaps longer. Celia rushed into the bathroom and bolted the door. For a while no sound emerged. I stood outside frozen as a statue. Then she began sobbing, there was the sound of running water. When she came out, her face looked old, her eyes were swollen and red. 'Don't go in there,' Celia said, walking past me into the bedroom. I didn't know what had happened. Was it all over? Did she . . . ? I was curious. So I walked in. And saw . . .

There was blood everywhere, on the floor, in the commode, bath and basin. Thick globs of dark-red jelly, bits of pink flesh where the water had washed away the blood. The smell was sharp, not like that in a hospital at all. But acrid, hurting. I leaned over the basin and threw up. Then for a while I stood there staring, my eyes moving from one spot to another. The blood had begun to cake in places, on the edge of the basin, on the bath tap. Coagulated lumps of jelly sat like pimples over the smooth slimy skin of scarlet blood that covered the floor.

I had no feelings, not any that I can remember anyway. I cleaned up the mess, putting the larger lumps into a washing bowl and throwing it down the incinerator shaft. I think I saw one little finger, about half an inch long, but I am not sure. When I had finished there were still spots here and there (perhaps they are still there), but I couldn't be bothered. Celia was asleep when I came back to the bedroom. I slid into bed with her and she put her arms round me, instinctively. I was too dazed to cry. I lay awake the whole night, waiting for her to open her eyes.

For the next three weeks we loved each other more intensely and obsessively than we ever had done before. But I knew that we had come to the end of this particular road. The happiness we experienced, the ecstasy of belonging wholly to one other person because there is no one else, because no one else knows and has shared the pain, the happiness and that ecstasy was suffused with hurt and a suffocating sadness. Those opposites lived with us like twins. When the twins were parted, when the memory of that agony was no longer immediate and sharp, and the hurt ceased to hurt as much, the happiness and the ecstasy went their way as well. What had held us so close together was the pain.

When the pain was diluted by time and conscious suppression, we became strangers, shy and awkward, as if each of us had been caught out by the other in a private act which no one else should have witnessed.

I don't want to detail the disintegration of our affair (perhaps because I can't) as there was no single point or event over which the break-up took place. It was a gentle drawing away, like the withering of an unwatered plant. In the last days Celia and I hardly ever talked with each other. When the time came I saw her off as she left for London, promising to see her again, soon. But both of us knew it was over and nothing we could do would ever stick the pieces together again.

Celia never went out with a man for two years after that. And when I returned to London, and met her accidentally on the street one day and asked her to have a drink with me, she screamed, drew the attention of two passing policeman to us, accused me of 'molesting' her, denied that she had ever known me before, and had me arrested.

After Celia left Copenhagen my period of sexual emancipation began. I stayed on for another three months, earned a lot of money (tax-free) and slept with twenty-five (or was it twenty-seven?) girls in that time. There is nothing I remember about Denmark, after Celia's departure, which is not in some way connected with sex. I formed no emotional attachments (though some of the women did to me), did not develop any male friends, gained no particular insight into 'the human condition', did not bother either to read or write, nor 'better' myself in any other way.

I did discover that I was considered attractive (very, by some), that dark hair and large brown eyes were a prize asset in Scandinavia, that women can and do take the initiative in the sex game, that failure to get an erection or ejaculating ten seconds after entrance does not kill your chances for ever. I learnt that sex was a commodity you could barter, that romance did not always enter into it, that women are just as capable of responding to the wholly mechanical and lustful aspects as men normally profess to do. I realized that in a bored and affluent society the need to seek variations on the sexual theme becomes obsessive, that marriages can and do last without the adhesive of sexual fidelity, that the act of copulation can be devalued and made unsacred by conciously adopting an anti-Puritan intellectual framework of morality and ethics. I suppose I could have picked up all this from books and none of it is either original or startling. But it is always better to 'experience' a thing directly, draw your own conclusions from the data you accumulate (even if the same conclusions have been drawn by scores of other people before you came along), rather than pick it up second-hand from the volumes that stack the library shelves. For perhaps there is going to be just that one experience, which no one else has had before you, which may be worth all the bother.

I got the sack from the factory, for arriving three hours late for work, two weeks before Christmas. The 'authorities' were informed, and I received a telegram ordering me to appear at the Danish equivalent of the Home Office the next day. Did I have any money, could I show my bank statement? Yes, I could, and did. It was duly computed that, after paying my rent, I would have a little over forty kroner left. (Obviously I had not saved any money.) If I did not produce evidence of financial viability I would be 'requested' to leave the country within twenty-four hours (after the deadline).

No money and an expulsion order! Train fare, pocket expenses and food? I had friends at work, a whole contingent of foreigners, who were also about to leave the country. Volitionally, that is. They would be going down to Spain. I could join them there said they. But how would I get to Barcelona? It was cold, ten degrees below zero in Copenhagen; on the Continent it would be warmer, of course, but how about the journey? Why hadn't I bought a coat? Simply because I never felt the need for it.

A Dutch boy who was evading military service said there was a nightclub in the centre of town where there were 'rich pickings'. Why didn't I go there? I still had two days, after all, to demonstrate my 'financial viability'. 'With your looks, you're sure to succeed,' he suggested. I discovered later that he was queer, which was why he lent me 200 kroner before I did actually leave. But I wasn't to know at the time.

It was Friday evening. I had a shave, daubed my cheeks with cologne and put on my suit. The club was near the Tivoli, cars drove in up to the porch, men and women in evening dress and fur coats slid out of leather seats, and the doormen took charge of parking the vehicles. I entered the premises without any soaring optimism. The lights were low, there was a brass band playing in the corner, the bar was moderately crowded with single gents. I asked for a table. The manager escorted me to an empty spot, a waiter pulled out the chair for me, smiled obsequiously as I seated myself and briskly thrust a menu into my hand. What would

I like to begin with, they had excellent snails for starters. No, not really, I wasn't going to have a meal, thank you. A drink perhaps, in that case. I gave a quick glance down the right-hand edge, the cheapest was fifteen kroner. I could only afford two, if this was going rate. Perhaps it was cheaper at the bar, I thought. But single ladies don't generally sit at counters in a place like this. And you couldn't really send over a drink from the bar, could you now? Besides, I had already sat down, ensconced in plush leather cushions, and there was a couple next door—the woman had flung a fleeting smile at me. So I thought I would dare. 'Yes,' I said, 'I would like a Scotch with plenty of soda in it.' The waiter bowed away and I was left to my stares.

The drink arrived, I took a sip and looked around. There were no single ladies in sight. Too early in the evening perhaps. or was it one of those places where people come only in pairs? Perhaps my Dutch friend was wrong, perhaps it was all a myth, a reputation based on the fantasy of starving aliens! Damn, blast! And fifteen kroner down the drain too! No, I was obviously not going to have another drink here, make this one last out as long as I could. I was not going to squander the remainder of my earthly fortunes on a swindle. While sipping my Scotch I would adopt an attitude of philosophic resignation, hope for the best, and then leave with as much dignity as I could muster. Perhaps I could even pick up something from one of the student bars and console myself with an animated hot-water bottle in bed for the night. What the hell!

Meanwhile the smiles from m'lady next door increased in frequency, the whisky began to take effect on an empty stomach, my cheeks burned. I must not lose sight of my original resolve, I reminded myself. I am here to find myself a 'rich picking', not to tease middle-aged ladies (and anything above thirty was middleage to me) into amorous states for the benefit of their spouses. Besides, I was simply not in that league. The man was at least thirty-five, if a day. He was suave, assured and handsome in his black tie. No, look elsewhere, young man, don't try to climb beyond your station.

The man waved to the waiter and whispered a few words. The garcon bowed, looking in my direction. Would I care to have a drink on the gentleman at the next table? Er . . . well . . . There was an ice bucket on the table with a bottle in it; the glasses in their hands were wide-rimmed and flat-chested, the liquid was fizzy. Obviously champagne. I recollected that a glass of champagne was priced at twenty kroner on the menu. At that rate how damn much was a full bottle?

The man noticed my hesitation, so did m'lady. And both of them beamed large full-bodied smiles at my tormented face. And, of course, by this time the waiter had disappeared from view, leaving no target at which I could throw my refusal. I was really and truly in for it this time. But what the hell, life was for living, wasn't it? I nodded to both Monsieur and Madame and returned their smiles with as effusive an oracular expansion as I could decently afford.

The waiter returned with a glass, filled it from the bottle at the next table and brought it over to mine. I raised the glass and said, 'Skol.' Monsieur and Madame did the same. Of course, we could not hear the word above the din of the music. But the lips had moved, Madame's more daringly than ever. Her eyes shone too, and I think she turned a slight angle in her seat to give me a better view of her half-exposed bosom. What was going on here, what would her husband say? (As a matter of fact the husband seemed blissfully unaware of his wife's treacherous glances, for his face did not show the least sign of discomfiture or rage.) I suppose they are just being nice to a foreigner (an Indian at that), I told myself. I shouldn't read lascivious intentions into gestures where none may be intended. Why couldn't I just accept a friendly overture, without colouring it with the lurid hues of sex? You have a dirty, one-track mind, Mr Ray, that's your trouble. Well! Meanwhile, here's to the queen of inebriating fluids.'Skol.'

Three sips of champagne (the whisky remaining half-intact), embarrassed aversion of glances from my side and repeated raising of glasses from the other. I was getting nowhere with my mission. Instead I was getting enmeshed in a situation which could only lead to embarrassment, perhaps worse. Take hold of yourself, Ray. This champagne stuff has always been a bad omen for you. Remember Rome. Yes, but every day is not Sunday. And Madame down there was no common tart either. You could see it from the clothes she wore, the way she held her glass, yes, and even the way she smiled. Warm and gentle, it was. Sensuous. That's it. She had a sensuous smile, not a whorish one at all. Besides, she was escorted, and this was no cheap pick-up joint either. It was the most sophisticated nightclub in Copenhagen. No, really, I had nothing to worry about, working myself up into a useless frenzy, I was.

Then she smiled again. This time there was no raising of the glass, just that long sensuous smile. I looked at Monsieur, his face was focussed in a different direction. No, he hadn't taken in that smile at all. Yes, I thought I could safely return her the compliment. So I smiled back. No sooner had I done so, she nodded, beckoning me to come and join them at the table. She touched her husband's arm, he looked at me and signified with his hand what she had done with her look. This was what used to be called, 'Invitation to a Beheading'. No, no, not quite, just an ordinary 'Invitation to a Beluting'.

I held the table with two steady hands, levered myself on to my feet, picked up the glass and strode purposefully towards Destiny. Introductions were completed (yes, they were man and wife), I sat down, some more champagne was poured into my glass, 'Skols' were exchanged, and the couple eased back in their chairs while I perched precariously at the very edge of mine, waiting for the thunder to break.

The man, like all educated Danes, spoke fluent English (if slightly accented). So did Madame. Polite conversation began. Had I been in Copenhagen long, where did I come from, how did I like Denmark, how much longer was I planning to stay, etc., etc. While going through the ritual, thoughts droned in my head. All hopes of a 'rich picking' dashed; fifteen kroner incinerated, with the blasted whisky not even fully consumed; the certainty of an embarrassing end to the evening (when the two of them would discover how ill-mannered I had been in accepting hospitality which I could not possibly reciprocate).

'You like dancing?' Madame enquired.

'Well, as a matter of fact . . . ' I noticed for the first time that there were couples on the floor and the music was 'swinging'.

'If you would like to dance with my wife . . . ' the man offered.

Madame got up from her seat, I offered my arm, we walked to the floor. Almost before we had begun, the music stopped. I wondered if I should lead her back to the table, when she smiled at me again. 'You have not come here before?'

'No,' I replied, shaking my head vigorously.

'It is nice, you will like it.' And then that smile again.

Look, I am not a brass statue, and I have had two glasses of champagne and half a whisky on an empty stomach. And this woman in my arms is no ugly duckling either. Middle-aged or no, she has the most gorgeous breasts, from what I can see of them. The music has changed into something soft, and she is holding me close, very close in fact. If she gets any closer, she will feel it. Damn her! Why in heaven's name should it rise up just now . . . ? Because I am not a brass statue, that's why. And there's that strong hefty husband of hers, sitting there at that table. Do you think he hasn't got any eyes? Do you really believe that he can't see her breasts pressed against your bloody chest? And oh, my God, what is happening? She is rubbing herself against it. Look, I can't really, I mean another minute of this, and I think it will shoot out. Fortunately, I am wearing underpants. Fortunately, her cheeks are rubbing against mine; fortunately, I can smell her perfume; fortunately, her hand is playing with my left ear; fortunately . . . Yes, very fortunately, the music has stopped.

Her arm was still around me, gently holding me by the waist. 'Hadn't we better go back to the table?'

'Why, don't you like dancing with me?'

'Yes, but . . . I mean, your husband . . . '

'Ladies do not always have to dance with their husbands, you know.'

The music started again. Well, I decided, this time I am going to take no chances, keep her firmly at arm's length, I mean at least six inches from the nearest point below my waist. Even if he was to inspect us through a pair of binoculars he would find no incriminating evidence, not from my side anyway. I couldn't really prevent the top parts of our anatomy from coming into contact, girls were much better equipped to do that sort of thing, just because it is the man who leads. But elsewhere . . . Right! I mean, any pressure from her side, and I would draw away, make my gesture without the slightest trace of ambiguity.

'Don't you like dancing with me? Do you not find me attractive?'

'Of course I do, but your husband . . . '

'Why worry about my husband? We are dancing here and we both like it . . . . ' That smile again.

'Well, look, if we are really going to dance like this, let's get a bit further away, to that corner behind that pillar.'

'If you like,' she replied, and laughed.

'It may be fun for you, but I don't want to be shot in the head or taken to court for enticement.'

This time she exploded with laughter. 'Danish law is not so uncivilized.'

I kept a serious face, while the music swayed her body against mine, sinuously fitting into curves and crevices. Her hands played with the nape of my neck, my hair and my ears. My prick stood in perpetual attention, while slowly, very slowly, I began to feel an ache in my balls. It was sheer muscular tension, trying to keep myself from ejaculating into my pants.

We did finally get back to the table. Monsieur got up from his seat, helped Madame into her chair, sat down again and topped up my glass. I preserved a fixed grin on my face, directing it mostly at him. Any moment now, I thought, there will be an offer of a duel or worse. He must have seen what was going on. I mean a husband simply could not be expected to tolerate this kind of thing, not in public anyway, in open view of the entire universe.

'Excuse me,' he said, a few minutes later, getting up. Well, here it comes, my heart pounded out the message to my brain. 'I must go to the bathroom.' Oh my God, what blessed relief, saved by a bursting bladder. My eyes trailed him all the way to the end of the room till he turned right and vanished from view. Her hand meanwhile had come to rest on my knee.

'Did you not like dançing with me?'

'Of course, but you really should be more careful. When we were on this side of the floor he could see everything.' She smiled and moved her hand further up. 'Look, please, I mean I really don't want to get you in trouble. And I would not relish being in any kind of mess myself either.'

'It is all right,' she said, continuing to stroke me, 'we may go to the other side. That will be safe. Come on.'

I suppose it's better than his coming back and finding his wife's hand on my crotch. Reckless woman this, quite, quite dangerous.

We were on the floor for nearly twenty minutes. The same sort of twisting and writhing went on as before. Her body, under the smooth velvet dress, yielded at every point to the gentlest pressure from my hands. Her fingers caressed my face and her perfume stimulated my olfactory nerves to the point of reckless abandon. When we returned to the table Monsieur was not to be seen.

I was mildly relieved. 'Takes a long time to crap, that man,' told myself. 'Must be suffering from the trots.'

Then Madame waved to the waiter, the empty champagne bottle was removed and an unstoppered one was on its way. The smoke from a not-too-distant fire became visible, my psyche began to rumble and alarm set in. Who was to pay the bill if Monsieur absented himself for the rest of the evening?

'You like champagne, no?' Madame queried, smiling.

'Yes, yes, I do . . . but . . . '

'It makes me feel like a young girl. Not like any other drink. It is so good to dance with champagne.'

True, all too true. But not so good to have to pay for two bottles of the stuff with forty kroner in one's pocket. After two more glasses of the bubbly inside me I forgot about Monsieur, my expulsion order, the grotesque fantasy of an unpayable bill, and I held her close, kissed her lips, wove my arm round her waist and caressed the small of her back. She clung to me, light, soft and sinuous. Her mouth melted on mine, her fingers crept up my neck and down again, raising hairs on my pores and tightening the strings to concert pitch. There was to be music.

'Where is your husband?'

'Are you afraid he will come back?'

'No, as a matter of fact, I was wondering . . . I mean, this place doesn't remain open all night and we can't go on drinking champagne for ever. Can we?'

She smiled. 'We can go back to my place if you like.'

'What? Don't you live with your husband then?' *What The Thunder Said*. What did it say? It said that I had been hooked once again, that Madame was a tart, that Monsieur was a ponce, that they were both getting a cut from the champagne, that I had compounded the felony of my pauperism with a bill which would be no less than 350 kroner, which, moreover, I couldn't pay. And to think that I had come here for a 'rich picking'.

'I have to go to the loo . . . I mean the gents.'

She held my arm firmly. 'You want to run away, no?' That smile again.

Madame beckoned the waiter once again, the bill arrived, she took out her purse and placed four crisp hundred-kroner notes on the table, got up from her seat and said, 'Come on, let us go. You can use the toilet in my house.'

We got into one of those small Triumph Heralds—flashy little things they seemed to me in those days. 'I would let you drive, but there is ice on the roads and you do not know the way. Normally, I like a man to drive.'

We arrived at an expensive suburb of Copenhagen (I have forgotten the name of the area), got into the lift, pressed the button for the eighteenth floor, emerged into a lengthy corridor and finally entered the most luxurious apartment that I had seen till then. Yes, Monsieur was indeed her husband, there was his picture on the piano. Besides, the place did not look as if it belonged to a scarlet woman. Very much a domesticated household, married, happy and cluttered with children's photographs.

'Make yourself a drink, the bar is on the other side of the kitchen. If there is no ice in the bucket, you will find some in the refrigerator.' She came over and kissed me on the cheek. 'I must change into something less . . . what do you call it? Less impressionistic . . . eh?'

'Please do,' I replied, resembling those legendary pillars of salt, my feet welded to the rug in the middle of the sitting room.

Madame disappeared into the bedroom; I looked around, transfixed. There was a large canvas on the wall, with gleaming strokes of red shooting diagonally across. It resembled a face, contorted, vicious and magnetic. A small plastic plaque, fixed at the bottom of the frame, carried the words, 'The Mistress'; the painting was signed—perhaps Monsieur, perhaps Madame, I couldn't tell.

'Would you like some music?' she asked, as she emerged in a silk kimono with transparent sleeves. 'I see you haven't got the drinks.'

'I am sorry . . . I was . . . just . . . looking around.'

'There is a lot of time for that,' she said, walking into the kitchen. I followed her. 'Why do you look so frightened? As if you had been kidnapped?'

'No, no, I mean . . . '

'You can go if you like. I could ask for a taxi.'

I took her in my arms and kissed her. There was a lascivious glow in her eyes; made me feel as if I had never seen a woman before in my life. I was not excited any more, my body was no longer taut. There was warmth there, as if one had just come out of a long hot bath.

We talked until five in the morning and then went to bed.

She had been married for eight years, had three children; the youngest one spent the weekends with her mother, the other two were in school. Her husband had a mistress, whom he went to see every fortnight. They had come to an 'arrangement'. He wouldn't let her have regular affairs; he also wanted to see the men with whom she went to bed. It suited her fine. She loved her husband, he was marvellous in bed, and he loved her too. Occasionally, she liked to make him jealous; he was so much better at love-making when he was jealous. He could go on for hours, seldom saying a word, his face knotted up, almost hateful. And then in the morning she would put him out of his misery. They would make love again but this time it would be much more relaxed, not as it was in the night; she belonged to him again.

'I liked the look in your eye,' she whispered, as I entered her, 'I knew you would be sexy.'

She was moist, warm and tight. I could not hold myself for more than a minute.

She smiled. 'It is better this way, you will not be so tense the next time.' She stroked my face running her fingers down the inside of my neck and over my chest, stopping just below my navel and then starting the journey from the top again. After a while she wove her legs around mine, caressed my thighs and the small of my back and the crevice between my buttocks. I wanted her to touch me, feel my penis and my balls. But her fingers skirted round, never pausing, never going far enough. In less than fifteen minutes I was hard again.

All that happened then was my initiation into the technology of sex and I was abjectly grateful to Madame for the lessons she gave me. The information and the experience took a long time to digest but at least I was no longer a novice. When I left the apartment on Sunday afternoon at five (Monsieur was due back at seven) Madame inserted two hundred-kroner notes into my trouser pocket and gave my balls one last squeeze while doing so. It was the only time in my life when I was actually *paid* in cash for 'fucking'.

I produced proof of my 'financial viability' the next day. The Dutch boy lent me 200 kroner, on the understanding that I would meet him in Barcelona in ten days' time. I took a train from Copenhagen to Eindhoven in Holland and from there to Paris. I changed the plane ticket (for Calcutta) to include the Paris-Barcelona journey. I stayed in Spain for three weeks in a small pension and then decided to return to London. I wanted to see Celia again (at least that was the ostensible reason I gave myself), wanted to try the 'London scene' once more. The Dutch boy made his amorous feelings for me quite clear on the first evening we spent together.

'Sorry,' I said, 'I wish I could reciprocate but really . . . '

'Why don't you give it a try?' he insisted.

'Someday perhaps,' I replied, 'but not yet, not now.'

SIX

~

LONDON STOP TWO

I arrived in London with the (by now) proverbial five pounds in my pocket. I had been away for nearly two years and most of my acquaintances in Earls Court had moved. Stanley had got married and migrated to South Africa; Sean had vanished from the scene; Sally was pregnant, unmarried and had started living with her parents. I knew I wouldn't get such a hot reception from Celia; she was not in London, anyway. By the time I had looked up all the possible contacts it was nine o'clock in the evening. Though I wasn't a pauper and could still hope to dig up another kind Polish landlady, my 'situation' wasn't exactly enticing. I decided to retire into the saloon bar of a public house, determined this time not to order a pint of Scotch.

Of course, there was one other telephone number I had on my list. And after the third Scotch I thought I would try my luck, without much hope of success. The number provided connection with an Australian, whom I had met in Copenhagen and who had worked in the factory for a few weeks. I had written two letters to him, principally because he had written to me first and I believed in returning courtesy for courtesy. He was a half-groomed architect and I was sure he would be living in a flat (instead of the sort of miserable cavern which I called 'my room' in Earls Court). I was not so sure about the rate at which addresses seemed to change for 'fringers' like myself and my so-called friends.

But I tapped luck, for once. He was home and, what was more to the point, he had bought a car and would be picking me up in half an hour. Leisurely I went on sipping my Scotch, contemplating an uncertain future with the resignation that comes only to those who have nothing to lose. I had done a few things since I left India but the sum of the component digits was perhaps a dubious figure. I had actually finished a book, whatever Gollancz might think about it. I had done a stint of 'down and outing' in typically Orwellian fashion, only there was no Eton to cushion the shit at the Studs Farm Long John garage. I had lived with a girl, made her pregnant, smelt the horrifying odour of an abortion. Paris was firmly on the biographical landscape and so was sex and Scandinavia. 'Not bad, Ray, not bad at all,' I told myself and ordered my fourth Scotch.

Geoffrey Burton walked in through the door, resplendent as ever, accompanied by a tall blond boy. 'How come you've popped up like this?' Geoffrey asked, after the introductions. 'Just did,' I replied, smiling. 'But let's lubricate the gullet before we go any further.' The blond friend asked for a pint, so did Geoffrey, I launched into my fifth Scotch with merry optimism. I insisted on paying for every round till closing time. By the end of the evening I was down to two pounds. But it didn't seem to matter very much. I had a bed for the night, a large volume of whisky in my stomach and this was London. What was mere money when there was a whole world waiting out there? After all, I was a genius and an artist, wasn't I? Do petty considerations like pound sterling and vitalizing comestibles ever cloud the thought of visionaries and prophets? The Bible doesn't say so, neither do I.

The name of the blond boy was, as I should have mentioned before, Iain McGuire; an Australian of Irish extraction, who worked in an air-conditioning firm in London, aged twenty and the unproud possessor of the rawest kangaroo accent I had ever allowed myself to register. Geoffrey had sensibly moved out of the Earls Court hive, reasoning that colonial conquest of one square mile of London earth was a worthwhile goal only for those who came from broken homes and were addicted to Blue Lager. The two of them shared a flat in Finsbury Park and were under the constant surveillance of Mrs Garfuncle, a noble lady of nobler proportions, who had a distinct edge over newly inducted Poles and other misdemeanours in that she had announced early in their relationship that though her name carried every note on the Yiddish scale, she herself was *not* Jewish, never had been and never would be. What she was or had been remained unrevealed throughout the six months the two boys spent in 'her house'.

I bring in Mrs Garfuncle, although her genealogy was of no particular interest to me, because on the fourth day of my tenure as an unpaying guest of my Australian friends, the self-proclaimed non-Jewish lady knocked on the door of the flat at about midday and was received by me in my pyjamas with not less than my usual courtesy. I don't think that there were any words that passed between us, save perhaps the usual Anglo-Saxon greeting from my side. Her face responded with the vehemence of psychic discovery and mystic illumination; she pounded down the stairs with as much alacrity, I suspect, as her suddenly overworked heart, which had sent that extra supply of blood up to her face.

When my friends returned from work they were stopped at the gate by the gentle woman and were informed of the apparition she had encountered 'in my house' earlier on in the day.

'Don't even have any clothes, these people,' she had exclaimed, 'and in my house, too!' How could they, two clean white boys like themselves, have a 'wog' staying in the same flat? Even if she didn't mind (which she most vehemently did—if not for anyone else's sake, then only for theirs), how could they put up with it themselves? Didn't they . . . well, didn't they feel . . . ugh? No, they would have to get rid of that thing and she would forget that the whole episode had ever occurred. After all she had *their* interests at heart and she was a forgiving spirit, if she was anything.

It is easy to argue abstractly for a cause, far tougher to stick to it in the specific. Convenience fights principle, the urge to accommodate and compromise comes into head-on clash with unflinching idealism and obdurate execution. I know that the new breed of 'liberals' would say, 'Well, it was a clear-cut case, wasn't it? She wasn't phrasing herself with any ambiguity at all. If they couldn't make her give in, there was only one thing left open to them: to get out.'

All very well when you are sitting out there reading your *New Statesman* and the *New York Review of Books*, surrounded by 'liberal' friends and progressive Jewish landladies who would even have a 'wog' at their dinner table, not to mention not objecting to his sharing a flat with their tenants. But what do you do when you are an Australian lad, rather new to London, doing a favour to an Indian you don't know very well and who, in any case, isn't going to stay with you for the remainder of his earthly life? You like the flat, it is cheap and convenient; the house is kept clean, and you generally like your landlady, except for this one quirk. I mean, which is easier? To go flat-hunting, move house and disrupt a well-organized timetable you have fallen into, for the sake of what some people choose to call 'principle'? Or ask very politely, if Amit could possibly find somewhere else to stay, taking care, of course, not to hurt his feelings, camouflaging the real reason with something about 'not being allowed to have more than two people in the flat'?

I think the answer is obvious. The easier course involved putting convenience before principle. And the whispers of Satan become strangely audible when the blasts of idealism are muffled. My Australian friends did not decide their strategy as a matter of course, I am glad to report. They would not be human if they had done so. But my own position was acutely embarrassing. If it concerned anyone else I could have argued the case with force. Since it concerned me and I was in no financial state to play the haughty wounded soul, I was forced without much conviction to play Devil's Advocate. 'After all,' I said weakly, 'she wouldn't change, even if you did move out, would she? Perhaps there's a better chance of influencing her, making her see things in a different way, if I left and you stayed on.' Perhaps the cause would be better served that way.

Iain put an end to the debate. 'Look, we're paid-up till the end of the month, and that's a week from now. She can't turn us out till then. We could take her to court if she tried. So we have a week and I'll look for a flat tomorrow. All this chundering on about it is just bullshit. We can't have her tell us who we should or should not have in the flat.'

I wonder just how bitter I would have felt if the decision had gone the other way?

A post fell vacant in the firm for which Iain McGuire worked. He said, 'Well Amit, you studied physics at university and worked for a refrigerator-manufacturing company in Denmark. Air conditioning shouldn't be all that difficult to master. Why not give it a try?' Why not indeed? I had nothing to lose. So Iain brought his technical manuals back home from the office, we sat up three nights going over them, and I appeared for the interview on the fourth day.

The theory of air conditioning was easy enough, I had learnt all that at college. It was the technical jargon, names of equipment and design, that was double-Dutch to me. But the man who interviewed me, the managing director of the firm, was a non-technical man himself, with only the most elementary idea of what the whole damn thing was about. I spoke of Oxford, my two year's experience in a refrigerator-manufacturing firm in Copenhagen, various odd jobs I had done in industry, and how I felt it was time I settled down to some really worthwhile work in a firm where I would become part of the 'family'. My accent was impeccably Oxonian, my suit carried the impress of bespoke tailoring, my hair was suitably short and I had shaved off my beard. A week after the interview the managing director telephoned me to ask whether I would care to join his firm at £1000 a year plus car and expense allowance. I said I would write to him after considering two other offers I had had. Iain returned from work and was ecstatic at having been able to find me a job.

The word had gone round the office that I had been selected, the first and only Indian in the firm. I had my doubts, wondered whether I could bluff my way through an actual job as I had done in the interview. But I accepted, of course; I had nothing to lose, even if they gave me the sack in three months' time. The irony was that Iain, who had been working in air conditioning since the age of fifteen, was earning the same amount as I had been offered.

I had no experience of office correspondence, did not know what a 'quote' meant, nor anything about 'tenders' and 'invoices'. Humidification, which was the special branch of air conditioning I had been asked to handle, was a word which meant two very dissimilar things in physics and technology. Iain was an invaluable help in those first few months. I would bring home all the work from the office, go over with him on every single detail, pore over the drawing board till late into the night, and next day I would turn out those designs and 'quotes' as if I was the most knowledgeable man in the business. I kept myself away from the other engineers in the office, even Iain, lest they discovered my fraud. When I was inadvertently drawn into a technical discussion I would deftly switch the emphasis to theory and hold forth with apparent confidence on the Second Law of Thermodynamics, etc. Everyone would be silenced, my stock would rise and they would leave me alone for another week or so.

I worked very hard for the first year. My job was to design humidification systems, advise clients on their use and then try to sell them. But it wasn't 'selling' in the door-to-door sense. It was a new thing in Britain and we held the monopoly on the equipment. Clients came to us instead of the other way round. I built up a string of contacts, all the way from directors of consulting firms and partners in architects' houses to the pin-man on the drawing board. No one 'liked' me, I was never chummy with any of my clients. But they respected me, felt that I knew my job and could be depended upon. In the four years I was with the firm the turnover in my particular department increased from £22,000 to £67,000; two other men were taken on (both of them some fifteen years older than I and British) while I remained the senior engineer in the group. My salary rose from £1000 to £1950 by the time I left. I was given a new car by the company every nine months, flown to Zürich every year (the equipment was made in Switzerland) and no one batted an eyelid if my monthly expense account shot up to £50. At the end of those four years I was worth at least £2500 a year, which was quite a lot of money in those days.

This sudden uplift in my financial condition had obvious repercussions on my social and intellectual life. Having a car meant that if you went to a party you could offer a lift to a girl, bring her back to your place and pour her a Remy Martin with the coffee. Instead of a one-room bed-sitter with a gas ring, you had a flat, where the loo was not communal and there was a fridge with ice cubes for whisky or gin. On a date you could take a girl to L'Escargot or Wheelers and charge the dinner to company expenses, instead of sweating it out on half a bitter and crisps. You could have your wines delivered from Berry Brothers, have your suits tailored in Savile Row, smoke the odd cigar and keep a stack of hard liquor in your cocktail cabinet.

Having experienced the life of a pauper for some years, I registered the contrast with attention. My Indian-ness seemed to draw less opprobrium because of the way my suit was cut and the occasional fiver that passed from my hands over the bar counter. I was no longer quite the misfit and loner that I had been in Earls Court; meeting girls and even taking them to bed became much easier. It did not happen overnight; my new-found wealth did not sit easily on me for some little while. But when it did I found my way into the Hampstead world of 'bohemians and artists' through a channel which such creatures normally profess to despise.

Iain, Geoffrey and I went looking for a flat. I didn't particularly like the idea of sharing rooms with the two of them; after all, I could now afford a flat on my own. And as Dame Fortune smiled and the path was brightly lit we found two flats in the same house. I took the basement, they installed themselves in the one above me. The house was right in the middle of Hampstead proper; my telephone number carried the letters HAM before the numerals. That seemed to put a respectable seal on my status both in the office and with friends and acquaintances. I was not living in Belsizia, the barren bed-sitterland of foreign students and au pair girls. The phone was in my name, I had the lease on a flat, with a bathroom, kitchen and garden all to myself. The car reposed right in front of my gate, there were at least a dozen bottles of wine on the rack at any one time. Guests were offered a choice of drinks whenever they popped in. 'Whisky, gin, vodka or vermouth? Or perhaps you'd like a glass of claret, St. Julien 1959?'

The flat was within a two-minute walk from the Bumble-Bee Arms on the High Street. And with such attractions emitting siren calls from such close proximity, my days, or rather my evenings, fell into a pattern, laced with alcohol, bohemian talk and delicious dollies. I would return from work at about six-thirty, collect the post from the flat, pour myself a pick-me-up whisky, give myself a shave and walk out into the Hampstead night with a wallet stacked with pound notes and promise. The public bar of the Bumble-Bee housed some of the 'most exciting young talent' in the district. I hoped that some of the talent might rub off on me by association. And to bring about that 'association' I was willing to pay a price. Mere money, as I had occasion to pronounce earlier, was no deterrent to visionaries and prophets. Right? Right!

The Bumble-Bee was and is a unique pub in Hampstead. It was the only public house in the area where the same landlord had managed its affairs for over a decade. In the public bar there were bums, layabouts and derelicts, living on National Assistance, wearing tattered clothes and unshaven faces, drinking pints of rough Devon cider. One man who used to drink there regularly in those days was known to have got a double first at Cambridge. But he had never worked for eight years and lived on the charity of friends and the Welfare State. There were others—painters, poets, sculptors—a kind of freemasonry of conspirators who were cocking a snook at the rough, garish, bourgeois world out there. The Bumble-Bee was a womb into which these unhatched foetuses would retire, play darts and wear out their livers on the rawest drink ever concocted on the British Isles—Devon cider. Their talk was smoother than the would-bes in Fulham Road; a number of them had known money and education sometime in their lives. But they were rebels of a genuine kind, perhaps not entirely possessed of a genuine talent but with no uncertainty about the life they had rejected.

I suspect that most of them would have been able to find jobs if they had felt so inclined; they were well informed and provided stimulating company. But few, very few, of these defiant drop-outs ever *did* anything; the sculptors did not sculpt, the poets did not versify, the painters never held a brush. It was as if the very act of rebellion, of repudiating the 'system', had exhausted them and they were going to doze through the remainder of their terrestrial existence in post-prandial haze, gelding themselves with daydreams and bile.

The private bar was an entirely different place, though separated from the other only by an interconnecting door and some eight feet of bar space in between. It was the political cockpit of Hampstead, headquarters of the local Labour Party caucus, where the man who finally wrenched the Hampstead seat from the Tories in Parliament often drank: Scotch and soda, gin and tonic, even an occasional brandy, would be some of the orders shouted from the other side. Rolls-Royces would sometimes drive up to the Bumble-Bee and disgorge their loads into the private bar. Though both the private and public bars housed left-wing devotees, there was an internal dialectic between the two—a kind of 'them' and 'us' built not entirely out of the financial hiatus (though that was there) but a feeling of revisionist versus the true radical. If you had made it or even wished to, there were hostile stares in the public bar; you were considered unclean, whatever your professed political position.

I occupied a special position in the public bar. Because I was a wog, an underprivileged entity by definition, I was accepted by the cider men. My stuffed wallet helped, even though there was professed contempt for worldly possessions. When it came to my turn to order the round, sneaky whispers of Scotch or vodka would often fall on my ears. Also, I ordered far more frequently than the mere contingency of my round would dictate. Consciously, unashamedly, I was buying friendship, an entrée into the kind of 'artistic' world of which I had dreamt about in India.

Of course, the habitués of the public bar at the Bumble-Bee did not see my so-called generosity in this light at all. They thought I was a bit of a fool, who 'had plenty of dough and didn't know what to do with it'. Which suited me fine until they finally discovered my identity. Naturally, hostility ensued. But that did not happen till a few years later.

With most of the regulars I came to be on first-name terms within a short time, for the simple reason that at one stage or another I had bought every single one of them much more than my share of drinks. None of them became close friends. I did not want them to. No one knew of my ambition to become a writer; that would have identified me with them too closely, and I didn't want that. I called myself an engineer, but no one knew quite what I did. They saw that I wore a tie during the week, drove a car, always carried a fair amount of money on me, wore my hair short and did not sport a beard. Nothing bohemian in my appearance, there wasn't. Later, when word got around that there was always a well-stacked liquor cabinet in my flat, only two minutes away from the pub, I would get unexpected callers at all times of the night or day, often in substantial numbers. It didn't bother me, I was getting to see a part of life I didn't know existed, and if my money had to be used as a passport to this domain, why not?

Iain once asked me, 'What do you get out of spending every night of the week with those bums down there?'

To someone who can ask the question there can be no answer. It is curiosity, it is fascination, it is desire to club with people who share your aspirations. Above all it is the writer's instinct to observe character, the same dreary endless talk night after night, hoping for that one day when, quite out of the blue, there will be an incident, one memorable human being, who will redeem the boredom and monotony of all that has gone before.

Buster Tuffman walked into the public bar of the Bumble-Bee early one Friday evening. I had heard of him from friends; he had written and published a novel based on a schizophrenic hero, and was known to be quite a 'character' on the Hampstead scene. Character or no, this breed of homo sapiens was rare to the Bumble-Bee environment; someone who had actually published a novel and was accepted, indeed welcomed, in the public bar was in itself a phenomenon worthy of celebration. I edged up to the group which surrounded him (he was obviously quite a hero) and when glasses were empty all round, offered to buy the august gentleman a drink. He accepted. But I have to add that there were visible traces of discomfort on his brow.

As I had bought my way in, having provided an entire round of drinks, I ventured tentatively, 'You write novels . . . ?'

'Yes.'

'Er . . . er . . . what kind are they? I mean, what do you write about?

'How can one answer a question like that? Better read my stuff and find out.' That seemed to be the end of that one. But no, he took a sip of his Scotch, lighted a cigarette and continued, 'I write about reality, the conditions of human existence, the parameters that determine the modality of our thought processes.'

'What does parameters mean?' I queried.

'Well . . . er . . . parameter is . . . refers to the boundaries of our being, the extent to which we experience ourselves in reality.'

I smiled and dropped the subject. Buster was to discover later that I had read physics at university and did in fact know what parameter meant as it is a common word in mathematics: it is simply the constant that determines the relationship between two variables in an equation.

Buster Tuffman was Jewish and looked it too. He exuded vitality, held the stage in conversations and was fond of spoonerisms: 'Not with a whang but a bimper'; '*A sotre vonte*'; 'Here we go round the bulberry mush, the bulberry mush'. In those days he was not notoriously successful with women. Having recently separated from his wife, he lived in a twelve by ten bed-sitter in upper Hampstead, eked out a miserable living from a translation agency he ran with a friend, transported himself from points A to B in an old Ford, which he inherited on the demise of his aunt's husband, to wit his uncle. He was not averse to practising prehistoric techniques in seducing dollies, as I was to discover later that evening. 'No woman really means no, even when she says it; just a game they play,' he announced over his third Scotch. As empirical validation of this theory was never carried out under laboratory conditions, I was left in some doubt as to its authenticity.

Standing next to Buster was a blonde Swedish girl, Liza, whom I had never seen before. She was fond of art and literature and had recently arrived in Hampstead to indoctrinate herself in these ponderous matters. 'We always live in a dream, don't we?' she offered, in her heavily accented voice, at the end of one rather longish monologue from Mr Tuffman. His reply to her pronouncement was to weave his heavy hairy arm round her slender waist and attempt contact with her oracular muscles by means of his own. The attempt was unsuccessful as she unwound herself lithely from his arm and looked up at her escort, a habitué of the public bar. He was six foot six and was called Big Bob by his friends. He had blue needle-like eyes under black bushy brows; he loped rather than walked and held the consecrated position of being 'possibly the only genius in Hampstead', an assessment which didn't seem to be shared either by his fellow sculptors or critics.

'I like holes,' Big Bob used to say, lubricated by several pints of cider, 'any kind, anywhere. Just so long as I can get my finger in.' And in this vocation he was remarkably successful. Often he would lift a girl up by the waist and throw her over his shoulder, and thus suitably estranged from Mother Earth (the bare boards of the public bar actually) by six feet and so rendered completely vulnerable, the girl would emit the obligatory scream. At which point Big Bob would go to work on her underpants with his other hand and push his long middle finger into her hole. Mission completed, he would let her down, bring his finger under his nose draw in a deep breath and say, 'Yes, it'll do, smells like fish 'n' chips.' Thus Big Bob was the resident canonized genius of the Bumble-Bee, due principally to his success with 'holes'.

The group that night, however, was more reverentially disposed towards Buster than to the household genius. Mr Tuffman had recently scored a success with a series of surrealist dialogues which had been put on at the Lamda Playhouse's 'Theatre of Cruelty' season, directed by none other than the great Peter Brooke himself. This had earned our struggling novelist one whole line in the *Sunday Times*, no mean achievement in the eyes of the cider drinkers at the Bumble-Bee. Reverence for artistic talent was one thing, however, reciprocation of erotic advances quite another, Fruitlessly, and incessantly Buster tried to draw one pretty damsel after another into close proximity with his somewhat rotund being. And just as unceasingly his efforts were repulsed while the drinks were guzzled.

One woman, known to be an 'easy lay', was the target of his next attack. Her name was Junifer; she had large green eyes which shot about like small fish in an aquarium, black hair and a dainty frame overloaded by a pair of oversize breasts which were only too apparent under her tight sweater. She was famous for the remarkable facility with which she could fall off bar stools after ten in the evening: the nominal fee for her feminine charms was a ride back home, two black coffees and another quick swig from a quarter bottle of whisky. Then she was willing and ready, whoever it was, whatever night of the week.

'Come on, Juni, give us a feel,' Buster bellowed.

'I'll give you a feel,' Miss Junifer retorted uncharacteristically, between clenched teeth.

'Come on, what's the matter with you?' Tuffman persisted, drawing her against him with one hand, while the other groped around her waist, hoping to drag the bottom of the sweater out of her skirt.

He was rewarded for his services by a resounding smack on his right cheek; the glass dropped from his hand and crashed on the floor. Junifer walked to the other side of the bar and poured glowing lava out of her eyes on the counter. The group looked at Buster for a moment, giggled a little, then conversation resumed as before. Buster adjusted his glasses and ordered a fresh whisky, muttering to himself, 'Must be having her monthly blues, poor girl.'

At this point a young man, with the wispy good looks of a latter-day Rupert Brooke, burst in. 'I want to read this marvellous poem I wrote at dawn this morning.' He was tall, blond, blue-eyed and, incongruously, smoked a pipe. His voice had that metallic nasal veneer which comes from minor public-school education in England. He had managed a poet's third at Oxford, lived 'south of the riva, old chap', and was experiencing the first draughts of the Hampstead wind. 'Must you?' Big Bob groaned in reply to his euphoric announcement.

'Oh yes, but of course,' imitation Rupert Brooke replied, digging out a whole sheaf of papers from the inside breast-pocket of his jacket.

'Vicky, old chap,' Buster interjected, essaying a sardonic replica of tone and phrase, 'don't you think . . . pearls before swine and all that?'

'Don't be silly, Buster old cock, I mean this is Hampstead, this is where it's all happening. Baudelaire used to *write* his poems on cafe tables and Joyce . . . '

The shaft having missed its target, Buster sighed and took an extra large gulp of whisky. Vicky began:

'O dawn thou harbinger of mysteries
Hidden in the deepest caverns of the night . . . '

Liza, the Swedish girl, exclaimed, 'That is beautiful!' Buster and Big Bob exchanged glances, and Junifer, who had been eyeing the poet ever since he entered the pub, returned to the scene of battle. 'Why don't you keep your trap shut?' she shouted. The boil had been lanced, grateful sighs rose like incense all round, and the surgeon continued, 'Thinks he can write poetry, poor bugger. Can't even fuck, the miserable sod.'

Silence reigned for exactly ten seconds. Then laughter. 'I think you deserve a drink just for that, Juni,' Big Bob said, putting his arm round Junifer. Rupert Brooke returned his dawn poem to its original abode and shook his head morosely at me. 'No audience, no audience at all. No respect for the artist. They are all pseudos round here.'

I nodded. There was a poetic beauty in the equation here. If people don't want to listen to your adolescent romantic regurgitations they were pseudos; if a man with blond hair and blue eyes can't fuck he was no poet. I wondered, with my mathematical mind, whether a curve drawn from such an equation would pass through the point at which I was located myself? I was sobered by the thought. I accepted that Hampstead was in fact a special place; everyone had 'artistic' aspirations of one sort or another. Yet the inhibitions on exposure, on being found out and proved a fake, were almost Victorian in dimension. The 'mode of living' was fluid, unstructured, but intellectual or creative efforts were veiled in thick armour. Confidence was lacking, the ability to say, 'Yes, I think this is good.' Or 'My

God, that is execrable!' You waited till the *Sunday Times* or the *New Arts Review* picked up someone or damned him to perdition. Then you came along and chorused an echo. Yes, in this sense, Hampstead was provincial, taking its cues from Fleet Street, BBC-2, New York or San Francisco, and therefore pseudo. Yes, I agreed with Rupert Brooke, not realizing that soon my unheard opinion would be vindicated in a test case in which I was to be the principle witness.

Big Bob sat on a high stool next to the counter; Liza leaned against him, with her head on his chest, her breasts being gently massaged by a pair of large bony hands. Having said her piece and deflated Vicky, Junifer continued to probe outer space with virulent eyes. Buster held his glass of whisky at arm's length, as if in a tableau, toasting Lucretia Borgia or some other equally inaccessible female. It seemed as if one particular rung of the evening's ladder had been climbed, and the group was drawing in its breath for the next assault. I ordered another round of drinks.

There were in fact two others who were on the outer fringe of the group. One of them was a small blond man, who had been around in Hampstead since neolithic times, carrying the identity card of 'con man and psychopath'. In times past he would ask for half a crown off someone, ten pounds from another, and juggle his finances with the agility of an acrobat. Recently, however, he had come into a small fortune, bequeathed by a rich queer whose failing sexuality had been revitalized by our con man's dexterous fingers. That evening Julian was thus dressed in a Savile Row suit, and stood his ground silently, with the authority of a man who knows the colour of five-pound notes.

The other man was a newcomer to the scene, a Jewish

art dealer named Jake. He was balding, leather-faced, always slightly on edge and given to emitting sprays of saliva while speaking. He had as little control over this phenomenon as an incontinent sage of eighty has over his bladder. Consequently he stood a small distance away from the rest of us and rationed his comment to monosyllabic interjections. Which, all things considered, was rather altruistic of him.

As the evening drew to a close, all eyes criss-crossed the room in hysteric frenzy. Weekend evenings were always marked by this ritual, the quest for 'parties' and 'birds' and 'booze' after the pubs closed. It was like a malignant sore, strenuously nursed and kept suppurating; surgery was unthinkable. To terminate a Friday night at ten past eleven on pub premises was anathema to anyone who was anyone in Hampstead. (Which was everyone.) The hours between seven and eleven might have been miserable, advances might have been rejected a myriad times, there may be no female under sixty within eyeing distance, the liver might be howling protests at alcohol lacerating an empty stomach, but there was something about those words, 'Last orders, gentlemen, please', which provoked a last-ditch effort by all but the most assiduously married couples. There was 'happiness' lying past the midnight hour, there was 'hope' in the next handshake, there was 'promise' in a quart of beer drunk at someone else's pad.

As I said, it was a ritual, and like all potent rituals, content had been replaced by form long ago, the raison d' être vanquished by habit. You had to have a 'party' on Friday night, you had to prolong the isolation for a few more hours, professing faith in the miracle of a possible connection, but convinced within that 'nothing ever happens round here', no one ever turns up with salvation on a salver, that neither Ophelia nor Prince Charming live next door. That the end comes as always with a single sigh before turning off the light in a ten by twelve bed-sitter, alone as ever, leering over a hangover and bad breath in the morning.

Big Bob said, 'Let's go back to Amit's place.'

Buster queried, 'Where?'

'To Amit's place,' Big Bob replied. 'Our Indian friend lives just round the corner from here.' Of course, I hadn't been asked, it was assumed that I would be only too happy to provide the facilities of my 'pad' to such an august assemblage.

'All very well for you,' Buster retorted, a sharp edge in his voice, 'you've got little blondy here. What have I got? An empty glass with no whisky.'

'Go on then, find yourself a dolly and bring her back with you. Plenty of them around, you know.'

Just then a girl in a mini-skirt came into the bar and asked for a packet of cigarettes. Buster's hand proceeded mesmerically to her small tight behind while his lips formed the words, 'Want to come to a party, love?'

Her head turned, her eyes shot venom. 'I fucking well don't. And take your filthy hands off my bum.'

'Not the right technique, not the right technique at all,' Big Bob sighed.

'Serves him right,' Junifer muttered in an aside.

Julian stepped forward and announced, 'I'll pay for a bottle of whisky, if there's somewhere to go.' Eyes rolled, grace descended and Junifer's lips relaxed into a grin.

I said, 'You can come back to my place if you like.'

'Well, look, if we have a bottle of Scotch, there shouldn't be much trouble getting hold of a few birds,' Big Bob offered optimistically.

'Yeah,' Buster agreed, 'shouldn't be any trouble at all.'

No one made a move, though, no one was going to bell the cat himself, not yet anyway. It was a good idea, the dying embers were fanned a little, but the latent conviction of doom, of desolation, remained unshaken. There had been too many such evenings before this one, and there would be numerous others to follow. 'Nothing really happens round here, nothing, nothing.' Then suddenly Buster began scurrying round the pub asking every female he could lay his hands on, 'Like to come to a party, love?' The same negative grimace, the same vehement rebuttals. Outside the pub the group hung around for a while, Big Bob and Buster accosting single girls walking up High Street. No one responded, no one melted into docile acquiescence. The group that entered my flat at half past eleven consisted of two women and six men, including myself, the same faces who had been eyeing each other at the Bumble-Bee.

I opened two bottles of wine and brought out glasses and ice from the kitchen. The ladies preferred Burgundy, the gentlemen Scotch; I poured myself a glass of red vino. Big Bob, who had visited my 'pad' before, put on some music, Vicky stood in a corner looking wistfully forlorn, Junifer seemed as adamantly hostile to Buster as ever. Liza got up to dance with Big Bob. Then Julian said, 'Let's have some action.' His words fell leadenly on the carpet, the music blared, Big Bob's risen cock was grazing Liza's thigh (through the clothes). Julian persisted, 'Come on, Rupert Brooke, let's have a look at your gun.'

'Costs money,' came the supercilious reply, while a cloud of pipe smoke blurred his face. I sat in the corner and watched.

'Come on love, just a little feel,' Buster pleaded with Junifer.

'Get your claws off me,' she rebounded, 'before I give you another one. And this time it won't be on the face either.'

'Women are funny, aren't they?' Buster ruminated, walking over to my corner. 'What do you do, by the way?'

'I am an engineer, work for a firm in the City.'

'Oh,' he replied, confirmed in his contempt. 'Nice pad you got here. Must cost a bit of bread.'

'I suppose it does,' I replied, smiling. 'Doesn't worry me overmuch, though.'

'No, no, I don't suppose it does.' End of dialogue with nonartist. 'Come on Liza, give us a dance. You can have him all night. Me, you can only get for ten minutes.'

'Don't strain yourself, Buster,' Big Bob said, grinning, handing over the blond girl. 'Never gives up, does he?'

Like a million other such 'parties' which had happened in the past, which were happening then all over Hampstead, and which would go on happening till the next Ice Age devoured the British Isles, nothing 'artistic' or 'profound' or 'witty' was said or suggested. Yet there was, in every single person present in the room, a feeling of smug superiority over the grey amorphous mass of bourgeois humanity which lived safely out there, behind closed doors, television sets and roast-beef lunches. A self-righteous bravura glowed from every face at the mere mention of Surbiton or Chelmsford; the nine-to-fivers, hidden behind their *Daily Mail*s and their *Times*, packed like bees in a honeycomb, jangling in their commuter trains, these solid citizens who made the world go round, were objects of immense condescension. Why? Because they didn't go to 'parties' like this on Friday evenings, because they didn't try to feel the bums of teenage dollies, because they knew nothing about 'the modalities of human thought'. More even than the Jews, the inhabitants of Hampstead were possessed of the supernatural knowledge that they were 'the chosen few'. Writers who got published and made money, engineers who worked in the City, married men who stayed with their wives and bred kids, any type of female who professed faith in chastity and monogamy . . . the list was inexhaustible; anyone actually who didn't drink at the Bumble-Bee or one of four or five other pubs in Hampstead, could not really be considered a suitable candidate for membership into this, the most radically orientated and artistically conscious club devised by mammal Man. If only as an associate on strict probation, I was proud to belong.

Then it all began to happen. The demand for 'action' having yielded meagre results, Julian followed the precept of the Master and walked to the centre of the room, stopped the dancing and started undressing. Conversation ceased as jacket and tie fell to the floor, Julian's eyes focussed piercingly on Vicky. Buster looked as if he had just seen the Queen and Big Bob put on his famous grin. Only Junifer seemed upset. Even Jake, who had been inconspicuously silent, made several attempts at speech, unsuccessfully. By the end of the third minute of reverential silence there was one nude man in the room who surveyed the assembled gathering with expressions ranging from downright contempt to cynical challenge.

'Come on, you prudes, what the fucking hell is wrong with you? Don't you know this is the middle of the twentieth century? Queen Victoria died long ago! Or didn't you know that? And that proper little gentleman there, says it costs money to show his gun. Well here, have a look at mine, feel it, here, this is how it's done.' Julian matched action to word, his penis responded half-heartedly. 'What's wrong with a little fucking, eh? All this bloody talk. The whole lot of you, every single prick in this fucking room, you're all the same, crap full of Victorian prudery. Come on, I want to see a few more cocks round here. And if it's money you want, if that's what really gets you turned on, well, I'll put a tenner on the table. Come on Buster, let's see what you've got.'

'Do you mean that?' Buster asked, eyeing Julian intently.

'What do you think I do? Just said it for cocktail-party chatter or what?'

'No, no, but about the money, I mean?'

'Of course I do. Come on, let's see it. Let's have a first night of Buster Tuffman's cock.'

'All right, put your money on the table then,' Buster replied, taking off his jacket, 'tenner you said.'

'What do you take me for? A cheat or something? When I said I'd put a tenner, I meant a tenner.'

'Right,' Buster chimed, about to take off his shirt, 'let's just have a look at it.'

'Look, Buster, I'm not hooked on bread, get me? When I say a thing I mean it.'

'Yeah, we all know that,' Buster grunted.

At this point Julian went off to have a pee. Caveman's attempts at denuding himself of protective apparel were halted. Junifer looked angry and Liza somewhat flummoxed.

Big Bob went on grinning. 'I do believe,' Buster announced gravely, 'that Julian is sloshed.' (Could well have been, there was an inch of whisky left in the bottle.) The whole group burst out laughing as the nude re-entered the room.

'All right then, if Buster won't do it, I'll give ten pounds to the first man who takes off all his clothes.' Julian picked up his jacket, extracted the wallet and drew out one, then two, five-pound notes, and added, 'Perhaps another one, as an extra bonus, if he can get an erection and keep it up for five minutes.'

The three fivers lay on the floor, new, crisp, and rather a rare sight in Hampstead. Vicky was quicker on the draw than anyone else, he had already taken off his jacket by the time the first note had floated down to the carpet. Buster said, 'Now, Julian, that's unfair, I didn't say I wouldn't do it. Just wanted to see the money.'

'Well, you had your chance,' Big Bob interjected.

Buster's face assumed a mask of frenzy, as Vicky's shirt came off. 'Can we share that, Julian? If I take off my clothes too? His hand was rigidly pointing to the money on the floor. 'I could do with the bread, really could.'

'The first man, I said,' Julian replied non-committally, eyeing Vicky's progress.

'That's unfair, I won't race, I simply won't,' Buster muttered to himself, convinced that he didn't stand a chance, now that the trousers were down too. 'It's vulgar to race in a thing like this.'

'Bravo,' Big Bob shouted, as the underpants came off and then the socks. 'Well done, Vicky.'

The tall blond boy stood in the middle of the room, pipe between his teeth, legs scissored apart, face carrying an expression of infinite disdain. 'You said another fiver for a five-minute erection, didn't you?'

'Yes,' Julian replied, his eyes riveted to Vicky's genitals.

'Well, I'll have to work on it, I think. But shouldn't be much trouble.'

His hand went down and began a gentle to and fro motion, Big Bob disentangled himself from Liza and put the music on again, Julian's cock began to rise in sympathy. Buster walked about the room, groaning to himself, 'Quite ridiculous. Just plain old-fashioned avarice. Nothing to do with being a prude or not.' Junifer sat on the sofa looking angrier than ever. Only Jake didn't know quite what to do with himself.

The erection finally happened. Vicky picked up the three fivers, put them in his jacket and relighted his pipe. Julian came over and kissed him on the lips, while his hands played with the minutest erect penis that could be humanly conceived.

'Certainly has guts, that boy,' I said to myself.

It was Miriam Makeba on the record; Julian and Vicky kept time, their half-erect penises rubbing against each other. Avarice or no, the two men had certainly electrified the air. I went over to Junifer and asked her for a dance. She didn't reply, nor did she get up from her seat. Buster wanted to dance with Liza but she refused. Big Bob offered himself as a substitute and the two of them began dancing, half in jesting imitation of the nude couple, half in earnest. Liza looked at Junifer and whispered, 'Perhaps we should do the same.' Junifer's eyes poured venom as her vow of silence became binding. I looked at Jake, he stared back at me, we shared a smile.

I thought it was time to open another bottle of wine. Liza wasn't drinking much but Junifer had finished one whole bottle all by herself. The whisky was done. Alcohol had heightened sensation all right; Junifer must be drunk, I thought. Even I felt a certain urge as I watched Julian playing with Vicky. The room seemed darker than before, Liza's blond hair shrieked to be caressed, her lips looked moist, her breasts taut and ready. Yes, the slow, viscid throb of sex was being felt by everyone in the room. Even Buster had got into the swing of the thing and wiggled his hips as Big Bob led the dance.

Then suddenly Junifer shot up from her seat and screamed, 'Stop it! Stop it! You lousy bastards! Stop it!' The couples ceased shuffling on the floor, Julian's hand fell away from Vicky's cock, surprise flashed through whisky-sodden eyes. I didn't know what to make of the outburst; even Big Bob was not grinning. There was hysteria in the voice, not just anger; her eyes were bulging, about to devour. 'I'll show you. I'll show the whole poxy lot of you.' Pushing the men away she stood in the centre of the room and looked at every male face in turn. Her eyes were no longer human, as if she was possessed. There was a thin sharp rasp in her voice, demonic.

Junifer lay down on the floor on her back, drew up her skirt, took off her underpants, spread her legs wide and went on in the same hysterical pitch. 'This is a cunt, see. Or haven't any of you pansies ever seen one before? This is my cunt, see.' She poked her finger in. We were all standing now, mouths agape, minds in a whirl; even Vicky had taken the pipe out of his mouth. 'And I want a nice big cock to get in here. Come on, let's see who can do it, come on.'

No words, no movements, as if fixed in a spell.

'Come on, you lousy bastards, fuck me. Fuck me, you poxy pricks. Fuck me, damn you. Fuck me, fuck me, fuck me . . .' The voice rose to a shrieking crescendo, then broke. Loud, uncontrolled, hiccupy sobs took over. No one ventured, no prick came to her rescue. The two nude men put on their clothes, slowly, reverently, noiselessly. And one by one the males in the group filed out of the room, without words, without pity, stunned into an expressionless silence.

Liza walked over to Junifer, sat down on the floor and held the crying girl in her arms. I watched the two of them as if I was in another world, of another time. I don't know what feelings I had, what thoughts went through my mind. Her skirt was still above her waist, her legs forked as widely as before. The tuft of hair between those white thighs looked inappropriate, indecent. I must have felt some horror, for I was still a stranger to such desolation. But there was fascination too, the carnivorous appetite streaked my palate. I wanted to see.

Liza rocked Junifer very gently while the jerky sobs grew less and less violent. Tears came tumbling down her face, the eyes were shut. The music still crooned and Liza's free hand began to caress Junifer's body, softly, tenderly, around her shoulder, down the arm, then back to the neck. Only the smallest squeeze, the gentlest pressure, and then very slowly over her breasts, rocking the baby all the while.

By now the sobs had stopped. Junifer had relaxed a little. She lay in Liza's arms, recovering, hoping, perhaps even dreaming. Her eyes were still shut; it was as if she did not know what had happened or was happening now. Liza's hand stroked her face, her ears and then her neck. And slowly, very slowly, the Swedish fingers went down Junifer's body, over the peaks of her bosom, over the upturned skirt and even further down.

The two girls seemed totally unaware of my presence.

At first her hand rested gently, then it stroked the hair as if it was warm fur. The whole of her palm covered it, then she moved further down one thigh and stroked the inside with her fingers, as if with a painters' brush. Later she did the same to the other. It was all so slow; she did not prod at first, only the softest, lightest touch over and around the curly brown-black hair.

Junifer shook her body, adjusted herself more comfortably against Liza's bosom and parted her thighs a little wider, keeping her eyes shut all the while. After a few moments Junifer's thighs began to tremble, her lips parted and her whole body seemed to vibrate.

'Come on, darling,' Liza said, 'let's go to bed. It's better there.' Junifer turned her head, opened her eyes and the two girls kissed each other.

At this point I thought it was time for me to leave. The two of them were so engrossed that I don't think they noticed me get out of the door. I walked out of the flat and looked at my watch. It was three o'clock. A strange evening, certainly. You don't see this sort of thing sitting at home and filling in the crossword. No, this was bohemian Hampstead all right. But did I want to live like this? Do the people who live like this really want to? I walked all over the Heath that night with two lines of an Auden poem buzzing in my head:

'Two by two like cat and mouse
The homeless played at keeping house.'

When it was dawn I trudged back to the flat. Junifer and Liza were still in bed, fast asleep.

Then I fell in love.

Winter came on hard that year; it had begun to snow before Christmas, the wind was as sharp as the cry of a new-born babe. The white bony branches of the rose tree in the garden spiked the air. While the clouds drifted away, steel shafts of mirrored light gouged the eyes. There was something stern and unyielding about that winter, like desert rock hugging a hidden spring to its bosom.

There had been women of course, minor thirsts quenched. But success with females reflected little on the kind of person I was. And since I was not exactly discriminating in my choice of bed companions, the outcome of every 'affair' was rigorously predictable. Till finally I stopped expecting more than a 'fuck' from any girl. I no longer hoped that Miss Right would turn up some day; I drove 'love' to the back of my mind, not expecting it, never giving it, perhaps not even wanting it. But as I said, winter came on hard that year, the frozen snow crunched under my feet and I felt a yearning for spring.

I met Ruth at the wine store on High Street. She was wearing a duffel coat, a pair of suede gloves and the cold wind had blasted her face into crimson red. I took my turn at the counter while Ruth and her companion ordered a dozen bottles of red wine to be delivered at their flat down the road. It was a Saturday afternoon, I remember; I had just emerged from a session at the Bumble-Bee. The thought of a dozen bottles of wine incited me to curiosity. There's going to be a party on tonight, I thought. Ruth's accent gave away her New England origins; her face, with its soft oriental curves and tassels of raven-coloured hair, set the drums beating in my head. I edged forward and said, 'You're not going to drink all of it by yourself, are you?' Fatuous remark, I thought, but the best I could do under instant notice. Unaccustomed as I am . . .

'No,' she replied, not even bothering to turn her face to me, and continued talking to the man serving her.

'A party?' I persisted.

'Yes,' came the laconic answer.

'Well, you'll need a few men round the place to make it a going concern.'

'Yes,' she retorted, firmly this time, and looking me straight in the eye, 'and we've got them, thank you.'

At this I burst out laughing. The stern words simply didn't match her face. Her eyes were soft and liquid, dark brown and giving. There wasn't a trace of the gnawed, hard-bitten American bitch in her look. Her voice too carried the mellow whispers of spring, caressing as a fur, warm as a brandy on an empty stomach.

'What's funny about that?' she queried.

'Nothing really. Just that you're determined to get rid of me and I am determined to come to your party. A strange face always adds an extra bite to the meal, you know.' We looked at each other for a minute without speaking. 'And you're not winning the battle, are you?' I dared, pressing my point.

'Depends . . .'

'Oh come on, I am not an untouchable, I don't have an infectious disease and I could well liven up your party.'

The girls finished their transaction and walked out of the shop; I followed them. The man behind the counter said,

'But, sir . . . ?' 'I'll be back in a minute,' I shouted and fell into pace with the two girls on the street outside. Ruth looked at her friend, then at me and finally made up her mind. 'Look, if you really want to come . . . We live just round the corner and it's at two o'clock tomorrow afternoon.'

'Two o'clock?' I asked, puzzled. 'On a Sunday afternoon? What sort of time is that to have a party?'

'If it doesn't suit you, no one is forcing you to come.'

'No, no, I realize that . . . but I just wondered. You're not trying to put me off, are you?'

'There wouldn't be any point. You seem quite persistent.'

The sparring went on for a while longer. Ruth accepted my intrusion as a fait accompli, without enthusiasm but, I suspect, with a certain amount of well-concealed curiosity. I took down her address and she my name and then I walked back to the wine store, pondering on the anomaly of two American girls in Hampstead, throwing a party at two o'clock on a Sunday afternoon. I mean, what's wrong with Saturday night, for example? 'Perverse Americans,' I said to myself, and thought no more about it.

I spent an hour at the Bumble-Bee the next day, lubricating my system for what was to follow. At quarter past two I strode out with a bottle of wine under my arm. The snow lay on the street, frayed at the edges, less than sparkling white in colour, without much sign of life, yet hanging on. The street in which Ruth lived was lined with trees, sharp bare branches meshing out the sky. I rang the bell of the house and waited. Five minutes went by and still there was no reply. I rang again, with thoughts of angry vengeance flashing through my mind. This isn't where they live at all. And even if they do, they must have had the damn thing last night. There wasn't a sound from anywhere; the whole street was as quiet as a morgue. You don't have a party with people sitting around under stern autistic vows, do you? No, you most certainly don't! I had been cheated, they had thrown me off the scent, they had. Trust American girls to be this cunning. Devious lot, they were, quite, quite untrustworthy. When all I had done was to tag on and ask to come to their party. I hadn't committed a crime, I had been perfectly respectable in fact. Then why the hell . . . ?

'So you finally did come . . . ?' Ruth said, opening the door.

'Well, of course. I mean there wasn't any doubt about that, was there? In fact, I was wondering if you lived here at all. There wasn't a single solitary sound . . . so I thought . . . '

'We live at the top,' she replied, leading me up the stairs. 'You wouldn't hear the noise, even if there was any . . . . But I'm glad you've come.'

'Didn't you expect me to? After all that . . . surely?'

'No, I wasn't sure if you would remember. I think you picked me up on impulse. So I . . . '

'Don't worry,' I replied, putting my arm round her waist, 'even if there wasn't any other bait, your being American was lure enough.'

'Really?' she said, turning her large brown eyes at me. 'I had never thought of myself like that.'

The room was full of young men in their early twenties, a few girls. Ruth told me she was working for a Ph.D. at the London School of Economics and the assembled gathering consisted mainly of her friends from college. Almost all the men were Americans; their strange metallic voices jarred in my ear. As I poured myself a glass of wine, Ruth whispered,

'Jeff, the one with the beard, is my boyfriend, so you will be careful, won't you?' That seemed to draw us into a conspiracy and I was pleased.

'Existentialism is not a philosophy at all,' one young man announced, rather more raucously than such declamations normally deserve. 'It is a way of life.'

'Rather like the American way of life, is it?' I interjected.

He seemed taken aback, not quite certain whether to take me seriously or ignore my intrusion. After a moment's pause however, he rose to the bait. 'Depends on what you mean by the American way of life. If you are talking of the Frontier psychology and the Puritan ethic . . . '

'I was referring to toothpastes and Elvis Presley actually,' I cut in.

Ruth laughed, one of the girls in the group smiled and I went on: 'Seems to me that existentialism is nothing but a licence to *fuck* whoever you want whenever you want.' The four-letter word stunned the audience into embarrassed silence, the embryo philosopher wriggled out of the group and Ruth looked imploringly at me. 'All right,' I said, 'but when is this damn thing going to be over? I want you all to myself.'

'There's no harm in hoping,' she replied, smiling. 'But you do give tall orders at rather short notice.'

The party did end, however. Ruth's boyfriend vanished much earlier, sulkily, muttering mild abuses at her. It was eight o'clock. The room-mate started clearing the glasses and Ruth was trying, with all her New England tact, to get me out of the flat. 'Look, I am taking you out for a meal,' I insisted, 'and we'll have no more debate on the question.'

'Do you always have your own way?' she asked, obviously less disinterested than she would have liked to show. 'And are you always so persistent?'

'Mostly, in answer to your first question. No, not always, in answer to your second: only when I consider the situation is worth the bother.'

'I guess in that case I shall just have to come,' she said, bowing as if in obeisance. 'If you can spare a moment while I put on some make-up.'

'Sure,' I answered, drawing her to me, 'put on anything you like.' She slid away from me, and turned to smile as she left the room. And it was at that instant I knew that I was going to love this girl.

Why should a pretty American girl in London abandon her boyfriend at a party in her house, pally up with a complete stranger and then agree to go out with him for a meal? Especially when he has said nothing very scintillating or bright, when his looks don't quite match up to Yves Montand or the late James Dean? Because I was an Indian with dark skin and Ruth had grown up in post-McCarthy America, graduated from an Ivy League college and had been saturated with 'liberal' sentiments on the east coast of the United States. Also, I spoke with an Oxford accent, was older than her colleagues at college and insisted on exercising my authority in a thoroughly undemocratic manner. The Fascist, even miniature versions of the genre, is an attractive creature to all women, especially at the start of a relationship. In addition to all this, I had 'charm', though it is difficult to describe this when one is writing in the first person singular. The reader will have to accept this assertion to be true because a lot of people have spoken of this quality behind my back and it has come to me through second- and third-hand sources.

I took Ruth to the Bumble-Bee and instantly the public bar stirred into frenzied life. A new female face, especially an attractive one with a foreign accent, on the Hampstead circuit was regarded as a communal windfall. The commodity had to be felt, weighed, prodded and ultimately passed as worthy of purchase. Like cheese or meat or any other nourishing comestible. Buster came over and offered to buy a drink 'for your new dolly'; Big Bob leered, grinned and disengaged himself from Liza, thus indicating that he was free for hire; even young Rupert Brooke removed the pipe from his mouth, straightened his tie, and proffered, 'Your enchanting face is like the first bud of spring.' I guess Ruth was a bit overwhelmed by all the attention she got; I stood aside and watched the show in self-satisfied mirth.

When the pubs had shut we went to the Huntsman. Ruth ordered pheasant, I duck; we shared a bottle of Nuits St. George. By the time the meal was over I was drunk. Driving home could not have been without its tense moments, especially for her. We entered the flat, she took off her duffel coat, I held her in my arms and we kissed. Her lips were soft and warm, responsive. I tried to go further but she resisted. I wanted to feel her breasts but she said no. I wove my hand down her back and attempted to sneak under her skirt; she held the errant palm firmly in hers and removed it from the vicinity of her groins. I was beginning to get annoyed. We kissed some more, holding each other close. Then I tried again. Once more the same firm rejection. Then I dragged her to the bed and pushed her down on it. We wrestled.

Perhaps for half an hour, perhaps longer. At long last I exploded: 'If you're going to play this ridiculous cock-teasing game, you can bloody well clear out of this flat. Go back to your mama or your milksop boyfriend or whoever your like.' She got up from the bed, tidied her hair and put on her coat, smiling.

'What's so funny?' I shouted.

'Just that you are a spoilt baby,' she replied.

'And you think you are a mighty adult, do you?' There was no answer, she was about to leave, about to slip through my fingers; I was losing. 'And I don't want to see you again, ever.'

'As you like,' she said, opening the door. 'And thanks for a lovely meal and a very exciting evening.'

'You're welcome,' I pouted.

When she had gone I noticed her scarf on the floor.

Next morning I woke up with a quivering feeling of anticipation, something like the kind of feeling I get just before I set off on a long trip, about to board a plane to a place I have never visited before: the lure of uncertainty and the call of the unknown. I dialled Ruth's number and waited, more nervous than I had been with a woman for a long time. Would she snub me, would she put the phone down? Of course, I had a perfectly legitimate excuse, her scarf. But I *had* behaved rather rudely to her, would she forgive me?

Finally she answered, 'Do you know what time it is? I am still half asleep.'

'But . . . but your scarf . . . '

'Yes, I know . . . . I left it there in case your pride didn't let you call me without a pretext.'

I was thrown off balance by this one. 'Scheming bitch,' I thought, my wounded vanity rising to the surface once again.

'Look, why don't you come over and have some breakfast with me?'

After a pause, she said, 'All right. But it's too early yet. I guess I could make it in about two hours.'

I agreed, we muttered goodbyes and hung up. I looked at the clock, it said eight. Two hours would mean going late to the office. She must have known that, the cunning devil. But there wasn't much I could do at this point. Just have to make sure that I don't lose this round. She is only twenty-two, for heaven's sake! Should be able to deal with a baby her age, surely. With my experience . . . No, really, I was building this thing up to undue proportions. All I would have to do is be polite but firm. If she didn't want to sleep with me that was all right by me, no hard feelings at all. But I just wouldn't see her again, that's all. I mean, I simply don't believe in platonic friendships, that's all. If she was going to be a child, then I should be glad to let someone else do the baby-sitting.

I rang up my secretary, said I would come in after lunch. That little problem settled, I had a long hot bath, washed my hair, had a shave, daubed my cheeks with cologne, pressed my suit, took out a freshly laundered shirt, selected a sober but expensive tie and decked myself out in my respectable best. The mirror seemed overly critical that morning: no, the right hand-side of the moustache was a bit thin; there was just the slightest trace of hair on the chin; and then the knot in the tie, not quite right old chap. After I had fussed around to the point of exasperation, I looked at the clock and it stubbornly insisted that there was still an hour to go. 'Damn her,' I shouted to the walls of my empty flat but there were no consoling echoes.

Ruth arrived at ten past ten, and those last extra minutes were agonizingly unendurable. Would she come, would she simply ring up and say, sorry can't make it? Or perhaps she would just let me wait it out in misery, like a fooled buffoon? Anyway, she did arrive. We exchanged hullos and other inane greetings. Then I took out a bottle of chilled champagne from the fridge, popped the cork and filled two glasses with the bubbly. 'Is this normally what you breakfast on?' she asked.

'Only on special occasions like christenings and devirginations and so on,' I replied.

'Doesn't look as if it's going to be either of those two things this morning.'

'One can always hope,' I retorted, 'for the worst, I mean.' I put out some crackers and smeared foie gras over them. We munched on silently for a while

'Aren't you going to kiss me?' Ruth asked softly.

My heart thumped, I could smell defeat in the air. 'I don't believe in kissing in the morning,' I said haughtily. 'In fact I don't believe in sex at all. Especially with virgins, Americans and four-legged creatures.'

'Good,' she replied, coming over to me, 'we agree on one thing at least.' Then she took the champagne from my hand, put it on the floor and wove her arms around me. Our lips met and that kiss thrilled me more than many a fuck I had had.

'Why are you teasing me like this?' I blubbered.

'I am not,' Ruth whispered. 'I just want to show you something you've never seen before.'

'Have you?'

'No, but I know it's there. And I think we could take a look together.' I held her to me in reply and kissed her eyes. I knew what I wanted to say but I didn't say it. Not then, not there.

When we had finished the champagne, Ruth suggested we go for a walk on the Heath. I agreed. Things had suddenly become so simple; there was no need to fight any more.

Yes, it was the contrast. But it was more also, far more. Ruth's body was soft and warm and yielding. Her face reminded me of my mother who had been so beautiful when I was young: silk black hair down to her shoulder, those large enveloping eyes and her voice. Yes, Ruth was the loveliest girl I had ever known, her words fell from her lips gently, without the sharp rasping sounds that laced the speech of so many women I knew. Is it grace, is it beauty or is it something called serenity, that makes a feminine woman? I don't know, I don't think it can be defined in words. When you see it, you know it's there. But you can't pin it down, you can't describe the individual components that make up the whole. Most Western women don't have it. The way they walk, the manner in which they carry their hands, the way they use their eyes, somehow every single movement they make, violates the notion of grace that brings out the woman in the female. Am I being too lyrical or unfairly chauvinistic? I don't think so, for many Western men feel the same way as I do.

Yes, Ruth was a total woman but she also had a mind. The two things rarely come together and when they do, the combination is explosive. If she held an opinion, she didn't scream it at you. Patiently she waited, picking out the flaws in your argument, filling in the gaps with additional data.

There didn't have to be a fight every time we differed. We would simply agree to talk it over till either the one or the other came round. She said one day, 'I feel we shall never lose each other because we touch each other so. I love talking with you. You give me so much.' I could have said the same thing about her and it was in the warmth of this knowledge that we began our journey.

A week after that Sunday party we made love. It was quite unlike any other experience I had ever had. Almost as if it was something altogether different, not just two bodies sealed together, of me being inside her. I had the feeling that I was meeting another person, a woman, for the first time in my life. As if all that had gone before was one long preparation, that love-making had never happened to me before. When it was over, we held each other in our arms, silent, loving, without the need for words that speak of feelings.

Then she moved into my flat and we started living together.

Hampstead, my Hampstead, was stunned at first, then violently jealous. They missed the rounds I used to buy, the Bumble-Bee lost a regular devotee. I did not feel the need to pour oblivion down my throat every evening. We drank at home, talked and made love. Friends were still welcome, but not at all hours. If Ruth and I were in bed, I would not answer the door. I started writing again, a reason for hoping and living had suddenly sprouted in the garden. Spring came and the cherry blossoms spotted the green grass. I was happy.

Gide says somewhere that there can never be a story of happiness, 'Only what prepares it, only what destroys it can be told.' I have tried to tell what prepared it: the barren, unfeeling existence of an encrusted man. And when there was warmth, the ice melted, torrents of love gushed forth and tenderness burst into flower. For six months I tasted the honey, probing here, softly touching there, discovering a new and loving me.

Then the worm began to turn, the green of spring dyed into an autumn brown, the leaves began to fall and float away. We began to lose each other, the Bumble-Bee beckoned me once more and the siren calls of brittle lust began to be heard by both of us. Ruth hurt me and I hurt her, and there was no way of stopping the slide down the hill. Another man shot fiercely through our lives, trust was broken and we dived into a well of tears. One afternoon I screamed at her, 'Why the hell don't you pack your bags and go?'

Three hours later when I came back to the flat, half-drunk and repentant, she was doing just that. She had called her parents in New York, the ticket would arrive in a few hours by cable, the flight out was at eleven the next morning. I cried, pleaded, begged. But she had decided, the rupture point had come and no healing was possible. When I kissed her goodbye at the airport I knew I had chosen my own misery and my own loneliness and a future without Ruth would be as bleak as an Arctic winter. She winged off into a dark and unspeaking sky, leaving me to wonder if happiness can ever last.

Years later we were to meet again. Thunder and gale had swept away the clouds; new stars, fresh constellations chirped in the sky. Haunted by another dawn, I looked at shadows trailing behind me, then turned and saw her broken face rising from the ground. Our hands met, we shared the secret of despair, and when the sun rose we started walking silently up the hill, hoping that we might explore tenderness.

Après Ruth, desolation! Hampstead was full of consoling sounds but the whimper of malice underlined the words 'The Brown Casanova has been taught a lesson. Serves him right too.' Snide aspersions about Ruth's loyalty, oblique questions about my devotion. Buster said, 'Could have had her in the sack anytime I wanted. But wouldn't do it to you, my friend.' Big Bob remarked, 'Couldn't have been much good in the hay, could she? Her tits were a bit on the flabby side, from what I could see.' I endured the cold with as unruffled a face as I could muster. But it was hard. Not only was Ruth no longer with me, they wanted to desecrate even what we had had together. Hampstead is full of vultures, they live on the corpses of other people's emotions. In all the time I have lived in this area of town I have never seen a 'happy' affair last longer than six months. Does it say something about the people who have them or is it the *environment* in which they live? The old chicken and egg problem: does the world make us or do we make the world?

The soft succulent flesh of my being had been scoured out, I became a shell once more. The writing stopped, alcohol regained suzerainty. 'Fucks' became the goal, a demonic urge not to leave a moment empty, not to allow my mind to ponder. Women drifted in and out of the flat with the frenzy of flies. I don't know how many one-night stands I had in the weeks that followed Ruth's departure. I missed her so intently that an unoccupied evening would drive me towards hysteria. A hairpin lying on the bathroom floor, the half-finished bottle of Breck shampoo, the odd letter from her parents with their New York address, every single memento of Ruth made me want to cry. I wanted her with me, I wanted to undo all the wrongs I had done her, retract all the bitter venomous things we had said to each other. But it was too late, she was three thousand miles and many 'fucks' away from me.

Let me not give the impression that Hampstead was full of dehydrated cynicism. On the contrary, it was stuffed with enormous quantities of sensitivity, warmth, tenderness and so forth. Only, the possessors of these saintly virtues did not have too many places in which to display their marvellous wares. More, of course, was the pity. For there was genuine Wedgwood lying just round the corner, Chippendale tucked away in the attic. Yes, there were bona fide emotions but not too many people to respond to them.

I thought that Buster Tuffman was one of those unique human beings in Hampstead with whom 'sensitive' dialogue, an interchange of ideas, might be possible. He professed all manner of esoteric things: 'Men and women,' he would say, 'are equal. We have been conditioned to think of women as property. The time has come to treat them as human beings.' Sentiments with which I (as an emancipated 'wog') was in fervent agreement. We got to know each other fairly well. He, as a published writer, enagaged my adulatory faculties. I have an idea that my quasi-aristocratic lineage (with the bit about the Brahmin underlined) incited him to more than mere approval. His greatest approbation for any individual was expressed by the phrase 'high-powered'; it applied to women doctors, nuclear physicists, oil tycoons and national celebrities with whom he was acquainted. I have it from the best sources that he occasionally applied it to me, though always discreetly behind my back.

Over the period that I knew him Buster emerged from a chrysalis to a butterfly: he actually became famous, if that is the word. His name was certainly bandied around in more quarters than one and his original raison d'être for frenzied bum-feeling of 'delicious dollies' seems to have suffered some erosion. But the shriek in his voice did not drop a note, his insatiable thirst for 'fucks' did not abate. Of course, 'motivational impulses', as Americans are wont to say, do not transcribe easily over a short time-scale, so we shall have to leave the issue unsettled. It is enough to say here that Buster's life-pattern and his professed ideologies co-existed in precarious equilibrium and led to events of considerable dramatic moment.

He was for ever asserting the need for 'love' and 'tenderness' between human beings. Yet once he tried to seduce a girl by telling her that he could not write without having a fuck. When the lady was persuaded to come back with him to his bed-sitter, he 'threw me on the bed, didn't even bother to take off my knickers, shoved the damn thing in, came in half a minute and then announced, "Thanks, that's just what I needed."'

Consistency was not Mr Tuffman's forte, nor was that quality which could be described as the antithesis to hypocrisy. He wrote a whole book extolling his 'deep love' for an erstwhile mistress, whose salient feature was not her beauty. After he had abandoned her, the woman (pushing forty) was wooed by a handsome French boy of twenty-two, persuaded to start living with him and eventually taken to Paris and introduced to his parents, with a view towards imminent marriage. Tuffman's lifelong desire for 'deep love' was instantly activated, telegrams shot back and forth across the Channel and the lady, not yet purged of her affection for him, was induced to return to London. On the second day after the rapprochement Tuffman deserted the quasi-marital couch for fresh pastures with the acrid assertion that monogamy did not agree with his constitution. Her chances of wedlock having been ruined for ever, the lady in question consoled herself with the fact that a eulogy of romantic devotion, Tuffman's testament of 'deep love', was dedicated to her.

I go to some lengths in describing this man because Buster epitomized Hampstead in a unique way. The credits and liabilities were equally balanced, Lucifer and the Lord were housed in the same body. He was a genuinely free spirit, yet inside the genial warmth there was a ruthless self-seeker perpetually struggling to get out. He professed to care, yet when the pinch came he opted for desertion. Contradictions abounded. If Hampstead is a state of mind, rather than an area of town, Buster Tuffman reflected it. He was unconstricted, open, equipped with creative talent; he knew where his heart ought to be even if he could not always put it there. Callousness, greed, prudery, in short all the weeds of Victorian Puritanism, wove in and out of the tapestry: loyalty coexisted with horrifying indifference, sexually emancipated ideas jostled in his mind with the worst excesses of Forsyte property-consciousness. He once hit me in the face when I put my hand on the *head* of a girl with whom he was out for the evening, while with all my girls he was always feeling-up breasts, cunts and other portions of the anatomy.

Above all, Buster was an ideologue: 'We should desanctify sex, make love on park benches and buses, wherever and whenever we feel like it. Strip it of that damn thing called "mystery". Machines are going to take over from us. It is no accident that within twenty years we have the fifth-generation computer, they simply evolve at a much faster rate. Therefore, art, which is essentially a human activity, has no future—art is dead.' 'When men are going to the moon, the notion of nationalism verges on crime.' 'Jews invented genocide but they got a larger dose of it than they ever administered, Zionism is the mirror-image of Nazism.' If Buster had had a long white beard he could have passed off as an Old Testament prophet. As it was, he had frilly black hair, an undistinguished nose and he was fond of announcing, somewhat perversely in attractive company, that 'beauty is not my strong point'. The tautology was never underlined but people found him amiable.

This portrait of a Hampstead version of Don Quixote would remain incomplete without an incident which combined slapstick and the macabre in equal measure. I used to know a girl called Julia, with whom I had had a brief affair. Then she had moved out of the house, fallen in love with a man and started living with him. But we remained friends and she would come to visit me once every fortnight or so and we would spend the evening together. I found her company congenial as she was bright, warm and possessed of a wry sense of humour; she valued my friendship and sought to refuel her feminine vitality by mild flirtations. But since she was obviously *in love* with her man and I was well provided with carnal comforts from other sources, it never actually got to coitus point.

On one of her visits I took Julia to the Bumble-Bee and Buster joined us for a drink. The first one led to the second and then a third. By the end of the evening the three of us had imbibed enough whisky to revive our faith in rainbows, the Holy Trinity and the Vernal Equinox. Julia was flattered by Tuffman's erotic attentions (not having discovered the Catholic nature of his tastes in this direction). I had reason to be pleased too—a distinguished author was making passes at 'my girl'. Except that Julia *wasn't* my girl, and the two of them did not cease to remind me of this salient fact. She said, 'Never had two men going at me at the same time, might be quite an idea.' He said, 'Don't like to give an inch, do you? You want to have them all, don't you?' Grudgingly, I gave in. But not without preliminary protests. I knew Julia, I also knew that she was not an empirical sort of person. The whisky had done its work, it had churned up curiosity. But there was in fact a whole load of past history—Methodist parents, non-conformist schooling, virginity till twenty-two, and then an L.S.E. education. 'Ain't got the right cocktail for these sort of adventures,' I said to myself. But neither of them took any notice. I directed my restrictive remarks mostly at Julia, for Tuffman was not to be persuaded. And she ignored me. 'A wet blanket, that's what you are,' she said, as we started walking towards Tuffman's abode. I resigned myself. What was to be was to be.

Tuffman had moved into a bigger room. It had carpet on the floor, large bay windows and contained a record player. We had bought some whisky in the pub, so ice and glasses were brought out and the drinks were toasted. Then to the serious business at hand, the homage to Eros. Music came on, the lights were dimmed and Buster and Julia began to dance, while I sat on the sofa and watched. His hands roamed freely over her body; first the breasts, then further down and finally up between her thighs. The lady did not object, in fact she seemed to like it all. So far so good. After a few minutes of under-skirt exploration, Tuffman's hand came up for air but this time for more onerous activities. The buttons on the back of Julia's blouse were undone, then the blouse itself was peeled off. Next to go was the skirt. In her bra and slip the lady looked inviting. Her face radiated that strange glow which women get when they know they are desired and want to reciprocate. The dancing went on, groin to groin, cheek to cheek, perhaps even tongue to tongue. Then the bra was unclipped and a pair of taut breasts budded into view. Buster took off his shirt and the hairy chest pressed firmly against two sturdily erect nipples. Then the slip and the tights came down. Julia was nude, her pubic region being massaged by Tuffman's none-too-dexterous fingers. Moments later Buster unzipped himself and took off his trousers. Julia's hand went to his cock while his fingers continued to perform over and inside her crevice. This state of affairs continued for approximately five minutes, at the end of which Julia cried, 'What's the matter with you? You are as limp as a boiled cabbage.' In reply, he held her tighter and started to rub his penis, instead of his fingers, against her brown fuzzy hair. When this new procedure produced no appreciable improvement, Julia rushed over to me, more than mildly hysterical, and unzipped me with a degree of roughness I had not seen her display before. Fortunately the erotic exercises of the couple had produced adequate results in me and Julia seemed to find the condition satisfactory. But an unexpected hurdle presented itself.

'I am not on the pill,' Julia said, as I was about to enter her.

If the full import of her announcement had been allowed to percolate into my consciousness, I too might have joined the ranks of boiled cabbages. But, quick as lightning and as altruistic as Buddha, Tuffman came to the rescue. 'I have a French letter,' he said, digging into his trouser pocket. 'Here, put this on.' I did as I was commanded and Julia sat astride me. The incongruity of the scene might have appealed to a cartoonist; it did not appear in that light to me at the time a nude woman, legs akimbo, hoisted over a fully clothed man, with his penis, sheathed by a borrowed French letter, inside the lady's vagina, while a third member of the party, a male, also nude, watches the rocking movements of the pair, with the acute attentiveness of a zoo-keeper observing a near-extinct species copulating for the first time.

Julia came and so did I. Buster meanwhile was playing with himself and had managed to induce a mild activation of his genital organs. I went off to the loo, with the ridiculous bit of plastic dangling between my legs. When I came back to the room, the two of them were dancing again. My watch said two and I thought it was time for me to leave. Driving home I felt dejected and morose. Something was wrong, though I couldn't tell what. At three-thirty in the morning, over an hour after I had returned, the phone rang. It was Tuffman on the line 'I've fucked her! I've fucked her!'

'Don't you think that piece of cosmic news could have waited till the morning?' I said, and hung up.

When I phoned Julia at work the next day, her words were, 'Look, I don't want to discuss anything. I just don't want to see you or your friend ever again. And don't ring me . . . '

'But . . . but I did warn you . . . ' I started saying, but the line was dead.

I have not seen Julia since then. Buster got a fuck, admittedly; I merely lost a friend.

The world I describe is not London, it is not even Hampstead. It is a world of fringers like myself who have no home, mostly through choice, partly by compulsion. It is a world where the pub dominates whatever 'social scene' there is. Next to alcohol comes sex, and both are used and abused in a way which would shock and revolt the holy suburbanite. Parties go on till the early hours, men think nothing of going on the dole or having women standing them drinks. Sex is cheap, love scarce. The capacity to put on masks exists in abundance. Professions of faith are common, execution rare. We would *seem* to be derelicts but we keep insisting that we are not. Occasionally, one of us writes a book, another a play. But the art is always about the *outsider*. We do not know what being inside means. We don't have egg and bacon for breakfast, we don't celebrate Christmas. Most of us have few family ties; marriages are almost always broken, affairs have a high mortality rate. There is nothing permanent or fixed in our lives to which we can cling. Living in this condition induces addiction, few of us are ever cured. The safe, planned, loving and caring world out there, for which all of us feel a secret longing, can never take us in. Because we don't belong. We have had to make a virtue of our déraciné predicament because we are addicted to a myth. Romantics all of us, we do not have the guts to strip the lie and live naked. Our epitaphs are written long before we die. For the lucky few who leave more than a mere memory behind, there is solace. For the rest of us, each new morning brings that terrible day nearer and we have neither the grace nor the passivity to accept defeat with a smile. Does that make us rebels? I wonder.

We want the 'things' that the burghers have; we merely don't want to fit into the mould of their lives. Like getting up in the morning and going to work at eight, like putting money away 'for a rainy day', like taking the responsibility of bringing up children. But we want status, we want money, we love children. If only we could get these things by proxy, if only there was a fairy godmother to scatter manna over our lives . . . . But it is also part of our 'philosophy' not to harbour rancour nor culture covetousness in our souls. I don't think anyone would exchange his life with a solid citizen of Surbiton. We take a pride in our address, our clothes, our broken marriages. For often when we peek a glimpse into that other world of order and bliss, we don't like the look of what we see—one set of broken dreams replaced by another.

And just as we yearn to live by proxy, so do they. We get invited to Knightsbridge dinner parties and Kensington cocktails precisely because we don't vote Tory and announce our engagements in the personal columns of the *Times*. We are exhibited as rare specimens of a mutant species, we are allowed to turn up drunk with tousled hair and rumpled trousers. We are forgiven for lapses of social etiquette; we can belch and burp to our heart's content. 'Isn't he charming?' announces the hostess, when the smell of a particularly virulent fart asphyxiates her guests. 'So uninhibited, don't you think?' And of course, we pay the price by having to walk home at one in the morning, all seven miles of a lonely rain-soaked road, while the inhibited ones switch on their windscreen wipers and motor back to their 'lovely shacks'.

I met one such 'lovely couple' at a dinner party one day. He was forty, balding, six foot two and smoked a pipe. He practised as a psychiatrist though he was really a general medical practitioner by training. She was thirty-three, blonde, married for seven years and a mother of a child of five. The two of them exuded happiness, called each other 'darling' all through dinner, and once we came down from the table she occasionally extended her hand which he gently caressed.

'Why do you say you don't believe in marriage?' he asked.

'I didn't say I didn't *believe* in marriage,' I replied, a little fatigued. 'I did say that it is absurd to pretend that two people can be thrown together for thirty-odd years or more, without any other sexual or emotional outlet which is legitimately accepted, and then see red if one of the partners gets up and walks off.'

'Obviously,' he retorted, puffing deeply on his pipe, brow creased in psycho-metaphysical ponderings, 'you suffer from a deep sense of insecurity and cannot ever commit yourself.'

That seemed like a neat summing up of my predicament, so I got up to get myself another drink. His carrying voice infected me however and I heard the following pronouncement from the other side of the room: 'We all *need* things. Women need babies, men need satisfying work, children need homes and loving parents. The trouble with our society it that we don't get the things we need.' Now, I can be as profound as the man next door but it suddenly burst upon me that this seven-guinea-an-hour Harley Street headshrinker was about the most dazzling example of human profundity I had ever encountered. No wonder they were happy.

I have to admit that the man radiated dependability. His walk was slow and heavy, his voice mellow like an after-dinner drink. When he shook hands you felt it, warm, rubbery and dry. Even the pipe helped. His wife looked at him as if he was a miniature version of Jesus Christ and Sigmund Freud rolled into one. I was intrigued by her blonde hair and thick out-turned lips. 'Wonder how many times they do it,' I thought to myself, 'if ever.'

'And do you believe in marriage?' I asked, sitting next to her.

'Of course I do,' she answered, as if I had queried whether the Queen had any African blood in her. 'I have been married for seven years. Of course I believe in marriage.'

'So you don't suffer from a deep sense of insecurity?'

'No,' she replied, allowing a smile to drift over her face.

'And you *can* commit yourself?'

'Yes.'

'No need to seek any sexual or emotional outlet elsewhere, in that case?'

She smiled again, a little more openly this time. 'I have a feeling that you are trying to flirt with me.'

'Perhaps your feeling is right,' I said, getting up. 'Women's feelings usually are.' I think she followed me with her eyes as I joined a group in the other corner of the room.

Half an hour later I found her at my elbow, while I was chatting up an American girl freshly imported from Berkeley. 'You are very sure of yourself, aren't you?' the blonde wife whispered.

'Unh, unh,' I grunted, 'I am the one with a deep sense of insecurity, remember?'

'You are over-playing that one. Drop it.'

'All right, I will, on one condition. If you come out for a lunchtime drink day after tomorrow.'

'You don't waste time, do you?'

'No point.'

'And supposing I say no?'

'I shall have to accept. With the deepest regrets, mind you.'

'And if I agree, what shall we talk about?'

'I don't know anything about the first two subjects.'

'Well, in that case I can teach you about those two, while you can teach me about the third.'

She held her cigarette in that special way that women do when they are weighing you up and want to conceal what their lips are trying to say. 'I have a feeling that you know a lot about the third too.'

'You do, do you?' I said, matching her teasing smile. 'Well, don't let hubby get wind of that feeling, will you?'

'How do you know . . . ?'

'What?'

'That . . . that I won't tell him everything?'

'Isn't much to tell, is there? Just asked you out to an innocent lunchtime drink. And you know nothing happens at lunchtime, don't you?'

'I want to . . . '

'What . . . ?'

'You are so sure of yourself. I wonder if it's all put on.'

'Find out. I don't mind. You've had an offer.

She turned away. 'I shall have to think it over.'

'Talk it over with hubby, you mean?'

'You don't miss a chance, do you?'

'No.'

'Well then, just leave me alone.'

'As Madame pleases,' I said, bowing. She walked away, twisting the brandy glass in her hand.

When the guests began to leave, the blonde wife fidgeted around the hostess, ostensibly to say her 'thank yous', while hubby walked out of the living room. I edged over to her and she said, 'The name is Zaiman, Anita Zaiman.'

'I'll remember,' I whispered and shook her hand.

I rang her up the next day. 'I didn't really want you to ring, you know.'

'Yes, I know. Where and when shall I pick you up tomorrow?'

'Wait a minute, I didn't say I would come.'

'Look stop acting like a Spanish virgin of sixteen.'

'Why?' she giggled, 'are the Spanish virgins different from the other kinds?'

The battle went on, she feigned excuses. Finally she agreed to meet me at the Camden Town Tube station at eleven-thirty the next day. 'I have to pick my son up from school at four. So I shall have to be back well before then.'

'Don't worry,' I said, 'you will,' and hung up. I didn't have a plan but I knew that she would fall in with the one I made.

'You know,' she said, getting into the car, 'I've never played truant before. It's a strange sensation.'

'You mean you have never slept with another man in all these seven years?'

'I wasn't talking about that,' she snapped back. 'I mean I have never gone out with a man like this, without telling David about it.'

'So now you have.'

'Yes, now I have. I most certainly have. I wonder why, though.' Then she turned her face sharply, as if she had been struck by a wave of cosmic illumination.

'Incidentally, I have no intention of sleeping with you either.'

I smiled and continued to drive.

'What are you so pleased with yourself about? And *where* are we going?'

'I am pleased because I have never had a gorgeous blonde sitting next to me in the car, who is as nervous as a deer and who feels as if she has dared Mahomet by coming out for an innocent lunchtime drink.'

'Not so innocent by the look on your face.'

'Would you be very disappointed if it were?'

'You do take liberties, don't you? Do you think I am trying to seduce you or something?'

'We shall see. You'll be put through the test soon enough.'

'What do you mean?'

'I mean we shall be having our innocent little drink in my flat and there will be no one else around except you and me.'

'Oh no, we won't! I am getting out at the next traffic lights.'

'What's the matter?' I said softly, turning my face towards her. 'Don't you trust yourself?'

'Trust *myself*?' she shrieked. 'I like that for a piece of cheek!'

'Well in that case, I don't see what you're getting so worked-up about. Do I give the impression of being a heavy-handed sort of bloke?' She kept silent. 'And you will agree that since you're playing truant, for the first time in your married life, mark you, it would be more "discreet" than a pub or a restaurant?' Silence meant consent, I drove on and parked in front of my flat.

'There's some paté, cold ham and a bit of roast beef, by way of food,' I said, opening the door to my living room. 'Crackers or thin Rye bread to go with it.' She didn't reply but stood staring at the water-colour on the wall. 'I call her "My Bride" for obvious reasons.'

'Is that how you would like your wife to look?' she asked, after a while.

'A bit naive, I would have thought, for the wife of a Harley Street psychiatrist . . . . '

'Oh, for God's sake stop it, stop throwing that at me!'

'Presumably,' I carried on, ignoring her interruption, 'that is precisely how I *would not* like my wife to look. And since I call her "My Bride", it substantiates the point about my incapacity for commitment.'

'Will you stop it . . . *please*!'

I smiled. 'Whisky, gin or wine?'

'What? Oh yes, whisky please.'

'A girl after my own heart.'

We raised glasses, I served the food, we finished eating in silence.

'Well, now that's done,' I said, clearing the plates away, 'to borrow a line from Eliot, I'm glad it's over.'

She looked sharp and steady at me for a long minute. 'You know the next line, don't you?'

'No, tell me . . . '

'Of course you do, you must . . . you're just pretending. You're such an actor.'

'Honestly I don't. Please do tell.'

'You know, most of the time, I don't know if you're having me on or what . . . I . . . I hardly know you . . . and yet . . .'

'Tell me the next line, please.'

Mesmerically, she recited the line, as if she was in another world: 'When lovely woman stoops to folly . . . ' She gazed into her glass, remote, unfeeling, hypnotized.

'Are you going to?' I asked softly.

'I don't know . . . '

'Why do you want to make love with me?'

'I want to find out.'

'What?'

'If it's different.'

'From what?'

She came out of her spell, shook her head and her hand went instinctively to her hair. 'You want to know too much. Come on, give me another drink. An innocent one.'

'Are you sure?' I queried, flippant, lacing the words with a suppressed laugh.

'Quite sure, thank you!'

'In that case, you've lost.'

She wheeled round, put out of balance. 'And *why*?'

'Because I'm not going to make a pass at you. And you'll never find out.'

Again she looked at me, intent, piercing, her eyes pulsating. 'I wonder if you really mean that or if it's just a line?'

'You will never find out, will you?'

'I might.'

'Well then,' I said, raising my glass, 'here's to curiosity.'

'And to its fulfilment.'

'And to its fulfilment,' I echoed, beginning to lose control for the first time.

We drank silently for five minutes at the least, she on the bed (there were no chairs in my room) and I on the floor with my back to the wall. 'Well,' she said, looking at her watch.

'Well . . . ?' I replied.

'It's well past one,' she offered, by way of filling in the silence.

'So it is,' I answered, looking at the clock. 'And you have three hours to kill before your son comes home from school.'

'Not three hours,' she cut in. 'I have to be home by half past three at the latest. . . . Anyway, you have to go back to work, don't you?'

'No, I took the afternoon off.'

'You mean . . . ?'

'Yes, I mean I am entirely at your disposal.'

'Well,' she said, getting up from the bed, 'well in that case, why don't we go and have a drink in a pub or something? You were talking so much about Hampstead pubs the other night. I would like to see the inside of one of them.'

'Nothing much happens at lunchtime, I am afraid. They start livening up in the evening.'

'But one could still go and have a drink . . . ?'

'Of course. But I have quite an adequate stock of liquor here and it's cheaper to drink at home.'

She suppressed an irritated sigh. 'Well then, since we've had our innocent drink, how about that lesson on cybernetics and God?'

'And how about that lesson on sex? A bargain is a bargain.'

'You're impossible.'

'On the contrary, quite possible, I can assure you.'

'You're so bloody English!'

'How do you know?'

'Just the way you talk and . . . '

'And . . . ?'

'And the way you behave.'

'You think I behave like a proper English gentleman, do you? Like ringing up a married woman, taking her out for a drink at lunchtime, then bringing her back to my flat, serving her food and liquor and talking of nothing but sex. You would say that that was normal *English* behaviour, would you?'

'No but . . . For heaven's sake! Why do you keep sitting there?'

'Just tell me what you want me to do. I did say I was entirely at your disposal.'

'You know very well what I want you to do,' she screamed.

'No I don't,' I said, getting up and facing her. 'I *do* know that you want to be titillated, I know that you would like to be kissed. And by the way, those lips of yours were the first things that struck me about you. You would probably enjoy being kissed, you'd like to get me all excited, you would also like to get yourself all juicy and moist . . . '

'Stop it, stop it, stop it . . . ' she shrieked, attempting a sob.

'But what I *don't* know is how far you would let me go, how far you can let yourself go. And you see, before I know that, there's nothing in it for me. I am having quite a nice time as it is.'

'You are a heartless, calculating, unscrupulous bastard.'

'And you?'

She turned round, took out the pins from her hair, shook her head, and those thick blonde mane-like masses fell around her face. 'Don't be cruel to me,' she whispered, as I put my arms round her.

After we finished making love, Anita said, 'It *was* different.' I got up from the bed, walked to the cupboard and started pouring out two whiskies. 'You see, that's what I mean. Most men wouldn't do that. They would put on trousers or something.'

'Really?' I asked, handing her a glass.

'You wouldn't believe it. As if they were ashamed of being seen like that. Makes them feel vulnerable, I suppose.'

I lighted a cigarette, puffed at it, while she sipped her drink. I knew she wanted to talk. Love-making does that to women, it loosens their tongue, more so than alcohol. They come out with things they would never dare utter in any other state. I suppose it's a kind of drunkenness and I was ready for her outpourings. Only, I was curious about a few things so I thought I would steer her along for a while.

'You've never had an orgasm, have you?'

'What? Why do you ask?'

'You haven't, have you?' I persisted, hard, unyielding.

She thought for a while. 'No, I never have.' Then she raised her face to me. 'But how did you know?'

'Because you didn't have one this time either, did you?'

'No.'

'Then why did you pretend?'

'Because . . . because . . . ' she started in a rant, then continued in a lower key, 'because men seem to like that. They get all upset if you don't come. So . . . '

'So . . . ?'

'So you pretend.'

'To everyone?'

'Everyone.'

'Even to . . . ?'

'Oh please stop. I can't bear to go into all that. I hardly know you at all. Perhaps I'll never see you again. There's no point, really.'

'I would have thought there was plenty of point. Besides, you *are* going to see me again.'

'Am I?'

'Hunh, hunh,' I replied, taking the glass from her hand.

'You know, you really are strange. You are so sure of yourself. I think that's what's so attractive about you. Most men . . . well, they sort of don't know what they are doing most of the time . . .'

It was coming, I could see that, and I was itching to get my hands on the tape recorder. I kept it under the bed, not for such dramatic occasions, but to put down a phrase or a poem that would come into my head at night. The microphone was always under one of the two pillows. But the damn thing needed a new reel and in any case I couldn't possibly switch it on without shutting her up for good. Fortunately, her bladder came to my rescue. She wanted to go to the loo and I reckoned that that would give me enough time.

She went off, I got the machine organized and turned up the fan heater to drown the noise of the purring wheel. I reproduce below an exact transcription of Anita's conversation with me for the remainder of that first afternoon we spent together. I have deleted lines but added none; the grammar is hers, spelling and punctuation mine.

'It's strange. If someone asked me a week ago if I would ever . . . ever make love to anyone (except David of course) I would have said, "Of course not." And then you come along. It's strange. I find it difficult to get used to the idea, I can't believe that it has actually happened. And the funny thing is I don't feel guilty at all. In a way I am glad it did happen. Especially with you.'

'Why?'

'Because . . . because . . . well because I don't think it could have happened with anyone else. You just didn't give me a chance, sort of just assumed that I would. I mean, most men would . . . beat around the bush, drop in when David was away and you know, sort of ask, not in so many words but as if they wanted my permission or something.'

'Don't tell me that you've never met men who have wanted to seduce you.'

'Of course I have. But it's different. For one thing there's Julian, he goes to school now . . . . I mean, it simply could not happen at home. Anyway, the situation just never cropped up.'

'Never?'

'Except once . . . that was just after Julian was born, he was about two months old. And David went off to a conference in the States. I had a nanny living in but she was away that night. And there was this friend of ours down from Manchester. He was going to stay the night, so we chatted till quite late. Then suddenly he got up and kissed me . . . . Just like that, without anything beforehand . . . you know, simply grabbed hold of me and put his tongue inside my mouth. I was absolutely furious. Told him to go and find himself a hotel. Of course he stayed. I cooled down after a while and he kept apologizing all through breakfast the next morning. It was so nasty, I just wanted to forget all about it.'

'Did you tell David?'

'No, but I nearly did. You see, David is a very straight sort of person. He just wouldn't understand. It simply wouldn't enter his head to think that a friend of his would make a pass at me. He would think I must have done something to . . . to egg him on, you know. But of course, when I thought about it afterwards, what happened was the most natural thing in the world. The man was married but away from his wife, my husband was in the States and there was no one in the house except a two-month-old baby. And I suppose I am . . . not ugly.'

'You may be many things but you are not ugly, no. In fact I find you devastatingly attractive.'

'Oh please stop. I can't take it again. Not so soon after . . .'

'Well then, go on.'

'Nothing really, that's all . . . . And I must put on some clothes,'

'Why? You've still got a good hour to spend. At playing truant, I mean.'

'I have done that, haven't I? Well and properly played truant.'

'You know what they do to girls like you, don't you? Smack their bottoms.'

'Ah . . . ah . . . that hurt.'

'It was meant to . . . . What's so funny, what are you laughing about?'

'I was just thinking of David's face if he saw this. You know he is very rigid about certain things.'

'Like what, for example?'

'Like proper times to . . . '

'Fuck.'

'Yes . . . . I don't like that word. Makes it sound like a brothel or something.'

'It's an old Anglo-Saxon word, very good pedigree.'

'I don't care about pedigree. I just don't like that word.'

'Very well then, copulate. You were saying that David has rigid ideas about proper times for copulation?'

'Actually he always talks about intercourse. You know, in that funny voice of his, the one he uses when he is up on the pulpit. He always puts it on with his patients. "In-ta-course!" Sounds so funny, makes me think of laboratories and test tubes and things like that . . . . '

'Stop laughing and tell me the story.'

'Well, you see he believes that the sun . . . '

'What about the sun?'

'The sun brings light into the world and "In-ta-course" is for the dark. In other words, you should never do it after sunrise or before sunset.'

'You *are* joking, aren't you?'

'No, he is very serious about it. One Sunday morning I got up feeling very sexy, you know, so I tried to wake him but he kept on snoring. Finally I gave up and got out of bed. And just then, he opened his eyes and you know the sheets were off and I saw that . . . that, you know, his thing was hard, as if it was standing up all by itself. So I jumped back on the bed, I just wanted it inside me, you know. I was all kind of liquid and oozing. But just as I landed on the bed, one of the legs gave way and we fell thud on the floor. Of course that put an end to my plans. The funny thing was that David didn't say a word, just got up and drew the curtains. And of course it was a bright day outside. You know, he didn't talk to me for two days after that, except to ask for the salt at table and that sort of thing. Then when I finally got him to break his vow of silence, he explained the whole thing to me. You see, what I had been doing was trying to go against nature by "desiring In-ta-course" after sunrise and then to cap it all, attempting to "symbolically" castrate him because he wouldn't play my game.'

'How did he figure out the bit about castration?'

'Well, you see, that's where the bed came in. The breaking of the leg was a "symbolic manifestation" of my desire to castrate him. Fortunately, instead of his . . . his, you know, penis, the leg of the bed gave way and so saved him from . . . '

That was where the tape ran out. Anita went on to tell me about David's obsession with his mother, how he felt that 'sexual In-ta-course' was a 'part of living' but did not have to figure too prominently in a 'good relationship'. 'The important thing is to connect, to satisfy need,' he would announce, over cornflakes at breakfast or Coq au Vin at a bistro. 'Altogether too much importance is placed on sex.' His own performance in bed matched up adequately with theoretical assertions. Anita said, 'You know, he gets me all worked up and ready and then he comes in and before I can really get the feel of the thing, he is out and away. I mean, how long . . . ? Mind you, I am not complaining, he is a very good husband, a lot better than some I know. But . . . you do have to have it a bit, you know.'

The fact is I didn't know and I was curious. The affair with Anita lasted a little less than a year. We met in the afternoon, at my place, and after about two weeks she had her first orgasm. She had stopped pretending after that first encounter, we stopped talking about it. Then when she came, it was totally unexpected, both for her and for me. I was scrupulously empirical. The throbbings of her vagina convinced me that it was a 'real' one. (I was not going to be cheated.) At the end of that afternoon, she clutched me hard and said, 'I don't want David, I want you.'

A long story about financial dependence, 'liberated' women and the like, followed. The house in which they lived was hers. David's income was meagre; though he had set himself up as a Harley Street psychiatrist he had few patients. He had failed at general medical practice; he had applied for a job at the W.H.O. and had been rejected. Literally, she supported him. Would I marry her, and if not, would I come and live with her?

No, I said. I had very firm ideas about marriage. And in any case, I didn't think I wanted to settle down just yet.

Tears, recriminations, bitterness ensued. I did not give in. I had a good job, I was not in need of money, and even if I was, this was not my way of getting it. I treated her too much as a 'case history'. The index of 'love' for a writer is the degree to which he ceases to observe. I observed Anita all the time. Even when I grew to be very fond of her I did not stop recording. I knew from experience that the only times I have committed myself totally the observer and the experiencer have merged. This never happened with Anita; I could not tell lies where it counted. Having an affair was all right but marriage was not, especially where there was a child involved. Old-fashioned? Perhaps. But who cares? I don't.

The end of the affair deserves description, if only as a tiny footnote to Indo-British relations. David was going away for a week, to Paris of all places. And he was driving there. Anita rang me up bubbling with excitement. 'We can have a whole night together.' I shared in her jubilation. We bought theatre tickets and met for a drink at the Salisbury at seven on a Wednesday night before going on to the play. It was one of Pinter's later efforts, a terrible disappointment, but the meal afterwards offered compensations. Anita loved snails. We got back to her house in Kentish Town at about ten to one. I hadn't taken my car so I got down from the taxi at the top of the Mews and Anita went on alone. 'A lot of curtain twitching goes on around here, some old widows have nothing else to do. If you and I were to get out of a taxi at one in the morning . . . ' So I waited a good quarter of an hour, walked down as softly as I could and entered the house—Anita had left the door open, so the bell wouldn't wake the neighbours.

'I took Julian over to my mother's this morning and the au pair is spending the night with her boyfriend. We have the house all to ourselves.' Anita jumped around like a girl of ten, hugging and kissing me. 'Isn't it marvellous to spend a whole night together?'

I nodded.

The kitchen and the dining room were on the ground floor; the child's nursery, the loo and the sitting room were on the first floor, and then further up the stairs on the second floor was the master bedroom. The au pair slept in a small 'guest room' next to the kitchen and of course it was empty. I wanted to go up to the bedroom, take off my clothes and get into bed. But Anita kept saying, 'Wait, wait . . . there's no hurry, we have the whole night.' There was a hint of incredulity in her voice, as if she had to repeat it again and again to convince herself that it really was happening.

We drank, chatted, made coffee and sat down again. I took down her tights, put my finger inside her and held her tight. She unzipped me, took out my penis and started playing with it. Then just as I was about to enter her, Anita said, 'Wait, let's have a drink. I don't like it standing up, it's much better lying down.' We drank some more and finally went up to bed at two in the morning.

Then we made love. Anita said, 'I wonder if it would be like this if we lived with each other all the time?'

I said, 'I wonder too.'

We lay in each other's arms for a while, Anita stroking my back and I feeling her nipples.

Then a taxi drew up, down in the Mews. I jumped out of bed, terrified. 'How the hell does one get out of here? I can't jump down from the second floor.' Anita laughed. 'Don't be such a scarecrow. David is driving, he isn't going to turn up in a taxi. Our car makes a special kind of noise, I know. Besides, I don't expect him back before Friday at the earliest.'

The taxi drove away. I relaxed. 'So long as you're sure . . . But it is a Mews and it is three in the morning.'

'Please,' said Anita, 'come to bed, he is sound asleep in his Paris hotel.'

I fell into bed again, she held my prick, it got hard and we made love.

'I didn't have it that time, you know,' Anita announced, with the hint of a complaint in her voice. 'But I think you're wonderful.'

I went to the loo on the floor below, drank a glass of water, washed my face and came back to bed. 'Sulky, sulky,' Anita whispered.

'Sh . . . sh,' I replied and shut my eyes.

Just then a car drew up right in front of the house. Anita shot out of bed shrieking, 'It's David, it's David.'

'Look, for heaven's sake, how do you know?'

'I know, I know that sound.'

'But you said he was in Paris, it's not Friday yet.'

'Yes, yes . . . but he is here, down there . . . he's come back.'

'At three in the morning?'

'I don't know what time it is . . . just put on your clothes . . . quick.'

'I'll have to switch on the light.'

'Don't, for heaven's sake, don't!'

My hands were cold, my teeth started chattering and I felt queasy in the stomach. David was six foot two and a good twelve stone. 'Is there a back door to the garden?' I asked, getting into my trousers.

'Yes, but by the time you get down, he will have come in. The door to the garden is at the other end of the hall. He's bound to see you.'

'So what am I supposed to do?'

'I don't know, I don't know . . . ' Anita screamed.

I couldn't find my socks in the dark, so I put on my shoes without them. The tie was at the head of the bed and I shoved it inside my trouser pocket. In the pale light that sneaked in through the curtains, I could see that Anita had put on her dressing gown.

'Is he violent?' I whispered.

'No, I don't think so. I have never seen him hit anyone.'

Electric pulses were dancing through my head. *Crime Passionel*, headlines in the *Daily Mirror*, a bread-knife stuck through my ribs. What should I do? Try to run, pretend that I was just chatting? Not a likely story, was it? Wife in dressing gown, man without socks and tie, chatting about Wittgenstein at three in the morning?

'You had better go and wait in the sitting room downstairs. And don't switch on the light,' Anita said, in a surprisingly controlled voice. 'If he comes up without suspecting anything, you can tiptoe down the stairs and sneak out . . . If not . . . ' The sound of the front door banging shut shook me. 'Quick, hurry before he comes up.'

I raced down a flight of stairs and rushed into the sitting room and knocked against a chair. David's voice echoed through the house 'What are you doing up there in the dark, darling? I'm back, thought I'd give you a surprise.' I heard his heavy steps climbing up the stairs. Anita ran down and met him on the landing, just outside the room in which I was trying to hide. 'Hullo, darling,' he said, and they must have exchanged a gentle kiss. 'Why are you so cold? Have you turned the heating off?'

'No, no,' she replied, in a hoarse voice.

'I thought I heard a noise here. Liza isn't up, is she?'

'No, look it's nothing, don't . . . '

It was too late, David came in, switched on the light and there I was. 'What's this? What are you doing here?' Then he looked at Anita, turned towards me and remained silent for a good ten seconds. 'I see . . .'

None of us spoke as David put down his suitcase. I looked through the corner of my eyes to see if I could get hold of something for protection in the event of . . . 'So . . .' he started saying. 'Well . . . ' I gulped down my breath several times, trying to extract a 'hullo' out of my lungs. 'Well, you had better come down, hadn't you?'

What was he going to do? Make liver paste out of me? Stick me inside the oven? Smash an empty bottle on my head? 'We had better have a talk, hadn't we?'

'Yes, yes . . . ' I stammered.

'And you go up to bed,' he said to Anita, firm and husband-like.

David led the way down the stairs, I followed. When we entered the kitchen, he looked at the empty glasses on the table and the bottle of brandy. 'I see . . . I see,' he repeated, nodding his head. 'Sit down . . . . I want to talk about this . . . . '

Anita was at the door, looking like a truant child. 'I said you go up to bed,' David shouted. She didn't move. 'In that case, perhaps we had better go and sit inside the car,' he said to me comradely, male to male.

'Yes, perhaps we had better,' I replied. I was beginning to regain consciousness; David wasn't going to create headlines.

The man of the house picked up the brandy (what was left of it), took out two fresh glasses from the cupboard and led the way out of the house. It was raining hard, we ran to the car, he got in and opened the other door from inside. I got in. Silence reigned as he poured out two brandies, stoppered the bottle again, put it down on the floor of the car and said, 'Cheers.'

'Cheers,' I responded.

'It's a terrible shock, of course,' he began. 'You understand?'

'Yes, of course.'

'We've been married for seven years and you know . . . '

'Yes.'

'Mind you, I am not saying that sex doesn't have its place. But it all boils down to a question of need.'

I could see what Anita meant by his 'pulpit voice'. I was still shaking a little but the urge to burst into a loud thundering laugh was as great.

'Obviously, you have had "In-ta-course" with her?'

He looked at me, expecting an answer. I didn't know what to say, so I took another swig of the brandy. 'Yes . . . ?' David said, 'well . . . cheers.'

'Cheers,' I repeated.

'I don't know if you understand Anita. One evening in bed is hardly enough. I've known her for seven years. Actually longer, I met her a year before we got married. She has an inexhaustible appetite for sex. I thought when we had the baby, it would dampen down a bit but actually it just got worse . . . . She needs treatment, and I as her husband can't really . . . but, of course, sex isn't everything you know, she has other needs too.'

'Of course,' I agreed, wondering if we were discussing stock-market quotations or a wife's flagrant infidelity.

'I hope it was warm and tender,' David continued. 'Tenderness is very important in sexual "In-ta-course". Without it the whole thing is reduced to . . . reduced to . . . lust.'

The conversation continued for nearly twenty minutes, we came to the end of the brandy, and I suggested that I ought perhaps to be going home. 'Yes, yes,' David said, 'It's quite late. And you have to go to work tomorrow, haven't you? Fortunately, I don't have to see anyone till next week. I took the week off, you see.'

'I see,' I replied, getting out of the car. It was still raining, David got out and we stood facing each other for a few seconds. 'Look, do you want a raincoat?' he asked.

'No, thank you. I'll be all right.'

When I had walked a hundred yards away, David shouted, 'Bloody Indian bastard, I don't want to see you again ever. And if I ever catch you inside my house again, I'll break your bloody neck.'

I started running. When I finally ran out of breath, I sat down on a bench, turned up my face towards the sky and drank in the pouring rain. Then I started laughing till I cried.

Anita rang me up the next day in the office. 'Can't you steal a couple of hours off from work? I really must see you.'

'I don't think we had better.' I replied and hung up.

David is still practising in Harley Street and the two of them are still married.

I have been cheating the reader for a while now, concealing information behind a bland veil of modesty. All during these years in Hampstead I had been going back to my writing. I wrote short stories, poems, notes for plays; volleys of literary offerings went off in every direction, only to be received by cold unresponsive editorial eyes. Unfeeling postmen kept bringing in my weekly ration of rejection slips and regretful refusals. Then I dug out *Goodbye to India* from the bottom of my drawer, rewrote the whole book and sent it off to an agent. The response was prompt and negative: 'It doesn't work,' the man said categorically. But I was undeterred. This time I was somehow sure that the book could stand on its own, that I had finally done something worthwhile. It's a strange feeling this, and I don't think many writers can explain it. Analysis and objective criticism do enter into it, but only peripherally. You develop a conviction that the stuff you've written is valid, worthy of an audience. And whatever anybody else says this conviction remains unshaken. Yes, of course, every schoolboy of sixteen develops a similar kind of mystic faith. The difference I suppose lies in how much he has done before he stands before the altar. The writer doesn't always have to worship the Muse, but he has to woo her. And the period of courtship is long and arduous.

So I tried a publisher direct and a long letter criticizing my 'heartlessness' came back with the manuscript. Then another and yet another. A year went by; two agents and five publishers sniffed their metaphorical noses at my work. I was beginning to feel despondent. Another winter came and covered the grass in the garden with snow. Then one short story got accepted in a literary magazine; offers from literary agents poured in. I selected one, sent off *Goodbye to India*, received an ecstatic reply within a week and the book was sold to a reputable London publisher within a month. Mecca!

Time, I thought, to go back and take a look at the old country. So I celebrated my tenth anniversary in Europe by buying a plane ticket for Calcutta. I resigned from my job, bade my friends goodbye and packed my bags. I didn't know how long I would stay in India; I had no plans. But I decided that from now on I would call myself a writer—I had earned the right to enter the club.

What made me go on through all those years, how did I know that I would ever get between hard covers? What was the urge, what kept me hoping? It would be easy and tempting to say that it was 'indomitable faith', a 'manic obsession' etc. In fact it was none of these things. It was merely a prosaic assessment of my talents—there was nothing else I could do with even a moderate degree of success, and certainly no other channel which could lead to even half-lit arcades of fame. I couldn't stand for Parliament, I couldn't make a million, nor marry Princess Anne. But I could write. And that is what I would do for the rest of my life.

For whom does one write? asks Sartre. I write for a few people I have loved, a couple of men I respect, and to whom I would like to say a few words. Of course I want an audience, I would like to be famous. But that grey amorphous mass, the thousands who will enter a bookshop and pick up my story—I don't know them, they will never know me. If the things I have to say prompt recognition, ring up the curtains, I shall be happy. But it is to a small few I address myself. I have their faces in mind when I write, I want to know what they feel when they read my words. There is a girl in India, another in California, a couple in New York and perhaps half a dozen in London—I would like to know that they have heard me talk, relived those experiences which were precious between us. It is the only way I know to make me feel that my life isn't wholly worthless.